Also by Teri Holbrook

Sad Water

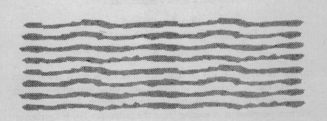

Teri Holbrook

BANTAM BOOKS

New York   Toronto   London   Sydney   Auckland

Sad Water
A Bantam Book /September 1999

ISBN 0-553-57718-2

Bantam Books are published by Bantam Books, a division of
Random House, Inc. Its trademark, consisting of the words "Bantam
Books" and the portrayal of a rooster, is Registered in U.S. Patent
and Trademark Office and in other countries. Marca Registrada.
Bantam Books, 1540 Broadway, New York, New York 10036.

PRINTED IN THE UNITED STATES OF AMERICA
WCD 10   9   8   7   6   5   4   3   2   1

To my mother-in-law Joyce Holbrook
whose stories of her mother's childhood among
the cotton mills of northern England were
the starting point for this tale.

ACKNOWLEDGMENTS

I'd like to thank the following people for their help in creating the fictional world of Mayley and its people: Valerie Gilbert, who was generous with her knowledge and sparing in her criticism of an awkward writer in her pottery classes; Trevor Leighton, fire investigation team leader of the West Yorkshire Fire and Civil Defence Authority, for answering all my niggling questions; Vyvyan Hughes and Robert Lowery for their assistance with all things photographic; Alicia Griswold, who shared her perceptions of the artistic spirit; Sabrina Wylly-Klausman, Scott Schmid, and Bob Coughlin for being steadfast friends and critics; May and Ted Fussey and all their friends and family members who put up with my nosiness; my editor Kate Miciak whose insight and patience is invaluable; and last but never least, Hazel Hinchliffe and Mike Meadow who opened their hearts to me and whose knowledge of the history of northern England never faltered. Any factual bobbles, either intentional or un-, are my own.

I would also like to note that, of all the books I read in preparation for this mystery, two were invaluable: Kirkpatrick Sale's *Rebels Against the Future: The Luddites and Their War on the Industrial Revolution* and *Pennine Valley: History of Upper Calderdale*, edited by Bernard Jennings. My deepest appreciation to the authors of both.

MICHAEL'S BOOK

16 February 1833

These things, it is said, have been caught in the quick current of Sette Water—a white lace glove, fingers full and pointing; a severed cat's head with a rat clenched in its teeth; a plate and spoon stacked as if the meal were finished. Once, a bride still in her finery fell into the stream. As water surged over her face, she smiled at the wedding party. The long ribbons on her dress turned to snakes, and they hastened her away, the song on her lips whisking down the valley.

These are hearth stories, old men's winks, and probably lies. My tale is true. This journal is its proof. It was a daring arrogance that I kept a record at all. "I, Michael Dodd, do declare and solemnly swear that I will never reveal to any person or persons under the canopy of heaven . . ." The oath I took with sincerity and broke in good faith. I thought we were proud heroes; we are instead criminals. Worse. We killed our young. What do they call creatures who do that?

The events I relate happened during the night hours of 30 April 1812. Thirty of us—twenty-six men and four women—met by prearrangement in Blandon Wood near Mayley

*in the West Riding of Yorkshire. From there we walked the few
dark miles to Yates Mill. We carried hammers, pikes, and axes.
Our purpose was to destroy the mill and stop the machines that
had stolen our livelihoods. Whoever reads this journal, given
what happened, may not believe we considered ourselves good
people. But we were not the first to fight; we were not the first to
murder. That is, I tell you now, a stillborn comfort.*

*The mill sat like a tomb on the banks of Sette Water. I say
"tomb" bitterly, and with the knowledge that no bodies rest inside its walls. That April night was moonless, and we nearly
stumbled against the rough stone before we saw its outline
against the sky. The fast slip of the stream covered our noise as
we rustled around the mill door. In our heads were thoughts of
Rawfolds, where a Luddite band had been surprised by a mill-
owner lying in wait with men and guns. Four had died. In the
coming months, eight would be executed. We would not be so
vulnerable. Across Sette Water stood the home of William Yates,
the owner of Yates Mill. No light burned within. At all costs we
would not awaken him.*

*Quietly, by a single torch, one of ours picked at the mill door,
trying to force it open. Another worked at a window. It was a
long and nervous delay. One man produced a great hog's head
from his cloak and, impatient, waved for five men to go with
him to find a rear entry.*

*The smell of water, even moving water, is strong, and I do
not recall now how long I detected the tartness before I compre-
hended its true source. Someone shouted, and I looked up to see
flames lick the front windows. Good enough, I thought. However it is done, it is done well.*

*We moved away, and I imagined the flames, fed by the hog's
tallow, crawling the planked floors and hunching up the throstle machines that spun cotton faster than any man. In my mind
I saw the fire leap from spool to spool, its red dancing legs ignite
fiber and yarn and cloth. Spinning jennies cackled and peeled.
No hired hands will grip them in the morrow, I thought. And
with the others I lifted my pike into the air.*

The first scream came from a girl, age thirteen, no more. She

*appeared at an upper window with her hair afire. Her clothes
rippled on her body—the flames ate them as we gasped helpless
from the ground. Behind her came a young man, his clothes also
ablaze. Racked with cough, he lifted the girl and pushed her
through the window. Her burning body fell into the rushing water below.*

"Mary!" someone shouted. "Oh, dear God, my Mary!"

*In all there were six, hurtling like torches, one after another
through the night sky. The water took them and carried them
downhill. We ran after, poor dogs howling and slipping on the
muddy bank, but the current was swift and their blazing bodies
glided away. We pounded down the river path, and as dawn
broke, rounded a bend and slapped into the frigid water ahead
of them.*

*Here is the miraculous sorrow. They came to us, these six,
backs still afire. In the grey light, they floated like baskets of
bright poppies into their parents' arms.*

*My son John, age fourteen, was among them. We never knew
why they were in the mill—clandestine meeting, lovers' trysts?
Their funerals were held in secret, at midnight in churchyards
where the curates would ask no questions. We did not warn one
another to keep silent. We were voiceless, soulless. What gentlemen failed to do to us with hangings and guns and starvation,
we had done to ourselves.*

*Twenty-one years ago I started this book as a defiant record; I
now end it as a document of grief. I want all to know we did it,
God help us, for King Ludd.*

1

Monday

Nadianna Jesup tucked her dress into her underwear
and thanked God for fog.

Back home in Georgia, her daddy had taught Nadianna and her little sister Ivy to believe many things.
Open the car door politely, and Jesus will climb in beside
you. Pray hard enough in church, and the Lord Himself will blast you, unharmed, from the back pew to the
front. There were other lessons, too—card playing led
first to gambling, then drinking, then dissoluteness;
women who wore lipstick spat at God; attending a the-
ater put one in the company of sinners who didn't
bathe. When Nadianna was nine and Ivy four, their
mother ran away. As Nadianna grew up, a movie stut-
tered through her head of her tall, red-lipped mother
throwing down cards and tossing back drinks, surrounded by a table of profligates with Good & Plenty
candy stuck in their teeth.

Her fallen mother might approve of what Nadianna

was about to do, but not her daddy. *Little girls' heinies are for sitting, not shining.*

Five thousand miles away from him, alone in a dark West Yorkshire wood, Nadianna blushed and patted her pouffed-up rump. Beyond the trees, water hissed; the smell of a million damp leaves rose from the earth. She took a deep breath to calm her nerves, but it didn't work. She shouldn't be here, not by herself before dawn. Wasn't that what her daddy's message had truly been— don't take too many chances? And in the end isn't that who Jesus was—a concerned local who warned visitors away from the bad parts of town? Even her profligate mother's sinful daughter ought to have understood that.

She jabbed a strand of biscuit-colored hair into her bun and, exhaling, took a tentative step forward. The hip waders she had borrowed slapped against her thighs. They were men's boots, but given her height they made a reasonable fit. She tightened her grip on the walking stick she'd found stashed in the cottage behind a box of coal. It was a curly piece of wood, like a snake. Her daddy's tut-tutting was mournful in her ear.

Whose voice are you followin', Nadianna Sara? Ain't no call from God. I told you before: God don't ask His children to lean on snakes.

Sometimes there ain't nowhere else to lean, she thought defiantly. Sometimes women gotta lean where they can.

The day three months ago when Nadianna got the letter from the Calwyn County Arts Council, she had run out the door without a glance at her daddy, over the railroad tracks that sliced through the town of Statlers Cross, and up the gravel drive to Gale Grayson's front door. She was out of breath by the time Gale answered her knock.

"They accepted it," Nadianna panted. "My Yorkshire project. They want it. Now what do I do?"

Gale's smile was genuine. "As they say over yonder, 'In for a penny, in for a pound.' You, ma'am, are gonna need a passport."

The notion had terrified Nadianna. Once as a child she had traveled as far away as Atlanta. A storm front had come in quickly with clouds so large that she forever after thought of Atlanta as a place where huge stones bowled through the sky. She had never repeated the visit. The idea of owning a passport, of packing a suitcase . . . The letter had trembled in her hand. Gale slid her arm around Nadianna's waist and, laughing, helped her into her living room. "You surprise me. What happened to that steady-eyed gal we're used to seeing around here?"

What Nadianna thought but didn't say was it's easy being steady-eyed in a tiny place like Statlers Cross. Fear may be deep here, but at least it was narrow. You could jump it like a crack in the sidewalk.

She didn't feel steady-eyed now. Last night the radio predicted the temperature to rise to sixteen degrees during the day—around sixty degrees Fahrenheit, Gale had explained, quite mild for early November in northern England—but now it couldn't be more than forty-five, if that. Nadianna fought a chill. Her daddy would tell her to put it off, to wait until the sun was out and the water warmed. Gale would have flat forbade it. But Gale was still asleep in the cottage and her daddy was out of all reach except guilt.

Her photographer's jacket, stiff and new, rested against a tree trunk. As she leaned to pick it up, she knocked over a rusting electric lantern. Light spilled across the leaf-strewn ground. Above her the trees were huge and purpled like bruised things.

Nadianna Sara, what kind of callin' puts you in a place of so much hurt?

Go away, she told her daddy's voice, then slid into the jacket, zipped it up, and headed for the water.

At the edge of the woods, the land opened out to a

grassy ribbon. Past that, the bank angled sharply downward. The water before Nadianna was too narrow for a river, too wide for a creek. In parts it bubbled white over the stones before flattening. She took a second deep breath. In for a penny, in for a pound. She skidded down the bank. Then Miss Nadianna Sara Jesup, six months pregnant and far from home, held her camera high and waded into Sette Water.

The current wasn't as fast as she had expected, nor as keen. The water swirled around her boots at calf level, then inched higher. She concentrated on her footing, poking the streambed with her walking stick to check the depth. Debris—a leaf, a twig—floated to her. She ignored it. Three more steps, then two . . . Twelve steps from the bank with the water trilling past her thighs, she stopped and turned north.

She had known yesterday as soon as she laid eyes on Yates Mill that this was where she would position herself for the photographs. Up close, the mill was obviously in cruel disrepair—shattered windows, boarded-up doors, busted stone stairs. And she would take photos of all that, never fear. But she knew those images would be incomplete without this special one. Before she had gone to bed last night, she had said a prayer for fog.

Now a heavy mist pressed on the water like thumbs. It is a marvel, she thought, how mere air can resurrect. Arrayed in the mist, Yates Mill was no longer a ruin. This was living rock.

She raised her camera and went to work while the light turned from plum to periwinkle to lavender. The fog was so thick, she didn't see the parcel until it was only a few feet from her. Her first thought, oddly, was of Moses. Moses floating in his basket among the reeds. Then she saw that it wasn't a parcel or a basket, just something humped and black in the water. She moved away. The water hurried the object to her. She took her snake stick and knocked it back.

Slowly, it rolled over. A strange coolness settled on her. It had no arms. It had no legs. But despite its charred and split skin, there was no mistaking the head or the angry, baked grimace of its teeth.

Chalice Hibbert parked her battered Escort at the top of Old Ground Lane in the slimmest slice of fog she could find. Beside her on the passenger seat of the car sat a large gold-painted basket from Hibbert Sweet Home Away Rentals, complete with cellophane wrapping, green and blue ribbon and a shiny card that read *To Mrs. Grayson and family. Welcome to West Yorkshire. May your sweet home away be your sweet home indeed.* Tucked inside were morsels meant to soothe the savage tourist—scones, macaroons, spice cakes, teabags, and one of Chalice's own special hand-made tea-bowls. With a few well-felt curse words, she hoisted the basket of comestibles and clambered from the car. Her older sister Totty, in a rare fit of disorganization, had forgotten to leave the basket on the table at Mill Cottage, and had, in no uncertain terms, commanded that Chalice deliver it before breakfast. "For Americans on holiday that means before eight o'clock," she said. "Use your instinct, Chally. If they're still asleep, leave it on the stoop. At least they'll know we made the effort."

Chalice balanced the basket on her thigh as she checked her watch. A bit past eight. Oh, well. It was only now sunrise. Knowing Americans, they'd have blasted her with a shotgun if they'd heard her knocking about in the dark.

With the basket wrapped in her arms, she crossed the road to the path that cut through the wood to the cottage. She had just stepped from the grass and onto the pebble path when she heard it. A queer noise—part sigh, part pant—deep within the fog. *Ahh.* A short pause. *Ahh.* An animal, Chalice thought. No—animal cries weren't breathy. And they generally weren't accompanied by the sound of someone being slapped.

The girl who struggled out of the foggy wood was less animal than apparition. Straggly hair, blond and wet, hung across her pale face. She wore only one shoe, which was caked in mud, and her blue denim frock was soaked in grime and clung to her swollen belly; with each step the fabric smacked against her legs with a sharp *thack.* Her mouth was opened wide, and she held her arms outstretched like a child who had fallen and now craved comfort. Without looking in Chalice's direction, she stumbled toward the road and the parked Escort. Fighting the impulse to run away herself, Chalice dropped the beribboned basket in the dirt and rushed to her.

The girl's fingers bit into Chalice's arms. A torrent of words came out, but it was a wasted effort—Chalice could understand nothing. She tried to twist free, but the girl tightened her grip.

"Wah-wta," the girl gasped. "Pleee . . ."

Chalice glanced down at the pregnant girl's stomach and swallowed her own panic. "Shhh," she urged. "Shhh." Her arms ached at the elbows where the girl clutched her. She's like a drowning person, Chalice thought. She'll take me and her baby down with her. With a forceful yank, she broke loose.

The girl began to tremble; Chalice wrapped her arm around her shoulder and made cooing sounds until she quieted. They were close in age—late teens, early twenties—and while Chalice was the taller, she recognized this girl as nevertheless quite tall. Together they huddled in the middle of the road, long limbs intertwined. To their left Chalice could hear sheep lowing. She knew that not five feet from them a drystone wall bordered the road, but in the fog it was invisible. We're invisible, too, she thought, and then remembered that, though remote, Old Ground Lane had become a favorite of Range Rovers and Vauxhalls making the morning commute to the train station at Mytholmroyd.

She guided the girl toward the safety of the pebble path. Mill Cottage was but a short distance. Surely the people staying there would help her use the phone.

It was then that she realized the girl probably was one of the Americans at the cottage, although she didn't speak any form of English Chalice knew. She certainly wasn't local. Old Ground Lane meandered for six miles over the valley, with only two working farms and a handful of isolated houses spread over the distance. Across Sette Water sat the town of Mayley, inhabitants numbering roughly three thousand, and Chalice had been enough of a fixture all her life to at least recognize most of them. Save for the ramblers who stopped at the pubs and B&Bs, the population was fairly constant. Even Mill Cottage was rented out so infrequently that its occupants rarely made an impact.

That would change now, she thought, but even as the thought formed, she knew how untrue it might be. What an irony that the first bit of strangeness to happen around Mayley in decades should happen not to one of the gregarious farmers who held court at The Crown & Drover, nor to one of the Liberal Club women with their raised brows and taut whispers, but to her. *She came out of the fog like a boggart, did she, hair streaming in her face and her mouth a red horror.* Chalice Hibbert alone had seen this apparition, and everyone in Mayley knew Chalice Hibbert would tell no stories.

At the edge of the path, Chalice stopped and looked down at the girl's shoeless foot. A muddy toe poked through a hole in her stocking, and even under the drenched cloth, the other toes appeared cramped and cold. After giving the girl what she hoped was a reassuring squeeze, Chalice knelt on the wet ground and undid

the laces on her left trainer. Gently, she lifted the girl's
stockinged foot, slipped on her own shoe, and tied the
laces as tightly as she could. The trainer hung from the
girl's foot as if hinged. By the time they reached the clearing where the cottage sat, the trainer had flopped hundreds of times, but it still held on. Chalice's own unclad
foot was sore and covered in leaves. And she, too, had
begun to tremble.

As they entered the clearing, the front door of the
cottage popped open and a little woman rushed out.

"Nadianna." The woman's voice was quiet but unmis-
takably urgent as she wrapped a blanket around the girl.
"Come—"

The girl grasped hold of the little woman and started
talking frantically. This time Chalice thought she recognized the words "stream" and "man." And "burnt." Surely
not burnt.

An odd expression crossed the little woman's face.
"You're mistaken, Nadianna. I'm sure of it."

The woman looked at Chalice. "Did you see it, too?
Do you know what she's talking about?"

Chalice shook her head. The woman waited a moment, her dark eyes locked on Chalice's, urging her to
continue. When Chalice didn't, the woman looked away.
Keeping her arm wrapped around Nadianna, she gently
took Chalice's hand. "I'm Gale," she said. "Y'all need to
come inside. We'll get you girls warm, then we'll call the
police."

The region's primary rock is millstone grit, which combines feldspar and quartz to produce a tough surface that never smooths.

—Notes, G. GRAYSON

2

Daniel Halford stopped whistling. He had been whistling off and on since yesterday evening when he rapped his knuckles in farewell on DS Maura Ramsden's messy desk, frowned at her devilish "Ta-ra, guv," exited the building's car park, and set about the business of forgetting New Scotland Yard and the Metropolitan Police for fourteen much-needed days of leave. After a fitful sleep that ended with a 4 A.M. clock alarm, he had resumed whistling in the shower and as he dressed in jeans and a dark blue sweater. It was only now, as his car purred northwest on the M1 and the dawn light hardened into morning, that his whistling ceased. He had not seen Gale Grayson in nearly a year. Their conversations had been few. But the prospect of seeing her, of actually being close to her—well, it was too worrisome to warrant whistling.

She had called him eight weeks earlier. A friend of hers, Nadianna Jesup (*"You'd like her, Daniel. You'd respect her. Some people don't give her enough credit, but one look at her work . . ."*) had received a grant to do a photo essay on an old mill in West Yorkshire. (*"It's an amazing thing. I never*

thought of buildings as having lineage, roots, but there you are.
A mill in rural Georgia can lead you right back to England.")
As a Southern historian, Gale was accompanying her to
write the text for the project.

Her voice had been almost indetectably hesitant. *"I'm*
bringing Katie Pru. We plan to be there for a month. Longer if
we don't finish. We've rented a cottage a bit off the beaten path.
If you find you have time off . . ."

He had damn well taken the time off. He and a
team that included Maura had completed a difficult
investigation—the sexual assault and murder of a six-
year-old girl found in a men's toilet in Heathrow's inter-
national departure lounge. It had taken weeks to identify
the child, and three months to locate her father in a
Toronto church shelter. In his knapsack had been a
bloodstained lock of the girl's hair. Halford had never
mentioned the investigation to Gale, even as it absorbed
him to the point of insomnia. He knew the reason. He
didn't want his image paired in her mind with a murdered child.

At Coventry, the motorway straightened and headed
due north. The traffic thinned. Signs of the industrial
north appeared—first a soot-stained wall, then a dark-
ened chimney stack, and finally, intermittently, whole
towns pocketed beside the roadway with blackened
spires and streaked rooflines. In the moist air, fields took
on the color of spring moss, broken by twists of trees and
the periodic white of a lone cow. The farther north he
traveled, the hillier the countryside grew; in search of
petrol, he exited the motorway and found himself puttering in the furrow of two great swards that shot up,
green and over-bright, on either side of him.

He didn't get to West Yorkshire often, but each time
he did Halford experienced the sensation of entering a
world both unknowable and familiar. His childhood in
Nottingham may have given him a kinship with this slightly
more northern region, but, like a child not wanting to

disturb his great-aunt's china hutch, he walked cautiously here.

A man who worked for his father had once told him about growing up in the West Riding of Yorkshire between the wars. He had painted it as a magical place, where fairies dwelled in gardens and the hill streams ran robin's-egg blue and daffodil yellow on the days the mills dyed their goods. But it was also the place, the man warned, where ghosts came in the form of squared stone buildings with black eyes; they howled at night as the wind whipped through their vacant chambers. Mills made this region, and as the economy went global, mills deserted it. Now abandoned factories pegged the moors; in isolated places, grass mounded over the neglected bones of drystone walls. And in his home village of Mytholm, the man whispered, you could go to the churchyard and see the skinny graves of mill children, packed so tightly that a weed trembling in the wind knocked tombstones on both sides.

The memory of the little girl in the Heathrow toilet, her face brutally broken, cut into his thoughts. As he left the motorway at Wakefield for the A638, his grip on the steering wheel tightened.

What was he doing—pursuing a woman who had offered at most a tentative friendship? It was a cussed minuet he and Gale Grayson were dancing, one in which Halford could touch her fingertips but never her hand. At one point several months before he had thought that was changing, and maybe it had, but he didn't know to what degree. Heading west into the hinterlands of West Yorkshire at ten miles above the speed limit, he had no idea what to expect.

What he certainly did not expect were black-and-white panda cars at the spot on Old Ground Lane where Gale had instructed him to park. Even as he emerged from his car, he told himself it had nothing to do with

Gale. It couldn't possibly. No woman could be so damned unlucky.

Two constables from the West Yorkshire police sauntered by, sloppy grins on their faces.

"Loony American."

"Not known for their smarts, are Americans? Bet she'll be out on the moors shouting for Lassie next."

Laughter. Halford reached for his warrant card, then stopped. Five cars sat on the verge—two police patrol cars, a new green Fiat, an older red Escort, and a black Rover. On the bonnet of one of the pandas sat a basket, ribbons drooping, mud dried on its colorful wrapping. Despite the haphazard manner in which the vehicles were parked, this had neither the feel nor the mood of a crime scene. And if it wasn't serious, the last thing the women at the cottage needed was speculation about a visit from the Metropolitan Police. He grabbed a sack from the passenger seat and, slamming the door shut, raised his hand to the PCs.

"Excuse me. I've some friends staying at Mill Cottage near here. Is something wrong?"

The taller of the PCs turned stern. "Nothing at the moment."

"No one hurt, then?"

The PC's assessing gaze swept over him. "No, sir. They expecting you at the cottage?"

"Yes. They knew I was driving up sometime this morning."

"Here you go, then, I'll escort you. The detective inspector there will answer your questions."

Gale had told Halford the cottage wasn't in much demand, and as soon as he and the constable stepped into the clearing, it was apparent why. Tourists might like the idea of solitude, he thought, but surely the notion stopped short of sepulchral. The cottage looked disused—the paint on the window frames was peeling; the odd shingle had fallen from the roof. The only sign of care was a brightly painted scarlet door, marred by a mound of unpruned ivy that arched over the entryway like a mustache. Halford reached up and carefully smoothed his own. He had seen the cheerful brochures luring holiday-goers to Britain's self-catering cottage industry. Mill Cottage wasn't up to standard. He wondered how in the devil Gale had found it, and more to the point, what had possessed her to take it.

The PC motioned him to stop at the door. "Let me have your name, sir, and I'll tell the DI you're here to see your friends."

He disappeared through the cottage's red door. Less than a minute later the door swung open again, and Halford was surprised to find a beefy hand gripping his.

"Bad penny, that's what you are. Every time I've got my nose in something odd-smelling, here you turn up." The owner of the hand laughed, his pulpy face shining. "Good as hell to see you, Chief Inspector."

"Mark Reston! Good Lord, it must be eight, nine years. I didn't know you were with West Yorkshire. How in the hell did I lose track of you?"

"You've been too busy wowing the city lads. And rising up the ranks like a good bugger. Bit of gray about the temples, old man." Reston's voice turned sober. "Rough case, that little girl. Sorry it fell on you, Danny. You did well."

Mark Reston, two years short of forty, was Halford's age—both had entered the Metropolitan force at the same time with roughly the same educational background and the same level of idealism. There, however, the similarities stopped. In their early years they had palled around together, earning the nicknames Frank and Igor for Halford's towering squareness and Reston's shorter, chubby-faced amiability. Both had opted for the detective branch, both dated women outside the force, and married within months of each other. Three years later Halford was divorced, and Reston, in an attempt to beat the odds against police marriages, had left the Met for duty in calmer pastures. That was all Halford knew. He recalled a couple of years of Christmas cards, a message once or twice on his answering machine, none of which he'd answered. It had been a miserable period and he hadn't wanted to deal with Reston's solicitude or hear about the strides he and his wife were making. Their friendship had dwindled to the sporadic professional encounter. But the meetings were always the same—a pumping handshake, a hearty welcome, and a niggling expression of concern.

Halford nodded his appreciation. "Thanks, Mark. How're Linda and the children?"

The detective beamed. "Couldn't be better. We've been here in Mayley now for six years and Stevie and Sally are like bean shoots. It took Linda a bit of adjusting. But she likes it well enough."

"Glad to hear that. I'm on leave here for a couple of weeks. It would be good to see them." Halford nodded toward the cottage. "What've you got?"

Reston's voice fell to a murmur. "I don't think we've got a damn thing, to tell you the truth. A girl out on the stream this morning claims she saw something in the water. A burnt body."

"A girl? You mean a child?"

"Ahh-uup, there you go catching me on my political correctness. Young *woman*, I should say. Twenty years old. An American. At any rate, if she saw anything—and it was damn foggy this morning—well, I think if she saw anything it was more than likely a rambler's rucksack, or at most some dead dog. Not very pleasant, of course, but at least it's not a human body. Still, I've got a team out searching. I don't want some fisherman downstream chewing my arse because he caught more than breakfast on his line."

"A bit below your rank, isn't it? Shouldn't you be comfy at headquarters, enjoying a cuppa?"

"Flu," Reston answered simply. "Thinned the ranks. Besides, I live ten minutes away . . ."

"So everyone is fine . . ."

Reston snapped his fingers. "My PC said you had friends . . . damn. Grayson. I knew I'd heard that name before. Your big case. Huh. So what is this, a little visit for old time's sake?"

"Something like that. Is it all right if I go in?"

"Sure. I've got everyone huddled about the fire. Go in and use some of that Met know-how to solve this one for me."

It took Halford several seconds to adjust to the darkness inside the cottage. A fire was going in the stone hearth, but it was a small one that barely licked the logs mounted on the grate. In the gloom he could make out a love seat on each side of the fireplace; seated in them was a collection of figures as still as pots. On the floor in front of the fireplace was what looked like a footstool, until it shifted, and he recognized it as a child with her rump in the air.

"I'm gonna see sheep today," she said. "I'm gonna name every one of them. They'll be dirty."

Halford grinned. "The sheep or the names, Miss Katie Pru?"

Katie Pru Grayson rolled onto her back and sat up in surprise. "I know you," she said. "From when I was little." She studied his face, her dark eyes serious beneath a fringe of brown hair. "You can't wash names," she said solemnly. "The sheep are what's dirty. My grandmother told me."

"Ah." He stepped past the figures on the love seats and knelt beside the child, placing the bag from his car behind him. In the sparse light, he could see she had changed. Her legs, which had been chubby and dimpled the last time he saw her, had grown muscular; her face had lost its roundness and was now a heart shape dominated by her round black eyes. He felt a twinge as he realized how much like her mother she looked. She even sounded like Gale—the babyish but detectable English accent with which she had left the country was gone, replaced by a soft American drawl he associated with only one person.

"Let me reintroduce myself," he said. I'm Daniel Halford. When I last saw you, you were three years old. That makes you about four now, doesn't it? I wanted to bring you a present, but I wasn't sure what four-year-olds like."

"Four-year-olds like toys," she said.

"Hmmm. Paints?"

"I like paints."

"Paper to go with the paints?"

"Yep."

"Turnips?"

She wrinkled her nose and slapped the floor, laughing. "Turnips! Did you bring turnips?"

"I considered it. Then I decided turnips were for old men and soups." He handed her the bag. "Perhaps there's something in there you would like."

Katie Pru stared at the bag for a moment before taking it and running from the room. When Halford looked up, Gale stood behind him, the flame lighting her face.

"She hates to be pleased in public," she said.

"I understand. I'm a bit that way myself."

She had changed, though subtly. At their last meeting Gale had been cold and hunched, her shoulders thin beneath a black sweater. Now she seemed relaxed. Even her peculiar black-and-white streaked hair, which would have made most women appear harsh, curved softly under her chin. He rose and put his hands in his pockets, resisting the urge to embrace her.

He was aware of Reston watching him from the door. He was aware of the motionless figures on the love seats, of the PCs outside, the search team at the stream. And he was bitingly aware of Gale, her distrust of police, her halting trust of him. He didn't know what to do next. So he did what seventeen years of police training had taught him to do. He waited for Gale's cue.

To his surprise, she laughed. "I bet you think I planned this. 'Chief Inspector Halford's coming up from the Yard, girls, let's make him feel at home. Somebody call the cops.'" She smiled sheepishly. "A cake would have been simpler, but I'm not that good a cook."

His eyes locked momentarily with hers. He tried to read her mood—bemusement, but also awkwardness. She was embarrassed.

Halford grinned. "A cake would have been nice, Gale, but this is more fitting. Thank you." He transferred his attention to the women in the love seat. "So I take it everyone's all right?"

A red-haired woman stood and adjusted the top half of her track suit. She was lean with a runner's body, but Halford's first impression was of a barely civil bull.

Her handshake was strong. "We're all right. Just a little confused." She didn't say "and irritated as hell," but the sentiment was obvious. "I'm Totty Hibbert. I own this cottage. My sister found Miss Jesup here coming out of the wood. Gave Chally a bit of a scare. Not the kind of thing one usually starts the morning with."

Gale had moved next to a young pregnant woman reclining on the love seat. Now she patted the woman's shoulder. "I'm sure it unsettled Chalice, Totty, but whatever Nadianna saw . . ."

"What I saw . . ." The pregnant woman spoke slowly, enunciating painstakingly; nevertheless Halford had to concentrate to understand the heaviest American Southern accent he had ever encountered. "What I saw was a body. A dead person. It was facedown in the water. It had teeth. It had a neck. Its arms and legs had been chopped off. I could see the bones." She glanced at Reston, still at the door. "It was not a dog and it was not a backpack."

Halford looked at Gale. She returned his glance, shrugged, then looked away.

Halford spoke gently. "If it was facedown, Miss Jesup, how do you know it had teeth?"

"Because I turned it over with my walking stick. I had waded out to the middle of the stream, and when it came to me I knocked it with a stick. I didn't want it touching me."

"You were actually *in* the water? Alone? Early in the morning?"

She looked at him, her blue eyes clear, and spoke calmly. "Yes. I know. I should have told someone. But I knew Gale would have fifty reasons why a woman in my condition should not be out in a river before daybreak. And I had to be. I needed the picture."

He caught Gale's eyes again. "A photograph of Yates Mill in fog," she explained. "The project I was telling you about—the grant Nadianna won. There's a connection between the old mill in Mayley and the one in our hometown. The grandson of the Mayley mill-owner came to Georgia in the late 1800s and built the mill in Statlers Cross, the one Nadianna's family worked in for decades. That's what her project is—an examination of her cultural roots through the architecture and history of the two mills."

"I see. And did you get your photograph, Miss Jesup?"

"Nadianna." She crossed her arms over her swollen stomach. "I won't know until I process the film."

"It might be helpful if DI Reston here could have the film. Perhaps you caught the object in one of the shots."

"I didn't catch it on film, Mr. Halford. I know—I was the one looking through the lens. And I'm not giving anybody the roll. You can have prints of the photographs, but I'm doing my own developing. I don't guess I'll be lucky enough to have another morning like this while I'm here . . . the fog, I mean. I'm not letting some detective lab ruin my film."

Reston broke in. "If we decide it's important, Miss Jesup, we'll let you know. Were you planning on developing your film here or in the States?"

"Here. I met with a photographer yesterday. He's agreed to let me use his darkroom."

Halford nodded and turned to the last figure in the love seat. The attractive, copper-haired young woman had sat wordlessly during the conversation. "And you are—"

Totty Hibbert broke in. "My sister Chalice, Chief Inspector. She found . . ."

The girl waved the other woman silent and rose to her feet. Involuntarily, Halford took a step backward. For a moment he was disconcerted. She was at least six seven, six eight. *There is no aesthetic category for her,* he thought. Had she been slim and pretty, one would have compared her to a model. Obese and ugly, she would have disturbed. Instead, she was simply . . . his mind shuffled for words . . . *abundant.* He found himself wondering where she bought her clothes, and in truth the loose tunic and skirt she wore could have been hobbled from a meal sack. But whatever blandness there was to the fabric was negated by the lengths of malachite beads that wrapped around her throat and reached to her pelvis, and the bright green and blue scarf she had tied around her waist. As she shook his hand, her sleeve wagged from a powerful, sculpted arm. The flicker of a challenge lit her green eyes.

Between her fingers she held a palmtop computer. She lifted the pen and wrote rapidly.

CALL ME CHALLY, it read. EVERYONE WITH A TONGUE DOES.

The general geography of Mayley vicinity: terraces rise 700 to 900 feet above the valley bottom; moorland plateaus (or wasteland) rise above terraces to 1,500 ft. Early settlements clustered on the usable middle ground of the terraces.

—*Notes*, G. GRAYSON

3

To Katie Pru Grayson, the grown-ups who walked solemnly from the cottage looked like toys she wouldn't want to play with—the funny little man with the roly-poly stomach, the skinny young constable who stumbled after him, the stern-faced woman whose red hair could have been chopped off by Katie Pru's own scissors. The last was the big girl who Katie Pru suspected could lift all of them in one hand.

Katie Pru sat on a stone by the corner of the cottage and watched the band of grown-ups head for the woods. In front of her were the treasures from Mr. Halford's bag: a tablet of paper, a plastic dish of paints, and beside them a china cup of water from the kitchen. The grown-ups stopped, and for a second Katie Pru wondered if they wanted to say good-bye to her, or, worse, wanted to stick their noses over her tablet to see what she had painted. Instead, they put their heads together and mumbled.

". . . wouldn't worry," said the roly-poly man.

". . . bother," said the redheaded woman.

"Ah, well," the roly-poly man said loudly. "Not as

much a bother as some things. You have a good day, Miss Hibbert. Call us if anything more comes up."

And then they formed a single line and disappeared one after the other into the woods. The very big girl lingered a moment, but then she, too, was gone from sight. Katie Pru gazed after them. They're walking through a whale, she thought. She wondered if they knew it.

With her brush she painted a gray hump on the paper. Katie Pru knew about whales. Grown-ups didn't believe her, but she had looked at the far edge of her grandmother's field in Georgia and seen them. They sat in the distance, their silver backs strong and round above the yellow grasses. If she stared hard enough, they wiggled and their wet skin flashed. They wiggled most in summer—Katie Pru had decided that whales, like her, hadn't much use for the Georgia sun.

"Those aren't whales," Nadianna told her one day as they sat on Grandma Ella's back porch. "You are too silly for words. Those are woods."

It was just like whales to disguise themselves as woods, and just like grown-ups not to see it. "I'll tell you about whales," Nadianna said. "Have you ever heard the story about Jonah? The man inside the whale?"

Katie Pru had not. She had seen Pinocchio get swallowed up and watched him set his raft on fire. But she had never heard of Jonah. So Nadianna told her—about this stubborn man sitting in the fish's belly, about the weeds wrapped around his head, about the fish vomiting him out. It was not a nice story.

Now, in England, Katie Pru again worried about whales. Around her stretched a thick circle of trees, and the gray sky over her head hung like animal skin. She turned her paintbrush upside down and poked it into the damp ground. Nothing jerked, nothing howled. Not that she was fooled. She had known they were entering a whale as soon as they stepped into the woods and started their long walk to his stomach.

She glanced at the red cottage door, cut in half so the top swung open. It was open now, and she could hear her mother talking.

"Look, Nadianna, I'm sure they'll do what—"

"They'll do nothing. They don't believe me. You don't believe me."

"That's not true . . ."

It was true. Katie Pru could tell by her mother's voice when she wasn't being truthful.

Mr. Halford spoke. "Nadianna, I've known Inspector Reston for years. He's very good. He'll—"

"He'll file it under 'Backwater Ignorant' and forget it," Nadianna said. "I'm going to take a nap."

Silence. Then her mother's murmured "Okay," and footsteps. Her mother stood at the doorway, leaning over the bottom half of the door.

"How's it going, K.P.? Are you cold?"

Katie Pru patted the buttons on her coat. "Nope," she said. "I feel good. Can I stay outside for a while?"

"All right, for a bit. Just stay close to the cottage. Don't go into the woods. I want to be able to look out and see you. If you go somewhere and I can't see you, you'll have to come inside for the rest of the day."

"Yes'm."

Her mother disappeared inside. Katie Pru poked the ground again and glanced at the woods. How funny that her mother thought it was more dangerous out there.

She waited a second, straining to hear the sounds from the cottage. When she heard nothing, she dropped the paintbrush and slowly made her way to the woods' edge. A small path led through the trees, and Katie Pru took a careful step into the gap.

She didn't know what she expected—maybe a yawning sound like the ground opening up, or the far-off clatter of teeth—but all she heard was a whisper of air and the clicking of insects. The woods smelled like the holes she dug so deep in Grandma Ella's yard that she could stick her whole head inside. She walked farther, making sure to keep the cottage in sight.

"Where have you been? Why were the police here?"

She stopped. It was a soft voice. She thought back to Nadianna's story. She didn't think Nadianna had said anything about the whale talking.

It spoke again. "Are you joking?" A pause. "The world's full of bleedin' nutters. Come on, then. You can tell me more afterwards."

The leaves rustled like an animal dragging its tail. Katie Pru stood still until the noise stopped. She listened to the air. She listened to the insects. But the whale was silent. He hadn't vomited her out, but he had had his say.

Gale Grayson dropped into a love seat and wrapped her arms around a worn melon-colored pillow. "I don't think I'm handling this well."

Standing by the hearth, Halford shrugged. "I think you're handling it very well, considering you don't believe her."

"Hmm. That's the troublesome part, you know. I ought to believe her."

"No, you ought to believe I'm glad to see you. And you ought to believe Katie Pru is cute as hell. Whether or not you ought to believe that a young woman alone in a foreign country saw a dismembered body floating in a foggy stream, well, that I think could undergo some debate."

Gale clasped the pillow tighter and studied him. The year apart had altered him, she thought. His stance was still commanding, his voice good-humored. Nevertheless, he was changed. His dark hair held more gray, and the lines along his cheeks had sharpened. His eyes were troubled; that she could discern despite the grin he now flashed at her. It could have been fatigue, and she wondered what had happened to make him so gratefully jump at an excuse to take professional leave. He hadn't confided in her over the phone. She wouldn't broach the subject first.

She tossed the pillow aside, stood, and did what she for days had wondered if she would do. She walked over and hugged him.

His embrace was immediate. The worsted yarn of his pullover was rough against her cheek; he smelled of soap and the darker aroma of coffee.

"It's good to see you, too, Daniel. I don't know what to say beyond that."

His arms relaxed, but he kept them around her. "I wouldn't expect you to." He paused, and then sighed. The fatigue behind his eyes deepened. "I'm tired, Gale. Are there any provisions in that kitchen of yours? I could do with some good old-fashioned American-made coffee and a chat."

Thirty minutes later they sat at the thickly polished kitchen table, an empty coffee carafe in front of them. Crumbs from a package of toasted crumpets speckled the table; a jar of orange marmalade filled the room with the smell of citrus. Through a small sash window set low in the wall, Gale could see Katie Pru standing at the edge of the woods; every now and then the child darted back to the side of the cottage, where Gale lost sight of her, but a low singsong allowed her to keep track. From upstairs there wasn't a sound.

Gale wiped her palms with a napkin and tossed it on the table.

"Ask it," she said.

Halford looked up from where he slouched in his chair, his empty coffee mug cupped to his chest. "Ask what?"

"You know. You've gone through every question that

was polite—how was my grandmother, how was everyone else in the family, how were Katie Pru and I adjusting. Now I want you to ask the question you've been too polite to ask."

His face was deadpan. "Oh. You mean who the hell is Nadianna?"

"Nay-dee-ann-a," she corrected him. "You talk like an Englishman."

"All right." He lowered his voice and, placing the coffee mug on the table, leaned closer. "Nay-dee-ann-a. Interesting girl. How many months pregnant is she?"

"Five, six. She either doesn't know or won't tell. Won't tell, actually, since I know she's been getting prenatal care. She won't say who the father is, either. 'Just some boy I met who's too young to be a father' is all she'll say."

"God knows there's enough of those around."

"Yeah." Gale tapped the knife against the marmalade jar. "She lives across the railroad tracks from us in Statlers Cross, in what used to be the mill village. She needed work as a childminder, and I needed someone to look after Katie Pru. She's really remarkable. Not well educated, not formally anyway, but artistic, insightful . . ."

"Religious?"

"Pentecostal. What made you ask?"

"Her clothes are . . . simple. Then there was something in her mannerisms. And her speech is difficult to understand. I dunno. Just something about her."

"Well, you're right this time, but if you think every Southerner with a heavy accent and plain clothes is religious, you'd be fair game on a country road. But, yes, Nadianna is from a religious family. She goes to church at least three times a week, more if she can fit it in. I've come across her telling Katie Pru Bible stories I just barely remember."

Halford nodded briefly and dragged the empty carafe to him. He played with the handle without looking at her. Gale felt a flicker of anger. He wouldn't say it,

whether out of loyalty to her or his policeman's reti-
cence, she wasn't sure. But she knew he was thinking it.
*And what do people think about her working for you, Gale?
What is it like for her, a religious, unwed pregnant woman who
refuses to name the father, to be paired with someone with your
past? How many taboos does the girl feel she needs to break?*

Gale knew what Halford was thinking because she
had spent more than one fitful night pondering it herself. Granted, the proximity of their two houses made
baby-sitting Katie Pru convenient, but Gale didn't live in
Statlers Cross untarnished. After a year there were still
the whispers, still the hidden smirks. A few months earlier, Gale had learned from an aunt that A&E had carried a documentary on terrorism in the UK. Her dead
husband had gotten a brief but pointed mention. Few
people in Statlers Cross had cable, but the curious looks
had increased nonetheless. The widow of a suicide may
have been entitled to a certain sympathy; the widow of a
suicided terrorist was certainly not.

Halford scooted the mug a few inches across the table. "So besides being Katie Pru's childminder, what else
does Nadianna do?"

"She used to work at a poultry plant, but she was laid
off a while ago. I know she makes a little money from her
photographs—she's won several competitions—but it
can't be much. She still lives at home with her father and
sister, so that must be a help to her. I've tried to talk
about her finances—I worry about her—but she cuts me
off. Very private. Independent."

"You must trust her quite a bit."

"If you'd asked, I'd have brought her résumé."

Halford looked at her, surprise melting to regret.

"I'm sorry, Gale," he said. "I've lectured myself off-
and-on for a month—no questions, take it easy. Old
habits. Policemen are hell on social occasions. I know
some who carry interrogation lamps in the boot of their
cars."

Gale felt her chest relax. A smile tugged her lips. "Or maybe I'm just a little uptight about all this."

"Hmm. Possible."

"The truth is, I feel awkward as hell here. The plane landed in Manchester and I kept thinking, 'Am I an idiot? What am I doing?' It took a helluva lot for Nadianna to convince me to come here. When I left last year, I swore I would never be back, at least not until Katie Pru was older and started asking questions. But Nadianna had never been more than a hundred miles from her home, and she was scared. Plus, her grant was provided under the auspices of the local arts council, but the actual money came from a private source. The condition was that I provide the project's text."

"A coffee-table book, then, is it?"

"No. An exhibit. If a book comes of it, well, good for both of us. The exhibit will feature her photos; I'll write the accompanying information."

"Seems a little simplistic for you."

Gale wrinkled her nose. "Is that a compliment? I don't think it will be simple at all. You know the history of this area."

"You mean the Luddites?"

"Right. They had a nice little lifestyle carved out for themselves—working at home, their own bosses. Then the Industrial Revolution came, and, poof, their whole lives were displaced by machines. So the Luddites banded together and fought back."

"And lost."

"And lost. The mill village in Statlers Cross is the result of their loss. I think it'll make an intriguing exhibit."

"I'm still having a hard time believing it was enough to get you to return."

"I had to, Daniel. Nadianna has the artistic talent to carry the project on her own but not the credentials—or the degrees. The art community, at least the level she's striving for, can be extremely suspicious of people without a certain education. It was damned hard for her to get this far. If I didn't come, I could have been crippling her future."

"Is she really that good?"

"You tell me."

Gale glanced out the window to see Katie Pru sticking twigs upright in the dirt, then she rose and picked up a tablet-sized portfolio propped against the front-room wall. She carried it back to the kitchen, careful to close the oak door behind her. Checking to see that the crumbs were brushed away, she placed it on the table in front of Halford, unzipped it, and flipped it open.

She had seen the photographs scores of times, had, in fact, helped Nadianna select the ones to bring with her. She was the first to admit that her knowledge of art was limited. It was not her particular interest. It was, however, Halford's.

"Not bad." He slowly turned the pages. "She does her own developing, printing? Where did she learn?"

"A couple of professionals took her under their wings. So she's apprenticed, taken classes. And she does volunteer work at the cultural arts center setting up and knocking down shows. All that, believe it or not, while plucking the feathers off chickens at the poultry plant."

"Christ. Her work's almost photojournalistic, isn't it?" Halford paused, and Gale watched, bemused, as he studied a photograph of two houses separated by a wire fence—one large and red with a roof shaped like a lance, the other squat and blue surrounded by a sea of grass. In the foreground ran the edge of a train rail.

"Sly girl," he said. "Take a look at this one. At first glance you think the social structure is determined by that fence—the red house to the left is power, the blue house to the right is subservience. But then you see the rail, and you realize that the real division is on the side of the tracks, between the subject and the artist."

"Statlers Cross in a nutshell." Gale rapped her

knuckle against the red house. "My grandmother Ella's," she said flatly. "Where Katie Pru and I live."

If he was struck by the oddity of the house, the combative shape and hostile color, he kept it to himself. His eyes roamed the photograph, his mouth set. He's already painted me in there, she thought, at one of the windows or waiting behind the front door. She could imagine the painted Gale as Halford saw her, wrapped in a winter coat with her hand on the doorknob—held there like a cold spot, never moving in or out. She felt a surge of panic. Reaching across him, she turned the page.

"There you are," she said. "The Statlers Cross mill."

It was obvious even to Gale that this was a lover's photograph, albeit one by a caustic partner. Unlike the houses, the mill was shot in black and white. It stood in ruins, with no roof and only two walls upright. A brilliant veil of morning sunlight fell along the walls. When she first saw it, Gale had thought it a wedding photo, the artist waiting in the wings to join the subject. But the more she looked at it, the more broken the stones became, the more sour the grounds. In the end she had decided it wasn't a wedding at all but a funeral, and Nadianna, by employing the forgotten tradition of photographing the deceased, was the artist as a widow.

"Strong stuff," Halford said.

"Yep," Gale replied. "That's why she's here. That's why I'm here. Not to have come would have been unconscionable."

Halford stared at the photograph, but Gale didn't think he was seeing it. "Yes," he said softly, "I think I can see why you're here."

MICHAEL'S BOOK

10 MARCH 1812

I start this record, as I end many of my days, with a tale. My brother Nathan scoffs at this habit—he knocks my arm at The Crown & Drover and shouts with drink and~~good~~ humour. "Sit down, Michael. No one wants to hear your dainties." But tales are not dainty. They sit in my hand like perfect stones, smoothed, rounded, full of heft. I launch them and they break through branches, walls, the thick sides of heads. That is the secret of tales—they build only after they destroy.

So I start with this one.

I was walking by the stream and met a man. (How many dark tales have begun with the encountering of a stranger!) He was winded, as if he had run a great distance, and he bent over, clasping his knees, spittle running from his mouth. Friend, I cried, let me assist you. He looked at me, and his eyes were bleak and haunted.

After he rested a time, he spoke. I come from a woman's house, he said. I am a weaver, and she could spin my wool. She has many children—her husband gone—and together they prepared the fleece. They mixed urine with hot water and soaked the dirty wool. They dried and carded it and shaped it into long rollags for their mother to spin. She would sit for hours feeding the rollags into her wheel, turning fibers into yarn. Some say she spun her own children, that they came not from between her legs but from between her fingers. There were many of them, it is true, and they had blond hair as finely teased as combed wool.

Here the man's face twisted, and he fell to the ground. I went to her house, he said, to gather my yarn. She was outside, sitting on a stone, with blood on her skirt and her cheeks. What is it? I cried, but all she said was Death now; death later. The silence from the house made my heart scream. I ran inside and found the children, all slaughtered, wrapped in blankets and stacked like bundles of wheat against the wall. I went outside to confront the woman, but she was fallen beside the stone, her dead eyes staring into the dirt.

I grabbed the man by the shoulders. Then we must go, I cried. We must call the soldiers and bury the children! No, he answered. It was very far from here. I have been running for days. I cannot stop. Look at me, he said—and he grabbed my collar. I am to blame. What I have not told you is that it was to be my last visit to the woman. I would not use her to spin my wool again. I told her I had found a spinning mill, a quick place. 'A quick place' were my words! And now they are dead!

He laughed at the hideous joke and let me go, and I moved aside so he could once more run by the stream.

Is my tale a dainty or a stone? Some will doubt its truth. Just as well.

This night I met with John Blaken, Robert Sawson, Liam Ward and my brother Nathan Dodd, at The Crown & Drover in the village of Mayley to initiate a Luddite band. We have heard these past months of the riots in Nottinghamshire, of the

*shearing frames smashed at Marsh, Golcar, Clough, Linth-
waite, and Hoylehouse. We have seen demonstrations against
unemployment and hunger. Last week a man from Huddersfield met with us. Beg no more, he said. We are not children. We
must break the machines. To the fight.*

*I confess at first I doubted. But it is spreading, the rage, the
fear. Three thousand English soldiers have been in the Mid-
lands since January, and thousands more are said to be on their
way to the West Riding. What was once my own known grass
will soon be a battleground. Parliament has made the breaking
of a machine punishable by death. By death! How wicked is a
country that bathes in its own blood.*

*I am a modest cotton clothier. My family lives by my hand-
loom, but it will end, we all know. Death now; death later, said
the woman.*

So tonight I stood in secret quarters and made this vow:

*I, Michael Dodd, of my own voluntary will, do declare
and solemnly swear that I will never reveal to any
persons under the canopy of heaven, the names of those
who comprise the secret committee, their proceedings,
meetings, places of abode, dress, features, complexion,
or anything else, that might lead to a discovery of the
same, either by word, deed, or sign, under the penalty of
being sent out of the world by the first brother who shall
meet me, and my name and character blotted out of
existence and never to be remembered but with contempt
and abhorrence. And I further do swear to use my best
endeavours to punish by death any traitor, wherever I
can find him, and though he should fly to the verge of
nature I will pursue him with unceasing vengeance. So
help me God.*

*So I pledged and became "twisted in" with the Luddite cause.
But in turn I twist my vow as gently as soft cotton flicked from a
spindle. I will be silent, but not wordless. Today I start this*

record. I will name names. I will write dates. I will do what I have vowed against so that my enemies may not twine me to their liking. Shall we leave only their records behind? So help me God, no.

Are my tales true? As true as stones in my hand.

4

On the day Chalice Hibbert stopped talking, her mother was in Blackpool, her knees to her ears. Chalice lived with her sister Totty in a flat in Mayley center, a one bedroom unit on the top floor of an old back-to-front mill cottage. The ventilation had been corrected from the days when circulation was so bad disease could get into the air and infect every family on the row. It had not, however, been perfected. The room smelled of dead fish, and on rainy days, an oniony odor filtered from the loo. No amount of cleaning changed the aroma, and when Chalice thought back on that day, her strongest memories were of two things: first, how invincible Totty had seemed at twenty-four; and second, how nauseating was the smell of the cottage when mingled with the salty taste of blood.

Across Totty's lap lay a small pink-and-white-checkered frock whose miraculous creation Chalice had witnessed over the course of two days, first as whole cloth, then as cut pieces, then, amid the starts and fits of sewing machine and needle, as this crisp garment with pearled buttons down the front and two big pockets on each side.

"There now, see?" Totty said. "I do tiny stitches for the hem. Fine work, handstitching is. If you get sloppy or fast, the stitching will fall out."

Chalice lifted the hem where it draped over Totty's knee and examined the crease. "If my hem fell out, then my frock would hang around my legs like an origami snake."

Totty laughed. "You're going to have a grand time in primary school, Chally. Much too smart for the others. Just you wait and see."

They sat in an oversized armchair by the window with Chalice's legs looped over her sister's thighs. She wore red denim pants, and her blue shoes were bright and fat as she clopped them together.

"Calm down, Chally," Totty said, holding the pink cloth high. "I won't be able to get my needle in unless you do."

It was midday; the sun shone through the uncurtained window and burnt a sharp odor from the cloth. The sun intensified everything—in the harsh light Totty's hair was the color of a brick, and the shag cut that brushed her neck looked as rough as horse's hair. As Chalice snuggled into Totty's lap, she detected the scent of hair lacquer and the less pleasant aroma of unwashed ears. The needle pulled a strand of pink thread in and out of the fabric—pink the color of her sister's nails and, before it was eaten off her mouth, the shade of her lipstick as well. With each stitch the hem grew anchored. The sun beat against Chalice's head, and her legs began to itch.

"I'm hot," she said.

"Get up, then," Totty answered. "Stretch a bit. I never said you had to sit and watch."

Chalice slid to the floor. Away from the frock and its seamstress, the fish smell became more pronounced. After a year of disinfectant, Totty had finally given in and done the room in a nautical motif. When she found a

mind sees something in the water and interprets it as a burnt torso with a head?"

"A highly impressionable one," answered Olivia. "And creative. It takes a lot of inner energy to see baked teeth in a—what was it the police said?—a rucksack, was it?"

"Yes, a rucksack. Although when I left they were admitting to the girl they hadn't found that, either. She looked at them like they were stupid dogs."

Olivia laughed. "That's generally how I feel about the police. They certainly can't come in here without leaving their slobber about."

Chalice placed her fingers inside the mask's mouth and gently pulled. The clay gave and the lower jaw extended a fraction of an inch. She glanced again at Olivia. The older woman was dressed in sweats, a dirty black apron covering her stubby body from neck to knees. Her graying blond hair was pulled back in a bun, and a pair of metalwork goose earrings dragged on her lobes and pecked her cheeks. The geese were Olivia's favorites, and Chalice often wondered if her employer knew her jewelry was redundant. Without makeup Olivia's narrow face was as unassuming as a farmyard fowl. Deceptive, is that, Chalice thought. When she was a child she had heard on the news about a goose who beat a toddler to death with its wings.

The clay felt dry to her touch; she walked to an expanse of shelves at the studio's far end in search of a spray bottle of water. Markham Studio took up one of six rooms in a crumbling mill-owner's house at the edge of Withens Moor on the bank of Sette Water. Across the stream sat Yates Mill and, together with Mill Cottage hidden in Blandon Wood, the three structures made up a rolling—and forgotten—textile triangle north of Mayley. On occasion, ramblers trotted from the Pennine Way and stumbled upon this picturesque juncture of buildings, stream, and green hills. For the most however, it remained undisturbed. The old home was now an artist's co-op, with Olivia, who had turned the upstairs into her flat, sharing space with a local photographer and a succession of other artists who set up a studio for six months, then departed, complaining of the cold and lack of custom. Lack of custom for them, that is. No one made the trek to Markham Studio unless it was to circumflect before Markham herself.

The day she had applied for her job, Chalice had stared slack-jawed at the gaudy clay pieces arranged in a glass case by the studio's front door and hastily slid into her overcoat pocket the simple tea-bowl she had brought as an example of her work. The interview had been crisp. "You will be my production assistant," Olivia had told her. "You will manage my pieces along the various stages—the leather hard stage, bisque, glaze—in other words, from raw clay to finished figure. You don't have as much experience as I would like, but"—and here Olivia had looked up at her towering new assistant with satisfaction—"you're strong. Clay's heavy. I hear you have some talent. Let me make this clear: My job is Art. Your job is order and completion. Your own projects must be done on your own time."

Chalice had wondered if, in addition to her height, her muteness had overridden her inexperience—to Olivia's mind an employee who couldn't talk couldn't infringe. Time had blurred their mutual lines in the sand; Olivia had become more encouraging of Chalice's work, and Chalice had grown more fond of the delicately curved objects she passed from shelf to kiln and back. Not that she would have referred to the red and purple flowers with which Olivia Markham had established her name as "Art." Neither would she have referred to them as flowers. If the police slobbered when they came into the studio, it was because even the dullest constable recognized a case full of engorged clitorises when he saw one.

the room Totty groaned. "I suppose the whole ing about 'the body' now."

"Yes, well, I was over to the greengrocer's this morning," Olivia said. "That Thornsby Person"—Chalice caught her sister's eye; Olivia never referred to the local evangelist as anything but That Thornsby Person—"was talking of forming his own team to search farther downstream and see if they could come up with something. Then the men started telling stories of the things they'd pulled from the water—a dead cow, a lorry. I couldn't follow it all. One of these days this West Yorkshire accent is going to be comprehensible to me."

Totty dropped her gaze to the Coke bottle on the desk. Chalice knew what her sister was thinking: *Not bloody likely.* But Totty would never say that to Olivia. Totty was too grateful. Beneath Chalice's fingers the lips on the mask cracked. She quickly dipped her fingers in water and ran them over the clay.

"So, Livy," Totty said slowly, "what's the news on the mill? The American girl was shooting pictures of the mill, you know. That's what she's here for."

"Hmm. Odd. I don't care—she can shoot all the pictures she wants as far as I'm concerned. Perhaps I can buy some for promotional purposes." Olivia took a swallow of her drink and carefully repositioned the bottle in the petals of water it had left on the desk. "The news is actually quite promising. The council seems to be going my way. There's even an arrangement for financing in the works. I told them it was an idiot's choice: either let me turn it into a artists' mall or watch it crumble into the water. Look at Hedben Bridge, I told them. Thirty years ago the town was so depressed, a house could be had for fifty pounds. Now Londoners go there and fancy themselves rugged. Not a bad little artsy community. And I have some very substantial artists interested in Yates Mill. Handled right, with some good publicity, the tourist money alone could turn this town around."

"So how close are you?"

"Very close. Between you and me, Totty, I've practically

gotten a handshake deal with everyone on the council. I'm optimistic."

"Good." Totty nodded, pleased. "I'm glad things are going nicely. Eventually this art mall of yours will be a good opportunity for Chally, don't you think?"

Olivia glanced at Chalice, startled, as if her underling were a door that had blown open. "Well, yes, it will. More jobs, perhaps. A lot of young people will benefit from it. They won't have to go into Bradford or even Manchester for work. And surely working in an artist's studio beats a dress shop."

Chalice's face burned. A damn dress shop. The mask's lips curled. She waited for Totty's rebuttal. *No, Livy, I meant from an artistic standpoint. Don't you think it would offer Chally an opportunity to market her own work? It's her compensation, you see. There's no loss without payment.*

Instead, Totty picked up her drink and sipped. The forced heat came on and filled the space with a burr.

Olivia stood. "Speaking of which, Chally, did I tell you that I want the kiln off-limits to your pieces until after my show on Friday? I'll have a batch to be loaded tomorrow, but until then I want the kiln free."

Chalice tried to keep her face noncommittal, but she failed. Olivia must have sensed her anger for her voice sweetened. "Let's have a look at what you've been doing today," she said. She stretched and moved her goose-legs across the room.

She stopped behind Chalice and studied the mask. "Not bad. I like the way you've conveyed a calmness in the eyes that's at odds with the brow and mouth. All right, then, when you finish up, look to my batch, will you? The leaves need glazing."

She turned to Totty. "Have you taken a look at some of Chally's recent pieces? I've arranged for her to display a few at a shop in Skipton. Mostly tourists, so her work should satisfy. I'll send her little tea-bowls, of course, but I'm encouraging her to do more adventurous work, like the masks. Simplicity may be satisfying to a potter, but if people are going to put money down, they want to know the clay's been worked. I think her masks could bring in a nice sum."

She walked to a cabinet where Chalice's finished pieces sat in the shadows. Reaching inside, she selected one of Chalice's masks and held it up for Totty to see. Chalice bent her head, focusing on her fingers as they pulled and pushed the clay.

"Ah, take a look at this one, Totty," Olivia said. "She calls it 'God's Messenger.' An angel, is that it, Chally? A young man, one side highly realistic, the other almost raw clay. As if the face were . . . evolving." She returned the mask to the cabinet and laughed in a way that set Chalice's teeth on edge. "Of course, I'd say that about most men, wouldn't you, Totty? By and large I find they're only half finished."

Peat bogs, caused by high rain and low evaporation, can be found on the moorland, sometimes reaching fifteen feet in depth and providing a hazard for hikers.

—*Notes*, G. GRAYSON

5

The Crown & Drover Pub & Inn perched on the crest of a steep cobblestone alley barely wide enough for a single car—this Halford had discovered earlier when he'd come to claim his room and promptly bashed his Ford's side mirror against a lamppost. In daylight the squat building had seemed the picture of staid comfort with its stone walls and dulled stained glass windows. Now, however, light poured from the pub's colored glass. Behind it stretched a row of blackened terraced weaver's cottages, so that in the dark the pub resembled a sparkly trinket atop a tarnished and not too reliable hat pin.

In defiance of the dropping temperature, someone had propped the pub door open, and as he drove past, Halford could see jean-clad teens beating on a video game; a queer greenish light, thickened by cigarette smoke, emanated from the interior. He pulled into a small car-park over the road and switched off the engine.

"Doesn't exactly look quiet tonight. But I have it on the best of authority—well, the innkeeper, actually—that their's are the best meals in miles. Shall we have a go at it?"

"I'm game." Gale unlatched her seat belt. "What do y'all say? You hungry?"

"Starving," answered Nadianna from the backseat. "I think I forgot to eat today." She reached over and unbuckled Katie Pru. "Let's go, katydid. Whatever you eat of your dinner, I bet I can eat twice as much."

Inside, the conversation was so loud that seconds passed before Halford recognized the wail from the jukebox as Patsy Cline. Groups of two and three huddled over tiny, water-ringed tables, and Halford was ready to dismiss them as world-weary youth until he noticed all the silvered and bald pates. As a yell rose from the teens, heads turned and scowled. The Crown & Drover, it seemed, was wavering between youth hangout and God's waiting room.

From the far side of the bar the innkeeper, Bertie Portman, stood to greet them. "Mr. Halford, good to see you. I trust your room is all right?"

"Yes, it's fine," Halford replied. "You were quite persuasive earlier—we've come for meals."

"Ah, good. That's what we like to hear. We won't disappoint, don't worry." On their right sounded a blipping noise, followed by a bellow from the teens. "Come this way, then," the little innkeeper said. "Most of us find that digestion prefers a little more peace."

They snaked their way through a second room, quieter than the first but only slightly less crowded. Tables ran the circumference of the room. Dark burnished wood covered the walls and ceiling; a massive stone hearth, still unlit, swallowed the whole of the room's southern face. A flushed young man emerged from a back hallway with two plates of sizzling mixed grill in his hands. He set them down in front of a well-dressed man and woman and scuttled back to the kitchen.

Portman waved them around a table left of the hearth. "Monday nights we offer a special fare—really draws 'em in. Menu's on the slate on the mantel." He ruffled Katie

Pru's hair and winked at Gale. "The kiddies like our fish and chips. The peas roll around tables and squash under forks brilliantly."

As Portman left, Gale helped Katie Pru into a chair. "Fish and chips sound good to you, K.P.? You stay here a sec while we see what else is on the menu."

"You and Nadianna go on," Halford said. "I'll stay and keep Miss K.P. amused."

"Good enough. Come on, Nadianna. Let's see what looks good."

A blare of laughter sounded from the woman with the mixed grill. Halford turned to see her collapsed in giggles on one elbow, a length of sausage dangling from her fork. Her appearance seemed at odds with the other, more casually dressed diners—a lavender-and-gold silk scarf draped over her blond hair, the ends stuffed into the neck of her lemon-colored blouse. Large silver geese hung from her ears. Right Grace Kelly-ish, Halford thought, although this woman was definitely on the stocky side, and, besides, he couldn't imagine the Hollywood princess sniggering in geese earrings. Her companion, a middle-aged man with dark hair pulled into a ponytail, looked vaguely familiar to Halford. Smiling but patently uncomfortable, the man took the fork from the woman's hand and rested the sausage on her plate. She responded by laughing louder, sliding her head down the side of her arm until it rested fully on the table. She was drunk.

Hoping the man would see fit to take her from the room, Halford focused his attention on a picture frame hanging above his head. Within the frame was a fac-simile of the *Leeds Mercury*, dated 2 May 1812. The head-line read "Atrocious Murder."

On Tuesday evening last, about half past six o'clock, as MR. WILLIAM HORSFALL, *a very extensive Woollen Manufacturer, at Marsden, about seven miles from Huddersfield, was return-ing from the market at that place, he was assassinated on the public road, on Crosland Moor.*

Halford let his eye drift down the newspaper page. The murder of William Horsfall was not unfamiliar to him. The wool manufacturer had been shot one time each by four men in dark-colored, coarsely woven coats, evidence, the paper noted, that the assailants were working-class men. The description of the wounds was graphic, a practice no doubt rendered obsolete by the gruesome immediacy of film. He had always felt that the murdered Mr. Horsfall was one of history's highly regarded bullies, relentless in his pursuit of the ill-fated Luddites. If his memory was correct, three of those four men were eventually hanged. High price for men whose cause had become a joke—families fighting the dehumanization of machines were not the same as lugs afraid of computers. But the article as eatery decor didn't surprise him. Tourists love regional tragedies.

"I heard a whale talk today."

Halford regarded Katie Pru's bright eyes. "Really."

She nodded. "He doesn't like policemen."

"Hmm. Why do you think that is?"

The child shrugged. "Maybe they sound too friendly when they talk."

"Ah. That is a problem. Should I change the way I talk?"

"I said po*lice*men." Placing her elbows on the table, she sank her chin into her palms. Her fingers drummed her cheeks. Halford waited for clarification, but apparently the conversation had ended. A strand of her dark hair was caught in her collar. Gently, he slipped his finger beneath it and let it fall into place.

"Lyle!" The scarved woman held up a piece of grilled beef. "What does this look like?"

The man looked hesitantly around the room. "Come on, now, Livy. Don't—"

"Don't 'don't' me. Just have a look. Guess."

"Liv . . ." The man's face reddened.

The woman's voice grew louder. "Guess!"

"Oh, honestly. I dunno—New Zealand."

"Guess again."

"A nicotine patch."

"You sod. No."

"Olivia, stop . . ."

"Why, Lyle. You surprise me. It's a *headless torso!*"

The woman brayed with malicious delight. Halford turned his head sharply. There was no mistaking her intentions; even as she sucked in her breath to laugh again, her eyes remained trained on the two Americans studying the menu at the hearth.

"Shhh," said her companion. His face was white now, and he brushed the sheen on his forehead. "Stop it."

The woman waved him quiet. "Quit being such a clot. The police didn't find anything, did they? Not like I'm being indecent to the dead."

Twittering started from the rear of the room. At the hearth, Nadianna looked puzzled. Halford had seen the expression before, the slightly cockeyed gaze that precedes realization. She didn't understand what was being said—either because she hadn't heard clearly or because the accent was unfamiliar—but a protective nerve was warning her. She turned to look at the couple. Her mouth fell open and her face flushed crimson. Halford saw Gale put her hand on the younger woman's arm, saw her murmur something.

"Don't you worry, luv," yelled a male voice from the far side of the room. "They's found stranger things in that water."

"Yeah, Bob." It was a woman in the back. "Like your bare arse after a bad night's drunk."

The room erupted. Nadianna dipped her head abruptly and rushed for the door. Gale caught Halford's eye. He nodded grimly and began gathering coats.

"Come on, Miss Katie Pru," he said. "Friendly talk doesn't seem to be a priority with some folk."

• • •

A cold drizzle fell on Chalice Hibbert. At nine-thirty the narrow lane that ran along her neighbors' back gardens was deserted. She skirted past the shadowed humps of garden walls, her ear sensitive to the sharp crick of drizzle hitting the stones. "Moor grime," Totty called this pecking Yorkshire mist, but since childhood Chalice had loved to venture out in the wet.

She was enjoying it less now. She could still hear Olivia's silken voice. *When you finish up, look to my batch, will you? . . . Surely working in an artist's studio beats a dress shop. . . .* She mimicked Olivia's goose waddle, not caring if the neighbors looked out and gasped at the gigantic silhouette cavorting past their garden walls. Let them smirk as they like. Olivia Markham was a shitty old bitch. Olivia Markham was a *cow*.

At the next to the last house on the lane, she flung open the gate and slumped against the wall. The lights from her own kitchen shone brightly, and through the back door window she could see Totty puttering in the kitchen. "Puttering" had been the word of Boyfriend Number Two, who had been part of the household when Chalice was six and was gone before she was seven. She had known by his tone the word was derogatory; she had also known that at least half the time it was true. She watched now as Totty moved from refrigerator to sink, a carton of eggs in her hands. Another holiday renter for Hibberts Sweet Home Away, thought Chalice. Good. Totty would be too busy baking for her baskets to want to argue. The fireworks could wait until later.

Chalice sighed and pushed herself away from the wall. In the garden's east rear corner sat a cramped shed. Built by previous owners decades earlier, it was no more than seven feet across both ways but big enough for her needs. She quietly unlatched the door, and was stepping inside when the garden light flicked on, and the back door opened.

"Chally?" In the light's yellow glow Chalice could see an egg in Totty's hand. "Are you coming in?"

"Uh-uh."

"Too cold for working tonight. I'd rather you came in." Her tone was sharp, but Chalice decided to be innocent. She shook her head and pointed her shoulder at the shed. Totty frowned. "Well, don't let yourself get frostbite, then. What would I do with you with frostbite? Lose work myself, in all likelihood." She paused. "Olivia rang. Said to remind you of Friday's show. She's left a list of things for you to do at the studio."

Of course she has, Chalice thought bitterly. She gave her sister a smile and pantomimed a big, smoochy kiss in the air. "You," Totty said, turning back to the kitchen. "Just take care not to work too late."

Chalice waited until the door closed on Totty before entering the shed. Out of habit she pulled a torn shade down over the shed's dirt-smeared window; then she switched on a desk lamp, illuminating the room's castoff furniture and storage boxes. There wasn't much room to maneuver, just enough for Chalice to collapse into a dilapidated cratch, relegated to the shed after Totty had purchased the entire cottage on Garrett Alley and, launching her business, decided that a professional woman's home shouldn't give shelter to worn-down chairs. Twisting around, Chalice checked first to make sure water was left in her cup, then reached beneath the table to pull from a plastic bag a rough ball of moist clay. For several minutes she rolled it around in her palms until the ball smoothed. She moved her fingers over the sphere, looking for cracks, unwanted folds. Then, convinced that the ball was formed to her requirements, Chalice sank her thumb into its middle and, eyes closed, began to pinch.

It was Totty who decided that Chalice's pinched pots

were really tea-bowls. *"Pinched pot" sounds like something you would call an old woman. You can't say it without snarling. They're too lovely to snarl about, Chally. Give them a more elegant name. . . .* Totty had been right, of course. The part-time potters who had taken Chalice under their wings before Olivia's arrival had marveled at the delicacy of her bowls. They had spoken of the *cha-no-yu*, the ceremonial tea of Japan, where the beauty of the tea-bowl was measured by its utility. They told her about the decline of British pottery with the advent of machinery, and the need of the hand-built potter to understand not only the concepts of gravity and balance, the intricacies of silicants and grog, but also the very human need to touch the earth. Some potters considered pinched pots unsophisticated, but Chalice knew better. She could have gone to art school, but instead she decided to become a studio potter. Totty had been livid. *I want you to do proper studies. In today's marketplace an artist doesn't have to starve. The route you're taking is one step away from a peasant potter. Is that what you want?* It was. Rather than lose herself in the fripperies of the art establishment, she, like the *cha-no-yu*, would search for art in use.

Her thumb, cigar-thick, felt its way around the clay's hollow, judging the wet mass in her palm, searching out its strengths and weaknesses. It was easy to misshape a pinched pot. Too much working of the clay made the walls brittle; too little and they were thick as pipes. Not enough control and the clay flopped in the potter's hands; overly controlled and the bowl was a lifeless thing. Chalice had the touch. Each one took hours to form, and glazed and fired, Chalice's tea-bowls were uncommon. Not perfect—she knew that would take a generation. But even Olivia had begrudgingly admitted her pots were admirable. *Fairly rare to make something that balanced without a wheel. Boring, too, I would think.*

She fell into a rhythm. She had spent the day glazing the woman's god-awful flowers, her own work neglected.

She had been experimenting with glazes herself, and twenty-four completed bowls, bright blue and luminous, stood hidden away in the dark of the studio cabinet. Another batch, however, the result of three month's work, waited on the shelves to be fired. She had gone late Sunday night to use the kiln, but Olivia, pissed off and boozy, shooed her away. Now she was saying that Chalice couldn't use the kiln at all until the weekend. Not acceptable. And the emphasis on the masks—in Olivia Markham's world, all roads had to lead to money or they weren't roads. As if the tea-bowls couldn't bring in money if they were ever taken out and displayed. . . .

It was getting absurd. She needed to leave the studio; she needed to find another potter under whom she could apprentice. Totty would balk—Olivia Markham might be an ass, but her art-mall scheme had glued Totty to her. She believed it would be Chalice's big break, as if there were such a thing as big breaks. Totty was able to overlook Olivia's put-downs, the little condescensions. Chalice couldn't. She was dead tired of it all.

The bowl went round in her palm as she pinched and turned, pinched and turned. She could feel the shape take form, the walls respond to her pressure. She thought of the day, the bizarreness of the phantom body melding into the inanity of Olivia's flowers. The hollow of the bowl grew wider, finer, the walls spreading out like wings. She began to rock. Her breath slowed. And behind the ill-lit shade of the old shed, in the deepness of her throat, mute Chalice Hibbert sang.

Katie Pru always slept with her feet stuck out from the covers. In books, children huddled under blankets, terrified of the monsters under their beds, but not Katie Pru. She stuck her feet straight out over the mattress, letting them dangle in the air all night long. I haven't lost a toe yet, she once told her mother. Her mother had

smiled. When it comes to messing with the Miss Katie
Prus of the world, her mother had replied, smart monsters know better.

Now she stuck a foot out from beneath a mound of
thick covers, pushing away the thought that the world
had *dumb* monsters, too. The night cold nipped, but she
kept it out for the count of five, then she drew it back in
and bunched herself tight until she was warmed.

Outside, the trees shivered. From her bed she could
see through a tiny window set low in the wall. The leaves
flipped back and forth—silver, black, silver, black—like
millions of minnows. It would be just like minnows, she
thought, to wake up when the whale was asleep.

From a bed across the room her mother's breathing
was even. Katie Pru stared hard, making sure her mother
was asleep. Then, tugging the thickest blanket over her
head, she slid off her bed and scooted to the window.

The window was so low, she didn't have to stand on
her tiptoes to see outside. The air was colder here, and it
grabbed greedily at her feet, so she scrunched her toes
in the blanket as she rested her elbows on the window's
narrow sill and peered into the dark.

The minnows darted around on the ends of their
branches like tiny dogs on leashes. They waved and
bounced, flickered and dipped, until Katie Pru's eyes grew
heavy and her head clunked against the windowpane.

It was the cold glass that waked her. She jerked up,
her forehead achy.

Outside, a light flashed. It could have been Pinocchio's fire, but Katie Pru didn't really believe that story.
It could have been the whale's eye. Only Jonah knew
what the whale's eye looked like from the inside.

The light blinked among the trees a couple more
times before going out. The minnows never stopped
swimming. Katie Pru gathered her blanket around her
and went back to bed.

MICHAEL'S BOOK

12 MARCH 1812

None of my "dainty" stones tonight:

My father was a cotton weaver and lived in a millstone grit cottage on an incline of common land outside the village of Mayley. Like his father, he kept hens, and close to the cottage a garden of vegetables which my mother tended to her satisfaction. My brother Nathan and I apprenticed under my father and learned the loom, while my younger sisters worked under my mother's supervision at the spinning wheel. My father kept four spinsters from Mayley employed with his need for spun cotton. We were well kept—food, clothing, and a regular pudding. A shilling a week remained to pay a clockmaker to teach my father's two sons to read and write. When work was necessary, we worked hard and long. When work was finished, we enjoyed our walks on the moors and spent many a village celebration with our friends in Mayley.

At the bottom of my father's incline ran Sette Water. The West Riding is blessed with water—the Pennines rise to our west and streams pour down them in abundance. And farther east the ground grows long fingers of coal. It is said that Dalesmen can scuff their toes and their shoes will turn black.

This was my father's Eden. He did not know that the merry beck tripping past his land was his serpent.

The common lands around Mayley have been enclosed by one of many thousands of Acts passed by Parliament. The gentleman to whom the land was given saw no need for a weaver, so my father was forced off. He and my mother survived for three years more. I was wedded to Martha Trench and for twelve years now have lived in a cold and cramped cottage in the center of Mayley, one of many in a row that stretches down Farrier Lane. The upper storey has wide windows and there I weave with my sons John, fourteen, and Will, eleven. On the floor below, my wife teaches our daughters to spin. We have no land for vegetables—we buy our food, as we must buy for all our needs. But for many years we eked out a fair living. We were content.

Will my sons have such contentment? Not if the gentlemen get their way. For with the streams came mills, and with the coal came steam, and what three hundred men once did by hand is now done by one solitary figure at a machine. Ten years ago I received twenty shillings a week for my labor at the loom. Now I receive ten, and there are times when the work does not come and my loom is still. Our food is meagre—Martha has learned that half a sheep's head, when one can be found, keeps us in broth for three days.

Imagine this one hundred times, a thousand times, ten thousand times over, worsen it for hosiers and the croppers of the woolen industries. Add the grim results of the blockades and deprivations caused by the war with Napoleon, and you understand the restlessness of the West Riding. From Lancashire and Scotland, petitions have been sent to Parliament begging for relief, but relief has not come. The Parliament, it seems, does not want to interfere with the employer.

My brother Nathan lives away from the village, in a cottage in Blandon Wood unwanted by gentlemen. He cannot afford a *loom, so he works as a farm laborer and steals what food he can. For his cottage he pays no rent, but that does not mean he lodges for no cost. Blandon Wood is parkland, and none but gentry may hunt there. Animals dart past my brother's door, but he may not kill them; the gameskeepers have keen eyes. His family is thinner than mine. We share what we can, but sharing is neither cause nor answer.*

So we smoulder. In dark corners we scheme. In my oath I pledged to pursue with unceasing vengeance the traitor, even though he should fly to the verge of nature. But it is not traitors I pursue to the verge. It is life.

Nathan told me tonight he thinks of seeking work at the mill. Yates is a cotton-spinning mill, furbished with throstles that spin cotton at incredible speeds. Few men work there; it is mostly women and children. The women suck the cotton dust into their lungs; the children grow twisted from crouching to work beneath the machines. You must not, I told him. It is what we fight against. Remember the oath. Nathan looked at me strangely, then his shoulders sank and he nodded. I understand his turmoil. His youngest son is ill. Tomorrow morning my Martha goes to help them. I will take our children to chapel to pray.

The local dual economy started in the 1400s when peasant families turned to the loom to augment farming income made adequate by the barren nature of the moors.

—*Notes*, G. GRAYSON

6

Tuesday

Head bent, Nadianna scurried across the clearing and into the woods. Yesterday the sky had been dark when she left the cottage—the entry into the woods had been little more than a shift in air. This morning, however, the immersion was immediate. The trees swarmed above her; the air moistened. She stepped carefully, using the snaked walking stick to guide her over slick roots. The droopy overcoat she'd borrowed from her father hung in awkward hanks by her sides, making her bulging belly cold. The farther down the path she descended, the thicker the trees grew. The light dimmed, and loose pebbles scrabbled like insects across her shoes.

The night before, she had gone to bed as soon as they returned from The Crown & Drover. Downstairs Gale and Halford had retreated behind the thick kitchen door, as isolated as in a soundproof booth. She imagined their conversation—*God, I feel sorry for her. What an embarrassing thing. Tomorrow I'll talk to her, buck her up.* She had pounded her fist into her pillow. She should never have left home. Her father had tried to tell her. Facing the unknown wasn't always a matter of faith. Sometimes facing the unknown was the pure result of being stupid.

Her sleep had been fitful. Several times she had awakened to the ticking of rain on the window. She'd closed her eyes and tried to imagine this English rain on her own window at home, but it couldn't be done; it was as if the change in continents had changed the laws of nature, too. The rain at home was full and openhanded. This was a sickly rain, pinching like an old aunt. She couldn't for the life of her figure out how it had the gumption to make the grasses so green.

Her thoughts returned to the rude couple at the pub. What had she done to deserve that? She couldn't make sense of it. By the time the sun rose, she was dressed in her father's coat, clutching the walking stick. She had to see the place again.

The path wasn't straight; instead, it twined through the trees so that after much walking, she found herself just a foot lower from where she'd been. The smell of the stream hung heavy in her nostrils and she could hear the water long before she glimpsed it. She didn't remember the path being so twisty—she wondered now if yesterday she had even stayed on the path, if in the gloom she might not somehow have wandered off and blundered to the streambed.

When she reached the bottom and emerged by the water, she knew that was exactly what she had done. This was not the place where she had taken her pictures. The mill was farther north, although more visible today in the fogless air. From here the structure seemed less like a monument than an oversized house, bland and suspect on its prime land. Tentatively, Nadianna stepped to the stream's edge. Nearby a log had tipped over the bank; bundles of swirled grasses and twigs gathered inside the crook where the stream first pushed then deserted them. She teased the debris with her walking stick. The police hadn't taken her seriously. Surely there were hundreds of such places along the stream, places where a corpse could get tangled.

Around her stick the water sang. In Statlers Cross there was a wide creek where she and her sister often fished, but she never recalled it singing. The water here sounded mournful, like a funeral song. No, that was wrong. She straightened, frowning. It sounded like "Blue Eyes Cryin' in the Rain."

She twisted around to spy an old man downstream from her, bent over and stirring the water with what appeared to be a mop handle. He was brown and spidery, as notched as the prickly bushes that obscured him. His voice shifted higher as he launched into the plaintive last verse. With his head angled skyward, he went on stirring the stream.

With the last note trailing off, he looked at her, and Nadianna realized he had known she was there all along. "I love that song. You know it?"

She nodded. "Sure. Everybody knows that song."

He grinned. He wasn't as old as she first supposed, probably no more than forty. His hair was the color of a mushroom and cut short; his clothes were baggy on his lanky frame. He pulled the mop handle from the stream and planted it on the ground.

"Not everybody," he said, "but many do. It's a bit of a hymn, don't you think?"

"I guess so. My mama used to sing me to sleep with it."

The words were out before she knew it. It was such a private thing—all her mother memories were private things—and she had shared it with this strange man by the stream. She remembered her grandmother telling her about spirits who lived behind gravestones and knew when children were telling the truth. For a fanciful second she found herself wondering if in England they lived among the damp reeds beside streams.

He must have sensed her discomfort. He smiled and idly examined the top of his staff.

"A sweet melody for a child, I'll tell you that. And I can see why your mother sang it to you—those eyes of yours must have been startling in a baby." He gripped the staff tighter and thumped it on the ground. "I'm Gerald Thornsby. It's a pleasure to meet you, Nadianna Jesup."

She frowned, her suspicions back. "How come you know me?"

"Everybody knows you. The tall preggers American who saw the body in the water. You're quite the curiosity."

"You tell them I'm not a curiosity. I know what I saw."

"I know you do. I saw it, too."

She had wheeled away from him, but now stopped and turned back. "What do you mean?"

Thornsby laughed. "Well, let me clarify that. I saw *you.* Up there, in the water. I was on the mill grounds and happened to glance out. It was quite a sight, really. Early morning, fog rolling off the water, and there you were, this pale creature in blue floating in the current. And I thought, ah, after all these years living in Mayley, Gerald Thornsby has finally seen a sight."

"I'm not a 'sight.' And I did see a body. It was close enough to me to touch." She studied his face. He was still smiling, but concern crinkled his brow. "You didn't see anything else in the water?"

He shook his head. "But I didn't need to. I believe you."

"Why?" she demanded.

"Because you were the witness."

The witness. Something in the way he said it—her memory flashed a picture of the altar at her church back home, the hand-hewn pine cross mounted behind the choir stall. Her daddy in the pew, leaning over her and her sister Ivy. *You witness for the Lord, girls. You witness for Him and He'll lift you in His arms and carry you to the altar.* She swallowed, forcing the nausea down.

"Yes, I was the witness," she said. "But somewhere that body's gotta come aground. If the police would just believe me, they'd find it."

"There's all kinds of finding, Nadianna Jesup. But you already know that, don't you?"

He had walked closer to her, and now she could make out the vivid green of his eyes. His face was unlined, open, and his accent was a crisped version of the West Yorkshire dialect she had heard last night at the pub.

"How come you understand me?" she asked. "Nobody else around has been able to."

"Not listening, then, are they? There's nothing wrong with the way you talk, Nadianna. Just takes a familiar ear." He paused, and for the first time his voice grew serious. "You should know you're among friends here, Nadianna. Don't let what happened last night discourage you."

Despite the chill rising from the stream, her face burned. "Were you there? Or is this another case of everybody knows?"

"I was there. It's nothing for you to think about."

"I knew one of the people there. I'd met him—I liked him. It felt like a betrayal." This was something else she wouldn't have told a stranger, but talking to this man was growing easy.

"This is a feeble town," he replied, "not much strength. It used to be healthy, in its way. Go to the center and look at the dust collecting in the shopwindows. There are items on the shelves that have rusted in place. Pick them up and they'll leave a stain."

Tears pricked her eyelids. "I come from a place like that. Never heard of anyone being treated rude."

"Ah. Either you aren't listening or it's a divine place you're from."

"Must be my listening's bad."

The water rasped in its bed; beside them, tall trees

shuddered. Thornsby clutched his mop handle in his fist and with his free hand rummaged in his coat pocket. He pulled out a small white card and handed it to her.

"I'm the pastor of the Mayley Christ Connect. We meet every Tuesday night on the mill grounds, just a social thing, to visit and pray a bit. We'd like to have you as our guest tonight, be part of our family while you're here. I could drop by Mill Cottage and pick you up around seven."

"I dunno. I need to work . . ."

Thornsby reached out and laid a finger on her hand. "I *believe* you, Nadianna Jesup," he said softly. "And Jesus does, too."

Halford drained the last speck of soaked tea leaf from his cup and stretched out fully clothed on his not-nearly-as-comfortable-as-it-looked bed at The Crown & Drover. The previous night Gale had asked him to ring her in the morning—the cottage didn't have a phone but the price had been so cheap, she had explained, that it more than justified a splurge on a cell phone. It was now nine-ten. He knew she had been awake for hours— she had said once that for her the most effecting minutes were those between full night and pre-dawn, when the sky accelerated into silver and cornflower. So she had been up since at least seven, coffee cup in hand, robe cinched and white socks pulled up to her calves as morning ascended. With Katie Pru asleep, she would have relished the freedom to sit in a silent house. Which was why he hadn't called—he didn't want to disturb.

It was bullshit, of course. In truth he was jealous.

He rolled onto his stomach, turning from the silent telephone on the night table. Nadianna Jesup was a rare talent, that was obvious by her portfolio. There was something in her photographs that he had not articulated to Gale, an unsophisticated element that one didn't usually associate with the technological art of the lens. If there was such a thing as a folk photographer, Nadianna Jesup was it. And last night at the pub had proved that she was little more than a lamb in the woods, a white-clad naif who had wandered too far from her home. How could Gale do anything but commit to her?

"Shit," he muttered.

Over the past year Gale had made it painfully clear where her priorities were. There was her work and there was her child. Only on the fringes was there a man in a foreign country with an ache for her. Moaning, he twisted around on the bed, grabbed the phone, and punched in a number.

Gale answered on the second ring.

"Finally," she said. "I was about to hunt you down."

"I was giving you some breathing time."

Her laugh was light. "Spoken like a bachelor. Katie Pru's been up since six, Nadianna was out to God knows where by eight. Later, we're heading to the mill. I want to see it up close before I start researching. Wanna come?"

"Listen, Gale, you're working. I didn't come up here to be in the way. I can keep myself—"

She cut him off. "You wouldn't be in the way, honest. To be truthful, I could use you. We're going to take Katie Pru with us, and a third person would be helpful. I don't expect we'll be able to go into the mill, but another set of hands—"

"So you need someone to look after Katie Pru?"

"Not what you had in mind, huh?"

What, exactly, had he had in mind? "No, that's fine. Katie Pru and I are like—that. What if I get there in about twenty minutes?"

"Twenty minutes will be fine. And if Nadianna isn't back yet, I'll fix you coffee."

She rang off. He stared at the phone, trying to decipher

his feelings. Too hard. He pushed himself off the bed, slipped on his shoes and coat, and headed downstairs.

The Bertie Portman sitting behind the Crown & Drover desk Tuesday morning was not the same cheerful bloke Halford had encountered at the inn pub the night before. This one was doleful, his shoulders slumped, a thick finger poking numbers into a computer. He gave the policeman a cheerless smile as Halford paused to button his coat.

"Weather's not bad out this morning, sir. Fog burnt off early. How did you sleep?"

Halford nodded. "Well. It was quiet. I take it I'm the only person staying here."

"Aye. Always a chance for ramblers on the weekends, but custom slows down a bit in November." Portman ran his bare hand over the desk as if he were wiping it down. "Look," he said. "Bad scene last night. I feel awful 'bout what happened to the girl. She didn't deserve that."

"No, she didn't."

"Folks get rowdy sometime. And Olivia, she was, well . . . Lyle—that's her fiancé—came up to me later and apologized. Said he had a touch of the flu and it was all out of control before he could stop it. Still, it shouldn't have happened. Tell your friend I'm sorry. You bring her back and I'll serve you supper in our private room, on the house."

"Thank you, Mr. Portman. I'll let her know."

Halford took a step toward the door. "So, I was just wondering," Portman said. "Well, some of us were talking . . . what are the chances there really was a dead man?"

"I couldn't say. Inspector Reston is in charge of the investigation."

Portman waved his pudgy hand. "Aye, yes, I know Mark. He's a good man. Stops in here now and again. Horrible gossip, though. Won't say a word."

Halford smiled. "Well, then, I can't go talking behind his back."

"Suppose not. Hoping you would, though. The idea of a chopped-up body floating out there . . . Chilling, you know?"

The front door rattled, stopped, then rattled again. "Dammit all," muttered Portman. "They're early. 'Cuse me, sir." He left the counter, walked to the door, and slid back a large wrought-iron bolt. "Good morning, all," he said breezily. "Weather's not bad out this morning, is it."

The couple looked only superficially different from the night before, although standing, they made a diminutive set. Beneath the bulk of a black parka, the man was compact, his dark hair again sleeked into a ponytail. Instead of a scarf, the stocky woman wore an orange-and-green-striped cape that reached below her knees; black leggings covered her thick calves. The large flying birds still dangled by her cheeks—one ill-timed collision with the man's shoulder, Halford thought, and the tip of a wing would impale her face. He felt again the niggle of recognition.

The woman's voice was as chirpy as her jewelry. "Hello, Bertie," she said, taking Halford in with a smile. "I've put my clay away early and dragged Lyle from his darkroom so we could make sure everything was ready."

"I believe so, Olivia," Portman answered. "Doreen's got the troops working on it now." He looked apologetically at Halford. "My better half is the organizer around here—left to my own devices, I'd have been out of business in a month."

Halford gave a brief smile and let his eyes drift over the newcomers. Olivia Markham and Lyle Botting. He had recently read a *Times* article that paired the two— the extraordinary young couple of the commercially successful art crowd. No starving artists they. Only, close up, they weren't that young, either. It had been a mildly offensive article, a bit snide in its assessment of talent. Botting, a nature photographer, had it; Markham, a potter, was, in the writer's words, "accessible."

The accessible Ms. Markham shook her head, sending her earrings dancing. "Don't sell yourself short, Bertie. Doreen couldn't do it without you. It's that jolly-innkeeper demeanor of yours."

Portman grimaced. "Jolly. Yes, well, I try." He turned to Botting. "I checked earlier and everything for the meeting seemed to be on course."

"Good," Botting said. "We just wanted to make sure there was nothing last-minute we needed to do . . ."

"Ah, no. We couldn't charge you money if there was. Now, if you two will go down and take a left past the door . . . The room will be on your right. Doreen's in there making sure it's up to standards."

The innkeeper waited until the doors had swung shut on the retreating figures before turning back to Halford.

"There," he said, dropping his voice, "goes one of God's lesser endeavors."

"Really? One or both?"

"Her. Troublemaker. Well, you saw that yourself. But she's worse than that. Troublemaker from London. Bad divorce, so she comes up here, thinks she knows what's best. She considers herself an artist, but if she ever had talent, she's squandered it. I've got a nephew studying art in Leeds—says she's a laughingstock. She used to be good, but now no decent artist respects her. She throws out the stuff like it were nursery leavings. But she pulls in the money, does Olivia. Makes you sick, what people will pay for trash."

Halford nodded. "I've seen photographs of her work, although never the real thing."

"Well, that's the problem, isn't it? Damn stuff looks like the real thing. Now, Lyle, he's a good-enough bloke. Local lad made good. Everybody likes him. But he follows her around like the back end of a donkey suit."

"So what are they doing today?"

Portman glanced at the hallway, where the artists had disappeared. "She's got this lunatic idea about restoring the old mill. Turning it into an arts and retail center. Another Saltaire, she says. They've got David Hockney, we can have her. Problem is, we don't want her. I don't know how you feel about art, Mr. Halford, but her stuff's obscene. What, we want people from all over the country coming to Mayley to buy women's body parts? What kind of people will they be?"

"So she's doing a bit of politicking."

" 'Ayat's right. Today she's having a private meeting to butter up some folks—community-leader types, or just plain thorns in her side. But she has no idea. For one thing, there's this local preacher with a regular Come-to-Jesus meeting going on up at the mill, and he's more than once said no pornographer's going to move him out. He may be loony, but everyone knows she's bats. I'll tell you what—she'll pay my fee, they'll eat my food, and they'll leave still knowing she's bats."

Halford moved to the door. "Not a bad deal for you."

"No, not a bad deal. I'm an honest man, Mr. Halford. I don't care one whit for Olivia Markham, but I'll take her money."

King Ludd, General Ludd, Ned Ludd —names used by
*Luddite groups to indicate the mythical figure at the head of
their "army."*

—*Notes,* G. GRAYSON

7

Yates Mill, built in 1793, was what was traditionally de-
fined as a small-sized spinning mill—three stories high
with a row of ten windows stretching the length of each
floor. It was rectangular, as could be expected from its
function, and built of local stone rubble, which gave it,
two hundreds years after its construction, the complexion of dirty wheat. Its only decorative features were
ashlar surrounds for the windows and an impressive
open arch on its ground floor through which water was
originally diverted for the massive wheel. All this Gale
learned from a phone interview with Nigel Pigeon, an
elderly member of the Mayley Local History Group, before she left Georgia. The roof was newer, the gentleman had added, rebuilt in 1820 following a fire and
comprised of a more fireproof combination of timber
and iron. The whole place shut down for good in 1884
during the Great Depression. "We had a Great Depression before the war, too," Pigeon told her. "All in all the
building's in decent enough shape, considering a century of neglect."

Gale stood on the grassy side yard of Yates Mill and assessed Mr. Pigeon's accuracy. Afternoon sun lit the mill's southern face, turning the stone a stained oyster-white. The neglect was evident—the windows, once mullioned, were now black and empty except for a few jagged splints of wood. In one corner the roof had caved in, and mounds of moss, still summer-lush, dripped into the cavity. There was no chimney stack, no pediment to provide relief from the structure's boxiness. Yet with the blue spill of Sette Water mere feet from its east wall and the tracery of bare larches playing on its west, the mill was somehow captivating.

"Beautiful, isn't it?" Nadianna asked.

"Very much. It's more of what I imagined Thrushcross Grange to look like than a mill."

Nadianna said nothing, just lifted the camera around her neck and fiddled with the lens. Gale mentally kicked herself. Thrushcross Grange. Why not just toss off the casual literary reference and see how stupid other people feel?

She picked up a pebble and lobbed it toward the stream. "Sorry," she said. "A house in *Wuthering Heights*. Not too much to do when I was a teenager except read and pretend I lived far away."

"Oh." Nadianna slipped off her coat and let it fall to the ground, revealing a long, white sweater over a black skirt. She fingered her camera in silence.

"So what do you think?" Gale asked, striving to correct her mistake. "Think this project of ours is going to fly?"

"I've risked too much for it not to" was the terse answer.

Across Sette Water sat a bulky stone house, the demarcations of its rough-hewn slabs visible even from a distance. As Gale watched, a red Escort pulled up to the building's entrance, and a large young woman stepped out. Her hair was wrapped elaborately in a bright green scarf, but there was no mistaking her identity.

"It's Chally," Gale said. "Not her house, though. I know she and her sister live in town."

Gale hollered, and both she and Nadianna raised their hands to wave. The figure across the water glanced at them, then ducked her head and hurried into the house. Gale looked at Nadianna, puzzled.

"Maybe we didn't make a good impression."

"Maybe," Nadianna said sullenly, "she just doesn't want to admit she knows the loony Americans."

A peal of laughter rang behind the mill, and Katie Pru came running toward them. Gale scooped her up and planted a kiss on her cheek.

"What's so funny with you, ladybug? And what've you done with Mr. Halford?"

Katie Pru bucked from her mother's arms and slid to the ground. "He's back there. We found some people. They have funny hats and weird shoes."

These last words she shouted as she darted toward the rear of the mill. Raising her eyebrows at Nadianna, Gale jogged after her daughter.

Halford stood in front of a small one-story structure sheltered by the mill's north wall. This building, Gale registered, was in excellent shape, the windowpanes intact and clear, the door painted a glossy white. But the state of this detached building was not nearly as captivating as the young man and woman standing next to Halford, both dressed in what Gale had to admit were funny hats and weird shoes.

Katie Pru took Halford's hand. "We found them in the little house," she explained. "I think they're clowns."

The man grinned sheepishly and took a dented fedora from his head. " 'Fraid we are at that. Sorting through stuff for a jumble sale. Old hats"—he held up the fedora—"old shoes"—he clicked a battered pair of wingtips as if they were Dorothy's slippers. "Got a bit carried away."

The woman removed a ratty picture hat from her hair and kicked off a pair of red spike heels that had been crammed over white socks. "Comes from a faulty child-hood. Parents much too easily amused." She held her hand out to Gale. "I'm Zoë Axon. This is my brother Alan. Most days we're quite respectable adults."

Respectability may have been achieved by these two, Gale thought, but adulthood, just barely. Both were fair-haired and light-complected in a way that usually vanished by adolescence; if Alan, who appeared the older, was in his mid-twenties, Gale would have been surprised.

"I'm afraid Katie Pru and I gave them a bit of a jolt," Halford told her. "I don't know which was more startling—us seeing them dance around boxes of old clothes, or them seeing us peek in the window like ghouls. I apologize. We were under the impression that the grounds were abandoned."

"Just the old mill," Alan said. "It's been abandoned since the mid-1800s. But this structure here, it's been kept in good shape. Plus we've done a bit of work on it ourselves."

"Just the two of you? What do you use it for?" Gale asked.

Alan chuckled. "Yeah. Just the two of us. We play dress-up and chase each other around the room." He rubbed his arm where Zoë playfully punched him. "No, actually it's a church. The Mayley Christ Connect. There are about fifty of us. We've been meeting here for a year now. The lease is cheap—we wash the windows, we get the space."

"That explains the painted door," Gale said. "Y'all have done a good job. Did Daniel tell you we're interested in the mill's history?"

"Aye, he did." Zoë pushed the hat back on her head and bent the rim to shield her eyes—from what Gale wasn't sure since the sun was blocked by the mill's high walls. "It's quite a place, isn't it? Alan and I used to come here as children and shout nasty things through the windows. Beastly, we were. Alan can tell you all there is to know about it. He's a historian—leastways, that's what he's studying."

"Really?"

Alan shrugged. "I'm trying hard anyway. University of Bradford. Mills are my particular interest. Well, I'm a Yorkshireman. Of course they would be. This mill is what got in my blood. While Zoë was shouting nasty things through the windows—I was taking notes studious-like."

He received another jab to the arm. "I'd appreciate it if we could sit down and talk sometime," Gale told him, and meant it. "We're here on an arts grant. The family that owned this mill came to the States in the 1800s and built a cotton mill in my hometown in Georgia. We're doing a photographic essay comparing the two."

Alan looked at her curiously. "You the photographer, then?"

"No, I'm doing the text. But Nadianna's here somewhere." Gale glanced around, but Nadianna hadn't followed her. "So," she said, turning back to Alan, "this support building here—do you mind if we take a look?"

He was peering toward the far corner of the mill. His brow puckered as he dragged his attention back to her.

"Ah, no, not at all. Zoë and I made a mess of the place, but perhaps you'll overlook that."

The space inside the building was limited to no more than twenty by twenty-five square feet. Worn planks covered the floors; the walls were comprised of bare stone except for a small coal-burning fireplace in one corner, a fact that no doubt made winter worship in this spartan space an act of faith indeed. Straight-backed wooden chairs lined the walls, freeing the middle of the room for a tumble of crates and clothes. Draped over the side of one crate was the head of a fox pelt. With Katie Pru cautiously eyeing the pelt from the doorway, Alan hurried to the crate and knocked the head inside with his foot.

"The church operates a few programs for the community—a food bank, a clothes closet," he explained to Gale. "A couple of times a year we have a jumble sale to get rid of clothes that not even the needy want. That's what Zoë and I were doing—sorting out the gnarly things."

"Interesting building," Gale said. "Any idea what its purpose was?"

"Carding shop, probably—the place where they prepared the cotton for spinning. I'm looking into it. I'd like to see the whole place preserved."

"It's a shame when architecture gets lost."

"Depends. I'd hate to see the place go, but nowadays, with this emphasis on nostalgia tourism . . ."

"What he's trying to say is it's demeaning," Zoë supplied. "People paying a quid for a tour and a tea towel decorated with cotton jennies and quaint-looking mill kids. Everybody says such things bring money, but it destroys the heart of a place. Preservation has its uses, but . . ."

Her brother waved her silent. "What I was trying to say is that it can warp the historical record. But you know that, Mrs. Grayson. Anyway, there's no hurry here. This little shop is protected by the church for now." He grinned at Zoë. "The little hoodlums who used to run up here and shout in the windows have all grown up. Now, the mill proper, that's a nightmare. Don't know what we're going to do about preserving it."

He reached into one of the boxes and pulled out a navy wool cloche topped with a cluster of plastic cherries. "Much too small for Zoë's big head," he said, crouching down and holding the hat out to Katie Pru. "Perhaps my new American friend would like to have it."

Tentatively, Katie Pru took the cloche and examined it.

"What do you say?" Gale asked.

Katie Pru crushed the hat to her chest. "Thank you," she said.

Alan grinned. As he stood, he winked at Gale. Then his face changed, and he stared past her. Gale turned around to see Nadianna standing in the threshold.

"Here she is," Gale said. "Nadianna, I think we've some folks here who can help us."

The silence in the building grew. Nadianna blushed as the other two young adults stared at her.

It was Alan who spoke first. "God bless you, Nadianna," he murmured. "Praise the Lord."

"God bless you," Zoë whispered.

"Don't do that," Nadianna said softly. "Please."

"What are they talking about?" Gale asked her, bewildered.

Zoë looked at her, youthful joshing gone, face serious. "The vision. The body in the water. It was a sign from God. And Nadianna knows it, too."

The area's ubiquitous terrace housing with its "weaver windows" was initially built to house outworkers, the textile laborers who owned their own equipment but made cloth for the more prosperous yeoman clothiers.

—Notes, G. GRAYSON

8

When Chalice was seven, the landlord installed a tub in the old terrace cottage on Garrett Alley. Chalice was delighted. She would recline in the cooling water for an hour, arms at her sides, her head smack against the top of the tub, her feet planted against the bottom. Every now and then Totty would come into the room and sigh. "Raisin fingers and raisin toes, not to mention a lovely cold. Come on, now. Time to get out." But Chalice would dip her chin below the water and burble in protest. "All right, then," Totty would say, relenting. "But you're a right spoiled child." And she would turn on the spigot and send ribbons of warm water up Chalice's legs.

It was another full year before Chalice recognized that her body filling the tub was a remarkable thing. She had always known she was bigger than the other children of Mayley, but she supposed she had taken it for granted that elsewhere children grew to her size or more. Totty's first job managing a rental property took them forty kilometers away to Wakefield. As a prize for good behavior while the contract was signed, they visited a playground, where Chalice dangled upside down from the climbing bars, her hair lapping at the ground, while the other children grappled with a merry-go-round. She watched their hands clamp onto the metal bars, their feet dig into the moist dirt as they ran the merry-go-round in a circle before jumping aboard. Their shoes left such small prints. Their knuckles were like the backs of tiny garden snails. *Their* bodies could not come close to filling her tub. Thus she realized that she was fully twice as large as they. She was the largest child alive.

The knowledge packed a wallop. From then on she felt her presence with every footfall. The cottage on Garrett Alley became a garment. She filled it until the buttons strained.

One night she stopped Totty in the middle of beating egg whites. *I'm the biggest girl on the planet,* she wrote on a tablet.

"Don't be absurd," Totty answered. "You're the right size for you."

I'll use up all the air in the house. You won't be able to breeth.

White foam dripped from Totty's whisk. "That b-r-e-a-t-h-e, Chally. Spell correctly. And I have plenty of air." But as she turned away, she breathed deeply. Chalice's sister had needed to check.

Chalice had no strong memory of her mother—a stringy-haired woman with shocked eyes who bustled in and out of the flat until one day Totty changed the locks and refused to let her in again. "We can't both be your mother," Totty had told Chalice. "So it's going to be me. You'll love me like a mother, won't you, Chally?" Chalice hadn't known how to answer, so she sat on the floor by the sofa, her stump of a tongue rolling in her mouth.

Now, as she approached the age where Totty once had her mother's daughter thrust upon her to raise, Chalice found her sister inexplicable. Well, she wasn't a

real creature, was she—part sister, part mum? The two of
them were twined unnaturally. Where was the competi-
tion when there was no parent to impress? Where was
the love without a parent to alienate?

Chalice relaxed her shoulder against the studio doorframe, thoughtful. Outside, she could see the two American women surveying the abandoned Yates Mill as if it
were already a photograph in a gallery. But she could
tell that Mrs. Grayson and Miss Jesup were not wholly
comfortable. She recognized in their crossed arms
and tilted hips two women bound together and still un-
sure. Ah, well, she thought, when were women bound
together ever sure?

She spied Olivia's yellow list of instructions tacked on
the studio wall, and sauntered over to ponder her day's
work—one hundred unfired flowers, pink and chalky,
that covered the worktable like a casket blanket. By Friday they would be bursting with color on the lighted
glass shelves of the posh Manchester Gloriana Gallery.
Invites had been sent out three weeks earlier; for the
past ten days Olivia had been receiving calls from cooing
patrons. All very chi-chi—endive boat hors d'oeuvres,
hundred-pound champagne. Olivia had even persuaded
some of her arty connections from London to make the
journey, and several publications had committed to coverage. It merely depended on Chalice taking the flowers
and slipping them into 1120 degrees Centigrade of heat.

Outside, she heard laughter. She turned away from
Olivia's flowers to watch through the window as the little
girl jumped into Mrs. Grayson's arms. From here Chalice had a clear view of the mill's stern eastern aspect—
the rear, where the little girl coaxed her mother to a
cluster of people, and the front, where the pregnant
photographer loitered. Chalice watched, but Nadianna
Jesup made no move to join the others.

Chalice cupped her long malachite necklace in her

hand and let the beads click like green water droplets. She was too honest to deny a tweak of satisfaction at Nadianna's unease. From yesterday's interrogation she had gleaned that the fair specter from America was being shepherded by Mrs. Grayson. She admitted to an unsportsmanlike comfort to see that the sheep felt alienated.

Eyes still on Nadianna, she removed the green scarf from her head and slowly, then more determinedly, crammed it up her sweater. It barely made a bulge, so she grabbed a dirty work shirt off a hook and stuffed it up her sweater as well. She pivoted sideways before the studio's glass-front cupboard. Her sweater pulled away from her breasts so that her reflected profile was a series of graduating slopes—forehead, nose, tits, belly. She patted her stuffed front in the manner of a happy mother-to-be. *Ooo, I don't know how I'm to feel once the little dear is here. I'm so content knowing he's safe inside me.*

She pulled the shirt out and tossed it on the worktable. Motherhood was not for her. She had been fairly surprised when it turned out that sex, in fact, was. Most of the girls her age who remained in Mayley did so because of pregnancies. She'd see them in the row of dilapidated housing on the west end of town, lank-haired and without stockings, sitting on damp stone steps and holding half-eaten sandwiches while their children rode tricycles in the road. She couldn't imagine her fingers pinching a dirty chin while she spit on a tissue to rub clean a face. She couldn't imagine the smells, the sounds, the sticky floors and soiled upholstery. Worse than that, she couldn't imagine being pierced and mounted by the skinny, ill-kempt men who had fathered those children. Thank God that wasn't her fate.

Unlike Nadianna. Yesterday Chalice had listened, bemused, as the girl emphasized *Miss* Nadianna Jesup to the detective making the report. No chef in the kitchen but a bun in the oven. Odd that a girl like that, talented enough to win her way here, would be so stupidly caught.

Too talented was Chalice Hibbert to be so stupidly caught; wiping a child's bum could never be as satisfying as sculpting a perfect bowl. Her eyes drifted to the cabinet that held her finished pieces. From the shadows, her tea-bowls glowed a luminous blue, a departure from her usual natural look but one that surprisingly pleased her. Along the back wall, two shelves were filled with soon-to-be-completed tea-bowls—more in her new blue series, bisqued and glazed and ready for a final turn in the kiln. They had been sitting there for weeks like dutiful handmaidens, waiting for Olivia's vibrant courtesans to be called to court. For so long, that had been okay with Chalice. Odd how the past twenty-four hours had changed her mood so defiantly.

She opened the kiln lid. The interior was washed and wiped out, as it sometimes was when Olivia had one of her famed "cleaning frenzies." A pottery instructor once told Chalice that potters were the most easygoing of artists because they learned quickly how limited was their control over their art—when a potter delivered her work to the kiln, she had to be prepared to see it destroyed. One week with Olivia had proven that a joke. In her frenzies, Olivia would yell and scrub and fume until the studio was spotless and she was emotionally spent. The frenzies usually followed on the heels of one of her drunks. Chalice blew into the kiln's chamber; not a spec of dust moved. Olivia had been drunk Sunday night when Chalice came to fire her bowls. No doubt a mini-frenzy had followed Monday morning.

She glanced at the studio clock. Two-ten. Olivia would not emerge sober from her meeting with the town leaders; indeed, she probably would be too drunk to come into the studio at all. Plenty of time before Friday to get to her flowers. Chalice walked to the shelves holding her unfired bowls. For once, she would put her work first.

She worked quickly, loading the kilns, placing the tea-bowls precisely five millimeters apart, fixing the temperature cones in place, checking their position, closing the door. She flicked the switch, feeling triumphant. By midnight her bowls would be finished.

When the studio door whacked open, Chalice spun around dumbfounded. Olivia breezed into the room, cape slung over her arm, Lyle Botting following in her wake.

"Want to know how the meeting went, Chally?" Olivia dropped her cape on the worktable next to Chalice's discarded shirt. "They sat there like wax figures. Rabbits. I'll have no trouble with them. Wouldn't you say so, Lyle?"

Botting shrugged. "I don't know, Livy. I think they're biding their time. A shrewd little native game. Gerald Thornsby—"

"Give over. Gerald Thornsby is a cricket. Watch me squash him, luv."

Botting's eyes met Chalice's. He winced and threw back his head a fraction of an inch. Olivia had been drinking, all right, but not to the degree Chalice had wagered.

A leather and tweed sofa reserved for clients was wedged next to the door. Olivia sank into it and stretched out, her short legs barely reaching the glass coffee table in front of her.

"Bugs, Lyle. We know what to do with bugs, don't we, darling?"

Botting's jaw clenched as he continued to look at Chalice.

"So, Chally," he said, forcing a smile, "been a busy day?"

Behind her the kiln made faint noises as the heat rose. She kept her eyes on Botting, willing her stare away from the unfired flowers on the worktable. He glanced at the table but remained silent.

"You've loaded the kiln, haven't you, luv?" Olivia murmured.

Chalice was aware of Botting's eyes on her, a strange stare, defeated and hard. He knew what was coming. They both did.

"Chally?" Olivia slowly rose from the sofa. "You did load the—" She staggered to the table. "What the hell is this? Why aren't the flowers in the kiln? I have a show on Friday. What the hell have you been doing?"

"Answer me," Olivia said. "What have you been doing all day?" She grasped one of the unfired flowers, the powdery pink glaze smearing her hand. "Do you think I can sell this? What do you think, you idiot, that people are going to pay me money for something like *this*?" She slammed the flower onto the table. "Bitch. Where the fuck do you think I get the money to keep you? You think I enjoy you? Smug bitch! I *protect* you! Think I'm as ignorant as Totty? Think I don't know about *you*?"

She was breathing heavily now. From the corner of her eye Chalice saw Botting start toward Olivia, then stop. He's going to let her spend her anger, she thought. And why not? It wasn't worth the bruises to him.

Olivia swirled around comically, arms outstretched like a witch's. "What's in the fucking kiln?" Without checking the temperature, she threw open the lid, and heat blasted from the top. She shielded her face and looked inside. "Goddamn."

In a fluid motion she grabbed a large stick used to stir glazes and drove it again and again into the kiln. Chalice could hear the clay break, the sound of the fragile bowls returning to grit. Olivia's face was florid. She threw down the stick and made her way to the cabinet that held Chalice's finished pieces.

Chalice heard her own voice moan, felt the worktable tip beneath her fingers. The flowers exploded into pink dust as they hit the ground. She ran toward Olivia, but

Botting intercepted her. They collapsed onto the sofa, her necklace tight around her throat, his fists in a clamp beneath her breasts. Her voice was a primitive howl as she screamed at Olivia.

The first tea-bowl burst into splinters. Olivia looked at Chalice casually as she flung a second and a third, the shards flying upward, outward. The hours of shaping, smoothing, caressing—crash after crash filled Chalice's ears. She counted them silently as they exploded. Four, five . . . Tears poured down her face as she grieved for each death, praying for the survival of the rest. At nine Olivia stopped. The last piece Olivia took out was the mask of the evolving face. She held it in front of her, her expression cold, terrifying. Jesus Christ, Chalice thought. She's going to kill me.

"God's Messenger, isn't it?" Olivia said. She stood over Chalice. "Fuck you."

She raised the mask over her head and threw it down with all her force. It caught Chalice in the stomach and punched the air out of her. Botting let loose of her and she rolled to the floor, gasping, stomach throbbing, as the mask hit the ground and broke into two even pieces.

"Mother of God, Olivia," Botting said. "Why did you do that?"

Olivia didn't answer him. She walked over to where Chalice knelt, gagging, on the floor.

"You're fired," she said coldly. "See what you can do with your so-called talent without me."

By seven P.M. it was well dark. Nadianna huddled in the passenger seat of Gerald Thornsby's aging Fiat, listening to the motor whine and chug its looping course up the valley's side. Stone walls hemmed the car on both sides; she flinched each time they rounded a curve, the rocks so close she waited for the scrape on her skin. At the rare points where the wall dipped to reveal the moor, she saw not the flicker of a lamp, not the glint of a star. For a while she concentrated on the path made by the headlights, but even that was unsettling. She kept imagining coming on a person unawares, and the terror of someone else's terror at being lashed with light.

She dipped her chin into her coat collar. "What do you do if you meet another car?"

The preacher shrugged. "Happens all the time. If you're lucky, you just pull to the side and wave the other fellow past. If it's a road like this, well, you say a quick prayer and mash the gas."

She sat bolt up. "No way."

Thornsby chuckled. "No way. There are little places along that you can pull into to let another car pass. You'll find that people are very courteous up here. Not like in the south, where everyone's in a hurry."

"Just the opposite from home," she said. The faint gold of the dashboard light bathed Thornsby's knuckles but barely lit his face. In profile his features were bold—nose strong, chin pointed.

She retreated deeper into her coat and stared out the car window. She had never seen a night so dark. When she got home, it would be the blackness she'd describe to her sister Ivy. Even in rural Georgia, where there were no streetlights, no reflectors on the highway, there was always the moony glow of whitewashed clapboard or the hulky shapes of buildings on flat land. Here the land was so hilly, it made a wall of itself, with not enough light to cast so much as a silhouette.

"You know some people think I saw a vision in the water." She said it abruptly.

She couldn't hear the sigh, just saw the rise of his shoulders. A wall appeared in front of them, and he shifted the car into first gear to make the turn.

"Is it possible you did?"

"No," she said firmly. "My sister Ivy speaks in tongues. They'll come over her in prayer, and it'll just start. Trills, strange words. It scared me the first time I heard her. She says she sees visions when the tongues come. But they're joyful visions, Mr. Thornsby. Her face just gets busted up with joy. They ain't horrors. And what I saw was a horror. God wasn't nowhere near that stream yesterday."

The road flattened; Thornsby picked up speed and shifted into second. Nadianna waited for him to answer, but he said nothing.

"What am I getting into, Mr. Thornsby, going to the meeting with you like this?"

He shook his head. "You'll be fine, Nadianna. It's just a prayer meeting. Some of the younger members . . . well, you know what they think. But they won't bother you." His hawk face peered through the windshield, jaw working. "So let me ask you," he said. "Why, if you have uncertainties, did you decide to come?"

"You're not gonna like the answer."

He nodded toward the backseat, where her camera case sat safe on the floor. "Anything to do with that?"

"I brought it just in case. I'm gonna leave it in the car. Maybe next time everyone will feel comfortable enough to let me photograph them."

"Ah, so we're being used."

"Turnabout's fair play, Mr. Thornsby."

Thornsby's laugh was rumbly. "I like you, Nadianna Jesup. I do."

"That's the rare thing. I think I like you, too."

"So tell me some more about this place you're from. You said it was small, reminded you of Mayley."

"Smaller than Mayley. But far from everywhere."

"Close-knit, is it? Your family been there for a long time?"

"Yeah, close-knit. We've been there since the 1920s. My great-great-grandparents moved there to get mill work. My family worked in the mill until it burned down. My daddy works at a plastics plant about twenty miles away. That's the farthest any of our family has ever been from Statlers Cross. When we were little, his car broke down, and for months he walked to work. He left so early and came home so late, Ivy and I didn't see him that entire time. We'd just leave notes on the table."

"That must have put quite a strain on your family."

"It did. Ivy was about seven. She thought we were orphans."

He glanced at her but didn't ask the obvious question— *Where was Mama? Wasn't she making home nice and comfy while Daddy was trudging to work?* "So that was the farthest anyone had been until you came here. No table to leave notes on now, though. They must be proud of you."

"Why's that?"

"No need to be modest, Nadianna. You wouldn't be here if someone important didn't think you were special."

"All different kinds of meaning of the word special."

"You mean your family isn't proud of you?"

"I mean they're proud of me in their own way."

He drove in silence, his face shadowed. "I'm sorry, Nadianna," he said at last.

She shrugged. "No point in that."

The road curved and banked, then slid forward in a steep descent. Thornsby slowed the car to a putter to round a corner, and the mill was before them, sudden and pearled in the night. Beyond it Nadianna could just make out the steady ramble of Sette Water. The carding shop, so unimpressive during the day, was now ablaze with light. But if anyone was inside, she noted stepping from the car, they were either wet blankets or Methodists. Sitting on the grass in front of the mill was a circle of a dozen people. Camping lanterns clustered in the center cast long streaks of light across the ground and up their faces. As Nadianna walked toward them, she heard traces of singing and something else that reminded her of the fevered prayer meetings in her church back home. The worshipers of the Mayley Christ Connect were laughing like hyenas.

"I'd say they were making a joyful noise, all right," Nadianna whispered. "Is this something y'all do frequently?"

Thornsby cupped her elbow in his hand. "Once a week. Light the lanterns and let the Lord do his work."

Alan and Zoë Axon, blond hair burnished by the lamplight, scooted apart as Thornsby helped Nadianna to the ground. Alan winked at her, grasped her and Zoë's hands, and raised them into the air.

"We have a visitor—pray with me," he exhorted. "Pray with me for Miss Nadianna Jesup, who's come so far to practice her art on the mill. Pray for her and her coming joy, her baby."

Prayers rose, surging back and forth in familiar waves. It was a peculiar sensation, this known rhythm backing such unknown sounds—like home, but strange enough that she felt unsettled, separate. *Je-susJe-susJe-sus.* The prayer slipped from spoken petition into song. She didn't recognize the tunes, couldn't understand the words. When Zoë rose in the middle of the circle and slid into tongues, Nadianna couldn't tell the difference. They could have been possessed by the blessing of the Lord all night, for what she could have told.

In the lantern light, Zoë's face was flushed. Her long hair wrapped around her neck and slipped between her parted lips. *Rrrrmoxnafadaadaleelent! Rrrrsolonilodallieny!* Her arms went stiff behind her and she hopped, straight-legged until her coat fell from her shoulders. She flung herself onto the grass and her body went stiff. As the group moaned and prayed, she bounced, her body a board slamming the ground.

Nadianna glanced at the faces in the circle. Eyes closed, mouths mumbling. Beside her, Gerald Thornsby's head rested against his chest, his lips fluttering. She thought hungrily of her camera in Thornsby's car.

At first the flicker in the distance barely registered. The gleam from the sweat on Zoë's face, the eerie cast of the lantern beams on the rapt faces, made her forget that out there, beyond the circle, all was dark. The glint was a blaze before her chest tightened and she grabbed Thornsby's arm.

"What's that?" she whispered. "Is that okay?"

He looked up, then scrambled to his feet. "The studio's on fire."

The worshipers were out of their trances instantly. They grabbed the lanterns from the pile and ran toward the swelling fire, leaving Nadianna struggling to her feet.

"Is there a phone?" she shouted. "Can I call someone?"

She heard only shouts and the sound of splashing as people piled into the water. But she knew from experience that no one moved quickly through Sette Water.

The cry was sudden in the dark, the crowd's single high note of surprise and horror. "A woman!" a voice screamed. "Oh, my God, help her!"

Dismay caught in Nadianna's throat. A form, fire pluming from all sides, fell from the studio's upper window and plummeted into the stream.

A shriek from the crowd. Sharp hissing, crackles. Then all was silent save for the swift rustle of water following its God-given course.

Michael's Book

30 MARCH 1812

Another stone for you, heaved lightly but with accuracy.

Two weeks ago my brother's son had rallied from his illness enough that Nathan left his bedside and travelled with me to the village of Longley near Halifax. We had heard how angry the women there had grown. No food for the children or jobs for the men. We sat at the public house, conversing with a man named Jacob Farnley, who claimed to have attacked a mill-owner's house, but he would not own whose. "The wife and children ran out the door screaming as if our hatchets were swords," he said. "We made shavings of their belongings, that which we did not want." Farnley was not a savoury man, and both Nathan and I were wary.

At midnight there came a loud clanging from the church-yard. With other men we ran to find a band of women, woolen sacks over their heads, banging on pots. They darted from the churchyard like spirits and we followed their sound, out of the village, down paths and up wide hills until we came to what we thought was a stone cross set on the moor. The banging was all around us, fainter now, and in the dark we could see only the hunched shapes of the women and hear a low, gravelly coo.

Then suddenly a blaze surrounded us, and we found ourselves in the center of a ring of torches. Before us loomed the giant figure of a man, straw for his hands and feet, a hat on his
head. The women banged their pots louder. One lifted the bottom
of her sack to reveal a painted mouth. King Ludd! she shouted.
Bow to King Ludd!

The women danced, wild, insane, wrapping like a snake
around this straw king's body. We men stood in a spell as skirts
flapped and swelled around us. A strong wind came, strong
enough to force our eyes closed. The flames went out and we heard
scurrying. When we looked again, we were alone on the moor.

What does it mean? Nathan asked. But I do not know. Are
all stones clear?

The next midnight there came a sharp rap on our cottage door,
followed by two low coughs. I opened the door to find a hooded man,
who led me onto a rise of wasteland due south of Mayley. There I
joined a band of fourteen men, some local, some from Sowerby
Bridge and as far west as Todmorden. Most of them I knew by
name or family—J. Thorpe, M. Cooke, C. Martin, J. Armstrong,
two men of the Bridges family, three Cowpers. All were twisted in;
all could be trusted. From the murkiness appeared a torch. Ludd's
men! cried a voice. I have come to train them who are honorable
enough to be King Ludd's men! A pot of lampblack was passed
around, and for an hour by the light of that torch we drilled,
marching in lines, retreating, following commands. We are not a
regular army, though we may encounter one. It was not until the
fourth night on the moors that I learned the name of the man who
trained us. Joshua Peters from Halifax. He claims to be one of hundreds who prepare brave men for what is coming. He produced
from his pocket a leaflet, found on a street in Leeds, which stated
that we Luddites are revolutionaries now, kin to the rioting citizens
of Paris. If it is all true, then I have hope we will succeed.

That was two weeks ago. Joshua has gone home; before he
left, he took me aside. They will do well with you, Michael, he
said. Angry men follow two things: their stomachs and their
imaginations. The stomachs of all these men are empty; they
will follow you.

In the daytime, we fret out our small lives. Alfred Corn chelps about to form a choir of Mayley weavers. From village to village we will go, he promises, dressed in humble working garments to sing Methodist hymns for the poor ransomed sinners. Come join us, he says. Join the true King. The Methodists gain favour here with their simple message of hope. But theirs is a meek army. What are we if we wait for eternal grace?

At The Crown & Drover our band met. I forced my son John home to his mother—he is too young, but how he hates his mother's protection. At the meeting I wrote a letter and we posted it at the homes of fellow workers.

> *Gentlemen, we of King Ludd's Army ask that you give us a reward for the trouble we take on your behalf. If you cannot do so, we will seek you.*
>
> *—Ned Ludd.*

In the past week our band has made two small raids on wagons carrying frames to mills in Erringden and Lumb. A month ago I would not have guessed myself capable of terrorizing women, but I have done; like the man at the Longley pub, we found justice invading a mill-owner's house, destroying at will, while his wife cursed us.

Are we pleasant men? We are judged harshly by some, lauded by others, as is just. But we do it for our own wives' pain, for the shadows that we fear for our children. If not pleasant, think of us at least as men.

We do as we must. These are mad days.

During the English Civil War, upper Calderdale was heavily Puritan. Later, John Wesley's Methodism found a foothold, in part because Wesley's belief that economic hardship was the result of personal shortcomings appealed to mill-owners.

—*Notes*, G. GRAYSON

9

It was eleven P.M. before the police let members of the Mayley Christ Connect leave the mill grounds. The fire was out, but the wind whipped the smoke downstream, causing Nadianna's eyes to burn and her nose to run. The congregants wandered over the grounds, murmuring, praying, clasping one another. Nadianna sat on the grass, a blanket from Thornsby's car wrapped around her. She listened to the voices, picking out what words she could.

"Hair aflame . . ."

". . . yes, her arms tight at her sides . . ."

"Horrible sight. I'll never forget . . ."

"God bless her . . ."

Two black running shoes appeared in front of her; she looked up to see Gerald Thornsby.

"Tired?" he asked gently.

She nodded. "And cold."

"I've talked with the detective sergeant. He said someone could take you home. I've got to stay, but Alan's ready to go."

She held out her hand and Thornsby helped her to her feet. "Does anyone know what happened?" she asked.

"Not really. The building's a pottery studio used by a local artist."

"A woman?"

"Yes."

Nadianna shivered hard. Thornsby put his arm around her and yelled for Alan. Across the yard the younger man broke off a conversation and jogged to them.

"Ready to go, Nadianna? My car is over here."

"I left my camera case in your backseat," Nadianna told Thornsby. "I need to get it."

"Go with Alan. I'll get it for you."

She crawled into the passenger seat of Alan's car, urgency beating away her fatigue. When Thornsby handed her the camera case, she gripped it tight.

"Get some sleep, Nadianna," Thornsby said. "This is a horrid nightmare. We all need to pray for each other tonight." He signaled for Alan to pull away.

Once the crowd was out of sight, Nadianna pulled from the camera case a piece of tightly folded paper and held it out to Alan.

"Can you take me here?"

"What is it, an address?"

"I need to go there. Do you know where it is?"

He switched on the roof light. "I can find it. Not the nicest street, Nadianna. Why do you need to go there?"

"I have some work to do. Really, it's okay. See?" She forced her fingers into her pocket and pulled out a key. "I have permission. It's nothing dishonest."

Alan smiled. "I wasn't thinking it dishonest. But it's late. Why not wait until tomorrow?"

"I need to go now. Please."

He drummed his fingers on the steering wheel. "How long are you going to be?"

"Maybe an hour."

"Tell you what, then. I have to go back to the mill and pick up Zoë. We'll come back and take you to the cottage."

Nadianna nodded. "Thank you. That would be very good."

The address may have been on a bad street, but in the dark the whole town looked deprived. There were no lights from the windows; even the streetlamps were muffled, their beams falling to the sidewalks like discarded dishwater. Buildings lined the narrow lanes on each side, long and flat and shuttered. They came to a stop before a stone building.

Alan unbuckled his seat belt. "I'll go in with you," he said.

"No. Seriously, it's okay. Just wait to make sure I get inside all right."

He looked at her, dismayed. "Look—"

"I said no. I don't want you with me."

"I'm not letting—"

"No." Her voice rose, and she fought to sound reasonable. "I'll be perfectly safe. This is something I have to do." She hesitated, bracing for her lie. "Mr. Halford knows I'm doing this. So it's perfectly safe."

"Nadianna . . ."

"Oh, for crying out loud. Do you think God sent me all the way over here, put me in that river yesterday, let me see that fire, just to have me knocked over the head somewhere? I'll be fine. Now, shoo."

"You're trying to convince me they build 'em tough in Georgia, aren't you?"

She hauled herself and her camera case out of the car. "Go pick up Zoë and come back."

Alan waited while she slid the key in the lock and pushed the door open. She flicked on the light switch and waved at Alan as he tooted the horn and drove away. When he had rounded the corner out of sight, she shut the door, locked it, and let the camera case slip to the floor.

It was as Mr. Botting had told her—rustic, the bare necessities. It had been his first darkroom, he had explained, the one he used before his work started to take off and he could afford a newer one with a higher technological capacity. He kept the old darkroom as storage and insurance, he said. "Someday another photographer is going to capture the public's fancy and I'll be shooting stock again. At least there will always be four walls that will know me." He had spoken with modesty, and she had instantly warmed to him. Then came the scene in the pub, the shame—she bit back the hurt and focused on her work.

The offer was that he would put the room in working order and she would have use of it for the full extent of her stay, paying only for what chemicals and supplies she consumed. He'd been as good as his word. The equipment was adequate if not sophisticated, the supplies basic but sound. She had spent the past three years scrambling for materials on a crunched budget—most of the time her darkroom consisted of her bathroom's tub and sink. By comparison Botting's no-frills setup was rich. He had evidently even gone to the trouble of giving the place a mop-down. A door to the right of the large sink led to a small room outfitted with a metal cupboard, a file cabinet, and an old desk, all empty. Nadianna pressed her palm against a set of bedsprings leaning against the wall; dust and rust came off on her hand. She had met several photographers before. Lyle Botting wasn't the only photographer who had spent his lean years living with his work.

Back in the main room, she knelt beside her camera case, undid the flap, and pulled out the film she had shot in the river. It had to be processed now. She wouldn't leave it to anyone else. Two burnt bodies now seen in the water—she had to face the possibility that tomorrow the police would ask to see her film.

She found a plastic spool and, light off, carefully

rolled the unexposed film onto it and placed it in a small metal tank. The room was frigid, and the developer too cold to use, so she heated it on a hot plate she found in the back room. Twenty minutes passed while she waited for the solution to warm. Impatiently, she checked her watch. She needed nine minutes for the film to develop. Thank God she told Alan to give her an hour.

The developer warmed, then she poured it into the tank and began the ritual of agitating and tapping. Thirty seconds of agitating, three minutes of waiting. Her fingernails were white—she should have felt cold, but the back of her neck prickled with perspiration. She had told Mr. Halford there was no corpse on her film. But what if she was wrong?

At nine minutes she poured out the solution and rinsed the film. Trembling, she opened the tank, removed the negatives, and held them up to the light.

The mill, the trees, the dark water spreading out like tar—that was all. No light-colored bumps in the stream's negative. Her camera had caught no corpse in the water, no confirmation of what she had seen. This was good and bad. Without confirmation, no one would believe her. But without an image on the film, perhaps she was safe. Perhaps, please God, they would leave her to her work.

Few one-cell dwellings, which housed working families and would have dominated the landscape in the 17- and 1800s, are left; however, many three-cells houses, the homes of wealthy yeoman clothiers and mill-owners, survive.

—*Notes*, G. GRAYSON

10

Wednesday

Katie Pru drew her legs together and scooted on her bottom until her back wedged against a big rock. Far above, water dripped on the leaves; trees, like surprised pencils, stood all around. She was so deep in the woods, she couldn't see the path or the cottage, but with her dark blue coat buttoned to the neck and her new wool cap with cherries pulled low over her eyes, she was pretty sure nothing could see her, either.

She waited for the whale.

She had decided during breakfast to wait for the whale, when she sat in the kitchen like Goldilocks with a big bowl of porridge in front of her and listened to the grown-ups in the next room. Something bad had happened last night, she could tell. There were five of them—her mother, Nadianna, Mr. Halford, and the two policemen from the other day. The door between the kitchen and the living room was open, so she listened while she dropped dollops of buttered porridge side-by-side on the tabletop.

"I want you to think carefully, Miss Jesup. What exactly did you see?"

"Something on fire fell out the window. It must have hit the water, because there was this hissing sound. But I didn't see nothing else."

"What was it that fell?"

A long pause. Katie Pru lined up three dollops next to her napkin.

"Let me ask you something, Mr. Reston," she heard Nadianna say. "If I said it was a body on fire falling out of that building, would ya'll go looking in the river again? Would ya'll believe me any more than you did the other day?"

At that Katie Pru's mother must have realized the door to the kitchen was open, for she hurried in, a bothered smile on her lips.

"Taste good, ladybug?" She looked at the mounds of porridge, but she didn't frown. "Clean that up, please, ma'am" was all she said. "I'm going to shut this door, but if you need anything, come get me."

The door closed and the voices became so muffled, Katie Pru couldn't tell who was talking. She looked at the mounds of porridge, wet and shiny, running in a line along the table's edge. Slowly, she scooped up the first and plopped it back into her bowl. It sat on the top of the remaining porridge like a humpback in water. That was when she decided to pay her whale a visit.

She pushed her chair away from the table and hopped to the stone floor. Her coat hung on a hook by the back door. Below it was what her mother called her "butt-stompin' shoes," a pair of thick-soled tie-ons that looked like the shoes men wore when they climbed buildings. The boots were caked with dried mud, and as she slipped them on, chunks fell. From her coat pocket dangled the cap with the bright red cherries. If a whale did spy her, she decided as she crammed on her cap, he would think she was a pretty shrub. Whales wouldn't mind a pretty shrub in the woods.

Now she snuggled closer to her rock, the cherries knocking against her head. Her butt-stompin' shoes pressed deep imprints in the wet dirt, and her corduroy britches were cold and damp. If she waited quietly, the whale would talk. She wasn't sure yet if she would answer, but she was certain the whale would talk. Whatever else did he have to do all day?

Ooooohhhhhh.

From behind the rock Katie Pru heard rustling, like the whale's tail was slapping about. *Aaaahhaaahhh! Ssssssss!* Swish, swish went the tail, back and forth over the woods' floor. Katie Pru wanted to peek over the rock to see the tail as it scattered leaves and twigs. Instead, she crouched, arms tight around her, stomach hurting. This wasn't what she had wanted. This whale was sad. He was aching.

"Stop, please, stop." The whale sounded stern. "This won't help. I'm telling you, stop this. You've got to get control. We've got to think."

The whale's cry dwindled to a whisper. Katie Pru buried her head in her arms. She didn't understand. This was frightening, a whale that both cried and talked. She squinched her eyes shut. Tears fell down her cheeks.

"Come with me, please. The police are at the cottage, do you hear me? Shut up and listen to me! The police are at the cottage. They will find you—they will take you. You've got to come with me. We can't do anything here."

The whale sobbed quietly. The ground gave a soggy sigh as the mighty fish moved away. Katie Pru waited, her breath stabbing her chest. No more cries from the whale, no words. Just the scary sounds of the woods. Too frightened to look over the rock, Katie Pru scrambled to her feet and forced her butt-stompin' shoes to speed her home.

Daniel Halford had watched other detectives interrogate witnesses many times. He had been present in both subordinate and superior positions as his colleagues probed, teased, tricked, frightened, and seduced information from bystanders who, out of happenstance, abruptly found themselves of interest to the police. But he had never felt the same unease as he did now, sitting beside Gale on one of the cottage's two love seats and watching Mark Reston peck at the defiant Nadianna Jesup.

"When did you first notice the fire?"

"I told you. While the group was praying. It had probably been going for a while before I figured out what it was."

"Who was sitting next to you?"

A hard stare. "Gerald Thornsby on my right, Alan Axon on my left."

"And you say neither one had his eyes open when you first saw the fire? Did you notice when they had closed their eyes?"

The interrogation had been going on for twenty-five minutes, and even Halford was beginning to wonder what Reston was fishing for, since it was obvious Reston was indeed fishing. The West Yorkshire detective had arrived at the cottage all beams and assurances. *This won't take long, so many witnesses to sort through. Mrs. Grayson, would you mind getting me a glass of water?* But from the start Nadianna had regarded him with suspicion and had fired back as many questions as she had answered. *Did you search the water? What do you think I've done in my life that I would know what a burning body looks like? If you've never stooped to attend a charismatic prayer meeting, Mr. Reston, how do you expect me to explain it to you now?*

The last one had been a potshot; Reston adopted a vacant grin and let it pass. He tilted his wooden chair onto its hind legs and swayed.

"So, let me go over it again, Miss Jesup, so DC Swain over there can make sure he has it in his notes. Gerald Thornsby picked you up from here at— What time was it again?"

Halford settled against the worn cushions. Gale was angled in the crook of the love seat arm, back stiff, her face a muddle of bewilderment and concern. He reached out and took her hand. She fixed her eyes on him, but he couldn't tell if she saw him or not.

"I don't want to answer any more questions." Nadianna's voice was tart. "That's right, isn't it, Mr. Halford? I don't have to talk to him anymore if I don't want to."

Halford started to speak, but the legs of Reston's chair hit the floor with a loud clack.

"You're absolutely correct, Miss Jesup, you don't have to answer anything. But I can't say that I think you've been one hundred percent honest with me. I'm sure that's something both Chief Inspector Halford and Mrs. Grayson would counsel you to reconsider."

Beside him, Gale flinched. He tried to squeeze her hand, but she pulled away.

Detective and witness regarded each other while Reston's long-limbed DC Swain sat awkwardly in a corner, scribbling in his notepad. The staring continued until the scribbling stopped and Reston stood. He reached into his jacket pocket and pulled out his business card.

"Call me if anything comes to you, Miss Jesup," he said. "Perhaps a little time is what we both need."

He gave Halford a pointed glance and left the cottage through the front door. Halford pressed his finger against Gale's knee, and when she nodded, he picked up his coat and followed.

Reston was lighting a cigarette as Halford closed the door and stepped into the brisk mid-morning air. The lit match flicked from Reston's fingers and sizzled between the damp pebbles surrounding the front stoop.

"What we say is confidential, Danny," Reston said.

"Of course."

"They're all nutters, then. Ride with me? I need your input."

"Unofficially."

"Of course."

Halford signaled a good-bye to Gale through the cottage window and with the two West Yorkshire detectives trekked through Blandon Wood to where Reston's white Mazda sat parked on the verge. At the road, Halford paused to look out over the drystone wall. Below him slinked Sette Valley, its willow-green turf already toughened for winter. The fog was just now lifting, and the upper portion of the moor was feathered with mist. On the other side of the valley, Mayley sat like a jumble of toy houses on the hillside. Below, in a narrow cleft in the valley bottom, Halford could just make out the tinsel glimmer of water and the heaped vegetation of well-moistened earth. From there it was evident that Sette Water was not a straight shot. It coursed through the valley's northern elbow, uncurled for a direct path past the town, then shifted into a meandering pattern until it flowed out of sight and into the River Calder. He had heard that during the middle years of the Industrial Revolution, the oil and pollutants in the rivers were so thick that floating debris would burn for days. The global economy had put an end to that. With the mills gone, the water was cleaner. Whatever Nadianna and the others had seen fall into the water had been quenched in short order.

Reston came up beside him.

"So," Halford said, "what does Olivia Markham make of her studio burning?"

"Ms. Markham has not made herself available for questions."

"Scarpered?"

"Wouldn't be the first to set her place of business on fire and scram. Make my life a helluva lot easier if she has. Can't locate the boyfriend, Botting, either. But I've got ten witnesses who say a burning body fell out that window. That's ten of them that were across the water at the mill who say the same thing, almost down to the last detail. 'It was a body, sir, with hair aflame, arms at her sides. Fell headfirst in the water, did she.' When was the last time that happened in an investigation—nearly a one-hundred-percent agreement?" Reston stamped out his cigarette and took a piece of gum from his pocket. As he folded it into his mouth, he jerked his head toward the wood. "Except that one in there. That one in there swears she saw a burnt body nobody can find in the stream Monday morning but weasels every time I ask her what she saw in front of witnesses last night. Bleedin' crackers."

A breeze blew the smell of peppermint in Halford's face. "So why does the wayward one bother you when you have the rest? Surely you've enough to justify an investigation."

The smile on Reston's face was strained. "You're sounding like a priest, Danny. And you know the answer to your question: I have enough to justify an investigation only if I provide results. This whole thing could end up with me looking like a damn fool. Was there a body Monday morning and if so, did I send out enough men? Was there a body last night and if not, did I send out too many men? I've had ten PCs since daybreak up to their waists in ice-cold water—and that's ten out of a force hit hard by this damn flu. Not a fucking thing. If there was no body . . ."

"But as you said, nearly a one hundred percent . . ."

"You taught me this one yourself, Danny. Remember the Chelsea teacher raped and murdered in her flat, twelve, thirteen years ago? Remember how seven people swore on their grandmothers' graves they'd seen her husband in a pub miles away at the time of the murder? Except there was this one boy who said the husband was at the scene because he recognized his footsteps. Didn't see him, just heard his bloody footsteps, for chrissakes. You went with the boy and proved the other witnesses wrong."

"Doesn't happen often, Mark."

"Bloody right, it doesn't. But it happens."

Halford decided to change the subject. "You seemed a bit concerned with the actions of Gerald Thornsby and Alan Axon."

"Not so much the boy. But Thornsby, yes."

"Why's that?"

Reston's gum popped as he leaned against the wall. "Gerald Thornsby is what you would call one of our local characters. Born here, moved to Nottingham and became involved with a theft ring, busted, served a year, came home and told his mum he loved her but Jesus more, then set up this little church group of his."

"Any trouble since he's been home?"

"Not a whit. Lived a virtuous life for the last two years. As far as I know, no one in the town even knows about his past, or if they do, they've forgiven him. But he and Olivia had a history to them. Her work was an abomination in the eyes of the Lord, y'understand. Can't say I disagree with Thornsby."

The wind bit again. Halford shoved his fists into his pockets and studied the path of the water. "Humor me a bit, Mark. Let's assume Miss Jesup actually saw a body Monday morning. Just from her description, do you think it would have fallen into the water while on fire?"

Reston snorted but his eyes were somber. "Not likely. Sounded like a regular crisp to me. Charred."

"All right, charred, then. What effect would water have on charred flesh?"

"If the body had been in the water for a period of time, you mean? Ghastly. Bloat. Puff up at the splits."

"Not what she described."

"No, it's not."

"So . . ."

"So the body hadn't been in the water long. *If* there was a body in the water at all. But that's supposition."

"That it is." Halford straightened and made for the car. "You wanted to show me something?"

"Aye, Chief Inspector. Wondered what you could tell me about the potter's art."

A sharp wind cut across Olivia Markham's property as Reston slowed his car to a stop. Blue and white police tape made a flapping perimeter around the grounds, starting at the waterfront and extending past a car shed to a broken wall that erupted from the grass like mucky teeth. The house sat on the water's edge, its severe lines pure bookshelf Yorkshire. Blocky millstone grit walls rose for two stories, capped by a sloping slate roof. Tiny sash windows peered from its front. Pity, Halford thought as he lifted the police tape and ducked under it. He once had heard an architecture historian comment that the famed "Yorkshire sash" with its horizontal slide was becoming endangered. Here had been four presumably fine examples. Now the glass was burst and the aged wooden frames seared black. If he had blown on them, the ashes would have whisked away. The air was rancid with the smell of burnt wood.

Reston nodded at a PC guarding the door and led the way into the studio's charred hull. The building was open to the roof save for the scorched beams that had once held the upper story. The fire had evidently been very hot. The metal shelves that lined one wall had melted until they drooped to the floor; the door of a wooden cabinet that had somehow survived the flames hung off melted hinges.

But these were cursory observations. In the center of the room Halford stopped. "Fantastic," he said. "How bloody peculiar."

"Isn't it, though," replied Reston. "If I were one of your imaginative men, it would keep me up at night. As it is, someone's a strange bugger to have gone to this trouble."

Halford crunched through debris to reach the kiln. Stacked on its closed lid was a pyramid of dingy white flowers, pistils extended. He tried to dislodge one with his knuckle, but heat had fused the glaze on the blossoms. He shook his head in amazement.

The flowers were everywhere. Clay blossoms were scattered among the soaked and denuded remains of a sofa like decorations in a maiden's hair. A metal stool lay knocked on its side, its heat-damaged legs curving from an amethyst-petaled mons. Circled like wreaths beneath the windows, strung like garlands along the floor—the room was covered in Olivia Markham's baked obscenities.

Halford gently rubbed the sooty tip of a blossom's petal. "Have Fire Investigation been here? Bagged some of these things?"

"Uh-huh. They implied in their oh-so-quiet way that yes, this was an unusual fire although it's still a preliminary investigation and yes, they believe at present that we are looking at arson, but no, there are so far no signs of human remains. Of course, there wouldn't be if the remains are floating a mile downstream."

"Damned odd," Halford murmured. "So, your witnesses say that sometime between seven-thirty and seven forty-five P.M. they look across the water and see the house fully on fire. About three, four minutes later a figure, engulfed in flames, tumbles from the upper floor. What time did the call go in to the fire brigade?"

"Eight-fourteen. No phone in the mill. Had to drive to the station in Mayley."

"Hmmm. And the fire brigade reached the fire?"

"Eight-thirty."

"And when was the fire officially out?"

"About three hours later."

"Hot enough and long enough, apparently, to effect the glaze on these pieces." Halford pointed at the cleared petal tip. "I know sod all about pottery, but the glaze is thick here, so the heat buildup wasn't sufficient to completely fire them."

"They weren't laid out in a—I don't know the term here—in a finished state, then. They weren't completed and ready to sell."

"Get a potter in here, but I wouldn't think so. The heat has to reach a certain temperature for a certain amount of time for the glaze to totally melt."

"We've had the Hibbert girl here—you know, that mute woman, although I'm sure I'll be reported for being insensitive for using that word—Chalice. She worked as Olivia Markham's assistant. She wasn't very helpful. A bit rattled. Her sister—her guardian, actually—acted like we had come to feed Chalice to the flames ourselves."

"Interesting. And understandable."

"I know. So you're saying someone laid these unfinished pieces out *before* this place was torched."

"It's possible." Halford stood and motioned to the sofa. "It appears they chose places where they knew the clay would be relatively protected. Ingenious, really."

"Rather desperate way to work," Reston said dryly. "More effective to use the kiln over there."

"Depends on what you were trying to achieve."

Halford glanced at Reston to find his old colleague studying him, his expression flicking between thoughtfulness and frustration. "Come on, Danny boy," Reston said. "Bizarre is just beginning."

Sette Water falls 190 feet per mile; to guarantee water flow during dry spells, the Yates family built a reservoir north of the mill. Reservoirs dot this entire region.

—Notes, G. GRAYSON

11

Chill and windy with evening rain—that was the forecast. "Chill" was a good English word; Gale, with her arms still browned from a Georgia summer, considered the turn in the weather downright hypothermic. The fireplace emitted a petty heat that warmed the small of her back but left the rest of her unthawed. She remembered this cold, remembered it colder, in fact, when her tiny cottage in Hampshire had grown so frigid the skin on her knuckles cracked, and a raw triangle perpetually spread from Katie Pru's nose to upper lip. There were nights after Tom's death when she would snuggle with Katie Pru, waiting until her daughter was warmed and sleeping, then slip outside to stand in the dark and inhale gulps of icy air until her lungs were seared. She'd never cried; crying was an act of heat, and she had wanted to freeze herself from the inside out.

She could hear the creak of a rocking chair upstairs, followed by the sudden thunder of Katie Pru's feet and Nadianna's soft *Come here, let's read this book together.* She thought back to the interview earlier that morning, and

Nadianna's recalcitrance in the face of Reston's questions. Nadianna was now doing what Gale had long ago mastered—hiding behind the needs of a child. Well, thought Gale as she plopped down on the floor in front of the fire, she'll learn. Katie Pru doesn't take well to grown women clinging to her skirts.

She picked up her notebook from the hearth, settled on the floor against the love seat, and, angling her feet toward the fire, slowly flipped through the pages.

She didn't realize Nadianna had come downstairs until she felt the *wump* on the love seat. She twisted to see the younger woman sitting with a blanket pulled around her, her blue eyes luminous in her face.

"I need your help, Gale."

"It's yours," Gale said. "What's wrong?"

Nadianna gave a little laugh. "This is going to sound a bit like everybody else is crazy but me and thee—"

"It's okay. I'm fully prepared to find the rest of the world crazy. What's up?"

Nadianna spoke in a rush. "There was no body fallin' out of that building last night. I don't care what everybody else told Mr. Reston about hair on fire and arms by her sides—I was there and there weren't no hair and there weren't no arms. It was something flat that fell into the water."

"Flat? Like what?"

"I dunno. A board from the roof, maybe. A shingle."

"A burning slate shingle?"

"Then not a shingle. But something flat and straight. It wasn't a body. I heard people last night calling it a 'she.' It wasn't no such thing." She paused, a film of sweat covering her face, and she finished weakly, "It wasn't, that's all."

"I don't understand. If you didn't think it was a body, why didn't you say that to Inspector Reston?"

"He wouldn't have believed me. He had all those other people saying it was a woman."

"He'd at least listen to you."

"No, he wouldn't. There'd have just been me—me, who told him there was a body floating in the river that he can't find." Tears sprang into her eyes. "I want to go home."

"Oh, no." Gale rose and squeezed next to Nadianna. "No, no, no, you don't want to do that."

"Yes, I do. I realized as he was questioning me this morning that he thinks I'm a problem. He won't leave me alone until he's proved me wrong." Tears fell onto the frayed blanket. "I need you to stand by me."

"Oh, God, Nadianna. I will stand by you. But not in this. You don't want to go home, honest. Your grant—"

"My project is ruined, anyway. What kind of work do you think I'll be able to do now?"

"Have you forgotten what it's taken for you to get this far? The work, Nadianna, the goddamn courage. Do you know the odds you've overcome? Because if you don't understand them, then maybe I need to tell you about them."

"I know the odds."

"Then why are you ready to give up? I know this isn't easy . . ."

"Isn't easy?" She looked at Gale in amazement. "I saw a dead body, Gale. A dead body almost bumped into me in the water. And nobody cared enough to really look for it. And now all these people think I saw a vision. A vision? Either they're crazy or I am."

"The police looked, Nadianna, but they can't keep looking forever. And as to who's crazy, they are."

Nadianna exhaled sharply. "I can't believe you're so cold."

"This isn't cold. This is damn well knowing that if you let this push you down, you will never get up. I know this, Nadianna. I know it for a fact."

"What about *me* letting *you* push me down?"

The words were nettle-sharp. "I'm not pushing you

down," Gale answered, incredulous. "What are you talking about?"

"You make me feel stupid."

"I don't—"

"But that's not the worse of it. You don't believe me. You haven't from when this whole thing started. How can I stay here if the one person I trust doesn't believe me? I gave up more than you'll ever understand to come here. Do you think Statlers Cross will be the same for me? It won't. I've lost my home."

"That's ridic—"

"No one's gonna treat me the same. Ivy told me. She told me that I'd never be accepted again if I left her and my daddy to go away with—with a woman and child who most folks would rather just leave alone. Ivy said I was turning away from everyone who loved me."

"What a terrible thing for her to say."

"But she was right. There's a certain way of life there, and by coming with you I told everybody I'm too good for it. And now you don't believe me. The person who believes me isn't the one I've put all my trust in, but a preacher who trusts me even when he didn't see what I saw. You, on the other hand, have no faith in me whatsoever."

They stared at each other. Gale felt the heat creep up her face. It was true. She didn't believe Nadianna. She didn't believe that the pregnant mill-village girl from Georgia had seen anything evil in the water. All her pats on the shoulder and reassuring hugs had been hypocritical. At her most generous, she believed Nadianna was mistaken.

"You know what they call y'all back home, don't you?" Nadianna's voice trembled. "Pariah and Child."

"Nadianna," Gale said softly. "Don't you see they'll say the same about you? Unmarried, pregnant, talented—they'll call you and your baby that, too. It had nothing to do with me."

Tears ran down Nadianna's knuckles where she clutched the blanket. "I want to go home," she insisted.

"Listen to me. I do believe you. Dammit, I'll make myself believe you. You saw a body two days ago. There was no body last night. I'll do what I can to help you prove both."

"Now it's my turn not to believe you."

"It doesn't matter. The truth is, if you return to the States now, there will be no way to save your project. You'll lose the grant. Your reputation will be scarred and you may never get it back. Is that what you want—to fail with your photography and rely on your family's pity to take you back?"

"They'll take me back."

"They take you back, and what will you do then? You've earned this chance, Nadianna. You've more strength than you know. Don't give up."

"I always thought I had strength. Now I don't know." She leaned toward Gale and Gale wrapped her arms around her. Nadianna's sobs were muffled. "Don't let me go back."

Halford and Reston, with DC Swain in tow, walked down five grimy steps to reach Gerald Thornsby's flat, located at the end of a narrow, rubbish-strewn alley. The minister's entranceway was more properly kept, the area swept, the door painted a glossy white similar, Halford noted, to the paint used to spruce up the carding shop. Beside the entrance, a ceramic plaque bearing the words JOY AND ABUNDANCE hung on a tenpenny nail.

"I just want you to see what I'm up against, Danny," Reston muttered as he knocked on the door. "Tell me you contend with this kind of thing down in the City."

Zoë Axon opened the door, her eyes swollen, her blond hair mussed. She looked at the three detectives uncertainly before her brow smoothed.

"Oh, right," she said, glancing at Reston's warrant card. "A WPC called earlier. Come in. Gerry's in the back."

Halford half expected to find Thornsby's abode done up in opulence. Instead, the flat had all the comfort of a petrol station. Most of the main room was taken up by a metal desk piled high with books and papers; a smallish brown clay bowl filled with liquid tottered on its edge. The room's only light was a desk lamp. A book cabinet topped with a stack of dishes and several mugs seemed to perform both literary storage and meal-taking functions. Five bright orange plastic chairs butted against a wall. In the middle of the floor was a shag carpet, its once-vivid greens and reds aged mercifully to more earthy colors.

Zoë gave Halford a bemused smile. "Didn't peg you as a copper. When I met you at the mill you looked more like a nanny with that tyke in hand."

Halford smiled, too. "Funny, when you have a child with you, no one asks your profession. I'm on leave from the Metropolitan Police. Just here observing."

"She your little girl, then, the kid?"

He couldn't read her mood. There was a challenge in her sleepy eyes, something subtly sexual. Despite the bare chill of the flat, she was dressed in a filmy wrap skirt that reached to her ankles and a buttoned-up cardigan thin enough to reveal the lace on her bra. On her feet were thick brown socks and leather sandals.

He widened his grin, hoping to draw her out. "No," he said. "She's a friend's. Didn't know I looked the Mary Poppins type. Another career waiting, perhaps?"

She didn't reply, but continued to smile at him as she rapped on a closed door at the rear of the room. "Ger," she called softly. "The police." An inaudible response sounded. She sat in the desk chair, picked up the clay bowl with both hands, and sipped. "He'll be out in a minute," she told them. "He's exhausted, I'll tell you that. So am I. None of us left the mill last night until almost dawn. Then it was back up this morning, answering questions from two of your lot. You have more, then?"

"Just a few," Reston replied. Swain sat in one of the orange chairs and opened his notepad. "Clarification, mainly." He looked around the room. "You live here, Miss . . ."

"Axon. Zoë. No, I live on Hall Street with my parents and brother. You just missed him, by the way. Ran out to get some groceries." She gestured at the stack of papers in front of her. "This is my job. I do all the office work for the Mayley Christ Connect—flyers, newsletters, that sort of thing."

"A paid position?"

"We don't have paid positions. All of our money goes to our works."

"No other wage-earning job for you, then?"

"This is my job," she repeated. "And I pray for what essentials I need."

"You . . . pray for your income?"

"It's amazing how the Lord provides."

She said it without sarcasm. Reston rocked lightly on his heels. Halford could guess what he was thinking. They had put away plenty of three-pint meals in their early days at the Met, railing on about the lay-about youths who cluttered up sidewalks and littered the hallways of the local Job Centres. Coming from a single-parent household with five children, Reston had been particularly callous. *Useless louts, can't make their own way. Living off their parents or the government. Either way, something's gone wrong. A job or the military, that's the only choice I'd give them.* Zoë Axon had evidently decided on a third way: menial volunteerism.

She lit a cigarette, the flame bouncing before the paper ignited, her eyes on Halford. What was there in her manner? A hidden excitement? A secret maybe? Halford pulled a chair out from the wall and placed it near the desk. He spoke to her gently.

"Tell me, Zoë, about your church. The Mayley Christ Connect, is it? I'm not familiar with that denomination."

"Maybe that's because it isn't a denomination, not in the sense that you mean it," she replied. "We're Christians, charismatics for the most part, although we have some evangelicals in our group."

"I apologize for my ignorance," Halford said meekly, smiling at her again. "I didn't realize there was a difference."

"Oh, yes—well, there can be. Evangelicals are much more rule-ordered. We charismatics—we're more receptive to the emotional aspects of the Lord. But we've all found a home with Gerald. Used to be chapels, mainly Nonconformist, all over the valley, but they're mostly torn down now. Not as many believers these days. Gerald saw that and decided to bring us all together. We're not affiliated with a larger church. We started as a house church—"

"A house church?"

"No chapel, no building. We just met in each other's houses. We believe in the power of prayer, and that God works through miracles. Can work, I should say. He works through other ways, too, like the power of tongues, the power of the Spirit . . ."

"And visions?"

Her excitement became palpable. Her eyes glowed. "Yes," she whispered. "And visions. You understand that, don't you?" She leaned toward him, but sank back quickly when Thornsby emerged from his room, looking less than exhausted in a fresh shirt and creased trousers. His short hair glistened with water, and he brought with him the muggy smell of a shower.

"Hello, Inspector," he said, holding his hand out to Reston. "No rest for the weary."

"I always heard it was no rest for the wicked—either will work, I suppose. I wanted to ask you some questions about last night's fire."

The smile remained on Thornsby's face. "I suspected you might."

"Really?" Reston asked. "Why's that?"

"Because I suspect you went over the notes your men took from my people and your policeman's intuition thought, hmmm, this doesn't quite fly."

Reston picked up the chair next to Halford, swung it around, and straddled it. "Lovely. I'd like to hear more."

Thornsby glanced at Zoë, who, fussing with paperwork, disguised her interest beneath a fall of blond hair. "So you don't mind if Zoë stays?"

"We can go in the back room," Reston said. "Or to the station. If you'd prefer privacy, we'll certainly—"

"Oh, no, I don't mind if she's here. Prefer it, actually." Thornsby sat cross-legged on the carpet and looked up expectantly.

"To begin with," Reston said, "we're trying to establish where everyone was prior to the fire. Can you tell us where you were yesterday afternoon?"

"I was with a family in Mytholmroyd. The father is dying—several members of house churches had gathered there to pray."

"About what time?"

"From around two to six."

"I'll ask you to give the family's name to DC Swain. And after that?"

"After that I left and went directly to pick up Miss Jesup so she could attend the meeting at the mill."

Reston turned to Zoë. "And you, Miss Axon?"

"I was working at the mill all afternoon. Sorting things for the jumble sale."

"Were you alone?"

"Some of the time. A few people brought things, left."

"Good. You can also give their names to DC Swain.

Now, I'd like to talk more specifically about last night, Mr. Thornsby."

Making a tent with his fingers, Thornsby stared vacantly at the carpet. "Something rare and wonderful happened last night, Inspector."

"Indeed. Tell me about it."

Had Thornsby been of a different religious persuasion, Halford would have expected him to close his eyes and recite a mantra. Instead, he continued to focus on a point near the inspector's ankle.

"It will be hard for you to understand this," Thornsby said slowly. "You are by nature a logical man—which is why you do what you do. Hard, cold facts, isn't that what they say? But facts become murky in the hands of the Lord, Inspector."

"I would think the opposite to be true, but please go on."

"What did my people tell you last night? That they saw a figure on fire falling from the upstairs of Olivia Markham's studio."

Reston was noncommittal. Thornsby raised his eyes briefly, then continued.

"But what if that was what the Lord wanted them to see, Inspector Reston? What if it was the Lord's purpose for us to convene last night at a particular time at a particular spot, and, while in the midst of prayer, for us to see just that?"

"My first response would be to ask who was the human agent who chose the time and location."

"Normal time, normal location. We meet every Tuesday night like clockwork."

"Then my second response would be to point out that God has more important things to do than act as your video machine and play movies for your entertainment."

Thornsby gave Reston a patient smile. "It wasn't a movie. More glorious than a movie."

Reston glanced at Halford in exasperation, then at

Zoë. She had given up pretenses and was watching Thornsby, rapt. "What, exactly, was more glorious than a movie?" Reston asked.

"Nadianna saw it first." Zoë said it softly. "The Lord wanted us to confirm."

Reston raised his eyebrows. "Confirm what, Miss Axon?"

"The vision," she replied. "It's why Nadianna is here. Why else would she have been sent this far?"

"What do you mean by 'vision'?"

"A visual message from God. Some people hear His voice. Others *see* His works."

"And what was the message, then?"

"Nadianna would be the one to answer that."

Reston sighed. "Spell this out for me, please, Mr. Thornsby. This is what you've told your followers? That they've been privy to some kind of vision?"

Thornsby shook his head. "They're not my followers. We don't operate that way. And I didn't have to tell them anything. They all understood."

"A burning body falling through the sky?" Reston didn't bother to conceal his disdain. "A burnt corpse floating in the water? Give over, Thornsby. What the hell kind of God would envision something so horrible for His flock?"

Thornsby smiled. "Whoever said the Lord's message was pretty?"

During the 19th century, transportation in the upper Calder valley grew to include canals and railways. Mayley, however, remains difficult to navigate, the lanes serpentine and steep and many still featuring the original handrails that make it possible to walk them.

—*Notes*, G. GRAYSON

12

Chalice Hibbert was seven the first time she ran away. Her sister had yelled—about what exactly Chalice no longer remembered—and in retaliation Chalice had taken a piece of white paper and a red ink pad from the kitchen desk. She had pressed her fist into the pad and slammed it onto the paper, time and time again, until she ran out of paper and pounded red onto the desk instead.

Totty had watched her in silence. She leaned against the kitchen doorframe, her face a mask. When her arm tired, Chalice turned to await her sister's comment, an apology perhaps, but the clear gray eyes stared at her, considering her as if she were a poorly executed sketch inside a pricey frame. Furious, Chalice stomped into her room and packed her suitcase. In flew shoes, gloves, hats—no clothes, as if it were only the parts that stuck out that mattered. She got as far as the bridge over Sette Water. There, her suitcase popped open, and a car ran over her pink knit hat and a new brown loafer. She hobbled home, the broken suitcase clutched under her arm, accessories spilling along the trail like bread crumbs.

When she entered the house sobbing, Totty sent her to her room. "You're lucky I'm taking you back," she'd said. "I don't *have* to be your mother, you know." She refused to walk Chalice back to pick up her clothes until the next morning, and by that time they were gone, as if birds had eaten them in the night.

Now, running was all Chalice wanted to do. She sat in her bedroom, the door locked, and squeezed her car key until its teeth left bite marks in her palm. Kitchen sounds—the clank of metal on the counter, the pinging of a spoon against a bowl—traveled down the squat hallway and up the stairs. Totty was baking again; new guests somewhere tonight. Never mind that hours earlier Chalice had been interrogated by the police; never mind that they both had stood slack-jawed at the burned-out door of Olivia's studio, Chalice's eyes darting, searching, taking in the macabre display within; never mind, as Totty herself had said as they climbed into the car to return home, "Shit, what are you going to do now?" Custom called.

Inspector Reston had faced her from inside the ruined studio while she stood behind the strip of blue tape like a museum-goer poking a pointy nose into a restored vignette. She was stunned by the damage, but not so stunned that she was unaware of his detective eyes watching her. *Tell me about this room, Chalice. Tell me what it looked like before, where all the furnishings were. And tell me about the flowers.* Totty had rushed to stop him. *I know what you can ask her. I know where the line is, and don't for one minute think I'm going to let you cross it.*

Reston had ignored Totty. *I don't know anything about pottery, Chalice. Tell me about the flowers.* But she told him nothing. Her hands trembled so badly, she was unable to write.

The key tumbled soundlessly to the carpet. She wanted to run away. She needed to think.

From the kitchen below came the whir of an electric

beater. Totty was making macaroons, a Hibbert company staple. The beater would continue for at least three more minutes.

She quickly retrieved the key, slipped down the stairs, and headed out the front door and through the garden gate. At four, the evening chill was building. She climbed into her Escort and, fumbling, jabbed the key at the ignition several times before it hit its mark.

The aging car shuddered as much as its driver as she eased it up the alley and through snaked streets until she emerged onto the road that led to the moors. This time she didn't need a trail of fallen possessions to direct her from town. A pulse of words beat against her brain and spurred her on. *Olivia's dead. Olivia's dead.*

By six-fifteen the sky had turned pitch dark. Despite the snug scent of store-bought lasagna, the cottage had sunk into a sullen chilliness. The dinner they had inhaled might have been warming their insides, Gale thought, but it was doing damn all for their flesh. On a love seat Katie Pru snuggled beside Halford, burying her fists and occasionally her nose in the crook of his arm while he distracted her with a book. Nadianna sat on a fireside stool, feeding finger after finger of kindling into a limpid blaze. The last one she tossed in hard, sending a puff of embers cracking against the masonry.

Gale sat down by the pregnant woman. She picked up the fireplace poker and pushed a piece of kindling into the flame. "Maybe an early night would be good. I can't imagine you've been sleeping well. Why don't you go to bed?"

Nadianna gave her a weak smile. "Not a bad idea. I'm beat. And it's bound to be warmer under the covers."

"Go ahead," said Gale. "I've got an interview tomorrow at nine-thirty—you don't mind watching Katie Pru, do you?"

In answer, Nadianna sighed. "Get me up at eight," she said as she headed for the stairs. "Hopefully that'll give me time to both think and sleep."

Gale listened for Nadianna's door to close. In the morning her own work was scheduled to start in earnest. She wondered if instead the day would be spent canceling appointments and arranging plane reservations.

"Is Babar a good elephant or a bad elephant?" Katie Pru asked Halford.

"Oh, a good elephant, I'm sure," he answered.

"Then why did he make all the elephants wear clothes? I don't think they like it."

I've lost my home . . . I've lost it because I left my family to go away with a woman and a child who most folks would rather just leave alone. . . .

Hard words, but Gale was certain Nadianna used them to convey hurt more than to cause it. Regardless, they were true. Gale was well aware of the special reverence with which she and Katie Pru were treated in the closed world of Statlers Cross. Suicide was one thing; suicide blended with privilege and the exotica of terrorism was something else. But what Nadianna didn't realize, perhaps, was that exotica dwelled behind all doors. Gale remembered her grandmother Ella's condemning glance when she told her she was hiring Nadianna to help take care of Katie Pru.

You aren't expecting very much, are you? Is a moving body all you want as your daughter's child care provider?

Ella, she's more than a moving body. I've monitored her, watched them together. She has a way with Katie Pru. Besides, I'll be in the house. . . .

"Besides." Let me ask you one thing, Gale: What is that girl's agenda? What is it she wants from you that the best way she can get it is through your child?

Ella had been right about one thing. Nadianna had wanted something from Gale, and she had gotten it. A guide out of rural Georgia, a connection into an artistic field that was complex and competitive and in all probability out of reach had she stayed Nadianna Jesup of Statlers Cross. Nadianna Jesup, whose sister was known for her glossolalia and whose father once stomped, sober, into a Methodist church to bellow to the female minister that all women were fallen and shouldn't be allowed behind the pulpit. Nadianna Jesup, whose mother still inspired gossip in certain cramped circles of Calwyn County. Three months ago Gale knew nothing about her daughter's baby-sitter; as she checked her background, she learned scarcely more. Even Alby Truitt, the sheriff, had eyed Gale curiously as he answered. *She's fine, Gale. Strong, I think. I'd trust her. But it's hard to know somebody till they're in your house. . . .* The rest had been only fierce whispers. *Don't nobody know where Nadianna's mother is now. Margaret Jesup ran off with some man—nobody knows where he come from. She never called them girls of hers, never sent 'em so much as a card. Margaret Jesup was a beautiful woman with wide red lips. Know why God gives women lips like that? To make 'em prove their virtue . . .*

Gale lifted her head and ran her fingers through her hair, frustrated. Nadianna had her mother's lips. Gale had no idea what the mother had looked like, or what level of anguish had driven her to abandon her young daughters and never look back. But she knew the woman's mouth. She had watched it sing her own child to sleep. There were leaps of faith everywhere.

Behind her, Babar's friend The Old Lady was bitten by a snake and fell wounded to the ground.

"Are there snakes in our woods?" Katie Pru asked.

Halford's deep voice was reassuring. "Not this time of year. Snakes like it warm."

Katie Pru fell silent. When Gale turned around, her daughter had pulled her sweatshirt away from her stomach and was pressing her hand to her belly button.

"Stomachs are warm," she announced. "I bet snakes like our woods."

Gale met Halford's eyes and shrugged. No decipher-
ing that child's mind. She wondered if she should tell
him Nadianna's quandary. Not yet, she decided, and she
grabbed the love seat arm and hauled herself up.

"Do you know what I would pay good money for? A
nighttime drive through the moors. Do you think I can
get one of those?"

Halford closed the book, leaving The Old Lady to ail
until dawn. "Not too cold for a bunch of Southern
women?"

"Not a bunch. Just two. And we bundle up just fine.
Katie Pru, run go get your coat and mittens."

The Ford sat on the verge outside the woods. Gale
raised her eyebrow, amused, as Halford retrieved a thick
fleece blanket and a down bedpillow from the trunk and
made Katie Pru a pallet in the backseat. "Stakeouts," he
said simply, buckling Katie Pru in. "Always prepared . . ."

He found a smaller blanket and tucked it around
Gale's knees before sliding into the driver's seat.

"Do you have a specific place in mind?" he asked.

"Not really. I just want to get out for a while. Any
suggestions?"

"Why don't we head north? When we get far enough,
we'll head south."

"Sounds like someone with no respect for the moors."

"Sounds like someone with an Ordnance Survey map
in the glove box."

The car heated quickly, and Gale found herself relaxing as the car ambled up the hillside. Soon the moors
rolled out on all sides; at night they had a curdled look,
the darkness spreading lumpy and cream-thick over outcroppings and hollows. In the backseat, Katie Pru quietly sang "Go Tell It on the Mountain" until the car's
warmth and the engine's burr won her over, and her
breathing grew deep and even.

Halford tilted his head toward the backseat. "Is that
what you had in mind?"

Gale looked at her sleeping daughter, her head surrounded by a cloud of pillow, the red cherries on her hat falling over her eyes. "No, but it's not a bad side effect. Of course, she'll wake as soon as I carry her in—and won't go back to sleep until midnight. That's the payoff for unexpected peace."

Halford drove in silence, kneading the steering wheel with his palm. "Was it a tough decision?" he finally asked. "Bringing her along when both you and Nadianna need to be free to work?"

"There was no decision to make. Nobody at home is really suited to take care of her. I mean, who could I leave her with for a month?" She pushed the blanket off her knees, suddenly hot. "You know, it's funny. For a couple of months now I've been reading everything I can find about the history of this area, about the Luddites, about the culture that was displaced by industrialization— there's not overly much, you know."

"I know. The Luddites were so good at secrecy, the written record is nil to none."

"True. But even of the day-to-day living within the cottage industry, there's not an abundance of written record there, either. Not like what came once the factory system was in place, with the time sheets and evaluations and financial documents. The domestic sphere's always been a concealed world." She bit her bottom lip, only half aware of the cloaked vista sliding by outside. "I keep making these connections between them and us— between the cottage weavers and me and Nadianna and Katie Pru, huddled in our houses, ekeing out a living in our rooms. Family and work and play are all tumbled together—no neat divisions, no hierarchy. Sometimes it scares the crap out of me."

"Why's that?"

"Because we're so vulnerable."

"Really? In what way?"

The burn in her throat was unexpected. She stared

out the window, surprised at the violent surge of emotion, hoping her words wouldn't thicken as she spoke.

"I asked Nadianna once how she saw herself in five years. She was quite adamant. She was going to raise her own child, be independent, and get some satisfaction out of her work—and she didn't care if she had to move mountains to do it. But it won't happen. There are too many obstacles. If she manages it at all, she'll end up doing what I'm doing. What so many women are doing. Compromising. Biting back our frustrations."

"Gale, women aren't alone. . . ."

"The hell we aren't. We've got so much secret anger. We don't even tell it to ourselves. If there were machines to smash, we'd do it."

The road leveled onto a high plateau, and suddenly stretching on either side of them were rows of towering windmills, their arms circling eerie white, their stick bodies looming against the sky. Fat drops of rain spattered the windshield. The burn in Gale's throat intensified until she couldn't breathe. Her eyes blurred and she dashed the tears away.

"Oh, dear," she said. "I bet that's not what you were after. I bet you brought the subject up because I've been shameless in pressing you into baby-sitting service."

"Not at all. I enjoy Katie Pru. She's . . . well, she's so *Katie Pru.* I try to remember what I was like as a child. I don't think I was as certain of my own head as she is. I dunno. I don't deal with children much. . . ."

Halford pulled the car to a stop on the verge and turned off the engine. The road was flat and graveled here; no lights save the moon and the glowing pillars of the Ford's headlights sparkling the rain. They sat silently in the dark, the only movement the whipped rotation of the windmills.

"I don't want you to be alone, Gale."

Again the burn. "Ah, well, Mr. Chief Inspector, sir. It's too damn far for you to do anything about it."

She had said it gently, but she could still hear the sting in her reply. He stared up at the windmills, and she realized that he was as far from her as he could get.

"Thornsby's group is convinced what they saw last night was a second vision."

The announcement was so abrupt, for a moment she was certain she had misheard.

"A what?"

"A second vision. Nadianna saw the first, they saw the second. God's backup, as it were."

"That's nuts. What—*all* of them say what they saw wasn't real?"

"According to Mark, and he's interviewed them all. They give the same basic details, and in the end they all want him to join in prayer to thank God for the blessed moment."

"You know, Nadianna doesn't believe it was a body at all. She thinks it was a board that fell into the water."

Halford shot her a glance. "Then why didn't she spell that out for Mark? She was damned uncooperative."

"Why should she have cooperated? He didn't believe her three days ago. He's just supposed to be able to come in and say, 'Look, we thought you were crazy the other day, but tell us your opinion *now*'?" She shook her head. "The point is, she thinks the other witnesses are wrong. The rest of the group was there for a prayer meeting—Zoë, from the sound of things, was in a trancelike state. That's a highly suggestive frame of mind. How much more suggestive if they believe that God had already communicated with someone among them?" She paused, the rain now steady. The windmills rotated as the breeze picked up. "But they *all* say they saw a vision?"

"Actually, under the circumstances, I can see it happening," Halford said. "Humans look for patterns in things. We're wired to do that. Doesn't mean, of course, that what we see is correct. If a dozen people under trancelike conditions want to feel a connection with God, what better way than to see a vision?"

"Particularly a vision that has been pre-screened, tested, and ready for their approval. Not a bad deal for Thornsby. Convince your followers that they've had a communication from God and that you were the person who facilitated it—nice way to consolidate a group. Damn, that's fascinating."

"Well, while you're feeling so invigorated, remember two people are missing—Olivia Markham and Lyle Botting."

"Any chance they were in the house?"

"The fire investigators haven't found any indications."

"So you think one of them may have been the falling body?"

Halford's fist lightly tapped the wheel. "Don't know what to think. Damned odd, is all I say."

From the backseat, Katie Pru raised her head. "Look," she said breathlessly. "What are those?"

"Windmills, K.P. Aren't they something?"

"Yeah." Gale heard the unlatching of a seat belt, the opening of the car door. "Let's go see."

"No, Katie Pru. It's raining and dark. Stay in—"

But she was gone, the car door yawning behind her. Halford unbelted himself and swung open his door. "I'll get her."

He sprinted across the road and into the moor grasses. The slap of cold when Gale leapt from the car was immediate.

"Katie Pru!" she hollered. "You come here this instant!"

If her child answered, the reply was carried off by the wind. The sharp blasts pummeled Gale's coat, forcing it from her body like wings. She struggled toward the windmills, her yells caroming back to her face.

The child's scream came to her as a faint *whoop*. For a second all she heard was the battering wind, then, more clearly: "Mama! Mama!"

The wind was so strong, she could barely keep her eyes open. Halford had vanished.

"Katie Pru!" she screamed.

Halford was ahead of her. He was reaching for something, and as he grasped it, he pulled, losing his balance and tumbling.

Out of the ground rose a tremendous woman. Mud coated her from the waist down, her long, drenched hair flapped like eels around her shoulders as she stumbled onto the bank of a bog.

Gale ran to them. From Chalice Hibbert's powerful arms she pulled a squirming and mud-caked Katie Pru. Halford helped Chalice to her feet. With his arm around Gale, he guided them, shivering, to the warm enclosure of his car.

According to Joseph Campbell, the myth of one technology conquering another is archetypal, including the story of Cain and Abel — the shepherd over the farmer.

—Notes, G. GRAYSON

13

Nadianna was tired. She had grown familiar with this type of exhaustion, the sweet twilight weariness of pregnancy. Her limbs were heavy, as if whatever mother's milk lay dormant in her glands had soaked flesh, muscle, bone. She crawled into bed with her shoes off and clothes on, not curious if the oven was off or the door locked. Beasties could come into her room tonight, she didn't care. She craved sleep, but she kept hearing Gale's frustrated voice. *The truth is if you return to the States now, there will be no way to save your project. . . . Don't give up.* And her own tart reply. *I've lost my home. Because of you.*

She pressed down on the hard crest of her stomach. Pariah and Child. *They'll say the same about you . . . they'll call you and your baby that, too.* When she worked at the poultry plant, the pregnant women in the lunchroom talked about their embryos as if they'd been pinched from Play-Doh. *They say what you do when you're pregnant marks the baby. It gets in their little brains and makes wrinkles in the gray matter. . . . Oh, Lord, don't tell my John that. He'll tell me I'm givin' birth to a carnival geek, what with what I do all day. . . .*

Nadianna drummed her fingers on her stomach, then slowly stretched them down each side, feeling the firmness beneath the soft white of her sweater. She remembered when her mother was pregnant with her sister Ivy. She'd been four and not nearly as taken with the idea of a baby as everyone else.

Put your hand here, Nadianna. Do you feel the baby kicking?

Her mother beamed down at her, but all Nadianna felt was the strange, severe roundness of her mother's body, hard as a pecan shell.

There's nuthin' there.

Of course there is, honey. Here, press a little harder.

I did. There's nuthin' there. It's dead.

The room had been full of people, and there was a silence, followed by a titter. But the look on her mother's face had stunned Nadianna, and she saw it still—shocked, angered, and tentatively, prayerfully, *hopeful.*

The next day she came upon her mother sitting in her prized flower-print chair, her shoulders heaving, a ghastly bark of sobs coming from her mouth. Sometimes Nadianna wondered if, deep in her dark swimming hole, wrinkles had formed on the unborn Ivy's brain that marked her as an unwanted child. It would explain her fear of being orphaned. It would explain, too, why she hated Nadianna so.

Years after the baby incident, Nadianna found her mother Margaret alone in that same living room, pulling the vacuum cleaner hose around her neck. It had been comical, straight out of Looney Tunes—her raven-haired mother standing akimbo with her knees poking her dress out, the hose's accordion pleats pinching her skin so tightly that Nadianna was afraid her head would pop off. As soon as her mother saw her, however, she let the hose go and dropped to the floor. No sobbing that time. Nadianna had been surprised by her own calm. "I'll vacuum, Mama" was all she'd said, and she scooted the vacuum cleaner head around the collapsed woman. When she finished, she gave her mother a kiss on her hair and fixed supper, knowing full well that somewhere between the relaxing of the hose and the plopping to the floor, Margaret Jesup had made a decision. Six days later, Nadianna and Ivy came home from school to find their mother gone.

She rolled onto her side, weighed down by her comforter, dress, and bra. She knew she was dreaming; she stood in the ruined walls of the mill in Statlers Cross, plump with child, the sky gray and fresh above her. Beneath her feet the grass was the color of winter bark. Her baby slept warm within her stomach, but the rest of her was cold. She looked through an empty window frame, the glass long ago shattered and trampled into the mill grounds, and saw the lights of her house twinkling in the distance. Her own hands smelled of soup, and she wanted to go home.

No.

She thought it was her mother, and she turned, angry. But it was Ivy, blond hair held back from her broad face with barrettes. Her hands were on her hips.

I have questions for you. What color is the door? What kind of spread's on my bed? How many chairs are in the living room?

Nadianna shook her head, irritated at having to answer. *You have no business asking me that. Get out of my way so I can go home.*

Ivy sulked, pressing the tip of a white shoe into the mud. *The door's blue, and the bedspread's the same yellow chenille as when you left. There's two chairs in the living room, one with a flowerdy print and one with brown minutemen soldiers.*

I remember all that, said Nadianna. *I couldn't forget.*

Liar.

The rain started slowly, little nits that Nadianna could hear but not feel. It fell on her shoulders, her belly. Soon it was streaming in torrents, sluicing through the broken windows, carving bowls into the earth.

The water rose higher and higher, around their ankles, their calves. Droplets spattered Ivy's face, her golden hair.

You left me, just like Mama.

Don't talk to me that way.

You left me. How could you do that?

Don't be stupid. Why should I have stayed? What did I have left to teach you? You know to wear clean panties, brush your teeth, watch for cars . . .

Don't laugh at me.

They were yelling, the rain falling so hard, it bellowed.

You abandoned me, Nadianna.

I'm not your keeper. I have one life, Ivy. Was I supposed to give it all to you?

And what will you give your baby?

What kind of question is that? I'll give her everything, of course.

You're a damn fool, Nadianna.

Nadianna pushed Ivy hard. Her sister fell backward, the rain racing her out the window, turning her over and over in its slick grasp. Nadianna screamed as Ivy's body blackened, and her charred remains washed from sight down the stream.

Nadianna awoke. Her heart stormed in her throat, her head, her lungs. She looked around the shadowed room, heard the beat of rain on the roof. She wouldn't go home, couldn't, no matter if it reduced her lonely sister to charcoal. She had to work. Dragging the comforter around her, Nadianna Jesup wept.

MICHAEL'S BOOK

15 APRIL 1812

A merciless time. God blinks with a cold eye.

Four days ago three hundred Luddites gathered in a field near Dumb Steeple, to attack Cartwright's Mill on the Spen River at Rawfolds. They came armed with pikes and hammers and the will to break the shearing-frames which have left so many without work. But William Cartwright has long proved himself a man without heart. My fellows should have known that he so admired the machine that he employed it to pump his blood.

The men overpowered the sentries and set upon the mill door with hatchets. But the mill was not empty. Cartwright had prepared it for battle as if he sat in a fortress and the Luddites were infidels and not this country's own. In addition to the sentries, six armed men and five soldiers lay in wait inside. He had covered the door with iron spikes so the Luddite blows fell useless. He had put the upper story flagstones on chains so that the soldiers could lift and fire their guns from behind them. Spikes covered the stairs, and tubs of acid waited to burn the heads of our honest men.

The men fought valiantly. The gunfire, we are told, lasted for twenty minutes. Many men were wounded. It is said that blood dotted the roads for four miles. Three of the soldiers would not fire—one called the Luddites his brothers and he is certainly ours.

The cost to us was high. J. Booth died on 12th April. Samuel Hartley died the next day. Both were tortured and promised a quick death to reveal the names of their accomplices. They would not. The oath stands.

Today Hartley was buried in Halifax amid public displays of grief. But our grief is closer. My brother Nathan's son, Benjamin, is gravely ill. His mother holds him, intent that he not leave the world outside her arms; Nathan's complexion is of a dead man's. What looked promising is now dim.

No stone. Sorrow. And an ignoring God without mind or heart.

By 1811, 45 cotton spinning mills, utilizing 106,735 mule spindles, 15,944 throstle spindles, and 1,590 jenny spindles, operated in upper Calderdale.

—*Notes*, G. GRAYSON

14

Thursday

The sumptuousness of Chalice's room impressed Gale. Vibrant brocades fell from the four-poster; damask curtains covered the windows. Careful not to disturb the sleeping girl, Gale fingered a coverlet hanging in a bundle from the bed. Velvet, the color of garnets. Chalice Hibbert had made her most private space medieval— and sexual.

Gale set a bouquet of daisies and a paperback novel on the bedside table and retreated from the room into the hall. Totty straightened from examining the leaves of a potted geranium gracing a lacquered library table.

"A scrape on her forehead and a deep cut on her leg. The tech at surgery assured me that all she needed was rest, and the rest is what she'll get."

Totty reached behind Gale and quietly pulled Chalice's door shut.

"I'm sorry about it all," Gale said. "But I'm also grateful she was there. I don't know . . ."

"Don't think about it. I'm glad she was there for your

little girl's sake. I didn't even know she was gone. She just took off. I know why, of course. She doesn't know how to process this business with Olivia. It's happened with Chally before—something disturbing happens and she just grabs the car keys and runs. When she was little I had to put a latch high up on the doors so she wouldn't leave without me knowing. I sometimes wonder if it has to do with being inarticulate."

"But she's not actually inarticulate," Gale objected. "She communicates well with her palmtop."

"Oh, sure," Totty answered, "but believe me, when you have to write down every word, you learn to take shortcuts. I figure those shortcuts diminish her ability to sort through things. So when something happens that needs careful thought, she has to focus hard. Hence a little panic and the need to get away."

Gale sighed, smiling. "You sound like me analyzing Katie Pru."

"Makes sense that I would. I raised Chally from babyhood."

"Really?"

"Oh yes. Our mother decided, at the age of thirty-six, that she didn't want a baby. She'd seen me to adulthood and that was all she was willing to do. 'Her time,' was how she put it. I was nineteen."

She said it without rancor. A brown leaf curled among the geranium's greenery; she plucked it and crumpled it in her hand.

"That must have been quite a responsibility for you. It's hard enough to have a child of your own at that age."

Totty dusted her fingers. "It was hard at first. It wasn't fair. I should have been doing by own things, living my own life. Then I figured I was spoiled, thinking it should be fair. You learn to do what you have to. You're a single mother. You know that's right."

"Absolutely." Gale looked around, taking in the hall's crisp yellow-striped paper, its Berber carpet—not all that expensive, perhaps, but displayed with taste. "So now you're a successful businesswoman. I bet you found some buried strengths."

"We all do," Totty said lightly. "And after all this, Chally will, too."

"Olivia's disappearance must be quite traumatic. I imagine they were comrades as well as employer-employee."

Totty's laugh was short. "Yes to the trauma, no to the comrades. Anyone's disappearance is disturbing, especially under these circumstances. And when it's someone you work with . . . But I wouldn't want anyone to misunderstand the relationship. Olivia is Chally's employer. They are not friends. They don't even see eye to eye on their craft. But they are good for one another. After a year, I could see growth in them both."

"We learn most when we teach."

"If one is smart enough to realize that. To her credit, Olivia is."

"So why would she run away?"

"Positive she did, are you?"

"The police seem to think so."

Totty's gray eyes didn't flicker from Gale's face. "Because the studio was arranged? That's what it looked like to me, anyway."

"So you saw it. I heard it looked like someone's idea of a statement. Or perhaps an artist's grand gesture."

"Ah, well, there are plenty of statements that could be made about Olivia Markham. And plenty of people to make them."

"So you don't believe she's run off?"

Totty shrugged, her lean shoulders sharp beneath her sweater. "I think it's possible. I think it's equally possible somebody did her in." At Gale's surprised look, she waved dismissively. "Don't mind me. Olivia's certainly the kind to make grand gestures. But I find that grand gestures aren't generally made by people without enemies."

"So Olivia had enemies?"

"Who doesn't have enemies, Mrs. Grayson? You'd have to live an inoffensive life not to have them. And then some people would hate you for being inoffensive. But yes, Olivia has enemies. It's her way of staying strong."

"All in all, she sounds difficult."

"All in all, she's a bitch."

The gray eyes were hard beans in the older woman's face. Perhaps, Gale thought, there was something to be said for leaving buried strengths buried. She glanced at her watch. "I've got to run—I've a nine-thirty appointment with the Mayley Local Historical Group. Tell Chalice thank you for me."

Mayley in the morning was a wet, mealy gray. She found the village's historical society nestled between a greengrocer's and an empty storefront at the bottom of a steep lane. The letters M.L.H.G. peeled off the glass door, and as she swung it open, it moved cockeyed in its hinges. A narrow flight of stairs led up to another door, and Gale knocked firmly.

She expected an elderly gentleman suited to the name of Nigel Pigeon to answer. Instead, the door opened and she faced the scrubbed features of Alan Axon.

Once again she was struck by how young he looked, the pale skin without lines, hanks of blond hair drooping boyishly across his forehead. He grinned at her. "Nigel rang to say he couldn't make it—damn flu. He asked me to meet you instead. Said it's the mill you're interested in, and I can help you as well as himself."

"Hope it's not a bad case of the flu. He sounded . . ." Here Gale hesitated, not sure of the correct phrase.

". . . old as water," Alan finished for her. "I know, he is, but he's also strong as a goat. This won't keep him down more than a few days. Still, he said he knew you were here for a limited stay and that we should be as accommodating as possible. He's given me a list of resources to hunt down—with luck I'll be able to bring them by your cottage later. Not often we get a foreign historian interested in our little corner."

Gale smiled and thanked him, but she thought she detected an edge in his voice. The pale skin was bluish under the eyes, and a sprig of uncombed hair stuck out near the back of his collar. More than likely the ailing Mr. Pigeon had contacted him at the last moment, pleading for a good lad to stand in for him. Then she remembered the intensity with which Alan had looked at Nadianna at the mill, the hushed respect in his voice when he spoke to her. And she wondered if she, Gale, was now considered the chaperone for one of God's debutantes.

If she had muttered her suspicions aloud, his response couldn't have been more on target.

"No need to thank me. I consider it an honor." He motioned her to a wooden chair and sat opposite her. "You brought Nadianna here. We're grateful."

Gale was opening her notebook, but promptly shut it. She leaned toward him, making her eyes serious. "Look, Alan. I'm going to be frank with you about this vision business. I live in a community not unlike this one. I thought I understood the impulses behind visions and voices and such. Frankly, I wouldn't have pegged you as someone who needed that."

"That," he said, "is rather arrogant."

"It is," Gale admitted. "But Nadianna's never been outside Georgia before, and I feel responsible for her. She flat-out doesn't believe she saw anything but an actual carbon-based body in the water Monday morning. She thinks that what fell from the roof Tuesday night was a burning shingle. And I'm likely to believe her."

"Likely, but not absolutely?"

"I meant absolutely. I believe her. I do not believe in visions."

"You don't. How much do you know about them?"

He kept his eyes focused on the invisible rings he sketched with his finger on the chair arm. The upper part of his body was relaxed, but his left leg jerked up and down.

"All right," she said. "I'd say the people I know who claim to have seen visions fall into two categories— charlatans who are out for something or people who are unhappy, maybe even trapped. I've never known a well-adjusted person with a fulfilling life admit to having a vision unless they were looking back to a time in their lives when they were miserable. And usually the vision is something uplifting. A burnt corpse . . ."

"Stop there. What if I tell you that I agree with you?" His eyes were still on the circles, and he spoke as if he were talking to himself. "Let's rule out the charlatans for a moment because they're too obvious. Unhappy and trapped. Would you say that described Nadianna?"

"But she didn't see . . ."

He scrutinized her sharply. "Think about it for a minute. Does unhappy and trapped describe Nadianna?"

"It describes a lot of people."

He leaned forward. "Listen, Mrs. Grayson. I know you're trying to say I'm young and you're right, I am. But I have seen things, done things, that might surprise you. And I've been with people who you'd surely call trapped and have witnessed the most amazing changes. I've seen drug users in the depths of a bad trip come out of it saying they had spoken to God—and turn their lives over to Him and never take another drug. And I've known people— women, mostly—who say that God visited them and gave them permission to do things they otherwise wouldn't have felt strong enough to do—leave an abusive home, turn in a criminal lover. Maybe even do something as simple as travel. For someone with few opportunities, traveling to a foreign country must be a tremendous act of rebellion."

"What makes you think Nadianna has few opportunities?"

"This is a small town, Mrs. Grayson. Strangers are simple to talk about. Given her background, wouldn't it be easy for Nadianna to say that God told her to come here?"

"Except you and your church are the only ones saying God sent her a message. She doesn't."

"So God has to say it again and again. Until she can turn to everyone and say, 'He told me to do this. I tried to ignore Him, but he kept turning my face to Him.' "

"Alan." Gale's exasperation remained gentle. "What is this that you and Thornsby have going? A little armchair psychology mixed with a little down-by-the-riverside religion? First of all, Nadianna has already left home. She's here."

"And feels no guilt?"

"Well, no, I can't say that. She may. Her family didn't want her to come. But she had the courage to do so. And second—" She broke off, feeling the heat rise on her face.

"Second?"

"Never mind," she said.

"You were about to comment on Nadianna's pregnancy, weren't you? The child's illegitimate."

"How do you know that?"

He held up his hand and waggled his third finger. "No wedding band. Now, I know some Pentecostals consider even that much jewelry adornment, but somehow . . ."

"All right," Gale conceded. "Then, second, Nadianna is carrying an illegitimate child. She's broken *the* taboo."

"That's an interesting thing about you, Mrs. Grayson. Why do you think that having a child out of wedlock is a bigger sin than leaving home?"

The earnestness in his blue eyes silenced her. Why, exactly, did she believe that? She tried to imagine Katie Pru, twenty years older and pregnant by a man who didn't want her. What, indeed, would be the bigger sin—being pregnant or leaving the family committed to loving them both?

"All right," she said. "I'll give you that point. But that doesn't explain the body falling from the burning building. Do all the people in your group need God's permission to stand up to their family?"

He laughed. "Well, seeing that some of them are near sixty, I would hope not, but they might. Have you taken a good look at this town, Gale? There are no jobs, least none that a person can raise a family on. I've seen all my mates move away. Families burst apart, the children desperate to find a life, the parents desperate not to lose them. I see it with my own parents. They want us on our own, but they fear the world will have no place for us. It's a damnable thing." He shook his head. "I'm not sure I can explain Tuesday night. Nadianna was there; we were flattered. We were washed in the Spirit. And then the fire, the falling object . . . Maybe it was nothing. From my point of view, it doesn't matter. Those people feel they were addressed by God. The night changed their lives."

" 'Those people'? You sound like you're not one of them."

"Oh, I am. You can have faith and still be objective."

It struck her then how much Alan Axon, in looks and speech and intensity, resembled her dead husband—the passion and conviction, things she'd loved most in Tom Grayson. What she hadn't understood in her brief marriage was that they had little to do with her.

A knot formed in her throat. "That's very self-serving."

"All belief is self-serving. That's its ruthless part."

"And what if," she persisted, "it weren't as benevolent as you suggest? What if it was, after all, a person falling into the water?"

"Then we witnessed a murder. All the more reason to have God on our side."

• • •

Katie Pru had sprung out of many things. She had sprung out of her bathtub at home, water dripping from her face. She had sprung out of the pool in the summer, and out of the clothes hamper in the washroom. But nothing beat springing out of a mud pit beneath windmills, carried by a big girl. That was a special kind of spring. And it made her brave.

So brave, in fact, that she decided to make the whale talk to her. She squinched her eyes closed and jumped with both feet so hard, her body jiggled up to her chest. Nothing. She tried it again. Nothing.

From across the woods' path she heard Nadianna call. "Katie Pru, don't go too far. Don't get so far you can't hear me."

"I can hear you just fine," Katie Pru hollered back. "Better watch out for snakes."

"There are no snakes in November. They're asleep for the winter."

"IS THAT RIGHT?" shouted Katie Pru. "WHY THEY WANT TO SLEEP FOR?"

"Not so loud, Katie Pru. You'll wake the angels."

That was an idea Katie Pru hadn't thought of before, but she decided that waking one creature a day was enough. She wanted to jump, and she wanted to be left alone where she could jump with nobody telling her not to.

She dunked down low and scurried between the trees. First right, then left, then a circle. She skittered over the path a couple of times, over a big rock, passed two fallen logs. When she came to a third log, she stopped and listened. Far away, she could hear Nadianna's footsteps. She looked around but couldn't see Nadianna's bright red scarf. Maybe I'll wait, she thought. I wouldn't want her to get lost.

She sat down on the log, then not liking the feel of the bark on her pants, slid to the ground. She heard the rustle of Nadianna's shoes, the whisper of her voice. "Katie Pru, don't you go hiding from me."

I am not hiding, Katie Pru thought, and she settled against the log. She flattened her hands in the dirt on either side of her. She squiggled her fingers, feeling the leaves crumble beneath her nails.

Her left hand hit something soft and wet. She grasped it and pulled.

The bag was thick and very colorful, covered with zigzag designs in red and dark blue. A string held it puckered at the top. Carefully, Katie Pru loosened the string and peered inside.

Sand, she thought. Sand and rocks.

She put her hand into the bag and rummaged around until she found the biggest rock. She pulled it out and wiped it off on her pants.

It didn't look quite like a rock. It looked a little like the dried wads of chewing gum she'd picked off the bottoms of restaurant tables, but when she stuck her fingernail into it, her nail didn't leave a mark. She lifted it to her face, studying the tiny holes and sharp edges. For a long time she pondered, trying to remember where she had seen something very much like these.

Then she knew. She put the object back inside the bag, pulled the drawstring closed, and stood.

"Katie Pru!" Nadianna's voice was closer and angrier now. "Come here this instant. I'm getting cold and mad."

"All right," Katie Pru answered. "I'm ready to go home now."

Katie Pru Grayson dodged through the trees to her baby-sitter. Inside her coat, safe from Nadianna's disapproving frown, she clutched a damp and lumpy bag of whale's teeth.

In his maiden address to the House of Lords in 1812, Lord Byron objected to a law that made frame-breaking punishable by death; a year later, his friend Percy Bysshe Shelley set up an orphans fund for the children of men hanged for Luddite crimes; in 1818, Mary Shelley's technological monster and maker fly to the verge in each other's pursuit.

—*Notes*, G. GRAYSON

15

Mark Reston had a fever; Halford could tell by the heat in his old friend's pudgy palms and the unfocused glance he shot in Halford's direction—first not recognizing, then recognizing, his colleague. The wind cut through the lane in front of the Mayley police station and Reston visibly braced himself.

"Mark," Halford said, still holding Reston's hand, "I think you could use a day in bed."

"Sure I could," Reston answered. "Me and about half the men available to me. I believe at last count that was three. What are you doing down here, a little sightseeing? Tell you what, Danny. I'll compromise. You pay for a cup of coffee and I'll come in out of this godforsaken wind for ten minutes. Then we can both tell my wife I'm taking care of myself."

They climbed the steep stairs to a tearoom above a chemist's shop. In addition to coffee, Reston ordered hotpot, but after two carrots he pushed it away. He sank his head into his hands and shook it slowly back and forth.

"Got a preliminary report from Fire Investigation.

The accelerant was most likely turpentine or white spirits—both of which, given the nature of Olivia Markham's business, could have been on-site. There's evidence that sheeting was used to start the fire."

"How?"

"Spread out, sprinkled with accelerant, and lit. That's the current theory, anyway. What am I looking at, Danny? Have I got more than arson here?"

The tearoom was empty save for an elderly man tugging at the hem of a curtain and singing softly and the server who sat at a rear table totaling receipts. Halford lifted the French press and topped off his cup.

"Any progress in locating either Markham or Botting?"

"No. Markham's Volvo is still parked behind the studio. We've searched Botting's home. His car is there, fridge a bit bare, but my DC tells me so is his own."

"Where does Botting do his work? I assume he has some sort of business premises somewhere."

"He has a darkroom across town—actually, it would be more accurate to call it a photo-processing center, it's so hi-tech and posh—but we didn't find anything suspicious there. We're keeping an eye on both places, just in case. So far the last time anyone saw either one of them was about one-fifteen Tuesday afternoon as they left a business meeting at The Crown & Drover."

"I was there that morning when they came in to check on things. Bernie Portman implied that Miss Markham wouldn't exactly be pleased with the outcome of the meeting."

Reston slowly raised his head. "You know about it, then? Well, I think she was pleased enough. There's opposition to converting the mill to an art mall, but I think there's damn all anyone can do about it and Markham knows it. No real good arguments against it other than nobody likes her. Can't make business decisions based on that."

"People do it all the time."

"Not when the economy is scruffy. You know how it is—inflation rises and the dandies down south fight it by laying off people up here. Mayley's down to two groups of people—pensioners who've lived here all their lives and young people who've already made so many bad decisions, they've got nowhere else to go."

"So if it were anyone else but Olivia Markham, people would be enthusiastic about her mill plans. Is opposition to it really that strong?"

Reston shrugged. "Depends on who you ask. Some don't care, some think it's foolish, some just want the work, and some are spitting mad. There's a faction in these parts that don't like all these outsiders moving in, buying up the old properties, renovating, and not giving a damn about local customs and such. 'Assault by nostalgia,' Linda calls it, even though she'll admit we're part of the ground forces. All in all, I gather Markham found the response at the meeting to be priggish but not condemning."

"Was Gerald Thornsby there?"

"Not likely he'd be invited."

"So what's the story between them?"

"Markham and Thornsby?" Another shrug, and Reston leaned over to blow on the steam rising from his hot-pot. "Same old. Preacher offended by pornography. He's written letters to the local paper claiming Markham's work is obscene and in this age of AIDS downright irresponsible. She, of course, claimed that he's a holy-rolling lunatic and art is Art. I think they're both right."

Halford smiled and took a sip of coffee. "And where does Chalice Hibbert fit in?"

"Hibbert?"

"We had an interesting encounter last night. She pulled Gale's little girl out of a bog."

Reston looked at Halford in surprise. "Out of a bog? The girl just ran into it? Damned nasty things, bogs. Whereabouts was this?"

"Haworth Moor—about twenty kilometers north— underneath the windmills."

"What the hell was Chalice doing there?"

"I don't know. It was about eight P.M. Raining rather fiercely. Gale and I had taken Katie Pru up there for a drive. We'd parked to look at the windmills and Katie Pru jumped out of the car."

"Was Chalice alone?"

Halford nodded. "She was evidently just standing by the bog. I never saw her car, although her sister Totty said it must be parked up there somewhere."

"What—Chalice was alone and outside in the rain?"

"Looks that way. She somehow hurt her leg and we took her to surgery. Totty picked her up. She seemed quite agitated. Apparently she supervises Chalice rather closely. Said she had no idea she'd left the house."

"Did she say why Chalice might have gone there? To the moor?"

"Not directly. She did tell us that she and Chalice used to pack a lunch and drive up to see the windmills being erected."

"Yes, well, by the way, if locals aren't complaining about outsiders moving in, they're complaining about the windmills. We need the power, but they are a damn eyesore." Reston dragged his bowl to him and idly stabbed at the chunks of lamb. "Well, now, that's worth thinking about, but I'm not sure how much. An artist's studio burns down, the artist and her cohort go missing, and twenty-four hours later her assistant leaves home without a word and pops out of a bog twenty kilometers away. I didn't get to interview Chalice proper, you know. The sister interfered. Bothersome old bat, is Totty."

"You know the Hibberts well?"

"Not really. Linda worked with Totty a few years back—some village to-do. She found her to be smart but a bit prickly. I'd be prickly, too, if my mother dumped a baby sister on me to raise."

"The mother dead?"

"Don't know. I always got the impression she just didn't want to be bothered."

"Cruel thing for a mother to do—to both children. Has Chalice always been so . . . well, her size?"

"She stands out a bit, doesn't she? I don't run into her often—rather reclusive, didn't go to school. In fact, I haven't thought of her for a few years, not since my own daughter entered primary school and I kept wondering what it would be like to never hear all that energy, that *babbling*. Blessed, I'd think sometimes. But most of the time, I thought, well, Christ."

"Chalice never went to school?"

"Totty taught her at home. Now, Linda has strong opinions about that whole idea, but I'm not so sure. Children's tolerance goes only so far. I can imagine what kind of taunts that child had to endure. Hard to know what's right when you're raising a child. It's a bleedin' crap shoot. How much harder when she's not your daughter at all." He poked at his vegetables, the stream darting with each strike of his fork. A fine sweat had broken out on his upper lip. "I better see about talking to Chalice again."

"Mark, honest, I think you ought to go home. A good rest might knock this bug out."

"Bloody hell. I'm beginning to think I made the wrong decision leaving the Met. Is there always someone to fill your shoes when you've got an ache?"

Halford picked up Reston's coat and helped him into it. "No. But there's a lot to be said for being one hundred percent during an investigation."

Reston motioned to the server and dropped several pound coins on the table. "One hundred percent. Too much to do to worry with the math."

Chalice's armpits ached, and between her legs it felt as if someone were grabbing fistfuls of skin and squeezing.

Her ten-year-old body filled the summer room couch; her elbow kept sliding off, unable to find purchase on the blue-and-white upholstery. She didn't like to open her eyes—every time the lamplight hit them it felt like a syringe stabbing. The voices in the hallway sounded distant and furry.

"She fell off her bicycle, I tell you." It was Totty's boyfriend, his voice high and angry. "You know what a clumsy ox she can be."

"Stop it. She didn't fall off any bicycle. What kind of idiot do you think I am? Who the hell did *that* to her?"

"Well, excuse me, then, Totty, since you know so much. I was sitting in yon kitchen and I hear a great kablang in the garden. Go out and she's sprawled on the road. The bicycle bars were on her funny-like. And she's bleedin'."

"Bullshit."

"Don't get tart with me. She fell, I tell you. You can ask her yourself."

"A real pervert you are. And so smart to molest a child who can't squeal on you."

"A righteous bitch you are, not to believe me."

"Get out of here."

"You'll starve. You're too bloody useless to make it on your own. It's why you keep attaching yourself to men."

"Bloody hell. Get out!"

"Give off, Totty. For God's sakes—look at her. She's big enough to be twenty. All the men talk about her. You're lucky she's not been banged by some fucking teenager who doesn't give a crap about her. . . ."

Silence. Then Totty's voice, cold.

"You're sick. Get out of here or I'll call the goddamn police."

Chalice rolled onto her side, trying to ease the aching. He had been Boyfriend Number Three, and if there was justice, he had gone during the night with his fingers rotting where they had ripped her. Miss Tipe, a nosy neighbor of the crocheted-lace variety, once asked Totty why she never married the nice young man. "Not enough food for three of us," she'd replied curtly. "Sent him out to gather his own nuts and berries." Later, by the fire, Totty had stroked Chalice's hair and murmured, "I'd have killed him, Chally, but I didn't know where that would have left you. I had to make a choice. You won. But not to worry. I'll always choose you."

The ache in her armpit deepened, and Chalice winced. She struggled to consciousness, the childhood memory retreating, her adult body sore. Gently, she touched the plaster on her leg, then bent her knees one at a time. Sore for sure, but not substantially more so than the day after a hike on the Pennines. She wouldn't have guessed that hauling a child from a bog would leave her muscles so griping.

She pulled herself into sitting position and cautiously swung her feet to the floor. On the white bedside table was a book and glass vase filled with daisies. Willing the headache away, she picked up the book and focused on the title. *A Whisper of Threads: Thoughts of a Southern Mill Girl.* A small card peeped from the pages. *Don't know how soon you will be up and about—thought you might like something to fill the hours. Gale, Katie Pru, Nadianna, and Daniel.*

So she'd managed to bring in the whole foreign brigade with last night's heroics. She closed her eyes, trying to remember the incident. But it was a blur of rain and bog and little girl. The only clear memory Chalice had was of the ride home, and the muddy child sitting next to her, playing with Chalice's green beads as if they were a rosary. And her thoughts—she remembered them. She had gone to the windmills to collect her thoughts, and she had done so.

Opening her eyes, she examined the book again. It was published in America and resembled a journal, although as she flipped through the pages it struck her as nothing much more than the collected ramblings of a young Georgia woman. Chalice wasn't a mill worker; she didn't come from a family of mill workers. What an odd choice to give a person for recuperation.

Of course, there was to be no recuperation. The first steps were hard, and she grasped the edge of her bedside table to steady herself. Using the bedposts for support, she made a U around her mattress, then back again, before feeling confident that her legs wouldn't buckle.

Trousers were more than she wanted to deal with, so she took a knit frock from her closet and slid it over her head. Slipping her bare feet into skimmers, she ran the tail of a comb through her hair and eased from her room.

". . . she's asleep, now." Totty's voice rose from the downstairs hall. "Chally never has handled difficult things well. Somehow I always thought it would be the opposite. . . ."

Chalice tuned her out. Whoever Totty was talking with, she hoped she kept her on the phone for a long time.

As silently as possible, she made her way to Totty's room. There were only so many places one could hide something in a house this size. No accessible attic, limited cupboard space. She opened the wardrobe, slid out the bureau drawers. She sank to the floor and looked under the bed. Nothing missing. Nothing, as far as she could tell, added.

She checked the lavatory, then gave a cursory look around her own room. Fairly certain now that what she was searching for wasn't upstairs, she started down the steps. Totty stood at the bottom, still holding the phone, watching her descent.

"She's up now, Flo. Yes, she looks a bit wrung out, even for a hero. Listen, could you drive me to retrieve the car? It's still up there. The sooner the better. Can't conduct my business without a car, now, can I? Later, then, all right?"

Totty put the receiver down as Chalice reached the floor.

"Well. Good afternoon." She gently touched the plaster on Chalice's forehead. "I didn't expect you up today. No need for it, you know. You can go back to bed."

Chalice smiled and shook her head. She jabbed her finger into her palm and looked at her sister questioningly.

"Oh, the palmtop. It's in the kitchen. None the worse for it. Come on, let me fix you a cuppa."

She clasped Chalice's hand. You can barely tell our hands apart, Chalice thought, both of them muscular from the work of dough and clay. She had watched Totty knead bread hundreds of times, punching it down with her knuckles, her long fingers bringing it back up, mounding and patting it to resemble a baby's bum. As an adolescent she had decided that image of a child's bum on a floured board was behind the Hansel and Gretel story. Women must create and consume their children. She had written an essay about it as an English assignment; she later found it in the trash bin, where Totty had crumpled and thrown it.

The sunlight was bright through the kitchen window, and she caught a glimpse of the pottery shed, water drops glistening on its roof. She sat at the table and listened to Totty's prattle, her own eyes darting from cupboard to cupboard, visualizing which ones were full, which ones had extra space. She knew from experience there weren't many of the latter. Baskets and the accessories of a Hibbert Sweet Home Away welcome crammed the cupboard shelves. The kitchen was a possible hiding place, but not a very likely one. Her gaze kept shifting past the windowpanes to the pottery shed with its collection of boxes and buckets and stray containers packed to the ceiling.

The palmtop sat beside the kitchen basin. Chalice

smiled again as her sister set down a cup of tea and took the chair next to her. Totty picked up a packet of cigarettes from the table and patted one loose.

"Now, I want you to drink that all up, and when you do, let's talk about what caused you to run up to the moors the way you did last night. I know you find the windmills calming. Is that it, then—you needed to calm down about what's happened at the studio? Tell me about it, Chally."

Chalice took a sip of tea so large it burned the back of her mouth and made her wince. What she had thought about under the windmills were her precious blue tea-bowls. They were missing. When she had looked over the police tape and into the burnt-out studio, she had felt sick, but not because of the destruction or the question of Olivia's fate. It was because of her tea-bowls. Olivia had destroyed nine, but that left fifteen remaining in the studio cabinet. She had had to fight her elation when she saw that the cabinet had survived the blaze. But when she had peered closer, she realized the interior was empty. Someone had taken the tea-bowls; who loved or despised her enough to do that?

Totty took Chalice's hand between her own and began massaging. The veins and sinews rolled beneath her sister's fingers. Who took my tea-bowls, Totty? Chalice thought. Who the hell took them, and why?

The only known "records" of Luddite activities consist of government reports from informants, court documents, newspaper articles, a few printed Luddite declarations, and contemporary folk accounts. No authenticated Luddite first-person record has been found to date.

—*Notes*, G. GRAYSON

16

By two P.M. a weak light straggled through the woods. Gale looped the top button of her coat as she followed Katie Pru's march down the path from the cottage to the stream. She had invited Nadianna to join them for a winter picnic by the water, but the younger woman had pursed her lips and shaken her head firmly. "Y'all are crazy. If I'm gonna be cold, I'm gonna at least be cold with a roof over my head and something soft under my rear end."

Katie Pru had found the picnic basket in the cottage mud room and together they had filled it—a stained damask cloth, paper napkins, two cups, a thermos of hot chocolate, and crustless butter-and-watercress sandwiches. In it they also stowed a copy of *Horton Hears a Who*, although, as they neared the fresh bite of the water, Gale doubted they would have the stamina or the warm fingers to turn the pages.

At the end of the path the land flattened, and they stepped out of the woods and onto the stream's grassy margin. Due north sat Yates Mill, its facade pewter in the afternoon's frank light. On the opposite bank stood a bosk, and Gale realized that it was only this tidy cluster of trees that shielded Olivia Markham's charred studio from view. Come nightfall and it would be forty-eight hours since the fire. No residual smoke curled from the treetops; no smell of scorched wood washed the air. From this small place on the edge of Sette Water, it appeared nothing had happened—there was just the mill and the patient dash of water.

With a deep breath, she set down the basket and with Katie Pru wrestled the damask cloth until it formed an airy mound on the grass. Katie Pru made a show of setting out the picnic precisely: a plate by their knees, a sandwich on each plate.

"You pour the chocolate, please ma'am, Mama. Everyone needs something to do."

"Good philosophy. Nadianna teach you that?"

"I thought it myself." Katie Pru tucked a napkin into her coat collar. "But Nadianna thinks I'm right."

"I bet she does."

Gale lifted a cup from the basket. It was one of six from the kitchen, holding places of pride on the open shelves of the pine cupboard. A small and delicate thing, it fit nestlike in her palm. Thumb marks were visible where the handle had been roughly pressed into the clay. Handmade, she thought, and she turned it over to read the initials *CH*. Next to it was the potter's mark, an imprint of a chalice, and a two-year-old date.

"Impressive, isn't it?"

She looked up to see Alan Axon, dressed in a baggy barn jacket, his blond hair flopping over his forehead.

"Very nice," she replied. "You know the potter?"

"Everyone knows Chalice. Hard to miss her."

"She worked at the pottery?"

"Olivia's assistant. But she's quite a potter in her own right. She comes over sometimes and helps at the mill. That's how I got to know her pottery. I think it's quite elegant."

Gale unscrewed the thermos. "Then it's fitting that you should drink from it. Care to join Katie Pru and me for a picnic?"

She waited until he sat cross-legged on the tablecloth before handing him the cup. He took it, then nodded toward the wood.

"I brought that information Nigel wanted you to have. Mostly locally written pamphlets, but you might find some of them helpful. I left them up at the cottage. Nadianna told me it was all right if I joined you." He sipped the hot chocolate and winked at Katie Pru. "Ah, Miss Katie Pru, you know what it takes to warm a body on a cold day. Thank you very much."

Gale poured a little of the steaming liquid in the second cup and balanced it on Katie Pru's plate. "Chalice must be good at straddling fences if she works with Olivia Markham and helps your church group."

Alan peered at her over his cup. His expression was teasing. "Just like Mayley. A visitor's in town less than a week and already she knows the local politics."

"No different than you knowing Nadianna's marital status. But, to let Mayley off the hook, it hasn't exactly been an average week." She pulled a bite from her watercress sandwich and popped it into her mouth. "I heard that Olivia's artwork is controversial, and that Gerald Thornsby is one of the people most opposed to it."

"That's true enough. Gerald's not a prude, and his ministry isn't either—he doesn't insist on chastity, although I know many of us practice abstinence until marriage. But the human body is sacred. Olivia's work throws that notion into our faces."

"So what does Gerald want to do about it?"

The teasing expression remained steady. "And this is going to aid you in writing the text for Nadianna's photos?"

"I'm just curious."

"Ah. Well, it's not privileged information. Gerald wants Olivia gone."

"Looks like that for today at least he has his wish."

"Too simple. No, I dare say she'll pop back up soon enough." He said it easily.

"So it's a theological disagreement they have, not a personal one?"

"That's an interesting way to put it. But I see your point. Theological versus personal. I don't know." He paused and drank from the cup. As he swallowed, he studied the clay rim, considering. "Olivia came over to the mill one day during a meeting. Walked right into the room, told Gerald to stop interfering with her business. It was rather vulgar, and odd—bothered me quite a bit at the time."

Gale glanced at Katie Pru, who was poking holes in her sandwich and eating the plugs from her fingertips. "Personal, was it?"

"Could be. She basically threatened him. Said a man with his proclivities should be more mindful of what he said." He dropped his voice to a murmur. "But she said it 'pro*clit*vities,' and started laughing. She grabbed Zoë and twirled her around and said it again. Well, she was obviously drunk. That's been a problem with Olivia. Gerald didn't even blink. I talked with him about it later. That's when he told me his life story. He used to be a thief. Spent some time locked up. He was quite open about it. Olivia, he said, is a bratty troublemaker and a bad punster."

"I'll say. So Gerald's been born again?"

"Yes." He smiled at her, and his hair fell into his eyes. "But you don't trust that sort of thing, do you?"

"Not true. Jimmy Carter was born again, and I think he's great."

"But you're skeptical."

"I'm always skeptical. Is Chalice Hibbert a member of your church?"

"Chalice? Nah. I wish she would think about it. She's a bit lost, I think."

"Why do you say that?"

"She doesn't have anyone, does she, except her sister and her boss. Imagine how lonely that must be." He held up the cup. "She doesn't do this on a wheel. It's hand-built. She takes a ball of clay and molds it with her fingers. But look at it. Perfectly balanced. Flawless, almost. You'd think it was machine-made except for the way she dug her thumbs in at the handle. Interesting—most of the time she doesn't make the handle. Must have done it special for you tourists."

"You know she was hurt last night. Just a few scrapes."

His brow wrinkled with concern. "No. How?"

"Helping K.P. here. Nothing serious, but if she's involved with your church . . ."

"Yes, we need to visit her. I'll let Gerald know."

He drank slowly, upending the cup. When he finished, Gale took it from him and refilled it. "So I'm just wondering, if Chalice knows y'all are opposed to the work she's doing for Olivia, why does she help with your group?"

"Chalice is a good person. Perhaps she helps us because of that. Or perhaps helping us is easier than going home to take a shower every day after work."

He said it lightly, not looking at Gale. Across from them Katie Pru had opened her holey sandwich and was picking out the watercress.

"What's the matter, darling?" he asked. "Don't you like it?"

"Looks like grass. Can I throw it in the water?"

"Let's not," Gale said. "That water is running pretty fast. I don't want you to get too close."

Alan hauled himself to his feet. "I'll take her. I've had long practice in keeping shoes dry near Sette Water."

He took Katie Pru's hand and led her to the stream's edge with Gale following. Kneeling, he grasped the child by her waist. "Go on, Katie Pru. Toss it in."

Katie Pru raised her fist and threw the limp and buttered watercress into the stream. It fell inches from the bank but was instantly caught in the current.

"You know there're stories around here about all the things seen floating in Sette Water," Alan said. "Now they can start a story about a piece of watercress, plucked from a sandwich because it looked more like what a rabbit would eat than a little American girl with bright dark eyes." He tousled her hair and Katie Pru giggled.

Gale drew her coat around her. "Stories. I like that. What kind?"

"Ah, too many to count, really. A mooing cow. A driverless motorbike skimming along all proper like. During the war there was one of a plane's propeller, buzzing past like it hadn't lost its purpose." He stood, his hand in Katie Pru's. "A grinning cat's head. A bride, singing as she drowns. It depends on what age group is telling the stories. There's probably a kernel of truth in all of it. In the old days—that's what Nigel calls them, 'the old days'—the stream was known as Sad Water. Some people still call it that. A corruption of Sette, of course."

"And now there will be the story of 'Nadianna's Vision,'" Gale said.

"Unless it becomes something more grim." Alan stared at the rushing water. "I pray to God not."

He seemed to gather himself and, pushing his hair from his eyes, gave Gale a good-humored grin. "Just one more charming thing about Mayley, Mrs. Grayson. You beginning to understand us here?"

Nadianna heard a squeal and looked out the cottage window to see Katie Pru dashing from the woods. Behind her ran Alan Axon, bent over and galloping like a bear. The two were guffawing by the door before Gale emerged between the trees, the basket handle over her arm and the tablecloth wrapped around her coat like a sarong. Through the cottage's thick glass their voices were watery. She couldn't make out a word as Alan bowed over Gale's hand, saluted, and dashed backward into the woods.

By the time the door opened, Nadianna was in her father's old brown coat, the car keys jangling in the pocket. She grabbed Katie Pru up in a hug. "You didn't freeze. I would've sworn you'd come back a Popsicle."

Gale placed the basket on the counter and untied the cloth from her waist. "Did you get some rest?" She took in Nadianna's coat, frowning. "Are you really that cold? I could stoke the fire some more."

"The first answer is a little. The second is, no, but I was wondering if you could take me to town."

Gale began putting the contents of the basket in the sink. "Sure. Where do you want to go?"

"I did something the other night that I didn't tell you about. I developed the film I took Monday morning."

Gale stopped, her hand in the basket. "You . . . ?" She shook her head. "Never mind. It doesn't matter. What's on the photos?"

"Nothing the police want." Nadianna hesitated, kneading the hard cap of her stomach. "I haven't done anything wrong, Gale, honest. There's nothing there."

"Okay, let's go take a look at them. Where are they?"

"In Lyle Botting's darkroom."

This time Gale didn't conceal her surprise. "Lyle Botting?"

"Sure. I contacted him a couple of months ago, remember? One of the photographers back home gave me his name. He agreed to let me use his facilities."

"I'm surprised the police let you into his darkroom."

"I did it before the police knew there was a problem."

"You should have told Reston."

"What business is it of his? I don't have anything to do with Mr. Botting running off."

Nadianna waited for Gale's scolding, but instead the older woman picked up a dish towel and wiped her hands. "Okay. Let's go to the darkroom and see if they'll let you in today."

"You think the police will be there?"

"I don't know. I have no idea how seriously they're taking all this. But the man is missing. It would be my guess . . ."

Nadianna felt the first tick of panic. "Do you think they've gone inside? Would they have taken my film?"

"Only one way to find out," Gale replied. "Come on, Katie Pru. Don't take your coat off yet."

Nadianna was surprised at how easily Gale navigated the roads, arriving at the bottom of Old Ground Lane in ten minutes. Another five and they were on the street leading to the darkroom.

In the daylight, Nadianna appreciated Alan's warning about the area. Unlike other parts of town, where the residents had invested in lace window treatments and rainbow-colored woodwork, here the cottage windows were cracked and the iron gates flowered with rust. Two cars were parked on the sidewalk, but Nadianna got the impression that this was for the most part abandoned housing. Gale turned the corner and there was the door to Botting's primitive darkroom—a fading but decidedly bold pink.

Nadianna dug into her purse and pulled out the key. "No sign of the police. Come on, Katie Pru. Let's you and me and your mama do some exploring."

The negatives hung safely from the wire, apparently untouched since Tuesday night. Relieved, Nadianna shrugged off her coat and lightly squeezed the top of Katie Pru's head. "Don't touch any of the chemicals, ma'am. We don't want your insides turning green. And stay out of the back room over there. It's a mess."

Nadianna unclipped the strip of negatives and handed it to Gale. "Take a real close look at the water. Nothing's there."

Gale held the negative up the light, her eyes roaming up and down the amber strip. "I don't see anything, Nadianna, but I really can't be sure."

"I know. I'm going to make a contact sheet. But it's not there, Gale. Trust me on this."

"A shame if you're right. It would have been helpful."

No, Nadianna thought, it would have been destroying. She hadn't told Gale her deepest fear, that had she caught the body on film, the image would at once make and end her. It would have been the signature piece of her project, a black-and-white shot of a hacked-up body, the decaying mill suspended in the fog as the corpse was suspended in the water. But she would have laid aside her camera forever. She had seen the accidental capture of death by other photographers—the suicide inches from the pavement, the child in instant from a car bumper—and she wondered about the shreds that forever after posed as the photographers' souls. Some reveled in the notoriety, but some surely died. It wasn't a circle she wanted to join. Better not to be believed.

A loud smack blasted the room. Katie Pru dropped a package of dried chemicals on the floor and jumped back.

"Lots of things in here will bite you if you fool with them, Miss K.P.," Nadianna said, picking up the package. "Let's leave these alone."

"Then there's always the roaches." Gale lifted a brown paper bag from behind a box. Grease stained the bottom and as Gale held it aloft, Nadianna caught a whiff of old banana.

Gale wrinkled her nose. "Yuck. We'd better toss this out."

The tick started again in Nadianna's chest. "That's not mine," she said. "And it wasn't here Tuesday night."

Gale's face became still. "Are you sure?"

"I'm positive. I checked this place out good. I don't like rats."

Gale placed the bag on the floor. In one movement she had Katie Pru by the shoulder and halfway to the door.

She said one word, but in it Nadianna heard all the nuances of alarm and anger and Gale's cool stubbornness.

"Out."

MICHAEL'S BOOK

17 APRIL 1812

At age six, my brother's son Benjamin has died. Tomorrow we bury him at Mayley churchyard in ground that opens regularly for children. Nathan and Nell have five sons—two will now lie under dirt blankets.

I am the bidder. Today I went from house to house bidding the folk of Mayley to come to the burying. It was a wretched pastime. The sky was heavy with rain, riding above me like the palm of a tired angel, pressing, following. The houses were filled with mourners. I stared into eyes as helpless as mine own. There is my child, they all seemed to say. Tomorrow they will look at the tombstones and the whisper will return. And there, and there, and there . . .

At Charles Noland's house they drew me in with a Wesley hymn.

> *He speaks, and listening to His voice.*
> *New life the dead receive;*
> *The mournful, broken hearts rejoice;*
> *The humble poor believe.*

I left with a nod.

I asked Tansy Baker what killed Benjamin. Mrs Baker knows the telling things, like which vines curl before the chill and the textures of sickness on a tongue. We stood outside Nathan's cottage, and she turned her coal-black eyes on me. The times, she answered. She spoke of her sister, a midwife in Leeds, who knits a small ring for every baby she births and puts it in a wooden box for the child's fifth birthday. Her wooden box will not close, so many small fingers buried before they claimed the gift. In the cities the problems of damp and cold are added to filth and crowds. So Benjamin, Mrs Baker said as we broke from wood to air, is not so much a loss as a list.

She smiled at her joke, but her eyes bore into me. I watched her walk down Ground Lane. She swayed from side to side, her thick body wrapped in woven cloth, a satchel of remedies on her arm. I wanted to stamp her out, to beat the flesh from her body for all the cruelty in her words.

I found Nathan wandering the wood. I called to him, but he did not speak.

The Luddite revolt did not stop the coming of mills; however, cotton power looms came to the upper Calder valley later than in other areas, the first recorded in 1829.

—*Notes*, G. GRAYSON

17

A rumpled blanket, a box filled with balls of cling wrap and empty drink bottles, a portable radio—that was what a detective constable found in the cramped storage space of Lyle Botting's darkroom. Interviews with the few people who still resided on the street found a pensioner who whiled away his afternoons watching with equal measure the clock and the carryings-on of a young, unemployed couple over the road. At around three P.M. the pensioner saw a green Fiat pass by with a little girl in the back. About ten minutes later, the Fiat passed again, heading toward town, going too fast for the winding lane. And about three minutes after that came a man in a black parka with the hood around his face, ducking down behind the garden walls and dodging into an alley.

"I saw Botting wearing a black parka earlier this week," Halford offered.

"Right," Reston said, and Halford had to press the cell phone tightly against his ear to catch the detective's words. "We've been able to confirm that."

"And the witness was certain it was a man?"

"Certain? The old fellow said he thought it was a man,

but the figure was on the short side and all bundled up, so he supposed it might have been a fubsy woman."

"Both Markham and Botting were below average height," Halford said. "But from what I saw I wouldn't have considered Markham overweight."

Across the ether he heard Reston sigh and imagined his colleague at his desk, dropping his aching head into his hands. "Who would have figured the sodding little bastard had *two* darkrooms? And here we were all staked out at his posh one."

"No sign of the man around town?"

"None at all. For all I know, he's stashed himself inside somewhere or taken off for the moors—assuming it's Botting. I hope for his sake he's gone inside. It gets bloody cold out there at night."

"He's a nature photographer. With luck he'll be able to take care of himself."

"Ha to that. A nature photographer with a keen taste for champagne, if you ask me. He wouldn't have had time to plan an overnight stay outside. It would make my week, Danny—first an unverified torso, then a suspiciously verified but now missing burning body, then a well-respected photographer dead from exposure. I'm too far away from retirement for this rot. And my damn head hurts. Who called aspirin the miracle drug?"

On the other side of the kitchen table Gale fretted a coffee cup, her calm face masking worry. Halford winked at her.

"No sign that Markham ever was in the darkroom?"

"No, though we're checking prints. According to Miss Jesup, the place seems to have been given a thorough cleaning before her arrival, so if we lift any, we can hope they're recent. I'm sending a WPC to the cottage to take Miss Jesup's prints for comparison."

"I'd be interested in hearing if you come up with anything else."

"Don't worry. Good sounding board, you. Ta."

Halford punched off the cell phone and gave it a nudge toward Gale. "It's possible that someone was in the darkroom while you were there. After you left, a figure was seen hurrying away. They don't know where the person is, although unless he has a car stowed away somewhere, he's either still in the town or off on foot. Either way . . ."

He shrugged, trying to convey a "what's-to-worry" attitude. It didn't work. Gale slapped the table

"I noticed a door. What the hell was I thinking not to check it? I guess I assumed the police had already checked the place out, and if they weren't worried, I shouldn't be worried. But, Jesus Christ, Daniel, what if I had opened it? What if I'd found him? What—"

He leaned forward, and took her hands in his. "Listen, Gale. This isn't my case and I don't know squat about Lyle Botting, but my guess is that whoever was behind that door was sweating bullets worrying the *you* would find *him*. Now, am I thrilled with the idea that you were in a room with someone who evidently is avoiding detection? No. Do I think he would have coshed you over the head and taken Katie Pru hostage? No. I think you would have all ended up screaming and he would have bolted, and we'd be exactly where we are now except that you would have finished your coffee instead of letting it get cold." He squeezed her hands before releasing them. "Let me make you another cup. Don't suppose you outfitted this place with a bit of brandy?"

"Alcohol makes me sleep too hard." She twisted in her chair to face him as he dumped her old coffee into the sink. "What will happen with Nadianna's negatives?"

"I'm sure Reston's wanting a look at them."

"She says there's nothing on them."

"That's information, too."

He poured coffee into her mug and laced it with

milk. From the front room he could hear the clack of
the fire and the more rhythmic pitapat of beans dropping on a wooden board. Nadianna and Katie Pru were
playing a fierce game of mancala. Passing the doorway,
he could see Katie Pru's dark head bent forward, her
pudgy finger poking the board as she tried to judge
her best move. Nadianna reclined on the floor beside
her, head resting on her wrist, blond hair spilling to the
carpet. She rubbed her stomach and gazed into space.
As Halford watched, she shifted her attention to her
charge, reaching out to stroke the child's nose.

"Why wouldn't there be something on them?" Gale
asked.

"Hmm?" He set the mug in front of her.

"Why wouldn't there be something on the negatives?
She was right there, in the water. According to what she
told Reston, she was snapping pictures up to a few seconds before she saw it. It almost touched her. Something
ought to have shown up on the film."

"You're assuming she saw something."

"No one's ever claimed that she didn't see *something*.
The question has always been did she see a body. Okay,
so what if it was a knapsack or a dead dog as Reston's suggested? It still ought to be on the film."

"Perhaps not. It could have floated just under the
water . . ."

"Have you been down there, Daniel? Current's pretty
fast. I don't think anything would just float underneath
the water like that."

". . . or it could have been outside the frame. That's
why a professional needs to look at the negatives, Gale,
to put their contents in perspective."

He meant to calm, but the words didn't register. She
was so distracted that when she sipped her coffee, she
burned her tongue and yelped.

"Could be a warning," Halford teased.

"Could be not enough milk. The problem I'm having

is that from the beginning the police didn't take her seriously. So how did they investigate the water? I'm guessing if they checked at all—"

"They did. I saw them."

"Then they probably focused on downstream, right? Looking for the object itself."

"I don't know how Reston conducted the search of the water. You're suggesting he overlooked the area upstream . . ."

"Well, face it, Daniel, if they thought they were looking for something like a knapsack or a dog carcass, would they have worried about where it may have fallen in?" She paused, scowling. "Or even if it had fallen in at all."

Halford tilted his chair on its back legs and reached behind to swing the kitchen door closed. The sounds of mancala and fire receded.

"Start from the beginning and tell me what you're thinking."

"Well, I'm working under the assumption there's nothing on Nadianna's film. If that is so, then it makes sense that the object, whatever it was, might have come into the water at a point out of the camera's range."

"Actually, I've been toying with that idea myself. The description Nadianna gave didn't sound as if the object had been in the water for a substantial length of time."

"Okay. So, if it was put into the water, could the person who put it there see Nadianna? I mean, she's pregnant. Surely if you saw a pregnant woman in the water, you wouldn't toss something in. And if you did, and it turned into this big uproar, wouldn't you come forward? 'Oh, that's my knapsack that fell in the water, or my dead cat. Sorry.' "

"Hard to get people to come forward sometimes. Or it could be the stream bends a bit, or the growth bordering it is enough to block sight of its center so whoever it was didn't see Nadianna. Nor she them."

"Could be. I wasn't really paying attention to that when Katie Pru and I were down there today."

They were murmuring, heads close together, Gale no doubt as aware as Halford that Nadianna lay quietly in the next room with only a child to distract her from the closed door.

"So let's say Mark and his men were a tad lax that first day. But with the studio burning, and two people missing . . ."

"I bet he hasn't gone back," Gale said. "I bet he hasn't thought about where someone might have stood on the bank to throw the object in."

"I'll discuss it with him. See what he thinks."

"If you were in charge of the case," she said, "you would have already checked it."

From behind the closed door came a peal of laughter and Nadianna's stern voice.

'Now, Katie Pru, what on earth possessed you to do that?"

"They're Mexican jumping beans. See, they've jumped all over the room."

"Well, you can jump all over the room picking them up."

Gale pushed back her chair, and Halford followed her. Nadianna knelt in front of the fire with her hands on her hips, the mancala board hanging upside down off the side of one of the love seats. Small black and white ovals lay scattered across the carpet, and as Halford stepped into the room, he felt a tiny lump imbed itself in the sole of his shoe.

"Katie Pru," Gale said. "Why did you do that? When you mistreat a game like that, you could lose the pieces."

Katie Pru looked around her at the carnage. "It's not interesting to play with beans."

"Well, it's going to be a whole lot less interesting if you can't play at all. Now, get down and pick every one of them up."

Katie Pru sighed through her nose, then dropped to the floor. Crawling on all fours, she gathered the beans together one by one.

"I wish they didn't have beans," she said. "I wish they had buttons or rocks." Suddenly she was on her feet, dashing up the stairs.

"Kathleen Prudence," Gale yelled. "I still see some under the chair."

"Wait. I have something better than beans."

The "something better than beans" was in a beautiful bag, colorful and hand woven, Halford surmised. Katie Pru proudly held the bag out to her mother.

"I painted them with Mr. Halford's paints. I found them in the woods. They're not rocks. Can you guess what they are?"

Gale loosened the drawstring and, giving Katie Pru an exasperated smile, peered inside. Then her brow furrowed with curiosity.

She handed the bag to Halford. He was aware of Katie Pru's delighted eyes on him as he withdrew one of her masterpieces. It rested in his palm, the size of a marble. Impatient, the child tried to take it from him, but he lifted his hand from her reach.

"I think it's a whale's tooth," she said. "See? I painted minnows on it."

They were minnows, all right, little black lines with tails, traveling in a field of blue. A fine dust clung to the rough surface.

"Just blow that off," Katie Pru instructed. "I had to wash the teeth to get them clean."

Halford gave her a quick smile and examined the contents of the bag. The dust clung to the interior fabric, but otherwise the bag was empty save for four minnow-decorated objects knocking together in the bottom.

"There was more dust, then, before you washed these?" he asked.

Katie Pru nodded. "They were very dirty."

Halford dropped the whale's tooth into the bag and gave Katie Pru a hug. "Sweetheart, you did a beautiful job painting them. Now, I'm going to ask you to show me exactly where you found these. But first I have to make a call."

Gale's face was confused as Daniel picked up Katie Pru and handed the child to her. In his peripheral vision he saw Nadianna struggle to her feet. "I think Babar's over there by the fireplace. Why don't you read a bit until I get back?" he suggested gently.

Reston had been fretting about his week. As he headed for the phone, Halford wondered just how the detective was going to take the news that a bag of brightly painted bone fragments awaited him.

The area continued as fertile ground for political agitation,
with calls for labor and welfare reform that culminated
in strong support for the popularist Chartist movement
of the 1800s.

—Notes, G. GRAYSON

18

The shed's desk lamp illuminated table, cratch, and little else. Usually the sparse light pleased Chalice. Tonight, however, it irritated her; she kept brushing her hand in front of her, trying to sweep the glow away from her face as she stared past it to the boxes stacked high in the dark.

She had never been clear on what was in the boxes. Linens, she knew, and some ashtrays from Totty's smoking days, packed up but not thrown out. Somewhere in there were also the remnants of Totty's pre-Chalice days—school papers, perhaps, old photos. Chalice had never thought to look at them. After all, they were Totty's childhood, not her own. She had read how other children were curious about their parents' pasts. Movies had been based on this notion, books written, but she wondered if it was true. It was hard to judge in her own case, since the mother/sister roles were so confused. Besides, she suspected that when children asked about their parents' past, they were really asking about themselves. *What in you made me? What path led to me?* In Chalice's case, there was no path. She had been born and handed over like Oliver Twist. Totty couldn't tell her any stories that interested her because none led to her. And when were the stories of the firstborn a source of anything but anger or boredom to the second?

More to the point, Totty knew Chalice didn't care about her past. If she had indeed taken the tea-bowls, where better for her to hide them than in the boxes that attracted no curiosity?

She lifted the cratch over the table. The roof was eight feet high, which meant when she stepped onto the cratch she had to crook her neck to keep from ramming against the top of the shed. It was an awkward fit, but she didn't fancy the idea of unstacking the boxes and then reassembling them to fool Totty.

The first box was from a department store—Marks & Spencer, no doubt—and had a lid that lifted off easily. For a moment she considered the possibility of insects, but the chair teetered sharply, and she slammed her hand against the shed's top for balance. She shoved aside her fears and gingerly reached into the box.

A smaller box, sharp-cornered. She tapped its lid and heard the crackle of thin plastic. Christmas ornaments, the ones Totty made from paper or straw—whatever was the latest craft—to give to her clients. The extras were saved for their own tree. She moved her fingers around and located four boxes in all. Packed about the sides of the boxes were velvet ribbon and garlands of fake pearls. Nothing amiss. She replaced the outer box lid and slid her hand down to the second box.

Totty didn't knock before entering, not that it would have saved Chalice. She steadied herself by wedging her head more firmly against the ceiling and managing a rueful smile.

"What are you doing?" Totty demanded.

Her sister was framed in the doorway. The desk lamp lit her coat buttons and the veins in her left hand.

"I'll ask you again: Why are you up there like that?"

An answer came to Chalice suddenly, and she smiled

widely at her sister. Rummaging in the top box, she pulled at the garland of beads.

See? She widened her eyes playfully and shook the beads in front of her. Wrapping them around her palm, she grinned and she pressed them into her flesh.

Totty visibly relaxed. "You scared me," she said. "You shouldn't be climbing around like that. The whole lot could come crashing, and you with it. Lucky I looked out and saw the light on. What would have happened had you fallen and I didn't know you were here?"

Totty reached up and wiggled her fingers. With the beads strung around her free hand, Chalice took hold of her sister's arms and leapt to the floor

"How are you going to use these?" Totty picked up the dangling garland and rolled a bead between her fingers. "Not on your tea-bowls, surely?"

Chalice shook her head. With her hands she made the outline of a pot, and once again pressed the beads into her palm.

"Ah," Totty said. "You're going to press a design into your clay. I'll be interested in seeing what that looks like. Not your usual stuff, is it? But then I've noticed you've been trying new ideas. Good." The cratch scraped the cement floor as she shifted it in place and, hiking her coat hem, settled herself down. "I know how you feel more comfortable out here. Even when you were little— I knew to check here first if I couldn't find you. Second place to check was the wood." She patted the tabletop. "Here. Sit down. We need to chat."

Chalice started to motion that she didn't have her palmtop, but Totty pulled it from her pocket. "You never bring it out here. Why should you? Your fingers have better things to do." She waited until the device was turned on and humming. "Now then, we haven't talked, you and me. About all this"—she waved her hand—"all this that's been going on. Amiss of me, really. I've been so focused on the practical—what are we going to do about your work, the bother with the police—that I haven't asked you how you feel about all of it."

In the shadows Chalice saw that Totty's body was only half relaxed, the left shoulder slouched, inviting. *Letmebeyoursisterletmebeyourfriend.* The right shoulder, however, was stiff and unyielding. Chalice kept the suspicion from her face. She picked up her palmtop.

I'M WORRIED ABOUT OLIVIA.

"Are you? Then you're a mite more compassionate that I am. It's you I worry about. Livy Markham can take care of herself."

Into Chalice's mind swam the school of tin carp, stubborn above her, unmoving no matter how hard she flapped her arms. It was an odd memory for the moment, and she tried to dispel it. In the pit of her mouth the stumped tongue ached.

PROVIDING SHE'S NOT HURT.

Totty set her eyes on her. "Providing," she answered. "I told Mrs. Grayson that I felt it was equally likely she was hurt somewhere as run away. What do you think?"

The carp were back, frozen, as if her memory were a lake in winter. Their mouths yawned open. She wondered if all siblings dangled such hooks.

Chalice shrugged. MOST LIKELY SHE AND LYLE WERE FUCKING WITH INSURANCE. NICE BLAZE.

Totty didn't react to the obscenity. The shadows made a stone of her jaw.

"Got a call from Flo Caster little while ago. Her dad lives over on Milesway. Police came round to see him. Seems there's some thought that Lyle Botting's been hiding out near there." Chalice's face must have shown dismay, for Totty nodded. "Aye. Flo's dad saw a man scurrying down the road, like he was up to no good. Word is it might've been Lyle."

Chalice jabbed her pen at her palmtop. THEY FIND HIM?

"No." Totty leaned forward and the light sliced her chin. "Chally. Tell me what you know about this."

NOTHING.

"You worked there day and night. You knew—you know Olivia better than anyone. Tell me what you know."

NOTHING!!!!

Totty settled into the chair again. "Ah. Well, luv, I hope you can say that good and true. Because somewhere in all that burnt debris is your lovely mask of Alan Axon. 'God's Messenger'—isn't that what you called it? At some point the police are going to find it, and you'll be a lucky lass if they don't recognize it. And I wonder when that happens if the police are going to have as many questions about it as I do."

Chalice pulled her teeth over her lips. WHAT QUESTIONS?

"Don't be daft. Olivia wanted the mill. Gerald Thornsby would rot in his grave before she had it. One thing you learn as you get older, Chally, is it's never the general who does the dirty work." Totty suddenly clamped her hands on Chalice's knees. "Alan does all kinds of dirty work, doesn't he?"

Chalice felt the air leave her chest. She let the palm-top pen drop to the table.

Totty's laugh was harsh. "You surprised, then? Thought I didn't know? Meeting at Mill Cottage, weren't you? Thought I couldn't tell when I went in to clean? You ought to tell your young man to be more careful. I picked up things that any decent man would have thrown away himself."

Her sister's squeeze tightened. "This was inevitable, Chally. Nothing good comes from what has to be done in secret. Think about it. Do you really think this man loves you? He's using you. And you are so much more important than that. If you know anything about this, you need to go to the police. I will protect you. You know I always have."

· · ·

Katie Pru didn't like the way the roly-poly policeman was looking at her. The skin under his eyes hung down like a puppy dog's and his nose was red and runny. He tried to smile at her, but she could always tell when grown-ups didn't really want to smile. Their lips were flat against their teeth and they looked everywhere except at her face.

Right now Mr. Reston was looking at her ear.

"Now, young Miss Katie Pru, you found some mighty interesting things out there in the wood. Why don't you tell me about them?"

When he finished talking, he shifted his eyes to hers, but it didn't count. He and the tall policeman, along with another man in white gloves, had come to the cottage after Mr. Halford called. They had mumbled to each other in the kitchen, and then the white-gloved man had come into the front room and winked at her. 'Wash something out in the tub, lovey?" he had said to her, but Mr. Reston had cleared his throat loudly and the white-gloved man had grinned and bounded up the stairs. She had liked the white-gloved man. Mr. Reston, she was sure, needed a nap. And a handkerchief to blow his nose with.

"I found 'em," she said. She opened her mouth wide and tried to see how far back she could twist her tongue, but she ended up just yawning. She made a little sigh as she let out her breath. "In the woods. Under a log."

"How did you know to look there?"

That got her attention, and her next yawn stopped in mid-sigh. "I didn't. It was just there."

"What was just there?"

"The bag. It was just under the log when I sat down. I was hiding from Nadianna. She couldn't find me if I was sitting down."

"Oh, I see." Mr. Reston scooted forward on the stool he was sitting on. "And could you see the bag when you were sitting down?"

She scrunched her eyes closed and tried to think. She hated it when grown-ups wanted her to remember. They would ask the same questions over and over again. There were so many things she couldn't remember, so many things that she did and forgot. Katie Pru knew she lived in a world of Did and Pretend, and the pretend was much more interesting than the did.

"No. I felt it. With my hand."

"Hmm." The roly-poly policeman frowned. "Come tomorrow morning, when it's light out, I'm going to come back and see if we can't find the log. But for now I want you to think very hard, Katie Pru. Did something make you go to that particular log? Did you see anything that made you notice the log before you sat down?"

Now she really frowned, thinking hard, knowing that her mother and Nadianna and Mr. Halford, who sat on the other side of the room, were hoping she would think as hard as she ever had.

"Oh, yeah," she said suddenly, and she scrambled from the love seat and ran upstairs.

They all ran after her. She could hear them bumble up the stairs, could hear, too, the white-gloved man humming in the bathroom as she raced into her bedroom. The room was dark, but she didn't turn on the bedside lamp. Instead, she ran to the small, low window and pressed her nose against the glass.

The wind blew, and the tree branches waved, but the light through the downstairs windows made the leaves outside look like themselves and not a million minnows. She stared through the glass, trying to see, but she couldn't. She turned to the grown-ups, disappointed.

"I thought maybe it was the light," she said. "Maybe the log was near the light, but I don't think so."

Mr. Reston knelt beside her. "What light, Katie Pru?"

"The light I saw the other night."

"The porch light?"

She shook her head. "A moving light. In the woods. I

thought it was the whale's eye." She thought of some- thing, liked the idea and felt better. "Maybe it was. I bet his eyes rolled a lot when he was losing those teeth."

"Let's think back a little, Katie Pru. Can you tell me which night?"

"No."

"What happened before you went to bed that night?"

She thought hard again. "We went to the rest'rant."

Mr. Reston looked at her mother. "Monday," her mother said. Her voice was very quiet.

Mr. Reston stood and held out his hand. His skin was warm as he clasped her cold fingers. She felt sleepy.

"Well, Miss Katie Pru, you've done good work."

"I want to go to bed now."

"Me, too. Let's shake hands on it and wish each other a good night."

MICHAEL'S BOOK

20 APRIL 1812

Let me tell of monsters.

I had heard them, you see. From my grandfather's mouth came tales of them, and I saw them as clearly as if they stood in full form by the firelight. Not just the common barguest, the beast who meant death to the poor soul who spied him. My grandfather's monsters had tricks to them, which in their playfulness made them all the more horrible.

Shaggybairit was one. He stood eight feet tall and had the chest of a man and the legs of a beast. His teeth stretched past his mouth and were so sharp, blood trickled from his chin when he talked. But he had the eyes of a beautiful woman, round and soft, blue as the summer sky. It was said he would flag down men in the moor, coquettish-like. The men would take off their hats and bow, only to have the backs of their necks slashed. Women, not so beguiled, threw stones and frightened him away.

His wife was named Croose. She wore a long skirt fashioned of heather, and her hair was a jumble of gosling feathers. She had a pleasant face and would smile at wayfarers and ask them the time. When they answered, she would whoop and upend herself to reveal a second head and face and a second pair of arms upon which she had been walking. This face was quite hideous, and she would cartwheel away—head, arms, head, arms—down the hillside, her cackling still heard when she was out of sight.

To a small boy such monsters were fearsome. But I never saw a man buried because of one. Or a child, either.

A second horror has befallen my brother Nathan. His wife Nell has taken ill. Violent cough. High fever.

Tansy the midwife tended her through the night. She said that Nell has been sick for a while, but for the sake of Benjamin had overlooked her own waning health. My Martha has gone to her, but I fear for my dear wife. The women of our small clan have not rested well since Benjamin took ill nearly six weeks ago.

By his fireside I talked with Nathan. Rather, I talked to him, his attention caught by the fire, not responding. We will avenge all this, I whispered. Do not lose heart. But it is not my child under the earth or my wife crying with each cough. Avenge, he finally murmured. Who, dear brother, shall be the target of my vengeance?

Why, the mill-owners! I urged. They are our monsters. Come with me. Tonight we will plan.

Monsters, Nathan said, staring at the flame. There are no monsters but Death and Time.

Oh, but there is, I cried. Human monsters, who would eat our flesh and souls. Come with me, brother. We will not let them wheel like Croose away.

At that small reference to our innocent past he smiled. Good ol' Croose, he said. Two heads, pleasant and vile. And with that his face grew dark again and the fire ate his thoughts.

I could draw no more from him, so I left, knocking on my fellows' doors—one knock, fast and sharp, two low coughs. Within an hour we were gathered at The Crown & Drover, and I listened to my fellows' reports. Matthew Cooke spoke first. Several wagons pulled up the steep hill to Yates Mill last night. The horses lurched from the strain; many times the drovers halted behind the wagons, shoring them up with their own shoulders to *give the animals rest. Matthew and John Thorpe hid among the trees and boulders until the wagons came to a stop at the mill and the blankets were tossed off. Power looms. We had heard rumours that Yates was installing the new looms, but he had assured his workers that it was not true. The man is a liar. The machines that have caused riots in Lancashire have now made their way into our notch of the West Riding. They will not be allowed to stay.*

So it is set. We will strike Yates Mill ten days hence. For Benjamin, for Nell, for too many others who breathe today but will not tomorrow.

According to testimony to the Poor Law Commission, by 1832 the diet of the average Mayley working family consisted of oatmeal, potatoes, and milk.

—*Notes*, G. GRAYSON

19

Friday

The sky was plum and starry when Gale rolled from bed. She dressed quickly, and gathering up her daughter, trotted across the hallway to Nadianna's room. There she wedged the child against the pregnant woman's back, thus ensuring that if one awoke, so would the other, and Katie Pru couldn't ramble unattended. By the time Gale left the cottage, the stars were gone, and a slate sky topped the circle of woods. Reston would arrive at ten to search the woods with Katie Pru. She still had time before then, but she had to hurry.

As soon as she entered the path, she was struck again by how unlikely it was that Nadianna had navigated it alone and in the dark that first day. At best, the path was ambiguous—it diverged, went uphill then down, joined denser, ragged paths that ranged out of sight only to reemerge beneath fallen limbs and stone outcroppings. And it wasn't well traveled; that Gale could tell by the bare tendrils that snagged her boots. How many other neglected paths led to Sette Water? And away from what other places did they lead?

At the bottom of the hill she broke into a milky light. She followed the stream north toward Yates Mill. Here the grass was high; she had to step broadly, water surging from the dirt and lapping at the soles of her heavy boots. If someone had thrown something into the stream from this side, they'd have to be more adept at tromping than she was.

After five minutes of hard walking she stopped and sucked in a breath. Directly across the stream stood the bosk of trees, their crotchety limbs wagging at the water. Past it lay the gutted shell of Markham Studio. Even at this distance the windows looked hollow; soot drooped from the sills. The wrecked house rose from its shoulder of grass like the face of a battered woman.

Gale shivered. Without wading into the stream she couldn't tell where Nadianna had stood during her shoot, but from what she could recall of the negatives, the bosk hadn't been in the frame. Perhaps Nadianna had stood angled away from the bosk, which would have given her a front view of the mill and effectively blinded her from any activity on the far side of the trees. No bushes or entwined vegetation bordered the stream. On this side of the water the only shelter was that of the cottage woods, where certainly someone looking to dispose of a body would have seen Nadianna standing mid-stream.

But on the opposite bank the bosk provided perfect camouflage. Someone standing on the studio side of Sette Water could not have seen downstream. They would be in full view of the mill, but not of Nadianna silently absorbed in her work.

In full view of the mill. Something tugged at her memory. She focused on the mill's lichen-crossed facade.

A stone hit the stream a few feet away. Jolted, Gale looked across the water to see Halford in his black overcoat, chucking another rock her way.

He grinned when he saw he had her attention. "Wait there," he called. "Give me ten minutes."

He trudged around the back of the studio at a brisk pace—much more brisk than she could have managed on the rolling terrain—and disappeared behind a hillock. Gale squished the sopping grass with her boots and flapped her arms for warmth until, very close to ten minutes later, he appeared on the west side of the mill and headed toward her.

He arrived only slightly winded. "Brilliant morning for a walk," he said.

"Brilliant." She looked down at his pants, dry and dotted with grass bits. "How did you do that?"

"Get across, you mean? Bridge. Just north. The stream curves once you get past the mill, and the bridge is past the crook. An old packhorse bridge, good only for walking. Found it on the Ordnance Survey map—shows two bridges in the vicinity, the packhorse and the main one at Mayley. According to Bertie Portman at The Crown & Drover, a nature club made a stepping-stone crossing farther south, but it's a distance away and downstream."

"Well-traveled, that packhorse bridge?"

"I suppose so. For ramblers, at any rate. Not that this is a popular route, from what I gather. The Pennine Way notches west of here. It would mainly be ramblers willing to go a couple of miles out of their way to use Mayley as a stopping point." He tilted his head at her. "Up early."

A breeze lifted her hair and pressed her scarf to her mouth. "Restless night," she said. "Between Nadianna's body and Katie Pru's 'whale's teeth' . . ." When she glanced at him, she found him studying her face, his mouth quirked in a half-smile but his gray eyes somber. "Those bones are going to convince Reston, aren't they? He's going to take Nadianna seriously."

"The bone fragments will have to be tested, need to be confirmed as human. But yes, I think this will convince Reston. He doesn't really require too much of a nudge."

"It's going to be horrible."

"Could be, yes."

"Well, dammit, then." She sank onto her haunches, balancing above the soggy ground. At her shoulder the stream cooed. Because she was frustrated and didn't know what else to do, she picked up a rock and hurtled it. It sank without ripples, swallowed by the current.

"You know the locals call this Sad Water. Alan Axon told me. There are stories about all the bizarre things that have fallen in the stream."

"I'd imagine that would be the case with any water community."

True. She thought of the pond behind her cousin's fish house in Statlers Cross. The pond had its stories—of the large-catfish, drunk-fool variety. Sad Water was not so comical. A cat's head grinning, a drowning bride singing. The victims themselves were sinister, and the water carried them like captains on its shoulders. Odd mythology for a dying village.

Gale stood up. She nodded toward the bosk. "Find anything?"

"No. It's rained since Monday, so if there is any evidence, it's going to require a careful going-over. But your suspicion was correct. Those trees act as a screen. From either there or the studio, you can't see downstream to where Nadianna would have been."

"But you can look across from the studio and see the mill." Gale felt a vague anxiety; she should remember something but couldn't.

"That's right," Halford said. "If someone had launched a body that morning, Nadianna in all likelihood would have seen them only if it happened from the mill grounds."

"And then it would have been caught on film."

"Perhaps."

A sound came tumbling with the stream—a frail thread barely audible above the water's burble. Exchanging glances, they headed wordlessly toward the source. At the rear of the mill they came upon a dozen people standing in a circle, arms raised, their voices warbling in the thin air.

The melody was reminiscent of an old Methodist hymn Gale recalled from her childhood, "Soldiers of the Cross, Arise." But in the clapboard church in Statlers Cross, the song had been rendered with vigor and punctuation marks. Here the music was humble, its natural marching rhythm muted. The chorus dwindled, and Gale was surprised to see Zoë Axon lift her voice for the solo.

Hers was a pure alto. She sang with strength, her wind-tossed hair the color of the two-hundred-year-old mill walls behind her.

> *Come, the miracle to see;*
> *Come to touch eternity.*
> *Wash your joyous face and cry*
> *Embrace the water's sigh.*
> *Fire and water, quenched, are one;*
> *All our hist'ry will be done.*
> *Raise our voices to the sky*
> *And bless the vision seen.*

The Methodist melody it may well have been; Methodist lyrics, however, these were not. The chorus followed, but the multitude of voices made it impossible for Gale to decipher the words.

Halfway through the chorus, Alan Axon noticed Gale, and broke into a wide smile. He started clapping; the tempo of the music changed. The group soared with him, knees bending, until they were scooting around the mill grounds in a fevered circle dance.

They finished in laughter. Grinning, Alan broke from

the crowd and jogged to Gale and Halford while the group returned to a song.

"Don't tell me," he said. "You could hear us clear up at the cottage and couldn't resist."

"Not quite as far as the cottage," Gale replied. "But as far as the stream. The sound was lovely."

The young man gave a short nod, pleased. "It occurred to us that moping about all that's happened wasn't the hopeful thing to do. Raise your voice in song, that's Gerald's motto."

"Some might call that a wee bit of denial," Gale pointed out.

Alan threw back his blond head and laughed. "Don't mind Miss Gale," he said to Halford. "She and I have a bit of a rib going on."

"Old hymn, new words," Gale said.

"That's the case with most of our music. We write our own lyrics to match our worship. More personal that way."

"So who's the gifted lyricist here?" Halford asked.

"Me, actually. By writing our own lyrics, I like to think we're continuing what old Charles Wesley started— bringing the faith to the people."

"And if you can give a boost to your ratings at the same time . . ." Halford let the sentence dangle.

Alan's cheerfulness faltered. "Sorry?"

"Well, it can't be bad for the business end to have the faithful gathering at the riverside to sing praises of the Lord's most recent visitation."

"You may think what you like, Mr. Halford," Alan said, his discomfort palpable. "We don't operate 'for the business end.' We're not in it for money."

Halford raised his hand. "Didn't mean to offend."

"Sure you did. But it's something we've well learned to handle."

The singers had their arms wrapped around one

another, and they dipped snakelike as they sang. Gale focused on the rhythm, the snake's undulating movement, and behind it all, the constant, humming psalm of the water.

Her reverie snapped. From where she stood, Sette Water glided straight and even down the incline toward Mayley. From here she could see the studio, the bosk. And had it been daybreak Monday morning, she would have been able to see Nadianna standing hip-high in the cold water.

The arms of two singers broke apart and drew Alan in as the snake plunged downward. His hands locked in theirs, and he was suddenly driving his arms to the sky. For a split second, the serpent looked as if its back had broken. Gale heard his voice above all others, exuberant and powerful, before the snake flexed smoothly and arched again. She turned away and slipped her arm through Halford's.

"Gerald Thornsby was on the river Monday morning," she said.

"How do you know?"

"Nadianna told me as much, but I tuned her out. She said the only person she could trust was the preacher who trusted her even when he didn't see what she saw. God! I can't believe I was paying so little attention to her."

" 'Didn't see what she saw'?"

"That's what she said. Has Thornsby ever mentioned to anybody that he was on the river that morning?"

Halford shook his head. "I'd say the man's not mentioned a lot of things," he said softly.

Bus drivers had nicknames for Old Ground Lane. Chalice had overheard a driver and his mate joking about it on a day Totty had taken the car and she had been forced to ride the bus for her rendezvous with Alan.

Chalice had been the only passenger, and the mate, sitting in the bench seat to the left of the driver, kept staring at her as they joshed.

"Bugger shoots straight up, doesn't it?" the mate remarked as the bus chugged the lane's steep incline to the bus stop. "Hell on an engine, I'd think."

"We call it Old Lady's Arse," the driver replied. "Round at the bottom and then straight up and down."

"How about K2 Tit?" the mate sniggered. "Reminds me of a girl I had once. Needed tackle and a good strong arm to reach the top."

His laugh displayed tobacco-stained teeth. The driver shushed him with a warning glance at Chalice, but the mate shrugged. "Can't hear me now, can she?" he said sotto voce. "I mean, they can't when they can't talk, right?"

"That one can hear," the driver insisted.

Chalice had stared stonily out the window, and since then she had taken the bus only when necessary. That she found herself in such a position today was part of her despair.

The bus stop was located halfway up Old Ground Lane and consisted of a gravel lot large enough for a handful of cars. In all the times she had passed the stop, not once had Chalice seen a car parked there, nor had she ever seen anyone alight from the bus. This was a forlorn stop, and she had often wondered why the local line continued it. There were only two habitations within reasonable walking distance: a restored country house on the down side of Witkin Hill whose owners had a surfeit of automobiles, and Mill Cottage. It was because of this solitude that Chalice had suggested the cottage to Alan in the first place.

NO ONE EVER RENTS IT. AND WHEN SOMEONE DOES, TOTTY HAS A SERVICE DO THE CLEANING.

"We'll still need to be careful," Alan had cautioned.

OF COURSE. BUT THEN, WE ARE, AREN'T WE.

Evidently not. But that was the ego of lovers: they seemed to think passion was invisible.

And now Totty was livid. Fat tears fell on Chalice's fingers. Who could she trust now? What in the hell should she do?

The bus lurched to a stop. Chalice slid her purse over her shoulder and stepped from the green-lit cocoon.

"Last stop here is five thirty-five," the bus driver said loudly before shutting the door. "A long slide down if you miss it."

The bus swung widely on the gravel, sighing once before retreating to the kinder roads of the valley bottom. Chalice stood solitary in the center of the lot; on all sides the rough land ran away from her. She squinted shut her eyes and raised her mouth skyward.

"Someone has betrayed me!" she yelled. "Someone is lying!"

But all that came back to her was the wordless echo of her howl. She turned and commenced hiking the green rise of Witkin Hill.

Twenty-five minutes passed before she entered Blandon Wood, another ten before she was seated on the millstone outcrop designated as their meeting place whenever Mill Cottage was in use. Here, out of sight of road and path and building, she and Alan truly were invisible. No one could come upon them undetected. Even wet leaves had a sound to them.

She tapped her fingers against her palmtop, pocketed in her coat. He knew to come. They had their code worked out. Five after the hour, any hour—one telephone ring, cut short. That was the signal for the other to return the call, during which Chalice used vocal sounds to agree on a time. They knew the other's schedule, knew where to call. This was all necessary to fool Totty, Chalice had explained. Alan hadn't understood. "Do I embarrass you, then?" he had asked. How to explain that it wasn't him, that her sister had decided that she was off-limits to all men?

She didn't understand why. Was it resentment toward their mother and her selfish abandonment? Totty's own poor luck with men? Chalice's worst fear made her stomach hurt—that Totty felt her somehow unsuitable for sex, that intimacy was meant for smaller packages.

She heard a man's voice, answered by a woman. Chalice froze, knowing how sound darted through the trees. They were too far away for her to understand what they were saying, but the rumbling diminished and finally disappeared in the direction of the cottage. She glanced at her watch—just now nine A.M. The Americans had surprised her in so many ways. They had brought all this with them as certainly as they had brought their suitcases and coats. Without the pregnant woman in the stream, would anyone have seen a charred corpse? And if no one had seen a corpse, would the studio have had to burn? Such innocent carriers of ruthlessness—a pregnant woman, a widow, a child—but carriers they nonetheless were, as lethal as a bullet.

She heard the sudden sound of feet crashing over the ground, and Alan appeared, his face flushed from running. When, she thought, had he known they were past secrecy?

He leaned against her and kissed her face. His breath tasted hot, metallic. Clutching the back of her neck, he kissed her again.

"God, Chally, I'm sorry. I couldn't leave the mill. A whole group of us met there this morning—I wish you would come. We sang my hymn, Chally. My words. It was so powerful. I wish you would come with me."

A sheen of sweat covered his face. He shoved his hair against the top of his head, where it stayed plastered, and Chalice sensed, despite his vibrancy, how tired he was. His eyes were bleary, and the red of his cheeks splayed over his skin like an old man's veins.

He moved his palms down her arms and over her thighs. When he reached her knees, he gently pushed them apart and knelt on the wet grass between them.

"All right," he said, kissing her with finality. "What's the problem?"

She dug into her pocket and pulled out her palmtop. TOTTY KNOWS.

He tickled her sides. She wriggled out of his hands, irritated.

"Great," he said. "No more skullduggery. I can live with that."

SHE'S ANGRY.

"I can live with that, too. For pity's sake, Chally, you're a grown woman. Who cares if she's angry?"

I CARE. SHE WANTS TO TALK WITH ME ABOUT OLIVIA.

She studied him, dissecting his reaction as he read her words. She had spent the night weighing what she should say. *It's never the general who does the dirty work.* Totty could be a demanding bitch, but it was part of Chalice's anguish that the bitch was so frequently correct.

His expression didn't change. "Not your concern anymore, is Olivia? She hasn't turned up yet. Gerald's take on it is she's done a bunk. Tried to pull an insurance scam—probably drunk on her arse at the time. Sobered up, couldn't believe what she'd done, ran off. We'll hear about her drunk and bragging in some dive in France. Wired tight, that one. She was going to go off, just a matter of when."

He tried to touch her chin, but she pulled away. Her fingers jerked as she wrote on her palmtop.

MY T-BOWLS ARE GONE.

His brow furrowed. "I don't understand."

15 BOWLS IN THE STUDIO BEFORE THE FIRE. GONE.

"Chally, really, you can't expect things like that to survive . . ."

NO! She was agitated now, anger overriding fear. THEY'D HAVE SURVIVED. SOMEONE TOOK THEM.

"All right." He shook his head, confused. "Maybe Olivia took them. Before she left."

WHY???

"I don't know. To sell them, maybe. More like it to pass them off as her own. Who knows with that woman?"

TO MAKE ME LOOK GUILTY.

"What? Don't be ridiculous. Why would she want to make you look guilty?"

SHE HATED ME.

"Well, yes, a jealous old cow, is Olivia. But what are you suggesting—that she stole the tea-bowls so it would look like you saved your own pieces before torching the place?"

She nodded. He took a long breath and sat back on his heels.

"I don't know, Chally. Seems a little subtle for Olivia. Never heard anyone accuse her of being that. If she wanted to frame you, she'd write it in red letters on the wall—*Chalice Did It!*"

SOMEONE ELSE, THEN.

She turned the palmtop to face him. With the pale hair pushed away from his face, he had no hiding place—nowhere to duck his eyes, nowhere to retreat while he contemplated. Whoever took her tea-bowls either loved her enough to save them or hated her enough to hurt her. Tears burned the back of her throat.

Alan hadn't lifted his eyes from her words. "I don't understand, Chally," he murmured. "What are you getting at?"

Her sobs came without warning, hacking from her chest, making her large shoulders spasm. Her pen slashed at the small computer; at that moment she wouldn't have cared if she pierced the damn thing.

OLIVIA DIDN'T BUNK. DEAD! THE POLICE WILL THINK ME GUILTY. WHY TAKE THE BOWLS? WHY???

Her body shuddered. She plunged again at the palm-top, tears streaming down her face.

YOU? YOU? YOU?

The pink of Alan's cheeks flamed red. "Shit, no, Chally! Why would I do that? I love you."

GERALD, THEN? GERALD TRIED TO FRAME ME?

Alan tried to grasp her hands. She jerked away.

"You think Gerald killed Olivia and tried to frame you? Look, I think you've jumped to some awful conclusions. All right, maybe your tea-bowls are gone. But there doesn't have to be a sinister explanation. Maybe someone came by and bought them—now, I bet you've never thought of that, did you? No one would have expected you to, not with all the excitement. There's a logical explanation. Don't—"

He paused, his breath shallow and soft on her face. His blue eyes widened, and he leaned away from her. "What has Totty said to you?"

She stared past him, no longer wanting to see his face. The wind had dried her cheeks; she sat motionless. He took off his barn jacket and placed it over her shoulders.

"Let me get you home. Walk with me to the mill, and we'll take Gerald's car. He's bound to be there by now. If not, we'll wait. Come on, Chally, it won't do for you to be out in the wood alone."

She pushed his jacket to the ground. YOU'RE LYING.

"Chally, please. I'm worried about you. Come with me."

She shook her head and pulled herself upright. She had four stone on him, and she topped him by a hand.

The muscles of his mouth sagged.

"I love you. You tell your damn sister *that*."

He picked up his jacket.

She listened until he was gone and the wood filled up the silence.

An economic cycle of boom and bust settled in. 1836 was prosperous; 1837 depressed. The "hungry forties" lasted from 1839 to 1843 and found Mayley with only 30 percent full employment.

—*Notes*, G. GRAYSON

20

Lyle Botting was found in the early morning hours of Friday, making his way along the Pennine Way. To Nadi-anna, the news was of surprisingly little comfort. She listened restlessly to Halford as he conveyed the story, her heels kicking the rungs of the kitchen chair. Two hikers had left their provisions spread out on a blanket and walked to a nearby stone cluster. There they dawdled, trying to decide if the stones were naturally mounded or intentionally stacked by villagers long ago. Maybe they debated it for thirty minutes, they told the police, maybe a little more. When they returned, a man in a black parka was crouched in the middle of their blanket, wearing their spare clothes and devouring the food they had rationed for the rest of their walk. They had no trouble tackling him—he wasn't very big—and with him cater-wauling and begging and bribing, the two hikers planted their rear ends on the man's back and called the police from their cell phone, which they never left home without.

It was a story that explained why the police had not shown up that morning to search the woods for the log where Katie Pru had found the bones. It was also a story that engrossed Gale and Halford, Gale pounding her tiny finger into the tabletop to make her points, Halford lounging, nodding, thoughtful. So engrossed were they, in fact, that Nadianna put on her coat and slipped out of the cottage without either one noticing. The discovery of the bones, now this—it was all too much.

She started down the path, but quickly veered off, not wanting to be led to the road and visibility. She high-stepped over brambles, around outcrops, avoiding all logs so as not to disturb anything of help to the police. She walked as silently as possible for a pregnant woman in winter clothes.

She came to a sudden stop. Chalice Hibbert stood deer-still in the woods fifty yards in front of her—back straight, hands in her coat pockets, her red hair conspicuous among the yellows and browns of the trees. She faced away, defenseless; if Nadianna had had her camera, she could have bagged her in one shot.

A twig lay on the ground a few inches from Nadianna's shoe. She rolled onto the ball of her foot and cracked it.

She expected Chalice to turn and wave. Instead, Chalice ducked her head and strode away.

"Wait!" Nadianna hollered, raising her arms. "It's me! Nadianna Jesup. You remember." The other woman stopped mid-gait. "I never thanked you for Monday morning. I appreciate what you did, leading me to the cottage like that. Who knows where I'd be wandering now if you hadn't steered me right?"

With this last she gave a half-chuckle, and Chalice turned around. Even at this distance, Nadianna could read her belligerence. But as they stared at each other, the Englishwoman's expression changed. Her big shoulders relaxed, and she trudged to Nadianna's side.

They stood facing each other, hands in pockets—one woman tall for her Georgia hometown, the other woman tall anywhere. Nadianna was aware of Chalice's gaze measuring her, and she shifted her feet nervously.

"See?" she said, trying to alter the mood. "I got both shoes on today. Running around in your stocking feet is something you do only once here, believe you me."

Chalice stooped slightly, squinting as if Nadianna's mouth were the small print on a bottle, and Nadianna knew that once again she was unintelligible. "I was just thanking you," she said slowly. "I wanted to let you know how grateful I am."

Chalice shook her head. From her pocket she pulled the hand-held computer she had used so expertly during the police interview Monday. She wrote for several seconds before holding the small screen up to Nadianna.

Digital letters covered the screen. PLEASURE. BOUND TO BE ONE OF THE MOST IMPORTANT DAYS OF MY LIFE.

Nadianna looked at her suspiciously, not wanting to deal with any more talk of visions or to speak with anyone else who didn't want her to trust her own sight. But if there was mistrust in this person, Nadianna knew in a glance it wasn't directed at her. Beneath their pale lashes Chalice's emerald eyes were clear and vulnerable. For whatever reason Chalice Hibbert was in the woods, it involved a new pain that had nothing to do with her.

"For me, too," she said. "It certainly wasn't what I expected when I woke up that morning. I expected other things—like, to be frozen from the hip down, to be swept away and drowned, even"—here she faltered—"even causing a miscarriage. Pretty stupid. What did I know of the water around here? But I decided the pictures were worth the risk, so I stepped into the stream."

She heard herself suddenly putting into words what she hadn't yet acknowledged—that when she'd seen the blackened bundle floating toward her, her first reaction had been to look down at her own belly to see if the baby's life flowed red away from her, and this charred object was the ghost of what she would never be allowed to birth—and she waited for Chalice's recoil. What do you say to a foreigner who has just told you she risked her baby's life? How do you answer a woman who has just admitted that for a split second she believed she had witnessed a vision after all?

But Chalice didn't recoil and she didn't withdraw. Her vulnerable eyes grew darker, and she hunched over her computer.

WE ALL TAKE RISKS SOMETIMES THAT STARTLE US.

Pain stabbed Nadianna's throat. "And if it hurts someone?"

THEN IT DOES.

"I think I've hurt someone." Nadianna murmured.

WHO?

"My sister Ivy back home. I've made her feel abandoned."

Chalice's mouth quirked. TRADE WITH ME. MINE COULD USE SOME ABANDONING.

Nadianna laughed. "I wish it were that easy."

NOT REALLY.

"No."

I'M SORRY ABOUT YOUR SISTER. BUT YOU HAD TO COME.

"I know," Nadianna whispered. "I just wish I could've come without hurting her."

LEAVING ALWAYS HURTS.

"What about you? You're still here with your sister. Ever thought of leaving?"

ALWAYS. CONSTANTLY.

"Why?"

No response.

Nadianna took a stab. "Does your sister not support your work?"

A laugh. TOO MUCH.

"So what's keeping you here?"

Chalice looked away, her palmtop momentarily idled. I'M NOT AS BRAVE AS YOU.

A bird shot through the tree limbs overhead, and a shower of dying leaves fell around them. Nadianna plucked a damp alder leaf from her hair. "Look, why don't you come to the cottage and let's fix some tea?" An uncertain expression crossed Chalice's face. "No, really, it's okay. Gale would love to have you, and Katie Pru, she's a handful but she's worth the world once you get to know her."

The electronic pen scratched at the screen. SOMEONE LEFT SOMETHING OF MINE IN THE COTTAGE. DO YOU THINK YOU COULD LOOK FOR ME?

"Sure."

Pen scratching; green eyes as large as taws. BUT IT'S A SECRET, PLEASE. PLEASE, NADIANNA. I NEED SOMEBODY TO TRUST. MAY I TRUST YOU?

When Halford entered The Crown & Drover, the two ramblers were holding court, stocking caps pushed askew on their heads, mud from their boots making skid marks on the floor. Few locals were in the pub at noon, but a sparse audience didn't dampen the performance. By the time Halford leaned against the bar and caught Bertie Portman's attention, the ramblers had turned gnomish Lyle Botting into a raging alligator they had wrestled to the ground.

"Strong back on him for such a little bloke," proclaimed one. "Just about bucked me off, he was fighting so hard. Had to hold on to his collar so I wouldn't fall off."

"Had a squawk on him as well," contributed the other. "I bet if you'd listened you could have heard him clear to here. Kept saying he would pay us. 'Oooo, I have a lot of money, I'll give it all to you if you'll just let me go!' 'Right,' I said. 'Which is why you're stealing our food!' I said it to him just like that."

"Mind you," said the first, "He was wearing a pricey parka. Seemed a bit odd. But you fellows say you know him? None of you are his mates, are you?"

Portman bent toward Halford, shaking his head at the ramblers and scowling. "Gits," he muttered. "It pains me to see someone like Lyle turned into a burlesque show." He sighed deeply. "So tell me, Mr. Halford. Want to join the buggers with a pint?"

"I'll take half a pint of ale, but I'll stay clear of the buggers." Halford waited until Portman slid the frosty glass to him. "Don't get many ramblers here, I'd imagine."

"Not many, but some. A bit too far off the path."

"Even more rare this time of year?"

"Oh, aye. But the truth is, a dedicated rambler will walk in any weather. And I don't complain when they come. We're the only show in town."

Halford took an appreciative sip. "What about last week?"

Portman pulled a cloth from beneath the counter and rubbed the counter's gleaming surface. "Well, now. Last week was unusual. Weather not as cold. Had a young couple—they ended staying the night."

"Any solitary men?"

The rubbing slowed. "Aye, did have one. Friday night it was. Had a meal and a couple of pints. I remember him because of his posh accent—not that we don't get a lot of posh folk here, but he was posh and demanding. Made a fuss because his cod was too hard. Don't mind when a patron complains, but he was rude. Had to hold Doreen back from walloping him."

"About what time?"

"He arrived around seven. Stayed an hour or so."

"Other than the cod, did he talk to you?"

" 'E did. Wanted directions to Markham Studio. I should have mentioned it before, but it was several days before the fire, so surely it's not connected. Besides, we get a fair amount of that. The woman touts her wares but can't be bothered to print out maps." He slapped the cloth over his shoulder. "That's ungracious of me. They rarely stop to ask directions without having a bite."

"And did you see this man after Friday night?"

"No. But I wouldn't expect to 'less he was staying."

"Can you tell me what he looked like?"

"Aah, just a bloke. About forty, I'd say. Dark hair. Beige overcoat. Glasses. Hiking boots—left mud all around his table. Nothing unusual about him except his manners."

"Pay with a credit card?"

"Cash."

Halford took a long sip and laid his coins on the table. "Thanks, Bertie. You serve the best ale in Mayley."

"Aye." Portman grinned. "Tell all your friends."

Halford took the stairs two at a time. Inside his room, he shrugged off his coat, tossed it onto the bed, and sank down on the mattress.

Chances were there was no connection—a man asking for directions to a well-known potter's studio, a bag of bones that may or may not be human found in the woods. And he was meddling by even asking questions. Still, it would bear checking out.

A complimentary savory snack of basil crackers lay on the bedside table. He had popped one in his mouth when his phone rang.

Reston didn't bother with preliminaries.

"I've spent the whole morning with Botting, Danny. You'd be in your element with this one. First thing he did when his solicitor entered the interview room was vomit. The rest of the time he just sat at the table with his head in his hand. Wouldn't look up, wouldn't speak to his solicitor. Only time he responded was when he heard his solicitor suggest a psychological evaluation. Perked right up then, the bastard. Wouldn't have it."

"Anxious? Depressed?"

"Bloody quivering in his boots, if you ask me. He's done something or knows something, and I'd be willing to bet my pension it isn't some well-planned arson of his girlfriend's place."

"I don't know, Mark. People invest a lot in their reputations, particularly their public ones."

"Shit. If this were some insurance scam, he'd be demanding his rights and complaining about the dust in his cell. He's scared."

"Well, if he's scared, the right nudge will get him to talk."

"Just a matter of finding it." Reston paused. "Talked with the super about the bones. I laid it out for him. Armless, charred torso possibly sighted Monday morning; light in the wood Monday night; what might be partially cremated remains found in the area Thursday."

"You might want to check the bag as well. It looked hand woven."

"Aye, we're on it. At any rate, the super's not convinced. Wants to wait for the test results to confirm they're human. People've been known to bag an animal, or even garbage, and toss it in. Doesn't want to commit more men until we know what we're dealing with. If I'd been more forceful from the beginning . . ."

"Listen, Mark, if I can help—"

"Thanks, Danny. I hate to disturb your leave and all, but hell, seems you're in the thick of it already." Reston laughed, but the sound was tattered with fatigue. "This afternoon, then, if you can. A couple of interviews. Frank and Igor revisited, what?"

"Name the time."

"Pick you up at two."

Halford rang off and immediately punched in his favorite number at New Scotland Yard. DS Maura Ramsden answered the first ring.

"Tell me," he said without preamble, "what is it about the artist Olivia Markham that I'm supposed to know but don't?"

His subordinate Maura must have instantly detected his seriousness; the teasing tone she adopted during their off hours was absent. "Sorry, guv," she said. "Not familiar with her."

"A potter. She's living here in Mayley with a photographer named Lyle Botting. Nice little setup, old mill-owner's house turned into a studio, lots of customers, notoriety, healthy income, big plans. Only two days ago she goes missing. Boyfriend was flushed out of hiding this morning."

"What's the boyfriend got to say?"

"Nothing yet. But something's bothering me, Maura. And since you're my better half . . ."

"Right. Olivia Markham, spelled M-a-r-k-h-a-m, Lyle Botting, B-o-t-t-i-n-g. Got 'em. See what I can find. Anyone else?"

"A preacher. Gerald Thornsby. He'll have an arrest record—burglary. See if anything strikes you as particularly interesting."

"Will do. Now, be a chum, Chief Inspector, and tell me none of this has to do with Mrs. Grayson."

From the bowels of The Crown & Drover came a blast of raucous laughter. "I would love to, DS Ramsden," Halford replied. "But then, you would have a good copper's sense not to believe me anyway."

Chalice Hibbert didn't want to be seen—that Gale could tell by the way she stood back among the trees, the collar of her loden coat pulled up to obscure as much of her red hair as possible. Standing outside the cottage, Gale watched Nadianna emerge from the woods and wondered how it was that a woman as commanding as Chalice had convinced herself she could be overlooked. For the moment, however, Gale decided to play along, and she bent down to where Katie Pru sat by the cottage steps.

"You used interesting colors." She pointed to her

daughter's still-wet watercolor painting. "Can you tell me about your picture?"

"It's a whale's mouth. See? It has all new teeth."

"Ah." Gale hadn't quite figured out the connection between the bone fragments and a whale, but she trusted her daughter's logic. "It makes sense that whales need new teeth."

"He got tired of the old ones. He wanted blue ones. I'm tired of mine, too."

"Don't go painting your teeth, Katie Pru. Your teeth are the right color for you."

"I like orange."

"No ma'am . . ."

Out of the corner of her eye Gale saw Nadianna turn to the red-haired figure in the woods and raise her hands in a gesture of frustration. Whatever the two were playing at, Gale decided, they were going to have to do it in plain view.

She stood. "How was the walk, Nadianna?" She raised her voice. "How about you, Chally? Could you use something to drink?"

Chalice stood stock-still, poised uncertainly between escape and disclosure. She chose the latter, and with a sheepish smile walked into the clearing.

"Good to see you again," Gale said. "So the cut on your leg is doing okay?"

The large woman smiled and scribbled on her palmtop.

WELL. THANK YOU FOR THE FLOWERS AND BOOK ON THE GEORGIA MILL GIRL. ENJOYED THEM.

"Really? So you've had a chance to look at the book?" When Chalice's eyes flickered past her, Gale shook her head apologetically. "It's okay. Don't feel you have to. I just thought you might like it. Not so much a diary as a collection of stories. Some people can do that, round their lives into tales. But I gave it to you for another reason. The author had an artistic way of viewing her work at the mill. I've seen your pottery. I thought you might enjoy her perceptions."

At Gale's feet Katie Pru dipped her brush into a cup of orange paint. "Miss K.P.," she warned.

"The whale wants orange lipstick."

"Just make sure it stays on the whale's lips."

When Gale looked back up, Chalice was staring at her; she raised her eyebrows in question, and the young woman looked away. Gale crossed her arms and gazed at the sky.

"It's chilly. How about coming inside for some tea, girls?"

"Gale." Nadianna's tone was pleading. "Chally . . ."

Alarm sprang to Chalice's face. She took a step toward Nadianna, her hand reaching out. Nadianna moved away.

"Chally needs some help," she continued pleading. "She doesn't want to talk to you about it, but I think she should. "Chalice, honest. You can trust Gale. You need to talk with someone who can help you. I can't."

The expression on the Yorkshire girl's face was extraordinary—anger directed at her betrayer, but also fear. And despair. A flush surged up her cheeks, and her mouth popped open.

"Hep." Her cry was pitiful. "Pees . . ."

The local economy was generally healthy from 1850 to 1861 with 29 new mills built in the region.

—*Notes*, G. GRAYSON

21

No one answered the door at Gerald Thornsby's flat, so Reston and Halford took the safe bet and drove to the mill. Thornsby's beat-up white Fiat sat on the grass outside the carding shop, but the shop itself was vacant. The detectives circled the mill, looking for a place within the decaying building that might satisfy a preacher retreating from the cold.

They found it through a door on the east side of the mill proper. Without knocking, Reston pushed the door open. Instead of entering a deserted weaving room, the two men stood in a cozy study filled with the scent of brewing coffee.

Thornsby looked up in surprise from a sofa. In front of him knelt Zoë Axon, a bowl of water on the floor beside her and her long blond hair wrapped around Thornsby's bare foot.

Thornsby shook his foot loose and scrambled upward. "Well, gentlemen, perhaps knocking would have been a good idea." He rubbed his hands on the back of his jeans, then awkwardly looped his thumbs in his pockets. "Foot washing. An old ritual."

"Really?" Halford shut the door and leaned against it.

"Yes, really. An effective ritual. I participated in it regularly while in America—showed my subservience."

"To whom?"

Zoë finished tying her hair back. "To God, of course. What else are you implying?"

Reston didn't respond. "Miss Axon," he said, "Chief Inspector Halford and I would like to ask Mr. Thornsby some questions. If you could give us some privacy . . ."

"As I've said before, Mr. Reston," Thornsby interjected, "nothing—"

"I'm requesting the privacy, Mr. Thornsby." Reston looked again at Zoë. "Miss Axon?"

"Fine." She grabbed a coat from a hook on the wall and wrenched open the door, dislodging Halford. "I'll be in the shop, Ger. Come get me when they leave."

Halford waited until Zoë closed the door behind her before turning to Thornsby. "How old is she?"

Thornsby laughed. "What, now are you going to make me out a pedophile, Mr. Halford? I assure you Miss Axon is eighteen. In addition, there is no sexual relationship between us. I don't believe in sex outside marriage. For the time being, you see, I am celibate."

Halford didn't blink. "Thank you for letting us know."

"Thought I'd clear it up straight off." He looked from one to the other, smiling. "How about some coffee?" When the detectives declined, he walked to the pot and poured himself a cup. Now, how can I help you?"

Reston took a seat on the sofa. "We want to know where you were Monday morning between seven and eight."

Holding his cup aloft, Thornsby sank into an overstuffed tweed chair. "Here," he said.

"Here?" Reston repeated. "You mean in this room?"

"Yes, and on the mill grounds."

"Is seven to eight on Monday morning your regular work hours?"

"I hardly have 'regular' work hours, Mr. Reston. I work as needed. But yes, I frequently come here early in the mornings to work. I do my best writing then."

Halford considered the room. It was smaller but better outfitted than Thornsby's flat—upholstery instead of plastic and chrome, a wooden pub table with four padded chairs, a David Hockney print over the sofa. "Nice," he said. "I wouldn't have thought there was a room like this in the mill. Appears too dilapidated from the outside."

"Looks are deceiving, Mr. Halford. There are a couple of areas in the mill that are still in fair condition." He pointed to a second door. "That, for instance, leads to a storage room. The whole place is in need of renovation, but sections are for the most part sound."

"The kind of renovation that Olivia Markham is planning?"

"No." Thornsby's smile was tight. "Exactly not the kind of renovation that Olivia Markham is planning. The mill needs to be treated with honor . . ."

"Why?"

"Why? It's a historical building, Mr. Halford. It means a lot to the people of this village. That point never seems to be understood by Olivia."

Halford leaned forward to examine the Hockney print. The Bradford native had splashed his shimmering palate over the rolling greens of West Yorkshire. "I can see why you prefer to write here rather than in your flat. More . . . homey."

"The flat is for business. This is my study."

"I would have thought it the other way around."

"It's easier for church members to get to my flat than to come here."

"But Zoë can do either."

"Zoë makes arrangements to do either. Extremely dedicated girl."

"What about the other members of your church? They all have cars?"

"Of course not. On the whole we're not an affluent group. The few who have vehicles help the others."

"So why the mill in the first place if it's inconvenient?"

"That depends on what you consider convenient," Thornsby replied evenly. "When we were smaller, we used to meet at each other's residences. As we grew, we needed a larger location. The feeling of the group was that privacy was more important than access. I'm sure you realize, Mr. Halford, that not everyone in the world believes people should be allowed to practice their religion as they see fit, despite what they may say."

"So you are battling Miss Markham over the property to preserve the privacy of your church."

"My battle with Olivia has to do with morals, not property."

Halford reclined in silence against the door. Reston took the lead.

"Let's put that aside for the moment. Monday morning you were here. Anything you would like to tell us about what happened?"

Thornsby took a long sip of coffee. "I suppose you're fishing for whether or not I saw Nadianna Jesup in Sette Water. So does this mean you now believe Miss Jesup saw a dead body?"

"I'm proceeding on the idea that there was a body floating in the stream that morning, yes," Reston answered. "So I would be grateful if you tell us anything you feel could help."

"But it's not an official inquiry. You haven't gotten a coroner's ruling yet."

"That's correct."

"What about the second sighting by my church?"

"We're willing to entertain the idea that Miss Jesup may have seen a body Monday morning. We'll leave it at that for now."

"Of course you will. All right. The answer is, yes, I did see Nadianna in the stream Monday morning. She was taking photographs. I figured her subject was the mill, so I didn't interfere. Not that I would have interfered anyway. Quite an unexpected sight to see—almost lyrical.

"Did you see anything in the water that could have been the body?"

"If I had seen such, don't you think I would have mentioned it by now?"

"I don't know," Reston answered. "You hadn't mentioned that you saw Miss Jesup. I would have thought our interest in that would have been obvious."

"I saw a young woman standing in the stream, taking photographs. I watched her for a few minutes, enjoyed the way the fog moved around her. Then I left."

"Where were you when you were watching her?"

"Just outside the door here. One has a fairly clear view downstream."

"I've had my team go over Miss Jesup's photographs. No sign of you anywhere."

"I was discreet. As I said, I didn't want to interfere."

"Did you see anyone else that morning?" Halford asked.

"Anyone else?"

"Yes. When you were walking the mill grounds. Did you see any other people?"

Thornsby settled deeper into the chair. "Let me think. No, I don't recall anyone."

"But not positive."

"Not positive."

"So on some mornings you do see other people?"

"Certainly. Some mornings, some of the church members come around to work. On occasion, a tourist or rambler. The mill is quite beautiful—"

Reston broke in. "Ever see Olivia Markham or Chalice Hibbert?"

"Olivia and Chalice? Of course. I can look straight across the water and see the studio. Olivia lived there, so

I certainly saw her on occasion, although I wouldn't say she was much of an early riser. But Chalice, yes, I saw Chalice that early rather often."

"This past Monday morning?"

Thornsby's brow furrowed. "No. I don't recall seeing her."

"What about on Sunday nights?" Halford asked.

"Sunday nights?"

"Well, I assume you have members of your church here during the day on Sunday. Does anyone come here on Sunday nights?"

"Not often."

"But sometime?"

"Yes."

"Who?"

"Well, me, sometime. Once everyone is gone, this place has an ethereal peace about it. So sometime I stay late."

"And last Sunday night? Did you stay last Sunday night?"

A slight hesitancy, but Thornsby's answer to Halford was direct. "Yes, as a matter of fact, I did."

"Alone?"

"Yes."

"About what time?"

"I returned home about eleven-thirty."

"And you didn't see anyone."

"Here at the mill. No."

Halford leaned toward him. "You saw no one at any time that night?"

Halford was aware of Reston watching him. Thornsby stared into his coffee.

"I might have."

"Pardon?"

"All right. About ten, maybe a bit later. I saw Chalice Hibbert drive up to the studio."

"Ten P.M. Was that usual?"

"I don't know. I rarely stayed quite that late. But I have to admit, it struck me as unusual."

"Why is that?"

"Well, you'd have to know Olivia. She's an alcoholic. I know for a fact that she regularly gets drunk in the evenings. So, you see, it actually wouldn't be strange for Chalice to come to work that late, knowing her boss would be passed out and she could get some work done."

"But you said Sunday night was unusual."

"What was unusual was I don't believe Olivia was drunk at all. Just fifteen minutes before Chalice arrived, I'd seen Olivia outside, pacing up and down."

"You're sure you'd use that word, 'pacing.'"

"Yes. I remember thinking, 'Good, maybe the woman's sworn off the stuff.' She just wasn't acting the way she did when she was intoxicated. But then Chalice drove up, and it was the most remarkable thing. Olivia started swaying and collapsing onto the car bonnet, her voice very loud—like she was utterly inebriated."

"You could hear what she said?"

"Just some. Can't remember specifics now, but I knew she was telling Chalice to leave. Which she did. And that was another odd part. Olivia went into the studio, lurching, while Chalice drove away. But then she opened the door and looked out. Like she was checking."

"So how long would you say Chalice was there?"

"Less than five minutes."

"And you're sure it was Chalice?"

"Not much chance you'd mistake her for someone else, is there? No, it was Chalice, all right. She can about carry that little Escort of hers."

Halford looked at Reston. "One more question, Mr. Thornsby," Reston said. "Ever see anything suspicious in the wood?"

Over his coffee cup Thornsby leveled his eyes at Reston. "Such as?"

"Specifically, we're trying to find anyone who may have seen a torch in use in the wood this week."

"I have no knowledge of anyone. Besides, it's an old wood."

"Meaning?" asked Halford.

"Meaning people in these parts have their traditions concerning the wood. It's not up to me to decide if they are suspicious or not."

"Nice answer, sir," Halford said softly, "but you'll need to elaborate."

"I merely mean I suspect some of our young people use the wood as a rendezvous."

"Can you tell me their names? We'd like to talk with them."

"Mr. Reston, I'm a figure of trust around here. I cannot betray that."

"We have no interest in disrupting anyone's privacy; we just want to question them about what they may have seen."

"I'm sorry."

"Mr. Thornsby . . ."

Suddenly the cushy room was cloying, the burlgar-cum-minister maddening. Had it been his own inquiry, Halford would have had to stick it out. It wasn't his, however, so without looking at either man, Halford opened the mill door and ducked outside.

At the rear of the mill, the door to the carding shop was open, and from inside he could hear Zoë Axon's clear alto.

She moved into the doorway, a beautiful young woman framed by coarse rock. He didn't recognize the tune she sang, but then, he knew little of music. All he could attest to was that it sounded Celtic and that he found it strange and lovely.

"I heard you sing earlier this morning," he said when she fell silent. "You have an accomplished voice."

" 'Accomplished.' " Her eyes teased him. "Is that an example of damning with faint praise?"

"All right, then. Quite beautiful. Your mother is fortunate. Mine always lamented that she didn't have a singing child."

"What an odd thing for a mother to lament. Mine couldn't give a rat's ass."

"I can't imagine that."

"It's true. Father as well. Not a useful skill, a pretty voice."

"They let you live at home and work for Gerald. Sounds to me as if they respect your choices."

"Job-training—that's how they view my work for Ger. They don't see it as a calling and certainly don't see it as a church. Strictly twice-a-year Methodists, are Mum and Dad. Christmas and Easter. And if you can't meet in a pointy building with a cross on top, then God can't hear you—that's what they think. The cross is like a damn cell phone to Jesus."

"You spend a lot of time up here."

"A fair amount. I help prepare for services—even something as informal as ours requires a little preparation. And I do some cleaning . . . organizing . . ."

"So you might notice if you saw something unusual."

She looked at him warily. "Like what?"

"I don't know—something that didn't fit, something that bothered you."

"Just because something bothers me doesn't mean it's anything."

"Ah." Halford looked past the water at the burnt hulk of Markham Studio. "Zoë, you know the complications of this investigation. We have one—perhaps two—reported bodies and as of now one missing person. Like it or not, your church is involved with this—by mere geography if nothing else. The sooner we can get everything cleared up, the sooner the church can regain its peace. If you think you know something that would help us, you should tell me—or Mr. Reston."

"No, you." The quickness of her words must have startled her, for a faint blush started in her face. "No," she said more slowly. "If I had anything to tell, I'd tell you."

Halford spoke gently. "So, do you have anything?"

"I'm sure it's nothing, but if you think it might help you . . . Tuesday afternoon—"

"The day of the fire."

She nodded. "I was here moving the jumble boxes from the carding shop into the storage room in the mill proper. I had just put down a load and was taking a rest outside. I saw Chalice stumble from the studio."

"Stumble?"

"That's right. She was clutching her stomach. And crying."

"You could tell from this distance that she was crying?"

"I had walked to the edge of the stream. I could see her quite clearly."

"Did she see you?"

"I doubt it. I gathered she was in pain."

"Did you call out to her?"

She hesitated. "I should have. But I don't know her that well. And this sounds terrible, but she frightens me. I've always thought it best to leave her alone."

"Why does she frighten you?"

"Just . . . look at her."

"It's her appearance that frightens you?"

"Yes, that and . . . well, if she's that big, she must be strong. She has to be strong to load that kiln all the time, don't you think? It's not good of me to feel this way, but, yes, Mr. Halford, I'm afraid of her."

"What happened after she came out of the studio?"

"She got in her car and drove off."

"About what time?"

"Mid-afternoon. Around three."

"What kind of car?"

"Red Escort."

"Did anyone follow her out of the studio?"

"No."

"Did you see any other cars there?"

"No. Well, Olivia keeps hers parked around the side, so I never see it."

"Anything else you want to tell me about?"

"No, that's all."

"You're sure."

"Yes. Very sure."

Halford gave her an appreciative smile. "Thank you. Zoë. We'll follow up on it." He looked out over the grounds, taking in the building, the stream. "This church means a lot to you."

"Of course it does. It saved Alan."

"Saved Alan?"

"Drugs. We thought—me and my mum and dad—we thought they were going to kill him."

"What kind of drugs?"

"It was a long time ago, Mr. Halford. You're not going to do anything about it. I was just talking—"

Halford raised his hand. "If it was a long time ago, then Alan's turned himself around. You saying the church did it?"

She shook her head. "Ger did it. He met Alan somewhere in Leeds, converted him to Christ. It was an overnight conversion—Ger stayed with Alan, kept him clean until Jesus visited him." She paused. "It's true, Mr. Halford. That's how I know about these visions. Jesus came in the body and saved my brother. Alan's never touched anything since."

The dreamy sensuality he had detected earlier in her blue eyes had vanished. She was adamant, serious. "I've known of such turnarounds," Halford offered. "I'm glad Alan made one. So, was it after he got off drugs that he started university?"

"That's right. He's always been smart. Mum and Dad wanted him to continue his education. They want him to get out of Mayley, have a future."

"And what about their daughter with the beautiful voice?"

"Oh, he'll take me with him. That would be the way with us. Of course, I don't know that I'll go when the time comes. I have my work now." She scanned his face. "I can tell you're skeptical, but my work is important. I'm doing important things."

"I'm not skeptical. I've seen enough of the truly awful to appreciate someone who gives themselves to others."

Her smile was radiant, and the sensuality had returned. "I figured that was the case. That's why I told you all this."

"Why is that, Zoë?"

"Because we're going to need a friend. We're vulnerable up here—we're vulnerable wherever we are. That's the plight of people like us. You'll be our friend, won't you, Mr. Halford?"

"You feel the church needs a friend, Zoë?"

She nodded. He studied her for a moment, then decided to take a risk.

"To counterbalance that fact that Olivia was not a friend?"

She crossed her arms over her narrow chest. "She was certainly not a friend."

"She didn't like Gerald much."

"No. He thought her flowers were obscene."

"I've heard a story about a confrontation between Gerald and Olivia. I believe you were there. It happened during a church meeting. Olivia came in, said something to Gerald. I was told she waltzed you around the room. Do you remember that?"

Zoë held herself as if she were cold, making a thin line of her body. "Of course I do."

"Can you tell me what it was about?"

"She thought she could threaten Gerald, maybe make us pack up and leave."

"She said a vulgar word, didn't she?"

"Yes. She made a vulgar pun."

"Was she referring to something specific?"

If she had been made of less than flesh and bones, she would have disappeared, so tightly had she drawn the sides of her body together. She was folding herself into nothing. "Olivia was a difficult person," she said carefully. "I don't want to remember anything about her."

Halford nodded and laid his hand on her shoulder. "Thank you, Zoë," he said. "You've been a help."

Boyfriend Number One had been Chalice's favorite, and why not? At three she had still been small enough to fit on a man's lap, all wavy red hair and emerald-green eyes. She had detected his delight in her, the way his grin would broaden when she ran into the room. He would lift her high—she could be lifted high, then—and collapse into a chair with her on his knee. *My Chally Chally, Sweet Gally, Gally, My Pally, Pally*—up and down, up and down, with her voice bouncing along in a monotone with his.

Boyfriend Number One hadn't abused her and left in the middle of the night like Number Three; he didn't constantly insult Totty and bang out the door like Number Two. He had come into the tiny half-room Chalice occupied in the flat and hoisted her onto the bed.

"I'm leaving, my Chally Chally. I don't want to. Not true, actually. I must leave. But I don't want to leave you. You're like my own little sister. You I cherish. And always will, Chally. You must promise to remember that."

She had promised, although she didn't know to what. For weeks afterward she would peek through the curtains, straining to hear his footsteps smack the wet pavement. Other footsteps she heard. Other voices in the

flats surrounding her. But he never came back and she
was eleven before she understood that he had never
intended to return. With this understanding came the
realization that she had forgotten he cherished her. She
had forgotten, in fact, his name.

Not a nice round story, she thought, not like what Gale
Grayson had talked about. It didn't have a circle to it—a
beginning, yes, but the end was murky, like algae, not a
strong, firm reed one could bend to meet its origins. She
knew what the theme of the story was; nice when one's
recollections had a theme. It was trust. At nineteen Chalice Hibbert knew she had been without trust since the
age of three.

So she sat discomfited in one of the worn love seats by
the cottage fire. It was a love seat more to her than to anyone else in the room—the place where she and Alan had
first consummated their relationship, too eager and driven to clamber upstairs to a bed—and she found herself
picking at its cording almost obsessively. Across from her
sat two females who had made a simple request of her:
trust them. They didn't know how much they asked.

She lifted her malachite beads and puddled them in
her hand. Gale took a deep breath and leaned forward.

"I wish there were something we could do to put you
at ease, Chally."

To put her at ease. Did the woman understand what a
Herculean labor that would be?

Beside the unlit fireplace Katie Pru stared at her, her
paints in little pots arrayed by her knees.

Chalice picked up her palmtop. DO YOU KNOW A LOT
ABOUT DIARIES?

"Diaries?" Gale looked surprised. "Well, yes, I suppose so. I've studied a lot of diaries in my research, from
a variety of eras. Diaries by English shipbuilders during
the Civil War period, by women from the American

South. I was researching the women, in fact, when I came across the book I gave you. Why do you ask?"

Over the years, Chalice had learned to tune out the awkward pauses that occurred as she wrote. Now she was acutely aware of Gale's stillness as she waited. Nevertheless, Chalice wrote carefully, forming her thoughts precisely.

She held up her palmtop. YOU'RE RESEARCHING THE LUDDITES NOW. READ ANY LUDDITE DIARIES?

"I don't think there are any. A few letters. Proclamations. But an authentic Luddite diary"— Gale shook her head —"as far as I know, one doesn't exist. As it is, most of what we know of the Luddites comes from the people who prosecuted them."

A LOT OF SYMPATHY FOR THEM IN THESE PARTS.

"As well there should be. They weren't wrong so much as poorly timed."

I DON'T SUSPECT ANYONE COULD HAVE STOPPED WHAT HAPPENED.

Gale was watching her, clearly intrigued. "You mean the Industrial Revolution? No, some things are just going to happen. It was simply more cost-effective for mills to take over the work of home weavers. I didn't know you had an interest in history, Chally."

IT COMES OFF ON YOUR HANDS AROUND HERE.

Gale smiled. "I know what you mean. That's true where I come from, too."

On the floor Katie Pru was making a large blue shape on her paper. Chalice watched as the child planted green dots in a line down the shape's broad side.

"So, Chally," Gale began gently. "What is it you need help with?"

Here was the invitation to trust. The Southern woman's voice held the softest of lilts; her brown eyes displayed a concern as deep and whole as one of Chalice's bowls. Next to Gale sat Nadianna, their elbows touching. A few days earlier Chalice had thought their relationship uneasy. Something had changed for them—not a perfect trust, perhaps, but a holding one—and she felt a wave of sorrow. Where was the trust for her? Not with Alan. Not with her sister.

Tears sprang again to Chalice's eyes; she felt them sting her broad face like salt chips. In the woods she had come close to trusting Nadianna, telling her about the tea-bowls and asking for help. But Nadianna betrayed her, didn't she? As well-meaning as she may have been, she invited Gale into Chalice's secret.

No such thing as trust in Mayley's dwarfed world.

Michael should never have trusted Nathan.

MICHAEL'S BOOK

25 April 1812

*A second funeral. A second bidder's turn through the village.
Mayley buried Nell Dodd yesterday. I watched my Martha over
the heads of mourners. I am not a man if I do not admit that the
spectre of loss terrifies me.*

*Nathan now has three surviving sons—ages, ten, nine,
and seven. Today he delivered his middle son to me. Dickie will
work for me and live in my house as my child, although how I
will support him I do not know. Nathan looked hardly human.
It will be all right, I told him. He shall live here until better
times. And when will that be, brother? he asked. We will make
our own better times, I answered. Do not fret. His eyes were hollow as he stared at me. What will you do? he asked. You are too
tired to know, I said. Sleep, and remember your fair children
whom we shall all protect. As he turned to leave, he said, Be
careful, Michael. Know what you do.*

I know what I do.

*A fierce riot took place in Middleton this week, over the bor-
der in Lancashire. Seven citizens were killed, many wounded.
Yesterday the Westhoughton Factory was burned. Two dozen*

*people were arrested, including two women and a crippled child
of twelve. We fear they will all be hanged.*

My son John went to The Crown & Drover today. I told him
he must not and gave him the excuse that he ignores his chores,
but the truth is that what we now plan could lead us to the gib-
bet. I will not have him imperiled.

Our plan is thus: on the evening of 30 April, after dark,
we shall meet on the edge of Blandon Wood. From there the
walk to Yates Mill is two miles. We will be well-armed and
well-manned—other Luddites have sworn to join us. We will
beat down the doors and destroy the machines. We will not fail
as happened to the others at Cartwright's Mill at Rawfolds. We
go prepared for treachery.

And of that man Cartwright—I say "man" with spit in my
teeth—we hear he was shot at in Bradley Wood six days ago. The
bullet passed in the air. Tuesday one of the soldiers who refused to
fire on the Luddites at Rawfolds was made ready before a large
gathering to receive 300 lashes as punishment. Cartwright
pleaded that his sentence be reduced to twenty-five, but do not
fancy it an act of mercy on the vile mill-owner's part. The gathering was against him.

What gathers now is with us.

According to the 1851 census, even the households with one handloom weaver relied on employment in the mills by other family members to survive.

—*Notes*, G. GRAYSON

22

The sky had the glint of mica as Halford rode with Reston off the mill grounds and onto the road to Mayley. Drizzle flecked the windscreen. Coughing, Reston fumbled with a cigarette and rolled his window down a fraction.

He blew out a puff. "So what were those questions about Chalice Hibbert Sunday night? One of the Halford hunches?"

"Not really. If a body was put into the water near the mill on Monday morning, it's conceivable there was activity in the area Sunday night. But I'm not convinced Olivia pulling a sly one over on Chalice constitutes activity."

"Pacing suggests anxiety."

"And sobriety could suggest import. Which could mean a number of things with someone like Markham."

"She was expecting some 'import' tonight, actually." Reston nodded at his glove box. "Take a look."

Halford removed a manila envelope from the glove box and shook out a small clipping from *The Manchester Guardian.* " 'Markham Show Cancelled,' " he read aloud, glancing at the issue date. "Today's paper."

"The reporters started calling the constabulary HQ

yesterday afternoon. Seems the owner of the Gloriana
Gallery has a big showing of Olivia's work scheduled
tonight and couldn't reach her. She called around, located Chalice's number, and Totty told her the news.
The gallery owner rang me *after* she called the bloody
papers."

"What did you tell her?"

"That the studio had burned and the fire was being
investigated as arson. That we couldn't locate either
Miss Markham or Mr. Botting—which was true as of last
night—and would she please contact us if she heard
from either of them. I must say she sounded more infuri-
ated than concerned when she rang off."

Halford scanned the article. "It appears it was going to
be some do. Does Olivia Markham strike you as the kind
of person who would pass up a good PR opportunity?"

"Not on your life."

Halford dropped the article into the envelope and returned them to the glove box. "I had a chat with Zoë
Axon just now."

"Learn anything?"

"Well, for starters I think both Zoë and Thornsby are
lying about their relationship. A few months ago Olivia
visited the church during a meeting. According to Alan
Axon, Olivia made a comment to Gerald about his 'pro-
clit-vities,' then picked Zoë out of the group and danced
her around the room. Alan's explanation was that she
was extremely drunk at the time; Zoë swears she doesn't
know what the comment referred to, but thought it was
Olivia pulling a power play."

"But you think she was sending Gerald and Zoë a
message?"

"Possible."

"Then she's a blackmailer."

"Or a first-rate manipulator. Something of that
stripe."

Totty Hibbert was bumping her red Escort onto the

pavement outside her house when Reston and Halford parked and climbed from their car. It was never a pleasant experience, Halford thought, to see lawmen descending, but there was no mistaking the sudden pallor of Totty's face as she flung open her car door. She calmed as quickly as she paled, and her expression settled into a no-nonsense shell.

She walked forward to meet them, immaculately dressed in a white wool business suit. "It's not Chally, is it? She's not hurt herself again?"

"No, ma'am," Halford answered. "But we would like to ask Chalice—and yourself—some questions."

"What about?"

"Ms. Markham and Lyle Botting. I don't know if you were aware of it, but Mr. Botting was arrested today . . ."

"I heard. Everyone's heard. So, has Lyle said where Olivia is?"

Reston motioned toward her front door. "Please, Miss Hibbert, if we could go in . . ."

She gave both of them an impatient glance. "I doubt Chally's home. And for God's sake, Mark, call me Totty. Everyone in town calls you by your Christian name. You could do the rest of us the favor."

As soon as he stepped into the cottage, Halford felt enveloped in a clean and inviting warmth. This was the home of a house-proud woman—no dust on the corners of the stairs, no cobwebs hanging from the lamps. The affable scent of vanilla and spices filled the air. Eight plates lined the foyer wall; Halford noted with interest that they weren't the typical commemorative royalty plates or scenes of famous places, but, rather, thick, primitively shaped disks made from coils of clay.

"Beautiful," he said, and meant it. "They almost look Aztec. Did Chalice make them?"

"I did," Totty answered, removing her suit coat. "Years ago. It was a technique I was experimenting with. I was

going to make an entire service—plates, cups, bowls—
but I never got around to it."

"So Chalice gets her talent with clay from you."

"Oh, no. She might have gotten her first taste from
me, but her talent is all her own."

Halford stepped closer to the plates. He could see
now they were only partially coiled—in addition, small
balls of clay had been roughly blended together to create a pebbled effect. The technique gave the plates
a solidity that Halford instinctively liked, as if, taken between his hands, they would have the heft of a small
child.

"I think you're being modest," he said. "You don't
work in clay anymore?"

"Not anymore. That's Chally's business. I don't remember a thing."

"Perhaps your fingers still do."

"I'm afraid I don't have time for that, Mr. Halford.
I've gone on to other work." She draped her coat over
the banister and yelled upstairs. "Chally? Are you
home?" She waited, then shrugged. "Didn't think she
would be. Too busy by half."

"Where would she be, since the studio's burned?"

"Errands, more than likely."

"Perhaps then we could have a word with you?" Reston nodded toward the front room.

"Make yourselves comfortable. I haven't much time. I
have to meet a couple at a cottage near Haworth."

The room was as tasteful as Halford would have
predicted—not plushy, as Gale had described Chalice's
bedroom, but by no means austere. The walls were
painted sky-blue, dramatically setting off a candy-striped
couch and beige-on-white houndstooth armchair. A
computer sat on a small writing desk situated before the
room's only window. In the grate crackled a token fire;
on both sides of the hearth, rising from the floor like

ornate andirons, were clay heads, the curled short hair of one and the broad face of the other making them instantly recognizable as the Hibbert sisters.

Totty perched on the couch and studied the heads, nodding to his murmured compliment. "Yes, well, you see why I'm so proud of her," she said. "But you're not here to discuss Chally's artistic abilities."

"True," Halford acquiesced, taking his seat in the armchair while Reston idly toasted his hands before the fire. "We're interested in what she can tell us about the show Miss Markham had scheduled for tonight."

Totty frowned. "The show. Poor Chally had been working on it for weeks. She had to find the caterer, arrange the invites."

"Excuse me," Reston said, "but how did she do that? Find the caterer, I mean. Arrange invites."

"How would you expect her to do it, Mark? Faxes. Email. There's more to communication these days than drums and smoke—and verbiage."

Halford interposed. "Of course. And did your sister use your computer to do her work for Miss Markham?"

"No. I won't allow it. My computer is strictly for Hibbert Home Sweet Home Away. I am willing to do whatever I can to foster Chally's art, but I'm not in business to subsidize Olivia Markham's factory."

"Did Chalice ever indicate to you how Miss Markham viewed tonight's show?"

"It was quite important to Livy. Chally told me she was spending a lot of money on it."

"What else did she say about it?"

"That it was a pain in the ass."

"When she's available, we'd like to talk with your sister about the arrangements she made. Now, I have another question—did Chalice mention anything in particular happening at the studio Sunday night?"

"She isn't likely to have. She wasn't at the studio Sunday night."

"We have a witness who said she was there for a brief amount of time. Her car was identified."

"Your witness is wrong. She was with me."

"You're quite sure?" Halford asked. "She couldn't have gone out in her car without your knowing?"

"Yes, certainly she can leave without my knowing. She did the other night when she rescued that child. But she can't stay gone without my knowing. That car is vital to both our jobs. I keep it tightly scheduled. Besides, I always make a point of finishing up my work so we can have Sunday evenings together."

"What time do you usually retire on Sundays?"

"About midnight."

"Really?" Halford let his surprise show. "I would have thought a woman with her own business . . ."

"A woman with her own business needs no more sleep than a man with his own business. I regularly go to bed at midnight and get up at five."

"I'm jealous." Halford grinned at her. "I get amazingly cranky when I have to go without my full eight."

She shrugged. "I doubt that's accurate, coming from a senior police officer. Nevertheless, you do what you have to do."

"True. By the way, I'd appreciate it if you'd thank your sister again for helping Katie Pru Grayson Wednesday night. I might have gotten to her in time, but those bogs are treacherous. I might not have."

"I'll pass the message on. I'm sure she would tell you that she was doing only what anyone would do if they saw a child in distress."

"It was a bit of luck that she was there."

"It wasn't luck at all. As I explained to you the other night at surgery, Mr. Halford, Chally goes to the windmills when she needs a quiet place to think. What with the studio burning and Olivia gone—she needed to get away for a while."

"That's understandable. And she took your car."

Totty crossed her arms. "I've already told you that. She left without my knowing."

"Since I drove her to surgery, her car must have been left there. How did you retrieve it?"

"A friend of mine took me up there the next day. What does this have to do with anything?"

"Did you notice anything about the car that seemed unusual, out of place?"

She regarded him calmly, and once again he was reminded of his first impression of her, a civil bull barely tolerating the fools around her.

"The car was fine. You, however, are being intrusive."

"Can we take a look at the car?"

She glanced at her watch, then stood. "Sorry. Not today. I'm late for my meeting. You've taken up enough of my time."

Mill Cottage was the first of Totty Hibbert's rental properties and remained the only one she owned. The place had started out as a point of pride, and Chalice had accompanied Totty during the early days on the biweekly housecleaning expeditions. With her sister inside scouring sinks and polishing floors, Chalice had roamed the wood, reveling in her body's sudden smallness.

As a result, Chalice knew all the paths in Blandon Wood. She knew the circular ones, the dead ones, the ones that started north and ended south. And she knew the nearly swallowed ones that, decades ago, allowed trespassers to skirt Mayley Mill unobserved.

Now she shouldered through the wood, dodging the slaps of young limbs. To her right she could make out the mill's pale stone, broken like a mosaic by the trees. She trod quietly, coming around the rear of the mill until she made out the wing of a car parked near the carding shop. She heard voices, one high and fluty, the other a low mumble. One of the speakers she could identify.

The question was which of Zoë Axon's two men—her brother or her pastor—was she speaking with? Not that it mattered. What mattered was that Chalice reach the pottery studio without anyone noticing.

She walked stealthily, and the voices continued without pause. Soon she was out of earshot, and she broke into a run.

The packhorse bridge was slimy from the rain and the season's decaying leaves. She slipped as she ran across and slammed heavily on her injured leg. The pain was unexpected and sharp, and she crammed her hand into her mouth to stop her scream. Pulling herself up, she hobbled to the other side of the stream and began an awkward lope to the pottery grounds.

At the base of the hill, she stopped. Ahead of her, the charred house sat on its sloping rise like a mutilated box. From there on, coverage was limited to crumbling drystone walls and two small stands of trees. She didn't know if the house was being watched—a suspected arson case was the scene of a crime, wasn't it? But she would have to risk it.

She bolted from wall to tree until she crouched behind the length of drystone wall nearest the house. Cautiously, she raised her head. Across the water she could see Thornsby's rickety Fiat, but the mill grounds themselves appeared empty. Likewise, the pottery studio itself seemed deserted. The tape that had cordoned off the property was gone, but she could see its stripe stretching across the building's rear entrance. It was still officially off-limits. She didn't give a damn.

She sprinted to the studio and in a single motion threw her weight against the back door. She fell into the kitchen, the splintering sound of parched wood cracking through the hills. Brushing herself off, she peered out the door at the mill. If anyone heard the noise, they had chosen to ignore it.

From the kitchen she hurried to the studio's workroom,

soot clinging to her damp shoes with every step. She checked the top of the kiln where the stack of flowers had melted. Cleared. Goddammit. The arson investigators had been back. Maybe they hadn't known what to look for. And if they had found it, maybe they wouldn't have known the significance.

At the couch she lowered herself to the floor, holding her breath so as not to disturb the ash. Sweat dribbled down her face, her back, between her breasts. She found herself praying. *Please, God, let it be here. Please, God, please.*

Resting her cheek on the cool flagstone, she squinted as she peered under the sofa. It was there. Both pieces. She reached out and with one hand dragged them to her.

The voice was soft behind her. "Miss Hibbert."

She sucked in her breath so sharply, she inhaled soot. She collapsed into a coughing fit, her head falling against the sofa's melted coils.

PC Swain was beside her, slapping her on the back. The cough subsided, replaced by a deep ache that pounded her chest. She refused to lift her head. She wouldn't look up. What could she say to him?

"Miss Hibbert," PC Swain said gently. "You need to come with me. I think Detective Inspector Reston would like to speak to you."

Bernie Portman was putting away glasses in the pub when Halford entered. "Ah, Mr. Halford," he said, walking from the noise of the pub to the check-in desk. "I have a message for you." He handed Halford a folded piece of paper. "Everything going well, is it?"

Halford flipped open the note and nodded toward the pub. "Everything seems to be going well here. More custom than usual, I guess?"

"Ah, yes. It's better than watching the telly, isn't it? Detectives scurrying around. I had three reporters call today—booked rooms for the weekend. It's going to be a good few days for me."

"Don't get attached to it, Bertie. There'll be something else to grab everyone's attention next week."

"Oh, I know it. Still, a holiday with the wife might be nice. Any spare change I pick up this week will be well spent soothing our savaged nerves, don't you agree?"

Halford rapped the desk in parting and hurried up the stairs. In his room he took off his coat and lifted the phone off the hook.

Zoë Axon must have been waiting by her parents' phone, because it sounded only once.

"Zoë, this is Chief Inspector Halford. I had a message you called."

"That's right." Her voice was tentative, nervous. "I wanted to tell you something I didn't before."

"I'm listening."

"It was the day of the fire—Tuesday. I told you that Chalice left at about three."

"That's right."

"Well, yes, except later, about six, I looked over and the Escort came back."

"What do you mean, 'came back'?"

"I saw it drive up to the studio again. But then it turned around and headed for the stand of trees just below the mill. It parked there."

"By six it would have been dark. Are you sure it was the Escort?"

"Fairly sure. Same shape, size. I looked at it quite hard."

"You didn't mention this to the investigators the night of the fire."

"No. Like I said before, it probably isn't important. But I've been thinking about it, and for the church's sake—the quicker it's all cleared up, the quicker we can get on."

"You're correct there, Zoë. I'll tell Mr. Reston what you've said. He'll probably send a constable out to talk with you."

There was silence on the line. Then, softly, "All right. I can do that."

"Thank you. We need all the information we can find. We need it to clear the innocent as well as to find the people who may be involved in a crime. You understand that, don't you?"

"Yes, sir," she whispered. "Good-bye."

He punched his phone off. He was still staring at it when it rang again.

Maura Ramsden started in without introduction. "Haven't got a complete rundown on your names, guv, but got something you might want to know."

"Listening."

"Did you know Olivia Markham is divorced?"

"I seem to recall hearing something like that. Go on."

"Mr. Richard Row of Chelsea. They were married in October 1991, divorced '95."

"All right. That's mildly interesting."

"What's *more* interesting is this. Seems Mr. Richard Row of Chelsea has a record. He served time for spousal abuse in '94."

"More interesting."

"And even more interesting: The landlady of Chelsea's Mr. Richard Row reported him missing yesterday. Rent was due two weeks ago and he kept putting her off. According to the report, the last time she saw Row was Friday morning."

Prior to the American Civil War, 80 percent of the region's cotton was supplied by the South. By the fall of 1862, over half of Mayley's cotton weavers were out of work and facing starvation. Period know as the Cotton Famine.

—*Notes*, G. GRAYSON

23

Lyle Botting was dismayed. As Halford watched through the interrogation room's observation glass, Botting repeatedly looked down at himself, as if his limbs had disappeared and he could no longer fathom his own form. His black pants were torn and muddied; a dress shirt, presumably white, fell wrinkled and grimy around his chest. The last time Halford saw Botting, the photographer's dark hair had been pulled into a ponytail. Now it hung in clotted ropes around his uncomprehending face. Simply put, Lyle Botting looked chewed.

His solicitor, a dapper man in his thirties, sat beside him at the table. He stood as Reston and a female detective sergeant walked into the room. After perfunctory greetings, Reston took a seat opposite the two men. Nodding at the DS to turn on a tape player, he announced the date, time, and subject of the interview, and placed a piece of fax paper on the table in front of Botting.

Reston's voice came crisply through the speaker into the observation room. "Mr. Botting. Can you tell me if you recognize this man?"

The fax of the missing Richard Row, taken from the photo in his police file, was shadowy, but it was like an electric current to Lyle Botting. He started trembling.

His solicitor put his arm around him. "Are you all right, Lyle?" To Reston: "I think we should . . ."

The howl from Botting's mouth was deep—a moon-howl that started in the captured man's chest and ended in a vicious growl. The solicitor dropped his arm with such alarm that his chair skipped back an inch.

"The bitch!" Spittle flew from Botting's mouth. "Jesus Christ, the bitch!"

The solicitor glanced at Reston, then cautiously leaned toward his client. "Lyle, I'd like to speak with you . . ."

Botting wheeled on him. "I know what I'm doing! I'm not going to sit here silently and let this happen. It was not my fault. *She* did this to me."

Reston spoke calmly. "Who, Mr. Botting?"

"Livy, the bitch." Botting looked at Reston with incredulity. "I didn't . . . it was all her . . ." His mouth bobbed open and shut, but there was no sound.

"By, 'Livy,' do you mean Olivia Markham?" When Botting nodded dumbly, Reston said: "Mr. Botting has indicated that the answer is yes. Are you also indicating, Mr. Botting, that you are giving this information freely? Mr. Botting is indicating yes. What is it Miss Markham did?"

It was like watching a man punched in slow motion. Botting's mouth popped open; his chest caved. He sank onto the table, his back heaving in his filthy shirt. The renowned photographer whimpered.

"I could . . . kill her." This was harder for Halford to decipher, but Botting turned his head sideways like a schoolboy resting on his desk, and repeated it. "I could kill her."

"What has she done?" Reston pressed.

"It wasn't my idea." Botting didn't raise his head from the table. "Will you believe it wasn't my idea?"

"I will believe it as long as I can. Tell me what happened."

It was a odd sensation for Halford, this man with his head resting awkwardly on the table, staring in his direction but not seeing him. It reminded him of his first crime scene, when it had dawned on him that the dead man who seemed to gaze straight at him was long beyond seeing. Only this dead man's mouth moved.

"He came for money. They used to be married, Row and Livy. It was the first thing she told me about herself—that she'd left London and a horrible marriage and come up here to remake herself. 'Olivia Markham Unbound'—that was how she put it. She'd been in the fire, she said. He'd abused her. But being in Mayley remade her into something strong. Then he found her."

"She never made an attempt to hide," Reston pointed out.

"Why should she? You aren't reborn to hide. She thought the distance would protect her. Besides, she thought he wouldn't dare approach her. Make herself powerful enough and she could flick him away like a bug if she needed."

"You say he came for money. Were you there?" Botting nodded. "Can you tell me what happened?"

"He showed up Friday night—late. Livy and I were asleep upstairs. Banging on the door, drunk, he was. Hell, she may have been, too, although it had been a couple of hours since I saw her take a drink. He wanted cash—a thousand pounds—but he was after something more than that. He wanted a piece of her mill project."

"Really? And what did she say?"

"She told him to piss off. But Row just stood there. 'I've seen you cry, Livy darling,' he said. 'I can tell stories about you . . . ' I told him to get the hell out, but he never looked at me. Kept threatening her. 'Leave,' I said. I even pushed him. But Livy stared back at him, told him he didn't have any stories on her. He said, 'But I do. And people will believe them.' "

Reston looked perplexed. "Know what he meant by that?"

"I didn't at the time."

"But you found out?"

"Yes."

"So what was Row talking about?"

"He was talking about destroying her."

Even through the glass Halford could see Botting's eyes redden. The photographer's face bulged, and Halford braced himself for the man's vomit. But Botting's head drooped again, and Halford had to strain to pick out the words.

"I didn't kill him," he moaned, and raised his head. "I went to the studio Sunday night. I walked in the door and he was sitting on the sofa like a proper chap. But his hands were tied with duct tape, and a plastic bag covered his head. Livy sat across the room, quiet, like she was . . . I don't know . . . studying him. I just went berserk. She stayed so calm. 'He would tell lies and people would believe him,' she told me. 'I'm respected, not loved. People will turn on respect. He wouldn't have to twist hard to ruin me.' "

Reston spoke: "So you think that was her rationale for killing him? To stop him from telling lies?"

Through the glass Halford could see the deadness in Botting's eyes.

"All Livy has is her reputation and the media's interest in her. She knows that. She's barely tolerated here. A little bad press and she could lose everything."

"So you came in and found him on the sofa—suffocated?"

"Livy had promised him money if he came back Sunday night. Instead, she got him drunk, put tranquilizers in his drink. When he was out, she . . ." He faltered.

"What time did you get to the studio on Sunday?"

"About five P.M."

"What happened next?"

"She had already decided what to do. She wanted to burn him in the kiln. But he wouldn't fit . . ."

The wheels on the tape player twirled; in the seat next to his client, Botting's solicitor recoiled, his lips parted in disbelief.

Reston: "And?"

"She wanted me to cut him up. I told her she was mad. I stormed out of the studio. I walked—maybe three hours."

"So you went back to the studio around eight? Why didn't you go to the police?"

His voice was a whisper. "I thought about it. I should have. But I couldn't . . . I mean, the murder was done. I couldn't bring him back. And he was a batterer. He would have never left her alone. People don't, do they, once they know they have you? Still, to kill the man . . . I went back to talk with Livy, to see if we couldn't work up some way to go to the authorities. But when I . . ."

"She had already done it."

"Done it?"

"She—the place—was an abattoir. The blood—it was more than she had bargained for. She was raging and I . . . Christ, I sent her upstairs to take a shower. I put the—the legs and arms in the kiln. What else could I do? When she came down, I made her turn it on. I couldn't do it. She just flicked it on like it was a lamp. Then Chalice came and I was actually relieved. She'll find us out, I thought, and it'll be over."

A dry sob racked his body.

"Did Chalice see what had happened?"

"No. Livy sent her away. But we knew then we had too big a mess. Livy said she could hose down the room—all that stone, she said, the blood would wash away quickly.

But the bones weren't burning fast enough. We tried the torso, but it took too long. So Livy cleaned out the kiln, put the bits of bone that hadn't burned in a cloth bag, and I put . . . him . . . in a large plastic one. I stuck the small bag in my pocket and slung the other over my shoulder. I headed out and started walking the moors."

"Where did you plan to go?"

"Nowhere. I was just going to bury him, somewhere, but I collapsed. I couldn't believe what I had done. Why had I helped her? Why did I think she was worth everything? I couldn't stop crying."

The solicitor had shrunk in his chair, ashen-faced and repelled.

"And then what, Lyle?" Reston asked.

"At daybreak I pushed on. Bodies get buried in the moors all the time, don't they? No one ever finds them. . . . But I tripped as I walked over the packhorse bridge, right against the side of the wall I fell. I heard the plastic tear, felt the body slip. I twisted around and by God the fucker fell into the water. He got stuck in an eddy, twirling round and around. Then he straightened and headed away."

"What about the smaller bag of bones?"

"I hid it beneath a log. I meant to go back later—I did, in fact, at night, but I couldn't find it."

"So what happened next?"

"I went back to my flat. I prayed. For a strong current. For underbrush. For a hundred reasons that the . . . abomination . . . wouldn't be found. But then I heard the American had seen it—Nadianna had seen it, the woman I was helping. And the church started drawing attention to it. . . ."

A hoarse laugh came through the speaker. "I've never believed in God, but He's got a damned fine way with a joke."

Reston stood and Halford saw how ragged his face had become. "So you decided your only way out was to murder Olivia Markham and burn the studio and all the evidence."

The fury on Botting's face was so piercing, it made Halford suck in his breath.

"Me? Christ, no, Mark. It was Livy who burnt the studio. She's not dead. She's run off. You know that. The bitch has run off and left me here to take all the blame."

By any standard, the Mayley police station was cramped—no more than a tiny anteroom and a not-much-larger space for interviews. Nevertheless, inside it Chalice felt small and overwhelmed. Detective Sergeant Swain sat across the table from her, his lean face full of concern, and he cocked his head one way, then the other, like a bird who had found a very strange animal in its nest.

"We've called your sister." He hesitated and started to tap a pencil against the broken clay mask which lay in front of him on the table, but stopped himself. "I mean, yes, I realize you've reached your maturity, but, well, she should have been called, don't you agree?"

No, Chalice thought, and she suddenly felt a small tweak of pleasure. Swain didn't know what to do with her. She watched him as he wrestled with his confusion. She wouldn't put him at ease. The English bobby would have to reach his own decision on how to deal with the village giant. She felt herself grow a bit.

He leaned forward, a skinny, earnest young man with a patient voice.

"Chalice, you do understand the purpose of the tape we use to secure a crime scene, don't you? We do it to protect the area—and to protect people. The studio fire's still being investigated, you see. The fire investigation team hasn't given us the go-ahead to release the site. And besides, it isn't safe there. You could have been hurt."

Her palmtop dragged on her coat pocket. She made no move to get it.

Swain ran his hand through his curly brown hair and motioned at the mask.

"So, tell me about this piece of pottery."

Silence.

"Well, can you tell me who it is? Is it a person you know? A boyfriend, perhaps?" He smiled as if he were asking the question to a child to whom the word "boyfriend" was a quaint notion. "Fine-looking chap. Someone around here? I do know the piece is important to you. You risked your safety for it. Why is that?"

Chalice was growing bigger by the second. Soon she would fill the room and be able to walk the moors with the police station as a hat. Totty had been wrong. It wasn't her pottery that was her compensation. Now, when she needed it, her reward was her silence.

The young police officer studied her, then sighed and tossed his pencil down.

"Ah, well, then. Why don't you wait in the other room? Your sister should be here soon."

And she was. Totty pushed her way into the station, her hair wind-tossed, her clothes awry. She barely glanced at Chalice as she strode to DS Swain.

"What's going on. Why are you holding my sister?"

The young detective tried to smile reassuringly.

"We're not holding Chalice, Miss Hibbert. She was found trespassing on Markham Stu—"

"Chalice wasn't trespassing. She works there."

Swain faltered, but quickly re-engaged his smile. "She might have worked there, Miss Hibbert, but you'll agree that it's not a feasible place of employment now. And she *was* trespassing. We clearly marked the property as a crime scene and posted 'no entry' signs. She had to break down a door to get in. I could quite properly charge her. I could, in fact, quite properly take her to divisional headquarters for further questioning."

"It wouldn't yield you anything of benefit," Totty argued. "She didn't understand what she was doing."

In other circumstances, Chalice would have found the assertion humiliating; in other circumstances, Totty would never have used it. Now, however, Chalice ignored the humiliation and focused on Swain's face.

"I don't know about that," he countered. "But I don't see the need in keeping her here." He moved to the interview room door. "Just a quick question, please. Could you take a look at that piece of pottery on the table and tell me anything you know about it?"

Totty walked to the doorway, looked in, and shrugged. "Chalice makes all manner of masks. I don't know anything specific about that one. Why do you ask?"

"Well, the mask is important to your sister. That's what she was trying to retrieve from the studio."

"And why shouldn't she? She created it."

"Because it's part of a crime scene, Miss Hibbert. Nothing can be moved except by officials."

"I'm sure that's a fine point of law that Chalice now understands perfectly. Is there any objection to my taking my sister home?"

Swain's bird head twitched sideways as he gave Totty a quizzical stare. "Not at all," he murmured. "Just remember we'll eventually need answers."

They'd reached the car before Totty jerked around and seized Chalice's arm.

"What in the hell did you think you were doing?" The words were half hissed, half whispered. "Breaking into a crime scene? Do you realize the danger you've put yourself in? What do you think, Chally, that the police are as stupid as you seem to think everyone is? Good God!" She unlocked the passenger seat door and flung it open. "Get the hell in. I'm taking you home."

Chalice stared at her sister, openmouthed, before wedging herself in the car. Totty slammed the door shut, marched to the driver's side, and climbed in.

"This isn't some fucking game, Chalice," Totty snarled, churning the ignition. "The studio's burnt. Olivia's missing. Lyle's been arrested." Chalice's shock must have registered on her face, for her sister beamed with satisfaction. "Didn't know that? Been out shagging your boyfriend all day and didn't know that Lyle was being held in Halifax? The police came by this afternoon—Reston and the tall chap from London. They want to talk with you, Chalice. They want to search our car."

Totty's fingers were suddenly on Chalice's face, pinching hard, forcing Chalice to turn her head. The nails were as barbed as the expression in her sister's eyes.

"I've asked you this before. What do you know?"

The eyes were terrified, terrifying. Chalice yanked her face away, and instantly felt her skin slice.

"Christ." Totty withdrew her hand, gaping at Chalice's blood making half-moons beneath her nails. "On top of everything else, we'll have to explain that scratch on your face." She reached into her purse and pulled out a tissue. "We'll need a story, Chally. And if you're smart, it'll damn well cover your arse from all sides."

Halford stood in the lane beside The Crown & Drover and considered forcing himself inside. The pub was packed, the noise blaring through the darkening streets. Through the open door he could see crowded tables— shaggy-haired men in photographer's jackets, fresh-bobbed women in tailored suits. Reporters and locals were feasting on one another's voyeurism—and this even before Reston had had a chance to release a statement about Botting's confession. It wasn't his case, he reminded himself. He could do as he pleased. He turned away.

He angled his way though Mayley's snug streets, no clear idea of where he was going—no clear idea of how to get somewhere if he had wanted to. His week in Mayley had taught him how to get around by car, but now he took wet alleys and clouded garden walkways, threading thru Mayley like an amiable animal, entering whichever hole and passageway would accommodate him.

If he had allowed himself to think about it, he could have predicted where he ended up. The debris made the final alley familiar. The ceramic JOY AND ABUNDANCE sign gave a clink as he knocked.

Thornsby answered the door wearing a worn blue bathrobe. Halford checked his watch. It was not yet eight P.M.

"I'm sorry. I was out walking. If I had known I would end up here, I would have called."

The minister stepped back to let Halford in. "Is this the intuitive approach to crime solving? Clear your mind and see where your feet take you? That, Chief Inspector, is very close to an act of faith."

"Oh, I use acts of faith all the time. I just have to make sure they're backed up by evidence."

From a cupboard in the corner of the room, Thornsby produced a bottle of Merlot. "I don't drink often, but on occasion . . . Care to join me?"

"A small glass."

The minister disappeared through a door and returned with two glasses and a corkscrew. Halford settled his frame into one of the hard plastic chairs, the wine spicy on his tongue. As before, Thornsby sat on the floor. He swirled the liquid in his glass.

"Zoë told me you asked about Olivia's little escapade at our meeting."

"Yes," Halford said. "I have the feeling Zoë wasn't being one hundred percent truthful with me."

"She wasn't. For that matter, neither was I." Thornsby grimaced. "Olivia came across Zoë and me making love in the mill. She was spying on us, actually. It was the only time we had relations—that I swear to. I said I preach celibacy before marriage, and I do. It was one small transgression." He frowned into his glass. "Olivia was a very unpalatable person."

"You sound as if you're certain she's dead."

"Dead, run off—it's all the same. If she's responsible for that fire, she can't return. She's cast out. And that's damn fine as far as I am concerned."

"Not a very forgiving attitude."

"Oh, forgiving has nothing to do with it. I've forgiven her. It's a matter of not wanting your life polluted. Olivia was a pollutant."

"So was she threatening you and Zoë when she broke into the meeting?"

"She thought she was. What she didn't realize—what I didn't realize until I found myself lying to you today— is that I've been through too much to give a damn any more about such silliness. I shouldn't have committed the act, but I did. I shouldn't have lied to you, but I did. And I shouldn't have put Zoë in a position where she felt she had to lie."

"Did Olivia bring up your relationship with Zoë any other time?"

"Not really. Every now and then she'd give me a look. One of those leering 'I know what you did' looks. Perhaps she felt that when the time came to oust the church from the mill property she could use it against me. But I'm stronger than that. Whatever I did, it won't affect my ministry."

"What about Zoë?"

Thornsby balanced his nearly full glass on his knee and folded his feet onto his thighs yoga-style. The glass never wavered. "That's the astonishing thing about Zoë, Mr. Halford. She is even stronger than me."

In 1873 the local textile industry posted a profit; by 1879 the entire country was in a "Great Depression" that would last twenty years.

—*Notes*, G. GRAYSON

24

Saturday

It was still dark—if the morning sun was climbing somewhere over West Yorkshire, it hadn't yet fired the round of sky above the cottage—but Nadianna wasn't interested in seeing. She sat on the stone step by the door, shoes loose and untied on her feet, and hugged her daddy's coat around her. So the body had a name—or, as Halford carefully explained, it had an alleged name. Tests on the bone fragments still needed to be done, but it was reasonable to assume that Lyle Botting hadn't made up such a horrific tale. And the hand-woven bag had been traced to a craftsman who had worked at the studio three months earlier.

Richard Row. Never, if she had thought for a century, would she have chosen such a simple name for the man with the baked grimace. Malachi Bowleggedy; Zephaniah Whiskercheeks—she would have gone on for years constructing fanciful names for her grisly Rumpelstiltskin. And in the end she would have had to give up her firstborn because Richard Row was too simple a name.

Behind her the kitchen light flared, illuminating the black band of ground between cottage and wood. A breeze ruffled the branches, bringing her the coppery smell of frost and dead leaves. Minutes passed before she heard the door open behind her.

"Here," Gale said, holding out a steaming cup. Nadianna took the cup and, smiling her thanks, tasted the strong, sweet tea.

Gale sat down beside her on the step. "Easier to think out here?" she asked.

"Not really. I just found myself walking and the floor creaking and decided I'd better leave before I woke the multitudes."

From behind they heard a pounding. "The multitudes have awoke," Gale said, and they turned to watch Katie Pru through the kitchen window. Unaware of her audience, the child took a painting from a stack on the table, spit on it, and pounded the picture face-out onto the glass.

"Nature's own glue," Gale remarked. She wrapped her arms around her knees. "So. I guess we get back to work today. Lyle Botting's confession means it's pretty much over."

"Pretty much." Nadianna wound a loose shoestring around her finger. She didn't say what she was thinking— that giving the corpse a name deeply troubled her, that he'd become almost a thing to her, like a map she could tuck away in a drawer. The name gave him a story, and that terrified her.

But she should have known that Gale always sensed such thoughts. As she took another warm sip she heard Gale say: "I wonder what kind of man he was."

It would be the widow of a suicide who asked that question; another would surely have been content to leave the dead a stranger. But Nadianna had another question: Now that she had seen him dead, would she ever be able to let him go? She didn't think so. Any more than she could let her mother go. Any more than she could let Ivy go. Or her baby. They were all tied up together now, committed to each other. All these abandoned souls.

Gale picked up a pebble and flung it at the trees. "So you don't feel relief at all?"

Nadianna considered. "Yes, I feel relief. But I'm never gonna be separate from him now, you know. I'm never gonna separate from Richard Row."

Gale opened her mouth to protest, but quickly closed it.

The cottage door puffed open and a flashlight beam jiggled over the trees.

"Mama," Katie Pru said. "I wanna dance."

"Go on," said Gale. "But stay on this side of the cottage. And in the clearing, please, ma'am. Don't go into the woods. It's another hour before daylight."

Katie Pru leapt off the step, her cherry hat on her head, her nightie flapping white beneath her blue coat. She ran to the middle of the clearing, where she sang and whirled in her boots, the flashlight beam darting across the trees like a threatened candle.

"What do you make of Chalice?" Nadianna asked Gale.

"I'm not sure. I've looked in the cottage for her teabowls. The only examples of her work I can find are the mugs."

"Something's bothering her pretty bad."

Gale flung another pebble, aiming it far to the left of Katie Pru. "We can't help her if she won't talk to us."

The beam arched and jumped from branch to branch. Katie Pru pressed the flashlight to the top of her head and spun in the night.

"I think she knows where Olivia is."

"I don't know about that," Gale mused. "But I think she knows something."

"You gonna tell Mr. Halford?"

A pebble flew from Gale's hand and shattered a leaf on a low branch. "Hell if I know," she said softly.

Katie Pru stopped her dance; the beam made a wide sweep of the sky and settled on the kitchen window.

"Hey, Mama," Katie Pru said. "Have you seen my pictures?"

"I was looking at them earlier, baby. You did a good job."

"Chally is the whale."

Gale had reached for another pebble, but halted with her fingers in the dirt. "What did you say, baby?"

"Chally is the whale." Katie Pru jabbed the light at the window. "See? I painted her picture."

The paintings were lined up tidily on each wavy pane—a large stick figure with wavy red hair holding a tiny stick figure in her arms; a face with huge green eyes wrapped in a green scarf. And then the whale pictures—a whale with a scarf, a whale with a green necklace, a whale with a wide-armed child riding its humped back.

"Now, why would you paint Chally as a whale?" Gale asked. "Did you do it because she's so big?"

"No. She isn't so big. She's just a grown-up. But she is the whale. I heard her. When she was crying."

"Crying?"

"Uh-huh."

"Where?"

Katie Pru pointed to the wood.

"Did you see Chally crying?"

"No. I hid behind a rock. I was scared to look."

"It must have been scary. I wonder why she was crying."

"She doesn't like policemen."

Gale looked down at her. "How do you know that, baby?"

"I heard the whale say it."

"How . . . did you hear the whale more than once, K.P.?"

"Uh-huh."

"More than two times?"

But Katie Pru was gone again, dancing in the grass, the beam flitting among the treetops.

"Katie Pru," Gale called after her. "Just one more question: Are you sure you heard the whale talk? Chalice can't talk, you know."

Katie Pru squinched her eyes shut and whirled with her arms out. "I know!" she shouted. "There must be a whole school of whales!"

The dawn promised rain when Halford met Reston on the grounds of Markham Studio. The scene-of-the-crime team was already working—two men on the inside, a man and a woman on the outside kneeling beside the pavement stones that fanned out from the front door. The woman scraped the edge of a stone with a razor and shook the sample into a small plastic bag.

"Bad odds," she murmured. "Wish we'd been called in the day of."

Reston's brow furrowed, but he said nothing. Instead, he took Halford's arm and led him several steps away from the house.

"Know how many times it's rained since Sunday night? Three, counting mild, don't-wear-a-cap showers. One really wonderful goose-drowner. We've got a bloody ninety-nine percent chance of finding absolutely nil."

"You've got a signed confession," Halford reminded him.

"You believe Botting's confession?"

"Most of it."

"It's the non-most part I'm concerned with. A very nice Christmas present would be to find evidence of two blood types in the crevices of those stones. And to have them match up with one missing body and one missing person."

The female tech opened a second bag and leaned so far over the stone to peer at its far edge that her head brushed the ground. "Hope you have a happy holiday, Mark," Halford said, "but you'll be the luckiest bugger in the world if you do."

"Thanks for the sunshine, Danny."

"The search on for Olivia?"

"Yes. I should have jumped on this earlier. Super was tough as old meat last night when I spoke with him. If Markham's alive, then she's had approximately eighty hours to disappear. If she's dead, the damn trail's icy cold."

"You're tired, Mark." Halford said it kindly. "Bet you haven't quite knocked the flu yet."

"Bloody hell. Didn't I tell you, Danny, that if I put too few men in the stream looking for that body I'd be in for it? And didn't I say that if I put too many men and couldn't produce results I'd be in for it? Goddamn catch-22. The super's talked to the Greater Manchester Constabulary—they're going help look for Row. Have to search the reservoirs and streams Sette Water feeds into. The super made sounds about removing me from this case, and I can't bloody blame him. I should have stuck to my guns—should have demanded more men and be damned for it."

But you didn't believe Nadianna, either, Halford thought. The male crime-scene tech had moved away from the pavement stones, carefully combing the ground at the base of the studio. He stooped, running his hand over a clump of grass, then moved a step forward.

"So what's on the agenda today?" Halford asked Reston.

"Got to follow up on the church members. Olivia may be guzzling champagne in Spain, but she also may have fallen from that rooftop. And I'm going to get a bloody warrant to search Chalice Hibbert's car."

"The bog's been bothering you?"

"Hell, yes, it's been bothering me. Do you really believe she was up there clearing her head?"

"It's possible. I like to go for long walks."

"But if you follow that car the day of the fire, what do you have? According to Zoë, Chalice was at the studio—with the car—around three. She told you she saw the car again at six. And then the car was up on Haworth Moor later that night, around ten. At best it's suggestive. A bog is a good place to dispose of things. Pity Botting didn't think of that instead of his ridiculous plan to bury Row's body."

Halford nodded. "The car is suggestive. But you might have a hard time getting a warrant without evidence of a body."

"That's why I pester the church members again. I want them to tell me what they saw wasn't something ethereal but good old-fashioned blood and bones."

The male tech crouched by the corner of the studio. Standing abruptly, he waved and shouted to Reston.

"Found something, sir. Worth looking at, I think."

The margin of ground next to the studio was mainly pebbles, punctuated by errant tufts of grass. Sitting in the middle of one tuft was an obscured blue form, shiny and round like an Easter egg. The crime-scene tech moved aside; Halford and Reston knelt for a closer look.

The bowl rested on its side among the blades, small enough to be dwarfed by Halford's palm. What was visible was perfect—no chips, no cracks—and grew from a thickened base to an aesthetically impossible thin lip. Machine-made, was Halford's first reaction, but when he hunched over to read the manufacturer's name on the bottom, he saw instead the potter's mark—a medieval chalice.

"No other pieces around," the crime-scene tech told them. "Not even shards. And look, no window here for it to have gotten blown out during the fire, if that were even possible."

"It's got a date on it. This year," Reston said. "Odd. I would've thought fire investigation would've made note of it."

"If it was here," Halford said.

"If it was here. How interesting if it wasn't." Reston stood and clapped the tech on the back. "Good work, Timmy. Get a photo."

*Luther Yates and his brother David left the unproductive
Yates Mill and moved to Georgia, where they built the
Statlers Cross Cotton Mill in 1890. Instead of steam, the
new mill ran on gas and electricity.*

—*Notes*, G. GRAYSON

25

Chalice was twelve when she found Michael's Book. The
cottage hadn't been the profit-maker Totty had hoped,
and the biweekly cleanings dwindled to every three
weeks, then monthly, then to whenever the place was
rented. One day Chalice and her sister arrived after a
long absence to find that some of its slate shingles had
loosened and crashed to the earth. A bird had flown into
a window and left a spider-web crack in the glass; behind
a clump of ivy, Chalice discovered a pile of of bones and
feathers. Around back, someone had tried to break in,
and while the door lock had held, the wood was frac-
tured, and water and leaves had blown inside. The two
sisters set about cleaning, and when Totty left for town to
get more supplies and a handyman, Chalice drifted upstairs, too tired to work.

She wandered idly, inhaling the faint smell of mold,
unfolding the mattresses to let them freshen. Bored, she
had opened all three upstairs wardrobes, steeling herself against more dead animals. She found nothing but
dusty drawers and dessicated insects. There was only one
built-in cupboard upstairs, where Totty kept a broom.

When Chalice peered in, she was surprised to find that the cupboard opened to the roof. Squeezing herself inside, she was able to look above and see rafters. At first, she didn't comprehend the strange rectangular box tied to a low beam. But as her eyes adjusted to the dark, she could distinguish the lengths of three weathered ropes that bound it, and then a latch that held it closed. Curious, she hauled herself up to the top of the cupboard with her hands, then hung on to a protruding ledge by her elbows while she undid the ropes and freed the coffined book from its hidey-hole.

The wooden box smelled of rot—left any longer, she told herself, and its contents would have been gone—but the book itself was dry and smelled of something she couldn't identify. Its cover was black; flecks came off on her hands and when she brushed the sweat from her eyelids, they stuck to her lashes and fell into her eyes. She sat half-in, half-out of the cupboard and rested the book on her thighs as she opened it. Brown stains covered the book's pages like storm clouds. Evidence of water, she thought, and she wondered if the person who had so carefully hidden it under the rafters had half a heart that wanted it destroyed.

Water stains or no, it was legible, and for two years Michael's Book remained her secret.

Looking back, Chalice couldn't say why she never told Totty. Maybe it was because she had considered the book her prize, courtesy of a height that allowed her to see what others couldn't.

But it was a dreadful secret to keep. One night, scared sleepless by the image of all the dead children in its pages, she had cried an hour, inconsolable. Totty had crouched by the bedroom door, tears of exhaustion running down her cheeks as well.

"Please, I'm tired, Chally. What's wrong?" When there was no answer: "Why are you doing this to me?" And then, cruelly, desperately: "God, what I've given up for you! And you're not even my child. Grow up, grow up, GROW UP!"

It was Chalice's first grasp that Totty's despair was no longer directed at her absent mother, or at the string of inconstant boyfriends, but had turned to her, Chally. She was resented as much as she was loved. Not long after, the house on Garrett Alley with its nautical theme began to lose air, as if a hole had been punched in its side and all that was sustaining leaked out. Chalice fixed up the shed, immersed herself in her studies. And she learned the bus route that would take her up the steep climb of Old Ground Lane so she could roam Blandon Wood whether Totty wanted a clean cottage or not.

On one such walk she ventured to the ruined mill, where she found two young teens running across the grounds, laughing and shouting through the broken windows. For an hour she stood in the trees and spied on the pair. She watched their golden heads dip together and their arms fling out as they ran. Something in their freedom drew her out, and Chalice Hibbert, mute fable of Mayley, had emerged from the wood and walked toward them.

She now emerged from the wood again. Hugging a wrapped bundle, she crossed the clearing and knocked at the door to Mill Cottage.

Nadianna answered. "I was wrong to break your confidence earlier, Chally," she said breathlessly, without introduction. "I was doing what I thought was right, but it wasn't. I'm sorry."

Chalice merely nodded and allowed Nadianna to usher her into the front room. Gale stood by the fireplace, but the child didn't seem to be around.

"Chally," Gale said softly. "I want you to know something. Katie Pru heard you in the woods with a man. And she heard the man talking about avoiding the police."

Yesterday such news would have panicked her, but yesterday she thought she had a man who loved her and a sister who, at the very least, had her best interests at heart.

She reached into her pocket, pulled out a piece of paper, and handed it to Gale. As Gale glanced at it, Chalice scribbled on her palmtop.

PLEASE, READ THIS.

Gale read aloud. *I don't know where to begin. We were just normal teenagers who had found a place where we could meet in secret—like the movie "Rebel Without a Cause," remember it? At the start, there was only the three of us—and a cottage and an old house, and a fallen mill that no one knew the story of anymore. We were so lonely, and we didn't think we were being destructive. But maybe, like the teens in the movie, we were. We just believed in three things: we would stay together forever, God would find us, and the book would bring us . . . something.*

Chalice watched Gale's face. When the older woman looked up, her face confused, Chalice sat in a love seat and placed the wrapped bundle on her lap. Carefully, she removed the paper and handed the book to Gale.

READ IT, she wrote. AND TELL ME WHAT'S GOING ON.

Halford quickly recognized the broken mask; there was no mistake in identifying the droop of hair and the good-natured smirk of Alan Axon's mouth.

Reston bustled into the interview room. "Got Totty Hibbert on the phone. She says her sister's in. I've asked Swain to go. I'm having trouble getting a damn warrant for the car, and I've got to get back to regional. Would you mind going?"

"Not at all." Halford nodded at the mask. "Recognize the Axon lad?"

"Axon? Really?" Reston scrutinized the two pieces, and shook his head. "If you say so. I don't see it, but then, I don't know the boy that well. If it's important, we better hope she volunteers the identity—it will be tough duty to prove it otherwise."

"When I talked with Zoë Axon I left with the impression that she barely knew Chalice."

"Maybe she doesn't. It's a rare pair of siblings who share everything." Reston turned again to the door. "Swain. Pack this mask up for evidence. Meet Chief Inspector Halford at the car."

It took less than fifteen minutes for Swain to re-bag the mask, lock it up, and drive Halford to the Hibbert house on Garrett Alley. Nevertheless, when they arrived, Totty met them at the door with her wet hair in a towel and the news that Chalice was not at home.

"I have no idea where she is." Totty leaned into the door, her voice offhand, but Halford noted that the skin under her eyes was swollen, and her spine was rigid. "When you called I thought she was in the shed. But she's not there. She could be anywhere, not that it matters. It's not like she's been clamped in leg irons."

"We just need to follow up on yesterday, Miss Hibbert," Swain explained. "A few questions, that's all."

"Well, you damn near scared her to death yesterday, dragging her in for questioning like she was something wayward. She's done nothing bad, you know. Her worst crime was being in the wrong place at the wrong time— with the damn wrong people."

"Could you tell me what you mean by that, Miss Hibbert?"

"Meaning Olivia Markham and Lyle Botting. Think we don't read the papers? They're full of Botting. Hope you've prepared for the press corps. They're covering these parts like maggots."

Halford spoke. "She didn't take the car, then?"

Totty trained her eyes on him. "What did you ask?"

"Your car—it's parked around the corner. If Chalice is gone, she isn't using her own transportation."

"So what of it?"

Halford glanced up at the neat cornice about the stoop, at the scrubbed stone steps. "You'd mentioned before that you schedule the car tightly, which was why you knew she was home Sunday night. But she doesn't rely on the car for transportation all the time, does she?"

"Of course not. She walks quite a bit, takes the bus . . ."

"Any friends with cars?"

Totty's face grew severe. "No friends. Not a good one with friends, is Chally. Children are notoriously intolerant of difference."

"Does that include Alan Axon?"

Halford had seen the expression before—the wise look of someone who had expected her secret to be revealed and was triumphant that her prediction had at last come true. "Why bring him up?" she asked.

"I saw the mask at the police station. You said yourself your sister is quite good with likenesses."

"You're a clever man," Totty said lightly. "All right, then. What of it?"

"Is she with Alan now?"

"I've told you I don't know."

"Do you know if she had access to the car Tuesday night?"

"That was almost a week ago. I have no idea."

"Take a minute to think about it, Miss Hibbert. It was the night of the fire. Chalice would have had the car earlier in the day for her work at the studio, correct? Would she have had it that evening, at around six?"

An unvarnished fingernail disappeared between Totty's teeth. "Tuesday. No, I was to meet a couple outside of Wakefield on Tuesday. I was still there at six."

"You left here when?"

"Five thirty-five. Probably didn't leave Wakefield until well after seven."

"You're sure?" Swain asked. "Do you keep an engagement calendar?"

"Of course."

"Would you mind showing it to us?"

The look she gave him was hostile and composed. "I mind a great deal," she replied. "But since you've asked . . ." She unlooped the towel from her hair. The damp licks stuck out like hooks. "Come in, gentlemen," she said, moving aside. "Whatever it is you think my sister guilty of, I can prove she's not."

They followed her into the front room with its blue walls and bold red stripes. Sliding open the top drawer of the mahogany writing desk, she lifted out a green leather organizer.

"There," she said, holding the calendar page out to them. "The Trippings, Tuesday, six."

"No phone number here," Swain said. "We'd just like to verify that you met with them. If you haven't a phone number, an address will be fine."

Totty shut the book slowly. "That would be more difficult. I never talked with them by phone. And I don't know their address. We met at a pub. The name will come to me in a while. On the west side of Wakefield."

"How did you correspond with them?" Halford asked.

"Email. Always email."

"Then we'll get their email address."

"That's a bit of a problem. The file for my email address book is corrupted."

"That's no problem." Halford smiled. "I'm sure the West Yorkshire police has a veritable platoon of able-minded computer types."

Totty returned the book to the drawer and slid it shut. "Ah, but you'd need to take my computer. And for that you'd need a warrant." She turned to Swain. "As I've made clear before, I know where the line is. And I'm not going to let you cross it."

•   •   •

It was a marvel how pain could dwell on a page. The wretchedness, the anger. But there was more to this decaying book than an old man's bitterness toward his young self's tale. Michael's Book was unfathomable. It was a vision. It wasn't supposed to exist.

Gale sat at the table in the cottage kitchen, the old diary resting on a fresh piece of paper from Katie Pru's paint tablet. Chalice sat in the opposite chair—had been there, in fact, for the past two hours as Gale squinted over Michael's minute letters. Earlier, Nadianna had fixed Katie Pru a sandwich and, camera over her arm, headed out the door for a picnic at the mill. Now Gale felt a sudden panic as she envisioned her daughter in front of the hot stones of Yates Mill. So much pain.

She pushed the book away.

"Chalice," she said. "You know what you have here."

Chalice's jaw muscle flexed, and her thumbs worked the table edge.

"From a historical perspective, it's outstanding," Gale continued. "Names, dates, plans, cells, organizational data. This is an important historical find—but Alan knows that, doesn't he?"

Tears built in the young woman's green eyes. Her nod was quick.

"How long have you known about it?"

Seven fingers shot up from the table's edge. "Months?" A shake of the head. "Years?"

The tears spilled and ran down Chalice's cheeks.

"Tell me about the three of you and the diary," Gale said gently.

No response, just thumbs kneading the table edge. Gale stood, walked to the counter, and tore another page of paper from Katie Pru's tablet.

She handed it along with a pen to Chalice, then knelt down beside her. "Look, you must level with me. Something's scared you. Isn't that what you said in your note—that the three teens were destructive? How were they destructive, Chalice?"

The point of the pen pressed the paper, lifted, pressed again. Then, finally, three words.

Olivia is dead.

Gale shook her head. "Mr. Halford told me of Lyle Botting's confession. He says Olivia isn't dead. And for what it's worth, Daniel believes he's telling the truth."

Chalice shook her head firmly and jabbed the pen at the words. *She'd never leave. Ego. Anger. Pride. She would make me leave, make Lyle leave. She'd make the whole town disappear before she'd go. She's dead.*

Gale sighed. "Chally, I'm having a hard time with this. Why did you bring me the book? What do you think the book has to do with Olivia?"

Chalice's mouth widened, tears rolling into it. Her eyes were pleading as she dipped her head and wrote.

We took an oath—me & Alan & Zoë. Like Michael. "To fly to the verge of nature to pursue the traitor." Olivia was the traitor. She was going to tell. To betray us.

"I don't understand what you're saying. Did Olivia know about this book?"

A nod.

"Did one of you hurt Olivia?"

The tears stopped abruptly, only the shiny trails left behind on her cheeks.

"Sisss," Chalice whispered. "Sisss."

Gale picked up the pen and put it in Chalice's hand. "Tell me. Help me understand. Do you know who hurt Olivia?"

Alan. Zoë. Please. See if it's true. I don't want to think about the other choice.

According to Mayley Unitarian church records, 25 men out of a congregation of 98 were killed in World War I. By 1927, church membership had dwindled and the church closed, a pattern repeated in churches throughout the region.

—*Notes*, G. GRAYSON

26

Totty Hibbert ended the questioning by standing, arms crossed, on the stoop of the Garrett Alley cottage and waiting until Halford and Swain nodded good-bye and trudged to their car.

"Naïve woman," Swain said as he swung open the door and climbed inside. "Won't be difficult to track down the Trippings—provided they exist. And all the more difficult for her if they don't."

As the car rounded the corner, Halford watched Totty; she never moved, her lean body as severe as a door. "I think she knows that alibi isn't going to hold up. She's buying time."

"She better be fast, then, sir. We're going to figure this one out, and she'd best not be on the wrong side of the law."

It was the kind of television comment Halford had long ago learned not to make. He smiled briefly at the young DC.

"Going back to the station, are you? Let me out at the corner. Tell DI Reston to give me a ring when he gets in."

"Yes, sir. Thank you, sir."

The smell of sausages clung to the air as Halford strode past a row of terraced cottages, but all the street windows appeared closed and he couldn't detect the source.

He had reached the corner of the High Street when his cell phone burred in this pocket. He flipped it open and his stomach clenched to hear Gale's nervous voice.

"Can you come to the cottage?" she said.

"Are you okay?"

"Sure." A deep breath. "Can you come now?"

He was jogging even before he punched the phone off, heading for his car parked behind The Crown & Drover. Within fifteen minutes he had pounded through Blandon Wood to find the cottage door unlocked.

Gale and Chalice sat silent in the kitchen. "Have a seat," Gale told him, the nervousness in her voice replaced by fatigue. "I'd offer you a cup of tea, but you'd have to drink it somewhere else." She motioned toward what resembled a stack of tobacco leaves wedged between two pieces of leather. "Can't risk a spill."

"It's all right," Halford answered, easing a chair from beneath the table. "That's quite an old book. Is it yours, Chalice?"

She nodded bleakly. Her large hands were folded on top of the table, her thumbs pressed so tightly, their knuckles were purple. He reached over and gently lifted first one thumb, then the other. "Not good for an artist's hands. It would be a shame for all of us if you wound them."

He had meant his gesture to be partly a kindness, partly a palliative. He wasn't prepared for the look of pure misery she directed at him.

He wrapped his hand around the girl's fist and looked at Gale questioningly.

"Remember the discussion we had about the Luddites?" she asked. "Remember what I said about the historical record—about how limited the source material is—at least from the Luddite point of view? That's a Luddite diary. Chalice found it tied to the rafters of this cottage seven years ago. I've read pieces of it. It's . . . well, it's heartbreaking. But it's also an extremely valuable find."

Halford felt Chalice's fingers move beneath his grip. When he lifted his hand, she dragged a piece of paper from the opposite side of the table and placed it in front of him.

My Confession, it read in stark letters across the top.

He covered it with his hand. "Chalice, you need a solicitor. . . ."

She grabbed his arm and pulled on it, her expression beseeching.

"It's not a confession of a crime, Daniel," Gale interposed. "Chalice hasn't done anything wrong." She paused and ran her hands over her face in exhaustion. "She believes Olivia is dead. And she feels she has an idea of who is responsible."

Halford looked at Chalice. "Why don't you come with me to the station? Mr. Reston needs—"

The crack of Chalice's broad palm hitting the table sounded like a bullet shot. She shook her head fiercely.

"Ree—" she said. She poked the paper with her finger. "Ree—"

"I've read it," Gale said. "In fact, I was here while she wrote it. So if there's a crime in that, then I'm involved, too."

"Tell you what, Gale," Halford said. "I'll read Chalice's note. But move the book someplace safe. And if you don't mind, I could use a cuppa."

Chalice's handwriting was tight, as if the owner had spent a lifetime cramming large thoughts in limited spaces. It wasn't at all what he would have expected from Chalice—something flowing and unencumbered would have been his guess, not these precise, measured figures. But then perhaps precision was what a potter's fingers aspired to. He began to read.

My Confession

The only people I ever told outright about the book were Alan and Zoë. I came across them at the mill. The first time I saw them I thought they were sprigs of light—so blond and lithe. I felt like something monstrous beside them. Then Zoë took my hand and made me run with them. They were my first and only friends.

I showed them the book the day after my fourteenth birthday. Alan knew immediately what it meant. "It's a rare book, Chally," he said. "People will want to read it, to publish it. They'll want to study it. Michael Dodd will become a hero. People will write about him in their own books."

We went to the library, read all we could on the Luddites. Nothing like Michael's story, of course. Court records, newspaper articles, old ballads. "See?" Alan said. "Nothing so detailed and personal. You watch, Chally. When we get older, this book will make us famous."

So we made a plan—and a vow. We would be secret siblings. We would meet in secret at the mill and never tell anyone about the book until we were old enough. Then we'd reveal it. The

*book would make us famous and admired, for unlike the girls
who saw the Cottingley fairies, our secret wasn't a ruse. Michael's Book was real.*

*So we played at the mill. It was our retreat, and sacred be-
cause of what happened there. We promised to protect it.*

*Totty heard that Olivia Markham was looking for space for
a studio; I didn't think about it until one day when Alan &
Zoë & I were eating lunch at the mill and saw Olivia drive up
to the mill-owner's house. Within weeks she was ensconced, and
we were forced to sneak around. By this time I was working for
other potters, but Totty wanted me to apprentice with Olivia.
When she heard Olivia needed an assistant, I applied.*

*For a couple of months it went well. But we were bound to get
lax. One day Olivia looked out her window and saw the three of
us skulking about. Suspicious, was Olivia. She was so blatant
herself with her art that the idea of privacy in others fascinated
her. I don't know how long she watched us before we saw her. We
just looked over at the studio and there she was, framed in the
window. After that she wouldn't let up on me. "What are you
doing there? You can trust me. Drugs? I won't tell. Kinky
brother-sister sex? What's your part, Chalice—watching? Come
on, you're all three too far grown to be innocent."*

*It was all done playfully, but you didn't have to know Olivia
long to know that she was never playful.*

It ended there. Halford was aware of Chalice's eyes on
him as he took a sip of tea.

"You stopped," he said. "Tired of writing?"

When she shook her head, he smiled. "A wise girl to
know when not to commit something to paper. So I'm
guessing Olivia found out about the book?"

The palmtop appeared on the table. She made a few
strokes and turned to him. I TOLD HER.

"Why?"

I DIDN'T THINK IT MATTERED ANYMORE. ALAN WAS
DOING WELL IN HIS STUDIES. MY POTTERY WAS DOING
WELL. WE WERE ALMOST READY TO MOVE ON.

"What did Olivia do when you told her?"

ECSTATIC. THE PUBLICITY. BUSES FROM BIRMINGHAM, GLASGOW.

"All centered around the mill?"

NOSTALGIA SELLS. TRAGIC NOSTALGIA SELLS BETTER.

"And no more paradise for you three."

NO. AND THE BOOK TURNED OVER TO OTHER SCHOLARS, NOT ALAN.

"That's what you believed?"

The pen hesitated. THAT'S WHAT ALAN BELIEVED. AND THAT SCARED ME.

"Why?"

Another hesitation.

"I know about his drug addiction," Halford said quietly.

I WAS AFRAID. WE PINNED SO MUCH HOPE ON THAT BOOK.

"Afraid Alan would slip back into addiction?"

A nod.

"I see." He looked at Gale, who stood by the kitchen sink, thoughtfully threading a tea towel through her fingers. "Well, Chalice, why don't you let me take you to the station so you can show this to Mr. Reston? You don't want to be in the middle if this is a homicide—"

The young woman stared at him, her face an angry mask. She ripped the confession paper from beneath Halford's fingers.

I'M ALREADY IN THE MIDDLE. I'LL NEVER BE OUT OF THE MIDDLE. PERHAPS IT WAS MY BEST FRIEND, ZOË. OR PERHAPS IT WAS MY LOVER, ALAN. BUT MY MONEY IS ON MY SISTER. OLIVIA FIRED ME. SHE HIT ME. TOTTY KNEW.

"When was this, Chalice?" Halford asked. "When did Olivia hurt you?"

She slowed, and tears splashed on her hand. TUESDAY.

"The afternoon of the fire?"

A nod.

"How did Totty find out Olivia hit you?"

SHE WAS AT HOME WHEN I CAME IN. IT HURT TO STAND.

"Do you remember the time?"

Her stare was deadened. She's figured it out before any of us, Halford thought.

SHE WAS THERE WHEN I CAME HOME AT 3:30. SHE LEFT AGAIN TWO HOURS LATER.

"Did she tell you where she was going?"

TO MEET A COUPLE IN WAKEFIELD.

"That's what she told DC Swain. And confirmed it with her calender."

SHE LIED. THEY CANCELED. I READ THE EMAIL. SHE LIED TO ME.

Halford frowned. "We're going to Reston. I'll take you." He turned to Gale. "Do me a favor. Keep Katie Pru and Nadianna away from the mill. Some of what Chalice has said doesn't fit with other information I have. Until Reston sorts it out, best hold off on the mill."

Gale stopped kneading the towel. "They're at the mill now. I sent them out for a picnic so I could talk with Chalice."

"How long ago?"

"More than an hour."

Halford was already on his feet. "Let's take the car."

Through her viewfinder Nadianna could see Thornsby's tired Fiat peeking from behind the mill. Not what she wanted for this shot, so she picked up the tripod and readjusted it to face the stream bank where Katie Pru made wet blowing noises with a piece of grass she held between her thumbs.

The child looked up in disgust. "I can't make it honk, Nadianna. You make it honk."

It was a good image—Katie Pru's blue denim overalls against the mossy ground, the contrast between the intense concentration in the child's eyes and her funny, puffed-out cheeks. Nadianna aimed her camera and clicked.

"Okay, K.P." Making sure the tripod was stable, she plucked a blade from the ground. "Let's see if this English grass can cut the mustard."

She positioned the blade lengthwise between her thumbs and blew. The resulting honk startled a pair of birds from the trees. Both squawked righteously and wheeled off in the air.

"What on earth was that?"

Nadianna spun around to see Zoë standing in front of an open door on the east side of the mill.

"Oh, Zoë, you surprised me. I'm sorry. We didn't mean to bother you. I knew someone was here, but I thought they were in the carding shop. We'll be quieter."

"It's all right. You're not bothering anyone. It's just me and Alan and Gerald. The final bit of work for the jumble sale." Zoë moved onto the grounds and raised her voice. "Katie Pru, isn't it? Enjoying yourself today, Katie Pru?"

Katie Pru didn't answer. She selected another blade, put it to her mouth, and blew.

"I can't make it honk," she complained. "It only spits."

"I can't help you there," Zoë told her. "But I have a kazoo inside. It's guaranteed to honk. Would you like to have it?"

Katie Pru scrambled to her feet, and after a nod from Nadianna ran to Zoë. With her tripod and camera bag in tow, Nadianna followed them to the mill.

Inside, she let out a surprised breath. "My word. I had no idea the mill was in this good a shape." She set down her gear and touched the back of the couch. "From outside it looks totally fallen apart."

Zoë smiled. "This is Gerald's study. Looks nice, doesn't it? Actually, there are a couple of usable rooms in the interior. Places that probably served as office space long ago. It's the upper floor that's so ragged." She pointed to a door on the opposite wall and reached out for Katie

Pru's hand. "Come on. Gerald and Alan are just through there."

The second room, although larger, was not nearly as elegant. No rugs had been laid down or pictures hung. It certainly could have used some artwork, Nadianna thought—the scrubbed space was windowless with two blackened doors offering the only visual relief. Plaster had fallen in thick chunks from the stone walls. Portable lights lit the room. Boxes crammed with faded clothes and household goods covered the floor, and one corner was crowded with battered paint and gasoline cans and a pile of rags. When Nadianna sniffed, dust filled her nose, and she sneezed.

"Ah, none of that," Thornsby said, lifting a box onto his shoulder. "You'll be going back home telling everyone you came down with pneumonia."

Nadianna gestured to the boxes. "This what used to be in the carding shop?"

"Yes," Gerald answered. "Sorted it there, stored it here. Alan and I are loading up the car and taking them down to Mayley Hall. We'll have the jumble sale there this week."

"I'll have to tell Gale. She loves that kind of thing. Personal history hunts, she calls them."

Gerald shifted the box on his shoulder and turned for the door. "Let me put this in the car. Seriously, Nadianna, if you need to get away from the dust, you're welcome to sit in the study."

"I'm okay." As Alan and Gerald hiked from the room with their burdens, Nadianna surveyed the space. "From what the man at the historical society told Gale, we expected no more than a hull. I'd love to take photographs of this. With the boxes, if possible."

Zoë shrugged. "Sure. They won't get more than a half dozen boxes in Gerald's car. I doubt they'll move them all today."

"My camera's in the study. May I do it now?"

"That's fine. If you don't mind the men stomping about," Zoë said absently. "Katie Pru? The kazoo's in one of these boxes over here. Let's find it. Then you can take it home and let your mother wash it out."

Despite Halford's assurances, Gale was certain it would have been quicker to run through the woods. The roads curled ahead of them; Gale crushed the shoulder harness of the seat belt in her hand, holding herself upright as Halford steered the car along the walled roads. She knew he regretted alarming her, but she wasn't going to assuage his guilt. She was too scared. She shot him a worried glance as he finished a call and closed his cell phone.

"I've talked with Swain. She'll be fine, Gale," he said. "Katie Pru knows Swain. If he gets there first, he'll be the cordial big brother and ride her on his back."

"I know. Just drive."

She twisted around to look at Chalice. "There's not a phone at the mill, is there?"

It was a stupid question—no phone at the mill was why it had taken so much time for the fire brigade to reach the burning studio. Chalice looked at her, and Gale sensed something painful in her eyes. If the woman knew something she hadn't told, Gale didn't want to know it at this point.

"Chalice," Halford said, "I'm interested in the rivalry between Olivia and Thornsby. Do you know anything about that? Not the newspaper feud—anything else."

But Chalice made no move to answer. On their right appeared the gravel lot of the Old Ground Lane bus stop. Without warning, Halford whipped the car into the lot.

Gale looked at him, stunned. "What are you doing?"

"Swain will get to the mill before we do. If there is a problem, he'll deal with it."

"I don't want Swain to get there first. *I* want to get there."

He laid his hand on hers and squeezed. "Chalice," he said. "You don't have to talk with me if you don't want to. But I wish you'd tell us if you think there's something the police need to know before we all get to the mill grounds."

No response.

"Daniel . . ."

The grip on Gale's hand tightened.

"Chalice, can you tell me why Zoë would have led me to believe that she didn't know you very well, that she was afraid of you?"

Disbelief spread across Chalice's face, but still she didn't answer.

"Do you know," Halford persisted grimly, "why someone would have planted one of your bowls outside the studio after the fire?"

Gale saw Chalice's face sag. It was the only word for it—the flesh gave away from her jawline, and she looked suddenly old. With Halford holding her hand so tightly her fingers ached, and with her own heart ready to burst, Gale watched Chalice Hibbert age.

Sighing, Halford released the brake and pulled the car from the lot. As they headed south down the hill, Chalice poked Gale on the shoulder and clamped her other hand to her ear.

"The phone," Gale interpreted. "She wants the cell phone."

Halford fished it from his coat pocket and handed it over. Chalice punched the buttons, pressed it to the side of her head, and waited.

After thirty seconds she shut it off and handed it back.

"Who were you trying to call, Chalice?" Gale asked helplessly.

TOTTY'S NOT HOME. GET TO THE MILL QUICKLY, PLEASE.

In 1956, the Yates Mill fire of 1812 was mirrored in Georgia when the Statlers Cross Cotton Mill was burned and subsequently closed because of labor disputes.

—*Notes*, G. GRAYSON

27

Kazoos that had to be cleaned by a mother before they could be blown were not fun. Katie Pru looked at the one in Zoë's hand, but she kept her own hands behind her back.

"Don't want it, then?" Zoë asked. "Back to the box it goes. I'm sure some other child will want it."

Katie Pru reached up and took it, eyeing it a second before putting it up to her mouth.

From the middle of the room Nadianna spoke. "Uh-uh, Katie Pru. You heard Miss Zoë. We'll clean that with soap real good when we get home to the cottage. I'm gonna take a few photos now—just a couple—then we can go. Why don't you let me hold on to the kazoo until then?"

Grass is better, Katie Pru decided as she picked her way through the boxes to Nadianna. No one ever told her to wash grass with soap. She handed Nadianna the kazoo.

"This will take just a minute, K.P. Go find yourself a place to sit down. Only a couple of shots, I promise."

"A couple means one, two," Katie Pru pointed out.

Nadianna fiddled with her camera, turning its dial, holding a gadget up in the air and reading it. "Well, okay, maybe more than one, two. How about ten? Can you count to ten?"

Yes, she could count to ten, but she bet Nadianna wouldn't. Grown-ups never counted the way children did.

She took giant steps past the boxes and sank down against the wall. No kazoo. No grass. She looked at the cardboard boxes, some of them flowing over with clothes or stacked with plastic dishes. Dishes were fun, and so were clothes, but then she remembered the fox's head she had seen growling from a box the first day, and she stuck her hands behind her back.

Nadianna was kneeling in the corner of the room. "One, two," Katie Pru said. The camera clicked, but Nadianna didn't say anything.

Katie Pru relaxed her arms and rolled onto her tummy. She didn't like a room that was filled with boxes and still didn't have anything that she could do.

From outside she heard voices—Alan and Zoë and the other man Katie Pru didn't know.

"This is all that we can take this load, Zo," she heard Alan say.

"We'll be back in less than an hour," the other man added. "Keep an eye on the place, all right, my girl?"

"Will do," called Zoë.

A car started, and Katie Pru shut her eyes and listened to the motor whine until she couldn't hear it anymore. She should have been in that car. She should have climbed among the boxes and let the car whine her away.

"Three, four," she said to Nadianna.

"In a minute. Zoë," Nadianna said loudly, "is there a chair in there I can stand on?"

"Just a second," Zoë said. "I'll bring one in."

A minute, a second. They were both grown-ups. And grown-ups didn't know.

She put her hands straight out in front of her and, with her eyes shut, scooted on her belly. She was a minnow, and she would be a minnow until she plowed into the wall.

But she didn't plow into a wall. Before she hit, her hands flew into something fluffy, frilly. She opened her eyes. It was a piece of cloth, probably tossed out from one of the boxes.

"Here," she heard Zoë say. "You can stand on this. Let me help you up."

Katie Pru made herself as flat as a snake and, crumpling the fluffy cloth under her arm, stretched out her hand and felt the place where the cloth had been. There was a hole in the floor at the corner, as if a family of racoons had dug for a night and made themselves a secret, secret place beneath the stone. The cloth hadn't been tossed from one of the boxes. Someone had put it there to hide what was underneath.

"I'll stand here and hold the chair for you," Zoë said.

"Thanks," replied Nadianna.

A board the size of Katie Pru's chest covered the hole, and when she peeked beneath it, she saw a box of bowls. Carefully, she lifted a bowl from the hole. It was beautiful, blue like the sky. She slid it into the neck of her shirt. And carefully, again, she lifted out a second. One, two, she thought, and she stuffed the cloth back into the hole and scooted away.

Nadianna held her hands out and let Zoë help her to the floor. "I appreciate that," she said. "Now let's hope my photographs were worth the trouble."

"I'd like to see your pictures when they're printed," Zoë told her. "I love this old mill. I'd like to see how a photographer sees it."

Nadianna frowned. "I haven't thought about how I'm

going to develop these now that Mr. Botting's studio is off limits. Hopefully, I'll be able to show you these photos before I leave the country. If not, I'll work out something." She gazed around the room, taking in the rough walls, the colorful boxes, the broken floor. "There's more life here than I ever guessed. To think I started out this essay with death. One of my instructors warned me about that—never predict your work."

"A kind of faith, isn't it?" Zoë hesitated. "I know you don't think you witnessed a vision. . . ."

Nadianna pressed a button and listened to the whir of the rewinding camera. "I didn't see a vision. I saw a man. He had a name."

"But still, you were there. Trip over a root on your way down and you would have missed him."

"I don't really want to talk about it."

"I just think . . . sometimes things happen that make it seem we're being given approval. Like you being there in the water at that moment. Maybe you were being given approval for doing your photography."

Nadianna shook her head and knelt beside her bag to pack her equipment away. "This is just bad stuff we need to get past. Katie Pru, ten minutes are up. Are you ready to go home?"

"In a minute," Katie Pru said. "I'm feeding the two bears."

"Oh." Nadianna snapped the lens cap on her camera and slid it into the bag. "I thought there were three bears."

"I've only got two bowls of porridge. So I'm only feeding two bears."

"I see. Feed 'em quickly and put the bowls back where you found them. Mr. Thornsby has to come pick them up and we've got to get home. Your mama's gonna be worried."

The child's reply was a murmur, and Nadianna looked up. "Come on, now, Katie Pru. Put them back."

"I said, Mr. Thornsby doesn't want them! If he had wanted them he wouldn't of hid them in the hole!"

"What hole?" Nadianna stood but paused at the sound of a car puttering to a stop outside the mill. It wasn't Gerald's car—Gerald's old Fiat had a plaintive call of its own.

"Y'all are busy on Saturdays," Nadianna said to Zoë. "Katie Pru and I better get going."

Zoë didn't reply. When Nadianna glanced at her, the golden-haired girl was walking toward Katie Pru, her face flushed. "What's wrong, Zoë?"

Outside, feet crashed through the leaves, heading for the carding shop.

"Lock the door, Nadianna."

"What's wrong?" Nadianna repeated. "Zoë, tell me what's wrong."

"I left the side door open," Zoë whispered. "They'll find us."

"Who? Who'll find us? Zoë, who's out there?"

The footsteps headed away from the carding shop, toward the side of the mill. Another few seconds and the runner would find the door that opened onto the study.

"What are you talking about?" Nadianna's anger grew with her fear. "Who is it?"

"Just lock the door, dammit."

Helpless, Nadianna ran to the door that separated the storage room from the study. She threw her weight against it as Totty Hibbert barreled through. The door slammed into Nadianna, sending her sprawling over the boxes. It felt as if a hundred snakes were biting at her back. She gasped, trying to pull herself up, but collapsed, tears stinging her eyes.

"Where's Chalice?" Totty demanded, ignoring Nadianna. "Come on, Zoë. I know she's with your brother. Tell me where they are."

Through her tears Nadianna could see Totty advancing on Zoë, and Zoë retreating backward, lips opening and shutting wordlessly. Behind them on the floor sat Katie Pru, fascinated, a bowl halfway to her mouth.

"Tell me where that scum of a brother of yours is, Zoë. I've called your house. Mummy and Daddy don't know where he is. I damn well know Chalice is with him. Tell me where."

Zoë's eyes blazed.

"Alan's not here, Totty. He's with Gerald in town."

"You're lying. Chalice needs to come with me. Tell me where they are, or so help me God I'll kill you."

Zoë said nothing. Nadianna lurched painfully to her feet.

"Chalice is at Mill Cottage," Nadianna said. "She's with Gale. Please, you two move away from Katie Pru. If you're going to fight, do it away from her."

Totty glanced around Zoë at the child on the floor. Her stare grew transfixed.

"Christ," she said.

"You heard her, Totty. Chalice is at the cottage." Zoë tried to take Totty by the coat sleeve, but the older woman, still staring, jerked away. "You need to go get her. You and I both know she's done a very bad thing."

Totty looked up. "Where did that child get those tea-bowls?"

Zoë tried again to take Totty by the arm. "I know all about what Chalice did. I saw. Totty"—and here she grabbed the older woman by her gloved hands, which were now clenched—"listen to me. You've got to get Chalice away from here. You know what will happen to her if you stay."

With her foot Nadianna nudged aside a box and stumbled toward Katie Pru, who sat motionless on the floor, mouth gaping. "Katie Pru," she said. "Come here."

"Where did she get the tea-bowls?" Totty tried to shake off Zoë, but Zoë's grip tightened.

They're going to fight, Nadianna thought, and she stretched out to grab Katie Pru. In an instant the child was in her arms and Nadianna was kicking aside boxes, lumbering to the door. From behind her, Totty began to yell.

"What in the hell are those tea-bowls doing here? They were gone. . . . Who stole them? One of you bastards . . . I want to know who stole them."

"Get them, Totty," Zoë said calmly. "You're free to take them."

"I will, goddamn you."

Totty's angry voice diminished to a muffle. Nadianna broke into the air and kept running downhill, Katie Pru's legs banging her thighs and slowing her to a frantic amble. When they reached the stream, she lowered Katie Pru and they started stumbling along the bank.

"Keep going, K.P.," she urged. "We gotta find your mama."

The scream sounded when they were a hundred feet downstream. It cut through the mill's pocked walls and echoed over the hills.

"Nadianna!" A car careened to a stop outside the mill; the passenger door flew open and Gale was on the gravel before the engine idled off. She ran down the embankment to Katie Pru and wrapped the child in her arms.

"Someone just screamed in there," Nadianna said. "Zoë and Totty are inside."

"Let's get to the cottage," Gale answered. "The police are coming. They don't need us. Come on, Nadianna. Let's go."

Gale buried Katie Pru's head in her shoulder and hurried down the stream. Nadianna started to follow, but turned once more to look at the mill.

What she saw she couldn't have captured on film—not in a photograph, anyway, and a moving image would have made its horror preposterous.

A woman, her clothes and hair afire, staggered out the mill door. She was twisting and jerking, her hands beating her face. Halford climbed from his car and raced toward her with his coat held out to smother the flames, but he never reached her. A tremendous figure loped across the open ground and hoisted the burning figure in its arms. There the woman was held suspended, the flames whipping the air. Then the giant figure was slipping, sliding down the bank, and in one huge thrust, hurled the burning woman into Sette Water.

Halford rushed down the hill as Chalice threw herself into the water after Totty. By the time he reached the bank, she had one massive hand around her sister's ankle, stopping the current from carrying her away.

"Don't let her go, Chalice," he yelled. "I've called the medics. Hold on to her." But before he could plunge into the water, Swain splashed in, grabbing hold of the twisting woman.

"Check the mill." Swain's breath was labored as he pulled Totty to the bank. "See if there's anyone else. Come on, now, Chalice. Let's get her to the ground. We can help her easier out of the water."

Halford gulped deep breaths as he ran uphill. Before he could reach the mill door, Zoë staggered from behind the building, coughing.

"Is there anyone else inside?" he asked, catching her in his arms.

She shook her head. Pushing her aside, he headed into the mill. The air was smoky but not dense. Inside the storage room, tiny flames burned in spits on the floor and dotted the jumble sale boxes. He found a fire extinguisher behind the study door; a few hits and the flames were out.

He hurried to the door at the far end of the storage room, but the space it opened onto was cavernous, damp, and free of smoke. Checking again to make sure the fire was out, he left the mill and emerged into the sweet air.

Zoë leaned against his car, her blond hair loose, her gossamer skirt unsinged.

"I looked around and couldn't see anyone else," he said. "Are you certain there was no one else in the building?"

"I'm . . . certain."

"How did the fire start?"

She looked at him, and without warning her eyes rolled back in her head. He caught her around the waist and gently led her head to her knees; after a few seconds she grabbed his wrist and pushed herself upright.

"Totty doused herself," she said. "Totty set herself on fire."

Down by the stream, Swain and Chalice crouched over Totty's still form. "She did it to herself? How?"

"There are cans of lamp oil in the storage—we use them for the camping lanterns at our prayer meetings. Totty took one. She threw it all over herself."

Her teeth clattered; her pallor was alarming. He opened the rear door of his car and helped her into the seat, positioning himself to block her view of the stream bank and its gruesome activity.

"Detective Reston will be here in a minute," he said. "He'll want you to tell him exactly what happened."

"I'm not exactly sure what happened. Nadianna and Katie Pru were there, and Totty came in, acting crazy, yelling about Chalice and Alan. I didn't know what to do. I told her . . . I told her she needed to take Chalice away, that Chalice was going to be arrested . . ."

"Why did you tell her that?"

"Well, I put it all together. I saw how it started, didn't I, when Chalice came out of the studio hunched over and hurt. And then later, when Chalice's car was there where there shouldn't have been a car. I told you that, remember? And I could tell you were surprised."

"Yes, I remember."

"So I finally screamed that at Totty. I said 'I know Chalice murdered Olivia!' Her face was dreadful—blotchy, red like it had swelled up. She slung her hand back and hit me." She tilted her head to Halford; the flush mark of a blow was visible on her cheek. "It still stings."

Halford pressed his hand against the tender spot, and Zoë leaned into it. She looked up at him, eyes reddening. "I told her how I knew, and she got so quiet, like she was thinking. Then she looked at me and told me to listen, that what she had to say was going to be said only one time and that I would have to be the witness to tell everyone else. And that's when she said she killed Olivia."

"What exactly did she say?"

"That was it—'I killed Olivia.' She said she went to the studio to talk to her and found her drunk. They argued; she hit her. Olivia fell onto the sofa. The pillow was there, and she thought, why not? So she smothered her. Then she set the studio on fire."

"She told you all that?"

"Yes."

A howl rose from the stream: Halford glanced around to see Chalice kneeling beside her injured sister, her own burnt arms stiff in front of her as Swain fought to comfort her. Halford shut his eyes briefly.

"Maybe you should wait to tell DI Reston the rest, Zoë. He should be here shortly."

But she continued, her voice soft and distant.

"She walked over to the corner, picked up a can of kerosene. I tried to stop her, but she threatened to do me as well. 'I've become very adept at this sort of thing.' That's the last thing she said. Then she pulled out a lighter—"

She had wrapped the strand of hair tightly around her finger so that the tip bulged an angry purple. Halford stooped down next to her.

"That's a horrible memory to have, Zoë. You're going

to need your family around you. Tell me your number and I'll give your parents a ring."

She looked at him, her lips now red and full, her blue eyes luminous.

"It won't be a horrible memory. God has let me see that it is all right. But you know that, don't you, Mr. Halford?"

Since the 1960s, the focus of the region's economics has been on tourism. Mills have been turned into museums; a Luddite self-guided tour takes a day.

—*Notes*, G. GRAYSON

28

Sunday

Grief has its own corrals—Gale discovered this when her husband died and she found herself on some nights bucking and slinging herself against the fencing like something wild. Other nights she was the docile animal, sitting tethered and numb in the middle of the round. Either way, grief had left her imprisoned.

Alan Axon hadn't suffered a death; nevertheless, his grief was the tethering kind. When, in the company of Halford and Reston, Gale found him, he sat in the cratch in Chalice's shed, running his finger around the rim of a beige-colored tea-bowl. After a nod from Reston, Gale stepped quietly inside the cramped space and placed Michael's Book on the table in front of him.

"Chalice left this at the cottage," she said. "I thought about taking it to her at the hospital, but I realized it would be safer with you."

Alan didn't look up. His finger ran over a bobble in the tea-bowl glaze; he scratched at it as if he could make it disappear.

"How did you figure I was here?"

"When you didn't come home last night, your dad went looking for you. He checked here—saw you through the window but decided to leave you alone."

Alan let out a dry laugh. "So it's all over town that Chalice and I are lovers. My parents wouldn't have enough imagination to figure that out on their own. Well, fuck it. Chalice is better than all of them."

"We went to the hospital this morning," Halford said. "We asked Chalice if you had been to visit her. She said you hadn't. Chalice needs you, Alan. She's going to need help to get her through Totty's death."

Alan didn't answer. He placed the tea-bowl rim down on the table and flicked it away with his finger.

"So," he said, "Chalice showed you the book. Broke the damn vow, did Chalice. No one was to know of the book. But she told, didn't she? She told Olivia, too. Only half a tongue in her head, but she blabbed to everyone she knew."

The pain was evident behind the cruelty. Gale leaned forward.

"You know that's not true, Alan. Chalice told me about the book because she needed my help. She told Olivia because she believed you were at a point where it wouldn't matter. All she wanted was for the book to give you some security in your career. And it will." She paused. "Some historians spend their whole lives longing for an original source like this. You found yours when you were a child."

"Yes?" He stood, wheeled around, and kicked the cratch away from him savagely. "And to what end? My burnt lover is in the hospital. Olivia and Totty are dead."

Tears started in his eyes, and he kicked at the chair again, but it was beyond his reach. He stamped the stone floor and rounded on the table with his fist, but the energy was suddenly gone. "God," he murmured. "I'm so damned tired."

Gale walked to where the cratch had hit the shed wall and dragged it to the table. Sitting, she opened Michael's Book.

"Ultimately, it's a story of betrayal, isn't it, Alan? Calculated betrayal for a cause. That's what Michael did, wasn't it? Kept his journal—wrote down the names, the plans—so that his enemies couldn't twist the truth, even though he knew doing so broke his oath. But it's also what Nathan did. And Nathan was victorious for a very long time."

The writing had faded badly—unlike his brother, Nathan Dodd had chosen not to write on the pages but on the inside back cover. The water damage there was severe. Gale glanced at Alan, who had buried his face in his hands. Then she started reading aloud.

3 March 1837

I found this book last week, among the effects of my brother's household. Michael meant it to be found. It was in a cupboard, and atop the box in which it rested lay my father's watch. Michael knew the watch was dear. He wanted me to know the book was dear as well.

So dear. But only half told. In the last years of his life, it tormented him that he did not know the truth of his son's death— that he could watch his son fall from a fiery building, watch his healthy body consumed by flame, but not know why he was there that night. He was eaten by guilt that all his careful planning could have resulted in the cruel deaths of so many precious ones. In the end, my brother's body, too, was consumed.

I shall now finish Michael's story. For I alone of all men living know the truth.

After the death of my son Benjamin and my wife Nell, I was desolate. One of my three surviving children had gone to live with Michael, so meager was my ability to raise him. I looked at my two remaining sons and could not think how to feed them, how to dress them, much less give them the living and the learn-

ing my father had given us. I thought, if my poor life is so wretched, what life will they have? And one night, staring alone into the fire, I decided Michael and his band were fools. The mill could not be destroyed. To what end? Did they think all the mills and all the mill-owners of England would bow to them so they could continue their old ways? Did they think power cared aught about their children and their homes? It did not. Power would win: power always wins. I could save my children or kill them, it would not matter to the gentlemen.

So I decided to save them.

I went to William Yates, the owner of Yates Mill, and told him of the planned attack. My brother Michael, for all his courage, did not keep his secrets safe enough. Perhaps he thought I was too lost in grief to mind the details. Or perhaps he, the foolish brother, thought that blood could be trusted. I could not be.

Yates wanted to arm the mill, to counterattack as Cartwright had at Rawfolds, but I wanted no bloodshed. Let me do this, I begged. I know these men. I know what will stop them. Man the mill, but man it with bodies they will not fire upon.

And so it was done. The night of the attack I persuaded Michael's son John, my nephew, to gather his friends for a secret meeting at the mill. At first John would not believe me—these children are raised to believe every mill is the devil's own home—but I explained that it was to prepare the way for their fathers, that they would go first so their fathers could attack the mill with ease. But it must be done in secrecy, I warned. Tell not even your father because he will surely stop you. He does not think you are a man yet, John. But I know that you have passed your boyhood. This will prove to my brother that you are a man.

Potent words to a fourteen-year-old. John agreed, and on the evening of 30 April 1812, he and five others, male and female, ages eleven to fifteen, hid themselves in Mayley Mill. I let them inside. Their instructions were to stay in the upstairs interior and wait for the attack to begin. The door will be left open, I said, so the Luddites will enter without struggle. They will break the machines. The mill-owner across the way will no doubt summon

*the soldiers, but many soldiers will not fire on Luddites. None
will fire on the six of you.*

*Those were my instructions. When I left the mill, I made sure
the door was locked—both inside and out. The Luddites would
discover their children locked inside the mill and decide not to
destroy it. That was my plan.*

*I do not know why the children did not run to the windows
as soon as they heard the axes hit the door. For surely that was
what happened—the door was locked, so to get in the attackers
hacked forcefully at the door. I do not know why the children did
not appear until the flames were already consuming them. If my
brother knew, he never confided in me, and to all my questioning prayers God has been stubbornly silent.*

*Did Michael ever suspect? If so, he was too broken to con-
front me. His body shrivelled, his children left him. His wife
died a bitter, godless woman.*

*My own children survived—more than that, they thrived.
My work at the mill gave them all they needed. My second wife
has provided me much happiness. I am blessed.*

*So what shall I do with Michael's book? Destroy it so there is
no record? Hand it over to the authorities so they may decide its
worth? It is twenty years since the children died, and information on the Luddites is still prized in some small circles.*

*Neither will be done. I will secret my brother's book away. Let
another age decide its value. May my betrayal make a fine feast
for distant others.*

Here the writing ended. Gale closed the book. Alan
stared at the shed floor, tears streaming down his face.

"Tell me, Alan," Reston said from the doorway. "Are
there betrayals working now?"

His voice was a whisper. "I don't know," he said.

"But you suspect."

"I am too thick in the head to suspect."

"According to your sister," Reston pressed, "Totty Hibbert died claiming she'd murdered Olivia. I'm trying to

prove it. Scanty little evidence in this case. I'm hoping you can help me."

Alan's only response was to wipe his nose with the back of his hand.

Reston continued. "Because as I see it, Totty could have done it. She had means, motive, opportunity. But so could several other people. Chalice. Zoë. You."

Alan shook his head. "Not Chalice."

"Make me believe that."

"The afternoon of the fire, I was with Chalice. She called me. At first I thought she wanted to meet in the wood, but she was crying like her heart was broken. 'My home,' she said. That's unusual for Chalice. Most of the time she refuses to use words, even the ones she can pronounce clearly. She scared me. So I went to her. She was hurt. Olivia had somehow hurt her. But mostly she was angry."

"What time was this?"

"Early evening. Before six."

"Was Totty in the house?"

"No."

"Did you happen to notice their car?"

"I don't think so. No."

"What time did you leave?"

"About six forty-five. I had to get to the church for the seven o'clock prayer meeting."

"Did Chalice mention anything about her sister?"

"Not that I recall. She just wanted me . . . to be with her."

"So she didn't tell you anything about Totty's canceled meeting?"

"I don't know anything about that."

"Anyone see you go into or leave the house?"

"I don't know."

Reston frowned. "It's a rather flimsy alibi, Alan."

Alan shrugged. "It's all I've got."

"You and Chalice both."

"Me and Chalice both."

"And Zoë?"

Spittle formed at the corner of Alan's mouth. He shook his head.

"You've heard Zoë's explanation of what happened in the mill?" Reston persisted. "Anything you'd like to say about it?"

"No."

"Something strikes me as odd. You know what our crime team discovered? There were three kerosene cans in the storage room—two in the stack of supplies in the corner, one in the middle of the room. We assume that one was what Totty used to immolate herself."

"So?"

Halford leaned toward Alan. "The other two cans were empty, Alan. Could have been coincidence, but it was rather bad luck for Totty that of the three cans, she picked the only one containing fuel."

His sobs came in great gulps.

"God, I can't believe it. Chalice's sister is dead and Chalice . . . her hands. Did you see her hands? They're burnt so badly. They were her voice. How will she speak now?"

"Alan." Halford said it gently. "Go to hospital and talk with the doctors. They might be able to give you some hope about her hands. With physical therapy . . . She needs you. You should be with her."

"You don't know Chalice very well. She won't stay with someone who pities her."

"And you pity her?"

"I pity all of us. We're a fucking pitiable band."

Gale felt an old rage shake her. "Stop it, Alan. She loves you. More to the point, she's in bad shape and she needs you. What *you* need, what *you* think . . . you can't dwell on that. You pull yourself together for her."

"And what if she's not the only one who needs me? What if someone else I love is going to need me, too?"

"Then you better get tough. Or you better choose."

She was unaware she was crying until she tasted the tears. She sensed Reston's stoniness in the doorway, Halford's eyes upon her.

"Whatever you believe," she said to Alan, "none of it matters besides her need for you."

Nadianna stood on the cottage steps, straining to hear the water. Somewhere in the dark, hundreds of yards below her past trees and briars and brush, it rustled in its bed, but she couldn't hear it. The sound was muffled by the rattle of leaves and the cool whistle of the wind. She felt a surge of anger. It had no right. It had no right to continue its course, leaving her behind as a witness, forever hurtling images into her head, flowing on without her.

She placed her hands on her plump belly and breathed deeply, relaxing every muscle as she inhaled. It was a trick Gale had taught her while they sat at the hospital the day of Totty's death, waiting for a doctor to tell her if her fall had hurt her baby. She breathed deeply and clutched Gale's hand while the doctor listened to the heartbeat. "Strong child," he'd said. "I'd put money on this one. And I *am* a betting man." She had broken down and cried right there in Gale's arms.

Behind her the cottage door opened and the clearing was tipped in light. Halford's voice came, deep and calming. "Katie Pru's asleep. You can come in now."

"I keep trying to think, but I can't. Too much jumbled right now. I'm so angry with myself."

Halford opened the door wider. "No point in being angry. Why don't you come in with me and Gale?"

Reluctantly, she went inside. Gale sat at the kitchen table, an empty coffeepot at her elbow.

"Did the fresh air help?" she asked.

"Not much. It's like I keep arguing with myself. What do I remember happening? What do I think happened? What was said, who said it? It's a good thing Mr. Reston took my statement when he did. I'm a mess now. So what do you think, Mr. Halford? Is there enough to make an arrest?"

She had spent the morning at the police photo lab in Halifax, worrying as a police technician developed the photos taken yesterday of the mill's storage room. She was so tired, she couldn't remember exactly what she had taken pictures of. She remembered a shot of Katie Pru by the stream, shots of the stark mill walls and the filled, bright boxes. She couldn't remember a shot of Katie Pru inside the mill, and when the film was developed, her fear had been correct. She hadn't taken a picture of Katie Pru and Chalice's blue tea-bowls.

"We'll testify at the inquest Wednesday, but I think the coroner is going to find the testimony sketchy," Halford said. "He may give Reston the go-ahead, but I don't know. There's Totty's confession and suicide. Missing tea-bowls, planted tea-bowls—it's too vague. It would make everyone happier and strain the budget less if they could all go home and forget about it."

"But I saw the tea-bowls. I didn't understand at the time what they meant, but I know I saw them. And Katie Pru's identified them from other ones found in Chalice's house—same except for the blue color. Doesn't that mean anything?"

Halford's smile was rueful. "She's a four-year-old. And you glimpsed them from a distance while you were preoccupied with other things. It would have helped if Reston's team had found the tea-bowls hidden in the mill— then we could have made a tentative link between someone planting one at the studio after the fire and hiding them in the mill. But the hole Katie Pru described was empty. And your recollection is simply not enough, Nadianna."

"But, Daniel, Chalice was worried about the tea-bowls being missing," Gale said. "She thought someone was trying to frame her. I think they were."

"Perhaps," Halford replied. "But Chalice also feared that Totty may have been that person."

"So you're thinking that Totty started to frame Chalice for the murder and then had a change of heart?"

"The coroner might be led to believe just that. Families do brutal things to each other." He paused. "You know that for a fact, Gale."

"But you said Totty's fingerprints weren't on the kerosene can," Nadianna objected. "And other people's were."

"Gerald's and Zoë's were on the can, both of which could be there legitimately. And bits of burned woolen gloves were found on Totty's hands. The weather was chill but not brutal. One could argue she was acting with premeditation."

"I didn't get a feeling of much premeditation," Nadianna objected. "Panic. Fury. Fear. She wanted to find Chalice."

"Look, Nadianna. I'm playing devil's advocate here," Halford said. "There are too many unanswered questions for my taste. For one thing, there isn't even a body. We don't know where Olivia is. There was hair that might be hers in the boot of the Hibberts' car, but with Chalice working at the studio, that would be nothing unusual. But assuming that Olivia was murdered, Chalice has at least a tentative alibi for the time and Totty does not. Zoë saw the car in the bosk, and at least one other witness says he might have done so, too. We know Olivia hurt Chalice and that Totty knew that. She could have driven to the studio to confront Olivia and things got out of hand. Combustibles were readily available at the studio. Totty had motive, opportunity, means, no alibi that we can confirm, and an alleged confession followed by suicide."

"So that ends it."

"Until something else shows up, more than likely."

"I keep going back to the journal," Gale said, "and

these three children—barely teenagers. They were all raised here; they had to know the stories of hunger, lost jobs, frustration. More than a century of troubles. And when they were growing up, tourism and nostalgia were the official paths to prosperity, but those paths were controversial. So here comes Michael with his tale of Luddite idealism and tragedy. That's powerful stuff, Daniel. Powerful for anybody. What an elixir for three bright children who feared they had no future."

Halford leaned over and brushed the hair from her cheek. "So what are you saying, Gale?"

"It's something Michael had written. His reason for keeping the journal in the first place—so his enemies couldn't 'twine' him to their liking. He didn't want the mill-owners and the government to have the last word on the Luddites because he knew the last word would be a half-truth. He wanted to have input into what people thought of him after he was dead."

She shook her head. "Totty doesn't have any input. All we know of her is Chalice's fears and Zoë's unsubstantiated testimony. Two young adults who, thanks to Olivia, saw their world coming apart. I would hate to have their words be my legacy."

"It's a question of evidence, Gale."

"It's also a question of intuition. Totty wasn't directly threatened by Olivia. The three young people were. Or at least thought they were."

Nadianna interrupted. "And Zoë lied to you about knowing Chalice."

"She said it was to protect their secret relationship."

"But she still lied. And she was alone at the mill at the time of Olivia's murder. And the two empty cans . . ."

"That's right, Daniel. Zoë kept up with the running of the church. She would have known which can still had the kerosene."

"All right," Halford said. "So if all that is true, why would Zoë have wanted to frame Chalice?"

"Maybe she was angry because Chalice broke the vow," Gale said. " 'Pursue with vengeance to the verge of nature.' Or maybe she knew that when it came time to choose, Alan would choose Chalice and leave her here, behind."

Halford wrapped his fingers around Gale's and brought her hand to the table. "It's a good argument, ladies. We'll see what the coroner says. But intuition is valuable only if it leads to evidence. And at this point that is in short supply."

EPILOGUE

Dear Chally,

   I hadn't planned on writing this, and half of me hopes that when I am old and you are blindingly successful I will come upon it and laugh at how foolish I was. But the other half of me is hopeless. If you find it when I am no longer around or am to the point of mental infirmity, decide for yourself what is to be done.

   This is my sin: on Tuesday, 6 November, you came home from work at Markham Studio bruised through an act of violence by Olivia Markham. As far as I know it was her first physical act, although certainly not her first abuse toward you. Olivia was a lazy, vicious woman who used your talent and devotion for her own gain. She was a witch, and she used you. I thought that together we could skirt her manipulation and ride her to success, but you saw her more clearly that I. You knew she would never let you rise above her.

Her ego was too fragile. I blame myself for putting you in such a predicament.

I left you crying in your room, an ice-pack to your injury. I intended on talking to her, to tell her I would call the police if she didn't treat you properly. I thought I could make it right for you. You, on the other hand, wanted a different kind of comfort. The first time I left the house, I forgot my keys. When I returned, I heard you upstairs on the phone quite plainly telling someone to come to the house. I couldn't believe it. I lifted the downstairs receiver and heard Alan's voice. Why did you never speak with me?

I drove to Olivia's feeling hurt, and perhaps that explains the strange feeling I had as I neared the studio. As soon as I saw it, I knew by instinct something terrible had happened. I backtracked and pulled the car into the bosk south of the studio. Olivia was already dead. She lay sprawled on the sofa with a pillow over her head. The place reeked of urine and booze. I lifted the pillow—I don't know, to make sure she was truly gone. There was a blue tea-bowl shoved into her mouth. Your tea-bowl, Chally. It's hard for me to imagine you committing such a sacrilege with your beautiful work. Then I noticed the other bowls were missing from the cupboard. Why would you take your bowls but leave something so incriminating behind?

I left the tea-bowl where I'd found it. The last person to touch it would have been the killer. Maybe you didn't do this. If not, I pray the killer left fingerprints and the proof is still in Olivia's mouth. If you did, then destroy this letter. No one need know.

I locked the doors and waited until it was totally dark to drive the car to the rear of the studio. I loaded Olivia's body into the boot. It took longer than I thought—dead weight is surprisingly heavy. Within ten minutes it was done. But I wanted to turn suspicion away from you, so I thought of the flowers—Olivia's horrid, vulgar flowers. If I arranged them in a dramatic fashion, the police would think it the grand gesture of a fleeing exhibitionist. I hope they did.

It took little effort to start the fire. I draped linens from upstairs around the room; turpentine and white spirits were under the cupboard. A flick of a match and the studio was gone.

It took me a day to decide what to do with the body. During that time I tried to keep the car out of your hands. You scared me one night by taking it to the moors without my knowledge. Had you had reason to open the boot, Olivia's missing-person case would have been quickly solved.

None of the above do I regret. I hope you didn't do it, that Lyle got fed up with her control, or that Gerald decided to end her bickering, or that maybe a stranger came by and she was offensive to him. But if you did, know that I protected you.

My first thought was to hide her in the bog by the windmills, because it was so familiar, but that was also the reason not to. So I buried her beside a stone outcrop on the downward slope of Rishworth Moor. From the outcrop you can look out over Booth Wood Reservoir. What you do with this information is for you to decide.

If you haven't committed this crime, then I am sorry, for I have misjudged you in a way that is unforgivable. The truth is I can see the greatness in you, Chally, but I also see the coldness. Growing up, you took so much from me. Not all of that was your fault. I am not willing for you to suffer because fate—and I—tossed you in a dangerous path.

I'm writing this so there is a record of what I've done in the event I'm not available to state the facts myself. I will hide this in a place where you don't go now, but *will probably go in the future. I haven't decided where yet—perhaps the boxes in the shed. At any rate, it will be hidden well, but not permanently.*

Please don't misunderstand anything I've done. It's because of my love for you. As everything was.

Your sister, Totty

ABOUT THE AUTHOR

TERI HOLBROOK is a former journalist who lives in Atlanta with her cartoonist husband and their two children. She is the author of two acclaimed mysteries, *A Far and Deadly Cry* and *The Grass Widow*. Both were nominated for the Agatha Award.